# Feathers in the Sand

## SEAHAVEN SUNRISE SERIES

## BOOK 1

## Anne Marie Bennett

Quote from Alex Elle used with permission by AlexElle.com

Published in the United States by KaleidoSoul Media
PO Box 745, Beverly MA 01915
AnneMarieBennett.com

Cover & Interior design by Kozakura @ fiverr.com/kozakura

Print ISBN: 979-8-9860503-1-7
Digital ISBN: 979-8-9860503-7-9

Library of Congress Control Number: 2022906813

# Feathers in the Sand

# Welcome to Seahaven, Maine!

The first book in this series invites you to savor a breath of fresh salty air in this feel-good story about one woman's journey to believe she deserves happiness.

Single mom Tess Gilmore has been moving so fast to keep her life together that she's hardly had time to notice how unhappy she is, and how distant she's become from Eva, her preteen daughter. An unexpected job opportunity offers a chance to leave her Connecticut home for Seahaven, the idyllic coastal Maine town where she spent her childhood summers.

With a reluctant Eva in tow, the two begin to carve out a new life in Seahaven, surrounded by colorful, quirky neighbors and soothing sea breezes. Within weeks, Eva begins to discover mysterious, brightly-colored feathers in surprising places.

As Tess and Eva are embraced by their new friends, they begin to work through their mother-daughter growing pains, but a surprising run-in with Tess's first love, Luca, has the potential to re-ignite their interrupted romance . . . or destroy her new and improved relationship with Eva.

Will Tess have to choose between Luca and Eva? Where are those beautiful feathers coming from? And how can Tess redefine her life in a way that includes true happiness?

Perfect for fans of *Gilmore Girls* and loaded with relatable mother-daughter moments and family drama, Feathers in the Sand delivers a sweet escape to charming small-town Maine for a second chance at happiness.

*For John and Joe,*
*the best big brothers*
*a girl ever had*

*and*

*For anyone who is starting over*
*somewhere new . . .*
*may you savor the light of each new day*
*and may you be aware of every synchronicity*
*that guides your journey*

*The Sun will rise and set regardless.*
*What we choose to do with the light*
*while it's here is up to us.*

*Journey wisely.*

*~ Alex Elle*

# Chapter 1

Tess Gilmore was having a day. She didn't like to call it a *bad* day because she had been intending to practice positive thinking. But *this* day? Her boss at the dental practice—the insufferable Justina—had put her down in front of the entire staff for a one-letter typo in a memo. And *this* moment? She was struggling to tote three bags of groceries up to the second-floor apartment where she lived with her kids, Micah and Eva. She could have used their help, but Micah was still at the high school, putting finishing touches on his Senior Class art project, and Eva was with her best friend. Not that Eva would have been much help if she *was* around.

She definitely did not want to go back down to her fourteen-year-old Ford Taurus to make another trip, so she was breathing heavily and all three tote bags were dangling precariously from her arms, not to mention the coffee travel mug gripped in her right hand. Finally reaching the landing for her apartment, she set down two of the bags along with the coffee, then inserted the key into the lock. Home at last, such as it was.

Tess quickly put the groceries away—each item in its proper place—and wiped down the counters with the citrus sanitizing spray that Eva particularly liked, then grabbed her purse and headed to her bedroom to get dressed for Micah's birthday party. Hard to believe that eighteen years had already gone by. She loosened her stick-straight brown hair from its plain elastic band and rubbed her hand across her forehead which was beginning to show frown lines and shallow wrinkles even though she was only forty. Sighing, she quickly headed into the shower and was out in five minutes. Task complete. Check that off the list.

There was still so much to do, and she wanted the party to be perfect. Micah had invited his two best friends plus two of his teachers, and Eva was bringing her best friend, Charli. Tess felt sorry for Eva because Charli was moving to California with her family in a few days. Sunny and warm, sure, but way too far for best friends to visit often. Eva had Googled the distance from New Haven, Connecticut to San Diego, California, and was quite dismayed when she realized exactly how far Charli was going. "Two thousand, eight hundred and sixty-two miles," Eva had announced sadly.

Tess's phone rang as she race-walked to the kitchen, heading toward the fridge to start making Micah's favorite meal: tacos with side dishes of Mexican corn, spicy refried beans, and homemade guacamole—as homemade as it could be when it came from the grocery store. She had no extra time to spend on homemade *anything*. Her mother had said she'd bring the birthday cake, but who knew what else she'd bring? Cecilia often brought food that only she was fond of instead of what was suggested. Tess frowned as she abruptly answered the phone. "Hi, this is Tess."

"Mom, you don't have to say that *every time* you answer the phone." Her daughter's exasperation bled through cyberspace; Tess could almost see Eva rolling her eyes.

"I know hon. It's just a habit I've gotten into."

"You can *look* at the phone screen and see who it is. If you see it's me, you don't have to say your name!"

"I understand." Tess rubbed her eyes and summoned up a trickle of patience from the base of her spine. "I usually don't take the time to look before I answer. Is everything okay?"

"Charli's mom wants to know if we can bring the desserts we made this afternoon. You know, for Micah's party."

2

Tess plopped a five-pound package of ground beef into a large skillet and turned on the heat, breaking up the meat with a wooden spoon at the same time. She glanced at her old-fashioned wrist watch. "Well, Gram is bringing the coconut cake that Micah asked for, so—"

"But these are Micah's favorite. Lemon squares and oatmeal chocolate chip cookies. *Please?* We made them for his party."

Tess felt a rare wave of happiness flow through her body. She loved how close her children were even though they were seven years apart. "Okay, Evie-Bee. Bring the desserts."

Eva's voice sharpened. "I've asked you a million times not to call me Evie-Bee."

"Sorry, hon," Tess answered automatically, busily chopping tomatoes for one of the taco fillings. "Is Charli's mom bringing you home soon? I could use some help getting ready."

"I'll ask. See you later."

Tess tucked the phone in the pocket of her khakis and frowned when she noticed the plain white T-shirt she had thrown on after her speedy shower. "What was I thinking?" she mumbled to herself, slicing rapidly through a few more juicy tomatoes. "I'm a stain magnet waiting to happen." She kept chopping; there was no time to change.

Her phone buzzed insistently again and she quickly wiped her hands on a towel before answering. "Hello, this is Tess." She grimaced, remembering Eva's admonishment, but the caller apparently didn't care.

"I cannot believe you left us in the lurch like this." It was Justina Waverly, the office manager at Waverly Dental Practice in Branford. In spite of the prickly Justina, Tess considered herself lucky to be the assistant office manager at a practice only fifteen minutes from home. She had started there as a receptionist when Micah was seven, worked her way up to dental assistant, and then been promoted to Justina's assistant after she'd finished her business management degree in December. Not that Justina had actually wanted an assistant.

Tess's voice wavered. "I told you yesterday that I had to leave early today because it's Micah's birthday. We—"

Justina cleared her throat so angrily that Tess had to hold the phone away from her ear for a moment. She wiped her sweaty forehead with a paper towel, then swiftly dropped it in the trash can. Justina continued, anger still evident in her reedy voice. "You didn't give me the proper time-off request form."

Tess tamped down her impatience. Add *this* to the "day" she was having. She didn't want to give in to her anger; she didn't want to spoil Micah's special day. "I'm sorry, Justina. I didn't have time to fill out the form."

"I don't know what we're going to do about this."

Tess understood that "we" referred to Justina and her husband, Dr. Jim Waverly, who ran the practice with two other dentists. Dr. Wave, as everyone called him, was a good guy, but when he and his wife disagreed, Justina always won. "I came in an hour early today and plan to do that again on Monday." Tess clamped her mouth shut as she urgently paced the floor, then stopped to stir the browning meat. Her stomach grumbled as the salty aroma flooded the kitchen.

"The end-of-month billing needs to begin and that's part of your responsibility."

"I know." Tess shouldered her phone and scooped the chopped tomatoes into a white bowl, then tapped the spoon to get every last drop of the juice.

"What on earth are you doing?" Justina demanded.

She tried to keep the exasperation out of her voice. "I'm getting ready for Micah's party. Chopping tomatoes, actually." She attempted a light-hearted connection. "He loves tacos because—"

"Tacos. You're making tacos. It's four o'clock on a Friday and you're making tacos instead of sitting here getting a head start on the billing. I'm going to have a chat with Jim about this."

Tess frowned. She needed this job. With the kids' father, Cameron, no longer in the picture, it was up to her. It was *all* up to her. The rent. The food. The college educations. All of it. Sure, Cameron paid the required amount of child support, and thank God for that. But with Micah now eighteen, those payments would be lessened by half. A distinctly disturbing thought. Also, there had been rumors in the building that rent was about to go up. "What if I come in tomorrow? I'm scheduled for 10-2 but I can do 9-3 if you think that will help." She hated to give up a whole Saturday, but she didn't want Justina and Dr. Wave to have a "conversation" because there's no way it would turn out in her favor.

She could hear Justina tapping her pointy, fake fingernails against the desk. "You do that. I'll be in at noon to check on how far you've gotten with the billing."

Tess wearily rubbed her forehead and pocketed the phone again as she turned off the heat under the sizzling pan on the stove. On days like this, she wished she could turn her phone off completely, but she doubted that would ever be possible because of Micah and Eva. There were no smart phones when she was growing up, but if there were, she seriously doubted that either of her parents would have answered on the first ring, like she did for her children. Always. Even when she was at work. One more thing for Justina to complain about.

She glanced at her watch. In less than an hour everyone would arrive. She pulled out the lemonade mix and grabbed a large pitcher, but her thoughts kept going back to the dental practice. She knew more about running an office than Justina, who was twenty years older and long out of school. Most of the time, Tess suspected that Justina was the long-standing office manager of Dr. Wave's practice simply because she was his long-standing wife. How he put up with her away from the office, Tess couldn't begin to fathom.

Popping the ice cubes out of a tray from the freezer and into the clear glass pitcher, she remembered Justina's reaction when Dr. Wave had promoted her to Assistant Office Manager—not a word of congratulations, not an iota of encouragement. This was probably the one and only marital argument that Justina had ever lost. Tess was more than competent at her job, and she loved it. Most of the staff were supportive; but Justina's disdain tended to outweigh everyone else's friendliness.

Judged and dismissed. That's how Tess felt a great deal of the time, and sometimes even by her own daughter. Granted, she hadn't been home much these last four years. The four years of night school to get her degree while working full time, and then the last several months after the promotion, had taken her away from the kids more than she wanted, but it was all for the long-term good of the family. Luckily, Micah didn't mind spending time with his little sister while Tess was at work, and Eva loved spending time with her brother.

Tess carried the pitcher of lemonade into the living room and set it in the center of the long, sturdy table that Micah had borrowed from the art department. After the kids left for school, she had covered it with a bright orange tablecloth that she'd picked up at a thrift store. Tess loved weaving her way through a thrift store; she would gladly never walk into a Target or Walmart again if she could get away with it. Thrift stores were the most joyful way to shop; she could spend hours looking at things that people had given away, and was often incredulous as to what some people *did* choose to give away.

Living in this small apartment for so long with two children, she hadn't been able to accumulate many extra possessions. She usually let herself buy only the bare necessities, but as soon as she'd seen this gingery-orange, textured cloth with colorful giraffes embroidered on the edges, she knew it would be perfect for Micah's party. Plus, it had only cost three dollars! She had a perfectly decent (albeit old) cloth she could have used, but it wasn't orange like this one, and it didn't have giraffes on it, nor did it have an African vibe to it. Micah was all about nature and art, and he'd made a vow to travel the world. After college, of course. She had insisted on that.

She stroked the edges of the cloth fondly, then headed back to the kitchen, glancing at her checklist on the fridge. Most people she knew had magnets and photos all over their refrigerator doors, but not Tess. She liked a clean surface. The only thing on her fridge was a never-ending to-do list. In fact, last summer for her birthday, the kids had given her an erasable board with magnets on the back, so she didn't waste paper. Now, Tess grabbed an erasable marker from a New York Giants mug on top of the fridge, and crossed items off the list: get groceries, take shower, make lemonade, cook ground beef, chop tomatoes. She stuck the pen behind her ear and plucked a rubber band from the closest drawer as she pulled her damp hair back. There. That was better. Now, on to shredding the lettuce and the cheese, warming the taco shells, heating up the Mexican corn, and putting the bottles of hot sauce on the table.

By the time Eva and her best friend got to the party, almost everyone was there. Eva had purposely told Charli's mom the wrong time because she didn't want to be stuck helping her mom get ready. For one thing, her mom was a neat freak and everything had to be done her way. For another thing, her mom would want

Eva to tell her about school, or about how she was feeling about Charli leaving, or whatever was going on in her life. As if anything was going on in her life besides homework, cheering Charli on at her soccer games, and helping Micah with his art projects. It had been so long since she'd spent any decent amount of time with her mom besides a quick breakfast in the morning or the short ride to school, that Eva didn't know how to talk with her anymore. It was so much easier to talk with Micah.

As the thought of Micah came into her mind, Eva immediately sought him out. He was standing in the kitchen doorway, talking on his phone. "Charli, look!" she whispered to her best friend in the entire universe.

"What?" Charli tapped her foot on the floor as she looked around. She was exactly the same height as Eva, but her face held a summery tan from so many soccer games, and her hair was blond with springy curls that tumbled across her forehead.

"Micah got a haircut. Look how short it is!" Eva knew that Charli had a little crush on Micah even though it was hopeless because after all, Micah was gay.

Charli blushed. "It looks sweet, don't you think?"

"I don't know about sweet," Eva replied. "It's almost a buzz cut. Makes him look way older. He's never worn his hair that short."

"But he looks so cute, and it'll be cooler for him in the summer." Eva knew that Charli would have loved to run right over to Micah and give him a hug while kissing him on the lips. Eva thought that was gross. He was her big brother, after all. The same brown hair as her and Mom, but lighter. Lots of laugh lines at the corners of his eyes—one blue, one brown. Micah smiled a lot.

"Maybe that's why he did it," Eva replied thoughtfully.

Her mother was standing by the food table, encouraging the guests to fill up their plates. The spicy taco smell made Eva's mouth water and she eyed the Mexican corn. Grinning, Charli nudged her elbow and motioned toward Micah's best friends, Philip and Javier, who were at the food table along with Micah's art teacher and guidance counselor. They had both helped him apply for a full scholarship to the Rhode Island School of Design. He'd be leaving in September. Eva frowned. She didn't want to think about life without Micah, even though Rhode Island wasn't that far and he had promised to come home most weekends. Who would she hang out with after school, now that Charli was leaving for California? Eva believed that eleven was old enough to stay home alone, but she highly doubted that her mother would agree.

Tess hurried over to the girls, kissing Eva on top of her head as she slowly squirmed away. "Hi Evie . . . Sorry. *Eva*. Charli, I'm so glad you could come."

"Thanks for inviting me, Mrs. Gilmore." Charli smiled widely, showing off her neon blue braces.

Eva held onto the dessert box and tried unsuccessfully to get Micah's attention. He was still focused on his phone. She looked around the room again. "Why isn't Gram here yet?"

# Chapter 2

Tess shrugged and took a step back, glancing at her watch. "But she's bringing Micah's favorite coconut cake from Maria's Bakery!" Eva set the box of oatmeal cookies and lemon squares on the orange tablecloth while secretly admiring the bold colors and African motif. She wondered if Micah had noticed it yet.

"I know." Tess rubbed one palm over the back of her other hand. Her fingers and wrists were unadorned. No rings. No bracelets. She hadn't had time to change out of her khakis and T-shirt, all of which remained pristine in spite of her time in the kitchen. "I'm sure Gram will be here soon." She glanced at her watch again. Leave it to her mother to make a grand entrance.

"Come on, Charli, let's go to my room until Gram gets here. I want to show you the book I got from the library yesterday."

"Girls! Aren't you going to eat? I thought you loved my tacos." Tess gestured hopefully toward the food table.

"We ate already," Eva lied, pulling on Charli's arm and giggling. No way was she going to listen to any more of her mother's incessant questions. Maybe later.

Tess stood alone for a moment, letting the bright sounds of music, people chatting, and taco shells crunching stream around her. Eva kept pushing her away and she wasn't sure what to do about it. Was it because her daughter was eleven now, or was it because of Tess's recurrent absence over the last four years?

Her wistful thoughts were interrupted by Mr. Pendleton, who politely tapped her shoulder. "What a lovely party, Ms. Gilmore.

You must be so proud of Micah."

Startled, Tess turned to face the older gentleman who was wearing a turquoise sport coat and purple polka-dotted tie. His slowly graying hair was slicked back with what might have been too much gel. Mr. Pendleton had been Micah's art teacher for the last two years and, along with Miss Yoshida, had been instrumental in getting Micah into the best art schools in the country. "I'm glad you came, Mr. P. We're all very proud of him. He's looking forward to—"

"Looking forward to what, Mom?" Micah loped to her side and kissed her on the cheek while pocketing his phone. "This is a great party, and the tablecloth is awesome. You know me so well."

Tess looked pleased. Micah was so different from Eva, or maybe it was simply that he was older. "I was telling Mr. P. how much you're looking forward to starting RISD in the fall."

Micah blinked a few times, then quickly moved toward the table and began heaping a plate with food. He looked over his shoulder at his mom and favorite teacher, purposely changing the subject. "After graduation in two weeks, I'll be free as the proverbial bird!"

"Except for watching Eva, right?" Tess asked nervously. She was depending on Micah to spend time with his sister this summer. She would have to decide what to do about Eva when he went off to college in September, but she had the whole summer to make a new plan.

Micah grabbed a napkin and turned back to Tess. "I've been meaning to talk to you about that—"

He was interrupted by the sound of the apartment door clacking open and the appearance of Cecilia Gilmore, holding a large box in one hand and gripping a carryall tote bag in the other. She was taller than Tess, an imposing figure with ramrod stiff posture. Her perfectly coiffed dark blonde hair was tastefully dyed. Her skin was fair, like Tess's, and her eyes were a cloudy shade of blue, like the watery veins under an old person's skin.

Tess rushed forward and attempted to kiss her mother politely on the cheek but Cecilia abruptly stepped around Tess and into the living room. Micah set down his plate and gave his grandmother a warm hug, then took the bag from her. "Hey Gram, thanks for coming!" He turned to the small crowd while giving Cecilia a bright thumbs-up. "She brought the cake!"

"I did, indeed," Cecilia declared as she carefully scrutinized him from head to toe. "Happy birthday. I didn't know you were getting such a drastic haircut. You look like my Uncle Simon when he served in the Navy. But I must say, it suits you." Before giving Micah time to respond, she briskly turned to her daughter. "Here you go, Tess." She thrust the brown bakery box into Tess's hands.

Tess breathed a sigh of relief and headed into the kitchen, listening to Micah introduce Cecilia to his friends and teachers. The last thing she heard before the kitchen door swung shut was her mother's starched voice asking if Philip and Javier were also gay. She knew her mother was "old school" and had had a hard time when Micah came out a few years ago, but she thought they had worked through all of that because, over the last several months, Cecilia seemed to have come to a place of acceptance.

Setting the cake box on the table, Tess went to a cupboard and took out the large, rainbow-striped cake platter that they used to celebrate birthdays. After Cameron left when Micah was eight, Tess had been too busy as a single mom to create many new traditions, but this was one that they stood by.

Eva and Charli ran into the kitchen, giggling at something on Charli's phone. "I heard Gram come in. Is that the cake?" Eva asked eagerly.

"It is! Want to help me get it onto the plate?"

"Nah, we'll just watch. I've done it a thousand times before."

The girls stood close to the table, looking eagerly at the box.

"Really? A *thousand* times?" Tess teased. "I don't think you and Micah are that old yet." But her attempt at levity was thwarted when she opened the box. All she saw was chocolate frosting. "Oh no!"

"Chocolate?" Eva was as bewildered as her mom, but perhaps not as surprised. Gram didn't always do as she was asked. Everyone knew that. "It was supposed to be coconut!"

The kitchen door swung open and Cecilia entered briskly, frowning. "Why isn't the cake on the platter yet? What's keeping you?"

Tess turned to face her mother. "This isn't the cake Micah asked for."

"Pfffft. Coconut. Chocolate. It doesn't matter. This one looked perfect. Once you cut into it, you'll see that it has a layer of candied cherries inside. They gave me a sample at the bakery and it's delicious." She carefully placed a plastic container on the table beside the disappointing cake. "I brought my potato salad too, so let's get this on the table. And speaking of the table . . ." Her voice rose to a level of pomposity that Tess was all too familiar with. "Where did you get that hideous tablecloth with the giraffes on it? It's so . . . multicultural." She shook her head in dismay and her pretty beaded earrings swayed with the movement.

Eva had always loved Gram's earrings. It seemed she had an unlimited supply. She had never seen her wear the same pair twice, but then, she didn't see Gram that often. Pretty earrings notwithstanding, Eva fervently hoped that Gram wasn't the one who would be staying with her once Micah went off to college in September.

Tess tried to control her voice but it seemed to get louder with every word. "The cake certainly *does* matter. This party is for Micah, and coconut cake is what he asked for." She glared at her mother. "I can't believe you would do this. Micah is eighteen years old today. *Eighteen*!" She knew that directing this long-simmering anger at her mother didn't have a bluebird's chance in the underworld of changing anything, but she couldn't help herself. "And in two months, he's leaving for college!" She slammed her hand down on the table and Eva quickly steadied the cake box. "This party is for him, not you, and you should know by now that orange is his favorite color and he's been entranced by giraffes ever since *you* took him to the Bronx Zoo when he was five years old!"

Cecilia crossed her arms over her chest and pursed her lips dramatically. "Teresa Marie! What is wrong with you?"

Tess took several short, sharp breaths. "This isn't about me. It's about Micah!"

Cecilia stared at her daughter, a baffled expression on her perfectly made-up face.

"Mom, what's going on?" Micah strode to Tess's side and put his arm around her shoulder, darting a questioning look at Eva. Eyes wide, she pointed to the cake.

Tess rubbed her forehead, unsuccessfully trying to assuage years of hurt and misunderstanding. "Gram was going to bring your favorite coconut cake but . . . it's actually chocolate."

He mischievously swiped a little frosting from the side and snuck a taste. Eva smacked him lightly on the arm. "Hey, it tastes good! I like chocolate as much as coconut."

"You do *not*," insisted Eva.

Micah leaned toward his sister and touched her forehead with his index finger. "Boop!"

Eva giggled at his pretend-squeaky voice; this was a special joke, just between them.

"You're right, Li'l Sis, but I like chocolate almost as much, and if it's from Maria's Bakery, then I know it's gonna be good. Thanks for bringing it, Gram." He hugged his mom a little closer while Gram observed the scene, arms still crossed over her ample chest.

Tess leaned into him for a moment, then straightened and looked her son in the eye. "I wanted everything to be perfect for you today."

"But it is perfect. Look, everyone I love is here—"

"Except for Leo," Eva interrupted slyly.

"Okay, almost everyone. Plus, your tacos are the best, Mom, and I see that my other favorite desserts are here!"

Eva gave him a thumbs-up. "You're welcome!"

"I love the tablecloth too, Mom. Bet you got it at a thrift shop!" He put his hand on her shoulder.

Tess exhaled slowly and rested her hand on his for a moment. "I did!" Then she turned to Cecilia and took a breath. "Mom, I'm sorry I yelled at you."

Eva frowned. If anyone should apologize, it was Gram. Why couldn't everyone just get along? And why on earth did Gram think that potato salad went with tacos?

While Charli helped Tess lift the cake onto the celebration plate and Gram took her potato salad into the living room, Eva grabbed Micah by the elbow and pulled him aside. "Who were you talking to on the phone when I came in?"

"Just Dad. No big deal."

Micah called him Dad, but to Eva, he was simply Cameron. He had left them right after her first birthday; she had no memories of him as a father.

"What did he want?"

"He wished me a happy birthday, told me about the kids."

The kids. Cameron had married a younger woman soon after leaving, and they had started a family. He and Tess had never been married. Whenever she had asked her mom about this, the answer she received was that Cameron's last name was Testa and she didn't want to be known as Tess Testa. Which kind of made sense, but even Eva knew that married women could keep their own names if they wanted to.

Eva sighed. It wasn't fair. Charli had the perfect family—a mom and a dad, plus four brothers and sisters. Charli's dad worked a lot, but her mom was always home, and they did things together as a family. Not just once a year, a *lot*. In comparison, Eva's family felt broken, incomplete. All she had was a mother and a brother. Correction. A mother who was hardly ever home, and one super-incredible brother who looked out for her.

Micah gently "booped" her on the forehead again. "Forget about them," he said, reading her mind. "The three of *us* are a great family." Eva raised her eyebrows doubtfully. "Someday you'll believe me, I promise. Come on, let's get ready for presents and cake."

# Chapter 3

The next morning, Tess woke before the alarm and set her feet on the floor with determination. She'd get to the office early and show Justina that she wasn't slacking off. The fact was, she hadn't slacked off a day in her life. Even those days in Maine the summer she was fifteen didn't feel like laziness or irresponsibility. They had been perfect days with her first real boyfriend—someone who understood her, who liked her for who she was. Even though their time together had been cut short—thanks to Cecilia—she had never forgotten him, or how she'd felt when she was with him. Special. Cared for. Seen and heard.

Tucking her hair behind her ears, she headed into the family's small shared bathroom, giving herself more than the five-minute rinse she'd had yesterday before Micah's party. She relaxed as the warm water rushed over her body. Maybe she'd request a week off in July so the three of them could take a vacation. As she rinsed conditioner out of her hair, she remembered times when the kids were younger, when she worked at Waverly Dental as a dental assistant. Life was so much simpler then. Cameron had left—for the last time—but she was working mother's hours and was always home after school. The partners had seen potential in her and offered to send her to business school at night. It was perfect because Micah was old enough to take care of Eva after school and into the evenings. Had she made a mistake by choosing to give up so much family time in order to get a better degree so she'd be eligible for a promotion? This question haunted her daily.

As she patted her body dry with a towel, Tess remembered agonizing over that decision. Cameron had left them. Yes, the three of them were getting by with his child support payments and her meager income, but she wanted to make sure that Eva and Micah both got college educations, so she chose to give up family time for the college classes, the better degree, the promotion.

And now? Now she was almost forty-one, struggling with two distant mother-daughter relationships, and getting ready to let go of a beloved son who was about to leave the nest.

Staring into her tiny closet, Tess realized that she didn't have many decisions to make as far as what to wear to work. Her closet consisted of several pairs of slacks—khaki, navy, and black—and several tops in differing styles of white, gray, and blue. Simple and uncomplicated, like she wanted her life to be. Not that it ever was. Today she chose a pair of navy pants and a short-sleeved white top. No earrings. Earrings were just one more thing to keep track of. God knew, her mother had enough earrings in her jewelry drawers to grace the entire cast of *Downton Abbey* for several years.

She slipped on her plain silver watch and clasped the necklace that the kids had given her for Mother's Day around her neck. Tess hardly ever wore jewelry—it was too fussy, and she couldn't afford it anyway, but this necklace made her feel warm inside. It was a plain silver circle pendant with three birthstones resting against the bottom arc: her own grass-green peridot for August, Micah's darker green emerald for May, and Eva's purple amethyst for February. Every time she touched the necklace, it felt like proof that Eva and Micah loved her, and these days, she craved proof, especially from Eva. Now, Tess briskly combed her wet hair and smoothed it back from her forehead with a plain black headband. There. Ready for the day.

She headed to Eva's room and paused in the doorway. Her daughter was sitting up in bed, reading a book. Jasper, their big gray cat, was curled into her left hip. Most of the covers were on the floor; the late May day was already warm. Books were strewn around the bed and her clothes from yesterday were precariously perched on the edge of the hamper which wasn't in the closet where it belonged. The walls were a drab shade of white, like all the other walls in this old apartment, but Eva had tacked up posters of cats, Katy Perry, and Ariana Grande. Tess also noticed two of Micah's art projects on the floor by the bookcase. Her son was a gifted artist through and through. "I'm leaving for work early. Let's have breakfast and I'll drive you to Charli's on the way."

Eva groaned and put down the book as she rubbed her eyes. "Do I have to go there today?"

Tess stepped into the room and sat on the edge of the bed. "It's your last day with her, hon. They're leaving for California tomorrow. This will give you a chance to say goodbye."

"Exactly." Eva lifted Jasper onto her lap, hugging him tighter than usual. His purrs vibrated through her chest; perhaps he knew how much comfort his girl needed. It seemed like he had always known, ever since Micah and her mom had taken her to the animal shelter on her sixth birthday and told her she could have any kitten that she wanted. The kittens were cute, but when she noticed a cage occupied by a fully grown charcoal-gray cat with inquisitive sage-green eyes and white whiskers, she held her breath and pointed. "This one. I want her."

Micah had pointed to the sign on top of the cage that indicated the cat's name was Jasper and that he was two years old. "You want *him*," he corrected gently, bending down to stroke the cat's dark fur through the metal slats. "This beautiful guy is a boy."

"Yes," she had replied firmly. "I want *him*!"

"Are you sure?" Tess had been doubtful. "I thought you wanted a kitten."

Eva looked at the crates of kittens who were tumbling over each other in a blur of orange, white, and tan fur. Yes, she had wanted a kitten, but now that she'd met Jasper, there was no turning back. "I'm sure," she had said with as much conviction as a six-year-old could muster. Ever since, she and Jasper had been practically insepar-able; his warm body was a comfort to her as she slept. Charli, Micah, and Jasper: her three best friends in the universe.

Eva blinked her eyes and came back to the present moment. "I don't want to go."

"Okay. I see," Tess said thoughtfully. She was no stranger to difficult departures, but saying goodbye to a loved one was not something her daughter had encountered yet in her young life. They had just celebrated Eva's first birthday when Cameron had left for the last time, and she was only four when Tess's father had died. This loss was going to cut deeper; Charli and Eva had been friends for almost half of their lives.

Tess chose her words carefully. "Goodbyes are no fun. Believe me, I know. But it's going to be hard for Charli too because she's going to a new place that's full of strangers. You're lucky because you get to stay here and move up to sixth grade with the kids you've been with since kindergarten."

Eva wrinkled her nose in thought.

"Try thinking of today as a gift you're giving to Charli, so she has one more memory of you to take with her."

"I wish she wasn't going so far away. I can't even visit her."

"Maybe we'll take a trip to San Diego next summer. In the meantime, you can use my phone once a week to FaceTime."

Eva mumbled into Jasper's fur. "Thanks, I guess. But it won't be the same."

"No, it won't." Tess hesitated before reaching out and stroking her daughter's brown hair, exactly the same color and stick-straight-ness as hers, but much longer. Her heart ached for Eva. *Welcome to the preliminary edge of adulthood.*

"I'll never have another friend like her."

"Charli is one in a million." Tess agreed.

Eva kissed the sleepy cat on his head, then set him beside her on the bed. "I don't even want another friend. No one will ever like me as much as Charli does."

Tess stood and moved toward the door. "I know it feels that way, but I have a feeling there are many people who would love to have you as a friend."

Eva slowly climbed out of bed and began picking up her clothes. "I don't know why. I'm not interesting. There's nothing really special about me."

Tess spun around, astonished. "Oh Eva, that's not true! Why do you think that?"

She shrugged and pulled on a pair of green shorts and a flowered T-shirt. "I'm just average." She stood in front of Tess and pointed to her bed-mussed hair. "Plain brown. Like yours." She pointed to her eyes. "Uninteresting." She flexed her thumbs backward toward her body. "I'm just ordinary." She sat on the edge of the bed and tugged on her sneakers. "Charli's good at sports. I hate sports. I'm not even good at art or video games like Micah is."

As they walked down the hall to the kitchen, Eva slipped out from under Tess's attempted one-arm hug and plopped into a chair at the table. "You don't have to be good at the same things as Micah or your friends. You can be good at whatever it is that *you're* good at." Tess took out two hard-boiled eggs from the fridge and placed them on a plate in front of Eva, then began toasting an English muffin.

Eva rolled one of the eggs between her palms, then cracked the shell against the side of the table. "I'm not good at anything."

"Not true! You've always been a good friend to Charli. Remember the time you and Micah brought her chicken soup and her favorite corn bread when she was sick? That was your idea, and it was so thoughtful. You were always at her soccer games and swim meets, cheering her on. Please don't tell me you're ordinary. You're a beautiful girl and you're going to be a beautiful woman."

Eva shrugged. "Like you?" Sarcasm ricocheted from each word straight into Tess's chest.

Stunned, Tess rubbed one palm over the back of her other hand as she struggled for words. *No wonder she thinks she's plain and ordinary. That's what I think about myself and she knows it.* She took a deep, steadying breath as she placed a well-done English muffin on a plate along with a jar of blackberry jam, Eva's favorite. "I know you didn't mean that the way it sounded. You do look like me, and there's nothing wrong with that. But you look more like Aunt Kit did when she was younger."

Eva took a huge bite of the English muffin, then used a napkin to wipe off the reddish-purple smear on her chin. "Aunt Kit? She lives in Maine, right?"

"That's right, my dad's sister. She's in a quaint little town called Seahaven. We visited her once when you were about four, right after Gramps died. Do you remember?"

"Nope."

"She was a famous model when she was younger, and often flew to New York for jobs and meetings with her agent. When she had time, she'd stop by here for a short visit but you were usually in school. She's in her early sixties, and has mostly retired from the modeling, but she's still beautiful."

Eva got a glass of orange juice from the fridge. "Can I see a picture of her sometime?" She highly doubted it was possible that she, Eva Gilmore, looked like one of those beautiful people in the magazines.

"Sure. We can look at the family scrapbooks tonight when you get back from Charli's."

Later that morning, sipping her third cup of strong, black coffee, Tess was working steadily at the monthly billing project. She had learned about a comprehensive new software program in one of her business classes and introduced it to the practice. The doctors were pleased; anything that made the monthly billing easier and more profitable suited them immensely. Justina, annoyed because she hadn't discovered the software first, had scoffed at the high-level praise Tess had been given for this innovation.

Now, Tess looked around and frowned. She had hoped to have her own office, but there was no extra space, so she was working at a desk against the back wall of Justina's office. She stretched her neck from side to side, wondering how Eva was doing at Charli's.

Renee, one of the dental assistants, tapped lightly on the open door. "She's not here yet?" she asked, inclining her head slightly toward Justina's desk.

"Not yet. She'll be in around noon."

"Checking up on you, eh?" Renee's feathery blonde hair glowed under the fluorescent lighting.

"That's right." Tess frowned. "Like I haven't been doing this by myself for months."

"C'mon down to the break room with me. The new reception-ist brought those bagels that you like." Renee gestured toward the hallway, a friendly smile on her face.

"I don't know . . . I still have so much to do."

"It's only eleven o'clock. You've got plenty of time. Please? I want to hear all about Micah's party."

Tess stood and closed the laptop with a snap. "Okay. For you, I will take a break." As they walked down the hall, Tess peeked into each exam room as they passed. Renee was chattering about the season finale of *New Amsterdam*, but Tess was breathing in the antiseptic, minty smell that never failed to thrill her. She knew it was strange, but she had always loved going to the dentist. Not just the fresh, clean smell, but how tidy everything was, how the staff wore white coats and picture-perfect smiles. She loved the order of it all, the sparseness, the shiny silver of the dental instruments and trays. In the Waverly offices, the hallway was a soft sky blue and each exam room was pristine white; the hygienists and assistants wore white pants and colorful smocks; the dentists always wore white. No exceptions. She liked that too. Here, unlike living with two children, the entire space was always clean; there was a place for everything, and everything was always in its place.

When Justina came into the office, exactly at noon, Tess had long been back at work. The asiago cheese bagel had been delicious, but her head was starting to hurt. She was scrambling to beat the clock because she had to pick up Eva no later than three-thirty so the Bedfords could finish packing. Justina dropped an expensive leather purse on her desk. Standing behind Tess, she silently watched her work.

Tess refused to speak first. She was doing an excellent job and she knew it. If she was the office manager and had an assistant, she would have walked in with a friendly wave and said, "Hi Tess, thanks for working extra hours today. Why don't you leave early so you can enjoy the rest of the day with your kids?" But there's no way Justina would ever say anything like that.

"Think you'll be done by three?" Justina asked, sauntering back to her desk and picking up her purse.

"Sure." Tess didn't look up.

"See you Monday." Justina flounced out of the room. And that was that.

Tess leaned her face into her hands for a moment. She wanted to cry but didn't have time. She needed this job, and the dental practice needed her. She was sure of it.

On her way to pick up Eva, Tess's phone rang; it was Aunt Kit. Pulling into the driveway at Charli's house ten minutes later, she returned the call, wondering what was up. Her aunt usually only called when she was planning a trip to New York, and that hadn't happened in over a year.

"Tess! Thank you for calling me back so soon. Are you at work?"

Her aunt's voice sounded clear and strong, as always. There was a special brightness to Kit that had always made Tess feel better. "No, I'm picking Eva up from her best friend's house. Charli's family is moving tomorrow, so they're saying goodbye." She opened the driver's side window to let in a sweet May breeze. "Are you coming for a visit?"

"No, but I'm hoping *you'll* be coming to visit *me*."

She heard the eagerness in Kit's voice. "What do you mean?"

"The office manager at Pearly Whites Dental in Seahaven is leaving and I think you'd be perfect for the job. Could you come up here next weekend for an interview? The Doctors Pearl are eager to meet you."

"The Doctors Pearl?"

"The dentists who own the practice are husband and wife— Max and Mimi Pearl. You'll love them! Please tell me you'll come up next Saturday for the interview, then spend the night at my cottage. Micah can watch Eva, right?"

Tess gazed at the small but tidy lawn in front of the Bedford's house. The air was fresher here than in the heart of the city, and she breathed it in deeply. Aunt Kit lived in Seahaven, a small coastal town in southern Maine. The air in Seahaven was easier to breathe too, but she hadn't been back in many years. Not since the summer she was fifteen.

"Are you still there, dear?"

"I'm here. Let me get this straight. You're inviting me for a weekend with you so I can interview for a new job?"

"You got it! What do you say?"

"Aunt Kit, I have a job already." *Along with an overpriced apartment in the city and a boss who can't stand me.* She glanced at her watch as she shifted in her seat and turned off the ignition. Eva would be out soon.

"I know you do, but tell me this—how happy are you in that job?"

She cleared her throat. "The pay is decent, and I'm actually very good at it."

"I don't doubt those things are true, but are you happy there?"

Tess stared down at her hands. Of course, she wasn't happy, but who had *time* to be happy? There were things in life that you just had to put up with, right? If her mother had asked her this question—not that her mother would ever dream of asking such a question—she would have agreed, simply to get Cecilia out of her hair. But this was Aunt Kit, and Aunt Kit was nothing like her mother. She sighed. "Not really."

"Then what's the harm of coming for an interview? I've told them all about you and they're excited to meet you! Even if it doesn't work out, you'll have had a mini-vacation, and I'll treat you to a delicious meal at Chloe's by the Sea. It used to be Seahaven Diner, but it's been completely enlarged and renovated. Beautiful views too!"

Eva and Charli were on the front lawn now, arms around each other's waists, walking as slowly as they could toward the car. Both girls were quietly crying. "But what if it does work out?" Tess asked. "If they offer me the job, we'll have to move to Seahaven."

"Would that be such a bad thing? I remember how much you loved it here."

"I was young then."

"It hasn't changed all that much, I promise. Listen, there's an apartment available in the refurbished Victorian that I bought a while back. It's close to town and I'll give you a lower rent than you're paying now. Perfect timing. You'll be happy to hear there's a sixteen-year-old girl in the other ground floor apartment who can babysit Eva when Micah is—" She hesitated. "When he leaves in September."

"But—"

"Tess, I'm serious. I want you to think about this. You'd be the office manager, not an assistant. It's a smaller practice than where you are now, but it would be a step up for you. Promise me you'll think about it."

"Okay," Tess replied warily. "I will think about it, but I've got to go now. Eva's here."

They said their goodbyes as Eva reluctantly got into the car. Tess handed her a tissue from her purse, then waved to Mrs. Bedford who was consoling her daughter.

On the ride home, Tess attempted conversation with her silent daughter. The tears had stopped and Eva was huddled against the passenger side door, her head resting against the glass, staring gloomily ahead. "How did it go with Charli today?"

"Mom, how could you even ask that? I had to say *goodbye* to her. It was *awful*."

Tess reached over and laid her hand on Eva's shoulder. Eva shrugged it away, and silence reigned the rest of the way home.

Later, after a quick supper of grilled cheese and fruit salad, Tess tried again. "Hey, let's watch the first two episodes of *Gilmore Girls* tonight. Micah's out with the guys, so it's just you and me. Remember, I told you about the show? Lorelai is the mom and Rory's the daughter." She attempted to smooth back Eva's hair, and again, Eva moved away from her touch. "After all, you and I are Gilmore girls too, right?"

Eva rubbed her upper arms, and fought back more tears. "I'm really tired. I just want to go to my room and wait for Micah to come home."

Frustrated, Tess let her go. Aunt Kit had sent her the entire *Gilmore Girls* DVD set when Tess was pregnant with Eva, and she had watched every episode, happily anticipating a Lorelai-Rory relationship with her own daughter. Heaven knows, she hadn't had that kind of relationship with her own mother.

She sighed as she settled onto the sofa now, clicking the remote to the National Geographic channel. There would be no *Gilmore Girls* tonight. Another episode of *Cosmos: Possible Worlds* would have to suffice.

Much later, when Micah came home, the only light in the apartment was spilling out from under Eva's door. He quickly made a peanut butter and banana sandwich in the kitchen, cut it in half and placed it on a paper plate. "Hey Evie-Bee," he whispered, knocking softly on her door. "You still up?"

"Yes." The word, laden with sadness, was muffled under the sound of the TV.

Entering, he glanced around the room which looked as if a cyclone had destroyed any semblance of order. Clothes, books, and games were scattered about. Yup, that was Eva's room, quite different from his. Micah's personality gravitated more to orderliness, just like Tess. He picked his way through the debris and settled himself next to her, back against the headboard, the sturdy bulk of Jasper between them. "Want a bite?" he asked, offering half of the sandwich.

Eva sat up, rearranging the covers to make room for him. "No thanks."

"What are you watching?" He took a bite of the sandwich and wiped his mouth.

"*Gilmore Girls*. It's the one where Rory and Lorelai are on that road trip to Harvard after Lorelai leaves Max."

He put his arm around his little sister. "It's getting late. I'll watch the rest of it with you if you promise to go to sleep when it's over."

"Okay." She leaned into Micah's side. He smelled like sweat and chai mingled with the cologne he always wore, reminding her of evergreen trees in the park. He smelled like home.

# Chapter 4

The next day, Tess spent some time rummaging through her dresser drawers. Aunt Kit's phone call had stirred memories that she had long since packed away—memories of meeting a boy named Luca when she and Cecilia had gone to Seahaven for two weeks the summer she was fifteen. He had been sitting in the shade of the big birch tree near Kit's house on Sunrise Beach one morning, reading *A Brief History of Time,* one of her favorite books back then. There was something about the inquisitive kindness in his brown eyes that dissipated her shyness; she had surprised herself by plopping down on the grass and connecting with him through Stephen Hawking's theories about black holes and arrows of time.

Opening yet another drawer, she smiled as she allowed more memories in—the two of them riding their bikes through the Seahaven Common, fishing at the pier, and always talking, talking, talking. Tess didn't think she'd ever talked that much in her life, except with her best friends Chiara and Quinn.

She knelt on the floor to more easily access the bottom drawer, touching the fingers of one hand to her lips as she remembered. Luca had been the best kisser. Not that she'd been kissed by a boy before that summer, but she had been kissed since, and it was never the same, not even with Cameron who had lived with her—off and on—for eight years.

Tess dug beneath a pile of winter cardigans in the bottom drawer and finally found what she was looking for—a long wooden box, the inexpensive kind that you find in souvenir stores. The word *Seahaven* was etched on the top in a nautical font, and the small latch appeared rusty and worn. She ran her fingers over the top and felt the rough wood, frowning as she remembered saying a hasty goodbye to Luca. Her mother had insisted on leaving three days early, using a museum fundraiser as an excuse. She and Luca had both wiped away tears as they promised to stay in touch.

On the ride back to Connecticut—which seemed to take forever—Cecilia had shared her views with Tess, an unwilling and captive audience. "That boy is not for you. Luciano Silva is the son of a Portugee fisherman, do you hear me?" She purposely mispronounced the word *Portuguese* while wrinkling her nose in distaste.

Tess knew, even then, that there was no point in arguing with her mother. She and Luca had managed to stay in touch via email for almost a year, growing closer with each long missive. In the spring, he and his family moved back to Portugal, but three months later, his emails abruptly ceased. Still, Tess kept trying, until the day her email bounced back with a formal message: *account closed*. Devastated, she had called Aunt Kit, having found her number in the family address book, but Kit had no idea how to reach the Silva family either.

Tess slowly opened the souvenir box now, rifling through the folded papers, each of which contained a printout of one of Luca's emails. Even now, almost twenty-six years later, she could still remember her teenage self's anguish tied in a double square knot at the pit of her stomach. She and Luca had been so close. To not know why the emails had stopped, or even if he was still alive had been emotional torture. She bit her lower lip and rummaged underneath the folded emails, searching. Ah, there it was. She pulled out a necklace, the inexpensive kind also found at souvenir shops. This one was made of tiny seashells with bits of aqua and bottle-green sea glass threaded through it. She held it to her chest, remembering the way Luca had lovingly placed it over her head, lifting her hair so it wouldn't get caught in the shells. She had worn that necklace for nearly a year, even though her mother frowned whenever she saw it. There were no more family trips to Seahaven after that.

"Hey Mom, whatcha got?" Micah was standing at the door, biting into an apple.

Startled, Tess turned. "It's a necklace that . . . a friend gave me when I was fifteen."

"It's pretty," he said, moving into the room. "Want me to put it on you?"

"What? No, that's okay." She touched the Mother's Day necklace which rested at the hollow of her throat. "I'd rather wear this one."

"You can wear both." He set the apple down on the bureau and wiped his hands on his jeans, then clasped the necklace around her neck. She shivered at the coolness of the shells and sea glass against her skin, but also at the memories that it called forth. She could almost smell the salt air as she stood, facing the small mirror on the wall. Micah placed his hands on her shoulders. "See? What did I tell you?" He kissed his mother on the cheek, then picked up his apple and began to saunter out of the room.

"Wait."

He turned.

"Thank you."

"No probs! Anything for my mom."

"Micah." Tess cleared her throat. "I'd like to talk with you and Eva. Do you have a minute? It's important."

He looked at her curiously; if she'd been paying closer attention, she might have seen a flash of guilt cross his face. "Sure, I guess. I'm headed over to Javier's to shoot some hoops. You mean right now?"

"Yes." Tess put the sweaters back in the bottom drawer and closed it gently.

"Okay, I'll get Eva. Meet you in the living room?"

"Here's the thing," Tess said, her voice a little shaky. She perched on the edge of the old green recliner, facing her children who sat side by side on the matching worn sofa. Micah was still munching his apple; Eva was playing with a wide section of hair that spilled over her shoulders and into her lap. "I might be going to visit Aunt Kit in Seahaven next weekend."

"Why?" Eva sounded wary. The only time she got to see her mom was on Saturday and Sunday and now she was going away for a whole weekend? It figured.

Tess looked down at her hands which restlessly played with the hem of her navy shorts. "Aunt Kit has arranged a job interview for me at a dental practice up there. They need an office manager and I'm qualified for that. It would be a promotion . . . if they were to actually offer me the job."

Eva stared at her mom, dumbfounded, then glanced at Micah who was chewing nonchalantly on the last bite of his apple. "You might get a new job? In *Maine*?"

"I might."

"But where would we live?"

"Nothing's definite yet, hon. It's just an interview. They might not even like me. I don't have to go if you—"

"It sounds like a great idea!" Micah elbowed his sister and gave her a stern look. She wrinkled her nose at him. "Mom deserves a promotion. Don't you think so, Evie?"

Eva frowned, kicking the heels of her bare feet against the bottom of the sofa. "I guess so. But if you get the job, we'd have to move to Maine."

"We would. Aunt Kit owns an apartment building close to the center of Seahaven, did I tell you that?"

Micah nodded as Eva shook her head.

Puzzled, Tess noticed Micah's nod. How did he know about this? She was sure she hadn't mentioned it to either one of them as Aunt Kit rarely came up in conversation. "We could live in one of the apartments, and the rent would be less than what I'm paying here, plus I'd be making more money."

"That sounds perfect!" Micah stood, moved to the kitchen doorway and tossed his apple core into the wastebasket. He grinned with self-satisfaction, then leaned against the door jamb, hands stretching upwards. "I think you should go for it!"

"Thanks, Micah." She turned toward her daughter. "What do you think? I won't go if you don't want me to."

Eva was quiet for a long time. She pinched a section of hair in her fingers and smoothed it over her upper lip several times. Talk about pressure. It sure looked like her mom wanted to go to this interview. Why couldn't there be an interview right here in Connecticut? But then again, what did she care if they moved to Maine, or Mars for that matter? Wherever they went—unless it was California—Charli wouldn't be there. And why did Micah seem so excited about it? She glanced up at her brother who smiled at her encouragingly. He was nodding his head slowly, up and down. She felt defeated. "It's okay, I guess." She forced a smile and sat on her hands. "Can I go now?"

Tess's heart caught at the discontent in Eva's voice. "Sure. Thank you both for understanding. It might not even come to anything. And Micah? Can you be here for Eva next weekend? I'm going to leave on Saturday morning."

Micah grabbed his wallet from the small table by the front door. "You bet! Evie, I've got one more art project to turn in. You can help me with it . . . we'll even make our own pizza."

Eva's face brightened. She loved helping Micah with his art projects.

Eva's face brightened. She loved helping Micah with his art projects.

The following Saturday, Tess summoned all her courage, slipped on a sleeveless navy dress with a white short-sleeved sweater. She brushed her hair, secured it with a thin headband, clasped the Mother's Day necklace around her throat, and headed for Maine, leaving the seashell necklace on top of her dresser.

She drove the three hours north on Route 95, humming along with Alicia Keys and Jason Mraz, then made a short stop in York to refresh what little makeup she was wearing. Almost there. She set the GPS for the Pearly Whites Dental offices in Seahaven.

On arrival, Tess stayed in her car, breathing deeply and summoning a bit of confidence, following through on her intention for more positive thinking. She wasn't sure if she wanted this job or not, but she hoped to at least make a respectable impression.

Entering the two-story modern building across from Seahaven Common, Tess was the one who was impressed. Yes, she had always loved going to the dentist. And yes, she loved the feeling of hushed healing that always pervaded dental offices, but this place had a brighter, more peaceful vibe than any she'd experienced before. The front door opened into a large waiting area complete with a massive stone fireplace, several comfy chairs and low tables covered with magazines. Two people sat waiting: one was reading a picture book to a toddler; the other was playing a game on his phone. It was a warm morning in early June, but Tess could also imagine how welcoming it would be for patients to walk in here on a cold winter's day.

"Hey there!" A receptionist wearing what was obviously a platinum blond wig called out to her. Tess, standing in the middle of the waiting room, had been admiring the large framed art pieces that hung on the walls. The soothing watercolor paintings depicted the sea at various times of day; each shone with a definitive Asian influence. "Do you have an appointment, hon?"

Tess hurried to the receptionist. "Yes, but not the kind you're thinking." She noticed the woman frown as she raised her dyed-to-match eyebrows. "I'm Tess Gilmore. I have an appointment with the Pearls . . . for the office manager position." She swallowed hard, wishing she'd brought a bottle of water or a cup of coffee.

The woman's face immediately eased and a warm smile lit her wide face. She reached across the desk and shook Tess's hand. "Tess Gilmore, I'll be! You're Kit's niece, ayuh?" Her Down East accent was quite strong.

"That's right."

The woman stood, plodded slowly to the other side of the desk, and hugged Tess.

Surprised, Tess patted the woman's back. This would never happen at the Waverly office. Their head receptionist was as stiff as a carving knife and wore a perpetual frown.

"We were happy to hear that Kit knew someone who could fill the position. Elsie Withers was here for forty years." Her eyes widened dramatically. "Poor soul. Her husband died and she decided to move to Florida. She has family there, you know."

"Oh, I—"

"Never mind," the woman patted Tess's arm reassuringly and went back behind the counter. "You're going to love it here!"

"But I—"

"Oh dear, I forgot to introduce myself. I'm Marilyn M. James. That's right. I was named after Marilyn Monroe." She struck a pose. "Do you see the resemblance?"

"That's—"

"What about you, dearie? Who were you named after?"

Tess blinked. "I guess my mom just liked the name Teresa, but she shortened it to Tess." *Except for Luca; he used to call me Tessa.* "Aunt Kit was named after Katharine Hepburn but we've always called her Kit."

"I'll be a monkey's uncle! That's news to me," Marilyn exclaimed, slapping her hands on her desk as she scrunched her hefty body back into the office chair. She peered at the computer screen. "You're right on time! Mimi and Max are all set to meet with you. I'll call—"

A middle-aged Asian man peered around the open doorway behind Marilyn's desk. He smiled at Tess. "Hi, I'm Max Pearl. You must be Tess."

"Yes, I'm so glad to meet you. Aunt Kit loves coming here."

"We love having her, although she rarely needs dental work. Is Marilyn bending your ear?" He winked.

Marilyn waved him away with a fast smile and turned to greet the next patient.

"Follow me. Mimi and I are eager to talk with you."

As they walked down the hall together, Tess felt like she was entering an enchanted dental fairyland. Each exam room they passed was painted a different inviting pastel shade. She was pleasantly surprised to see that the theme of each tidy space revolved around a different book or movie, appealing to both children and adults. The seafoam-green hallways were adorned with photographs of satisfied, smiling patients.

Max led her into a small conference room with a round table at the center. It looked like it had been made from a ship's steering wheel and covered with a thick glass top. A petite Asian woman sat at the table, busily typing on her laptop. She closed it and stood as soon as she saw Tess and Max in the doorway.

"Tess, I'm so glad you decided to meet with us. I'm Mimi. Please, have a seat." She gestured toward one of the velvet-tufted chairs. "Would you like something to drink?"

"Water would be great, thank you. I love your office; the patient rooms are so inviting!"

Max brought her a bottle of water from a small fridge under the window that looked out onto flowering dogwoods. "Thank you. That was our intention." He bowed slightly to Tess. "We wanted to create something different. Something special."

Max's black hair was short and combed back, revealing a high forehead and deep-set eyes. Mimi wore her dark hair tucked behind her ears which were dotted with tiny pearl earrings. They appeared to be in their fifties, with many laugh lines around their eyes. Tess felt immediately at home with them.

Later, she met up with Aunt Kit at Chloe's by the Sea, the new restaurant on Seahaven Harbor. One side of the dining area was open to a large terrace where customers were enjoying the view. The inside walls were stained in dark crimson; the tablecloths were pristine white, hand painted around the edges by a local artist who used bold strokes depicting brightly colored flowers, seabirds, feathers, and sailboats. Similar art hung on the walls. The whole effect was striking. There was a certain elegance to the place, but the atmosphere was open, casual, and friendly.

After the young waiter brought their wine and took their order, Kit raised her glass, inviting a toast. "Here's to new beginnings!"

Tess hesitated, then gently touched her glass to Kit's and took a sip. "Mmm . . . This is exquisite."

"Tell me all about the interview." Kit leaned back in her chair and waited patiently.

Tess admired her aunt who had just turned sixty-four and didn't look a day over fifty. Her silver hair was long and thick; she wore it loose today, past her shoulders. For many years, Kit had been a model; her hair had been dark blonde back then, but Tess thought she looked more beautiful now. Beautiful, but also wise. Kit had experienced a tremendous loss at the vulnerable age of twenty, and it had changed her. Having lost the love of her life before the wedding could bind them together in marriage, she had thrown her energy first into her career and then into creating a new life for herself in Seahaven.

"It went okay, I think." She took another sip of wine and gazed past the open deck to Seahaven Harbor. "Pearly Whites is a special place, and I really liked Max and Mimi."

Kit ran her fingers over one of the sunflowers painted on their tablecloth. "I sense a 'but' coming." She raised her eyebrows.

Tess gazed into her wine glass as if she expected it to have all the answers.

"What is it, Tess?"

"They offered me the job." Her voice lowered to almost a whisper.

Kit leaned closer. "That's wonderful!"

"They didn't even interview anyone else. How can they be sure—"

"Max and Mimi are intelligent, decisive people, and they recognize a hard worker when they see one." Kit smiled gently. "What did you tell them?"

"That I needed time to make a decision."

"Good. No need to rush into this." They both sipped their wine thoughtfully. "What did you think of the office? And did you meet Marilyn?" Kit chuckled.

"Oh, I met Marilyn all right!" Tess laughed as she remembered the receptionist's nonstop chatter and warm hug. "I loved the office. I've never seen anything like it."

"Yes, Pearly Whites is special. It sounds like your kind of place."

The waiter brought their entrees and lit the candle on their table even though it wasn't near dark yet. Tess speared a scallop and bit into it. Sweet and juicy. "It *is* my kind of place," she replied between mouthfuls. "But Eva wasn't happy about me coming up here for this interview. I don't know if I want to uproot her . . . us . . . right now."

Kit nibbled on a piece of grilled salmon with pineapple salsa. "You told me that her best friend moved to California, so this might actually be the very *best* time."

"You're probably right, but she's already upset about the years I spent working fulltime and going to night school. We've hardly had any time together at all and she's growing up so fast."

"All the better to make the move now," Kit said sensibly, resting her elbows on the table a moment before scooping up some wild rice. "Pearly Whites is a smaller practice, so you'll be able to spend more time with Eva. Micah will be in . . . I mean, he'll be gone soon, and Seahaven is the perfect place to spend time with her again. You loved coming here with your parents when you were little, remember?"

"Yes. Every summer for a few weeks. I was happy here, especially when I met—"

"Luca Silva. The two of you were together a lot that summer. You were, what? Sixteen?"

"Fifteen. He was seventeen. You're right, we were together, until Mom dragged me home, three days early. I never found out what happened to him."

Kit savored another piece of salmon as she gazed thoughtfully at Tess. "What about dating? Have you met anyone? It's been a long time since Cameron left."

"Tell me about it," Tess replied ruefully. "The truth is I haven't had time to date. What little time I've had over the last four years, outside of work and classes and studying, has gone to Micah and Eva, and I'm telling you, that has not been much."

Kit laid her hand gently on Tess's arm. "I hope you'll consider taking the job and making this move. It could change everything for you."

"That's exactly what I'm worried about. I'm not sure I want everything to change." She speared another scallop and enjoyed the savory sweetness that played on her tongue.

"Of course. You've gotten used to your life and your routines, but sometimes we need to haul ourselves out of our comfortable little ruts." She chewed thoughtfully. "You always liked making lists. Remember Rory on *Gilmore Girls*?" Tess smiled. "Of course, you do. She used to make hard decisions with her lists of pros and cons. Why don't you do the same? Take your time. The Pearls can wait a bit."

Tess wiped her mouth with the cloth napkin and was about to reply when the waiter returned to whisk away their plates. "Are you interested in Chloe's Delight?" he asked, making eye contact with each woman. He looked like a college student on summer break—as handsome as Owen Wilson: tall, blond, and tan.

"Chloe's Delight?" Tess asked.

"It's a special dessert that Chloe bakes, and every day it's different. Today we have Blueberry Peach Cobbler with Honey Vanilla Ice Cream. I can bring the dessert cart around if you want to see the other choices."

Aunt Kit leaned forward. "That is my absolute favorite thing that Chloe makes. I'll have one. And an herbal tea."

"Make that two Chloe's Delights," Tess added. "And a coffee please."

When the waiter left, Kit said, "Sometimes they also serve Chloe's Secret."

"What on earth is that?"

"It might be a main course; it might be a dessert. But there's always a secret ingredient, and if you can guess what it is, then your meal is on the house!"

"That sounds like fun," she murmured automatically, glancing around the restaurant again. When was the last time she had eaten in an upscale restaurant like this? For that matter, when was the last time she had left New Haven? Last October with Chiara to visit Quinn in Vermont? Yes, that was it. It had been way too long.

"Moving here could lighten your load a little. We've got fresh ocean air and friendly people. You'll love Jasper Goodman; he lives in one of the apartments in my building and works at the theatre. Also, Glory and her grandkids; Kalila is sixteen and Samuel is five. And do you remember the sunrises? We're famous for our sunrises."

"Aunt Kit, the sun rises everywhere. How can one little town be famous for the sunrise?" They both laughed. "I did love watching the sunrises with you. Mom never wanted to join us but I brought Luca once.

Kit's eyes crinkled into a smile. "I liked him."

"I really liked him too."

The waiter came by with their tea and coffee. "Your Chloe's Delight will be out in a minute." Tess frowned. She was looking forward to the dessert. But why did the word *delight* make her so uncomfortable?

# Chapter 5

*E*va was stuffed to the brim from supper and didn't want to even think about food for the next hundred days. She and Micah had slept late, then gone to the movies with Philip and Javier. Back at the apartment she helped him with his final art project—a mixed media piece that was as big as the kitchen door. She loved helping him glue all the parts down once he decided what went where. This one contained hundreds of pieces of colored paper and fabric, glued into an amazing design like a kaleidoscope.

After the art project, they had made pizza from scratch. Her half was sprinkled liberally with cheese, mushrooms, peppers and sausage. There wasn't much that Eva didn't like to eat! Micah's half consisted only of cheese, ham, and pineapple. He named it Aloha Pizza and they gave each other a high five. She ate a piece of his and he had a bite of hers but picked off the peppers and mushrooms.

The whole apartment now reeked of a disgusting combination of epoxy glue, tomato sauce, and melted cheese, so the windows were open to let in the light June breeze. Eva was in bed, reading a Nancy Drew book for the third time. She closed the book when she started to get sleepy, rubbing her eyes with one hand and Jasper with the other. She kissed Jasper on the head, enjoying the soft, happy purr that vibrated through him. The dolphin-shaped clock beside her bed showed 12:15 a.m. She loved it when Micah let her stay up as late as she wanted.

Heading to the bathroom down the hall, she wrinkled her nose at the obnoxious odor leftover from their day of art and pizza. The light was on under Micah's door and she could hear him talking. Curious, she knocked lightly on the door. "Micah, who's there?"

The door opened and Micah waved, his phone caught between his shoulder and ear. He held up a forefinger, then turned away. "Yeah, it'll be hard for all of us, but you understand, right? And I already told Jasper about the—" She could see him nodding his head, then running his hands over his super-short hair. "Eva's here, I've got to go. I'll talk with you before I . . ." He turned around and glanced at Eva. ". . . you know." He paused, listening. "I will. Thanks for everything."

He tossed the phone on the bed, turned to Eva and began tickling her. "What are you doing up, Evie Bee? It's waaaaay past your bedtime!"

Giggling, she sank down on the bed, long hair flying around her face. Micah tucked it behind her ears. "Who were you talking to?" She licked her lips; they were dry from the movie popcorn, the pizza, and the laughter.

"Aunt Kit."

Eva was surprised. "Aunt Kit? Did you call her or did she call you? Is Mom okay?"

"Lots of questions, Li'l Sis, lots of questions!"

"Can't help it. I'm a curious girl."

Micah chuckled as he grabbed her hands and pulled her to her feet. "Mom is fine. Time for bed, Curious Girl."

Eva headed for the door, then turned around. "Why were you talking to Aunt Kit?"

He hesitated, put his hands to his cheeks and looked at her thoughtfully. Finally, he said, "I talk with her every week."

"You're kidding! Why?"

"Remember that summer when you and Charli went to Girl Scout camp? Aunt Kit needed help painting her house on Sunrise Beach. Man, that's a big house! I spent a month in Seahaven and we hung out together. She owns a gift shop downtown; it's called Coastal Soul. She even sold some of my art there, remember? I gave you a commission on the piece you helped me with—the one with all the feathers and the Emily Dickinson poem." Eva nodded. "Kit is cool. You'll like her."

Eva thought she'd have to see about that. Besides, Mom might not even get the job. Maybe they wouldn't have to move. "Does Mom know you talk with Aunt Kit every week?"

"I'm not sure, why?"

"I mean, she's *Mom's* aunt. I don't think Mom even talks to her that much."

"Hey, she's our aunt too. Related by blood, right? That makes her family." He lightly poked her shoulder with one forefinger. "Boop!"

Giggling, Eva swiped his hand away. "I guess so, but why were you talking about Jasper? Does she even know I have a cat?"

"Jasper Goodman is Aunt Kit's handyman. He's also the props guy at the theatre, and an actor. He and I painted Aunt Kit's house together that summer and we got to be friends."

Eva yawned. This was all so strange. Micah had spent a whole month in Seahaven and talked to Aunt Kit more than their mother did! If that wasn't enough, there was a guy there with the same name as her cat. She was now the teeniest bit curious about what it might be like to live there. "Okay, I'm going to bed now. See you in the morning."

"If I don't see you first!"

"Talk about the crack of dawn," Tess said at four-thirty the next morning, sipping hot coffee from a silver travel mug. She was in the passenger seat of Kit's green Forester; they were headed for Seahaven Harbor.

"Yes, my dear, the dawn is starting to crack!" Kit, dressed in a pair of soft blue yoga pants and a flowing white sweater, looked stunning. Tess smoothed her hair back and hoped that she didn't look too disheveled in her wrinkled jeans and plain black T-shirt.

They arrived at the harbor, noticing only a few other cars. Tess yawned as they spread a blanket on one of the large flat rocks that made up the jetty. She hugged her knees to her chest and took several deep breaths of the salty air. Kit's other rental property stood back a bit from the beach, an imposing structure of weathered gray shingles and sky-blue shutters. No lights were on although there were signs of occupancy: towels hung over several Adirondack chairs, two red bikes sprawled listlessly in the grass. Tess thought that if she was lucky enough to live there—or even rent the place for a week—she would be sitting out on that generous wide deck to watch the sunrise every single morning.

When Tess was little and had visited Seahaven with her parents, Kit had been living in that same beach house, and they had stayed there with her in two of the guest bedrooms. Tess clearly remembered how spacious the rooms were, how uncluttered the house was, and how the salt air flooded her senses even on rainy days when the windows were closed. On one of those rainy days, when she was nine, she had wandered into an upstairs room that happened to be Kit's meditation space, or "Quiet Room" as she often referred to it. Young Tess had been moved by the feeling she got when she entered that room. She remembered sitting cross-legged on a blue and green woven rug for several minutes, allowing a simple peace—although she didn't have a word for it at the time—to soak into her body and mind. She had been inexplicably drawn back to that room many times during her summer visits, sneaking in whenever she knew her aunt was out of the house.

The sky was starting to lighten around the edges now and the silvery moon high in the sky began to fade as daylight claimed the starless sky.

Aunt Kit, sitting next to Tess on the blanket, leaned toward her niece until their shoulders were touching. "Did you dream all night about Pearly Whites? Or Chloe's Delight?"

Tess groaned and placed her hand on her stomach. "Wow, that was incredible."

Kit leaned back, resting her palms on the cool stone beneath them. "The best Blueberry Peach Cobbler I've evah tasted, that's for sure."

Tess chuckled at her aunt's slight Down East accent, and they watched as the horizon began to display a shimmery orange and pale-yellow stripe. "Actually, I don't dream."

"Not at all? Not ever?"

"I used to, when I was younger. But I haven't, not in a long time." The sky lightened a little more and they could see the barest hint of the sun's halo as it began to brighten the horizon.

"We all dream," Kit replied kindly. "But we don't always remember. Have you thought any more about the job offer?" Kit loosened the lid on her ceramic flowered travel mug and took a sip of tea. A trail of peppermint wafted in the air around them, then disappeared.

"Haven't thought about much else." She shaded her eyes as the sun rose up, bright and magnificent. "Wow. I'd forgotten how amazing this is. Do you come out here every day?"

"Nearly. Once in a while I like to sleep in. I usually stay home when it's raining."

"Or snowing."

Kit nodded.

"Are the winters up here brutal?"

"They can be, but we haven't had a bad one in a while. Not much worse than what you've experienced in Connecticut."

"I wondered. I mean, it's so perfect here in the summer . . ." They turned sideways on the rock to avoid looking directly at the blazing sun which was now striping the horizon with intricate shades of russet, raspberry and gold.

"Our summers *are* just about perfect." Kit lowered her voice to a whisper. "But the tourists? Well, that's another story." She waved her hand toward the parking lot which was now a third full. People were chattering loudly, exclaiming over the sunrise, and settling in on the sand with their beach chairs. "We love our tourists dearly, of course, because the money they bring in the summer and fall keeps us afloat during the winter. But they can be noisy."

Tess noticed the crowd that was growing larger by the minute. "It seems they think sunrise starts after the sun has already risen."

"That's why I like to come out here when it's still dark. Less distraction. More peace."

"It is peaceful," Tess agreed, taking a deep breath and exhaling slowly. "But I'm not sure I can move here."

Kit patted Tess's arm as she slowly stood and stretched her tall, lithe body into the yoga tree pose. "Even if you decide not to take the job, I'd like it if we could visit more often."

Tess stood beside her and tried to imitate Kit's posture. Her own body was tight, not used to such gentle, flowing movement, but she could feel some of the tension freeing itself as she began. "I'd like that too."

"You and Eva could stay with me in the cottage—"

"And Micah too?"

Aunt Kit hesitated. "Of course. Micah is always welcome. You know, we talk almost every week."

"You . . . what?" Tess dropped back down to a seated position on the rock, legs stretched out in front of her, warming in the sun.

Kit eased herself back down next to Tess and took a sip of tea. "Yes, ever since he came up here two summers ago to help me paint the house. We hung out, your son and Jasper and me."

"I didn't know that."

Kit was silent for a long time as they savored the warming June air and the pale blue sky that showed off a now white-hot sun. "I always look forward to Micah's calls because I like being reminded that I'm still connected to your family. After your father died . . ." She tented her fingers pensively for a moment. "He was a good brother, but I think your mom only put up with me while he was alive. After he died, she pretty much cut me off from the family."

"I always wondered about that." Tess turned to face her aunt. "I'm sorry I haven't reached out to you more."

"It's all in the past, Tess, all in the past. At one point I thought I might move closer to you. There are lovely small beach towns in Connecticut. But—"

"Cecilia." Tess glumly finished Kit's sentence.

"Right. When I was younger, she thought I was a bad influence. To be honest, I don't blame her. I was living the high life in New York, traveling the world. Life in the fast lane, and all that."

"I can't imagine you being a bad influence."

"In my younger days I did my fair share of partying and that's what Cecilia objected to. Smoking. Drinking. Playing around. But in my forties, I stopped all of that and stuck to the modeling gigs. By then, she . . ." Kit leaned forward and touched fingers to toes. "She didn't want to have anything to do with me. To be honest, I was glad to be away from her, because who wants to be around someone who dislikes you so much?"

Tess thought of Justina and realized that what Kit said made sense. Why should she stay in a place where her own boss frowned every time they crossed paths?

"Enough of this gloomy talk about disagreeable people." Kit slowly stood. "I'm getting hungry. Come on, I'll treat you to breakfast at Sunnyside Up. It's a new place, right around the corner. They open at sunrise every day, rain or shine, and only serve breakfast."

"Sounds good," Tess agreed, following her aunt back to the car, releasing all thoughts of her life in New Haven. For now.

The next week passed in such a blur that Tess had a headache every other day. Between meeting Justina's increasingly unreasonable demands at the office, getting ready for Micah's graduation party on Friday, and trying to comfort Eva who was acting more and more depressed now that Charli was gone, she hardly had time to think about her weekend respite in Maine or the job offer. And when she did think about it . . . that's when the headaches were the worst.

The only relief she experienced was early on Wednesday morning during her monthly Zoom check-in with Chiara and Quinn, close friends who called themselves the Mutual Admiration Society. Chiara had been in Tess's fourth grade class and they quickly bonded over their unusual addiction to the National Geographic Channel and mocha milkshakes. Quinn had moved to Connecticut in their freshman year; the girls quickly clicked with her sunny personality, and the twosome became a threesome. Chiara was now teaching fifth grade in Stratford, not far from New Haven. Even though they lived twenty minutes apart, Tess and Chiara rarely found time to see each other, but the three of them made time to get together one weekend every October. Quinn was an artist living in Vermont, married to a farmer named Pilgrim, and that's usually where they gathered; autumn in Vermont was a lovely place to be.

Daylight was just starting to edge in through her bedroom curtains as Tess sipped her coffee. A swift wave of relief and gratitude rushed through her body when she clicked the Zoom link and her friends' faces popped up on the screen. Lorelai Gilmore only had one best friend—Sookie the chef at the Dragonfly Inn in Stars Hollow. Tess felt lucky to have *two* Sookies to turn to when life's dial flipped to overwhelm—Chiara the teacher, and Quinn the artist.

They did their special ritual at the beginning, the way they always began their Zooms: palms open to the screen in welcome, then hands to their hearts.

"Who's going first?" asked Quinn, her blonde hair caught up in a bright flame-colored scarf.

"Everything's copacetic here," responded Chiara, nodding slowly. "School's almost over and I'll be glad when I'm out from under the end-of-year paperwork." Her long hair was black and wavy, bangs casually swept to the side.

"How are the kids?" Tess asked.

"Oh, they're fine. Macy's already whining about her summer job, but once she gets to the YWCA, I know she'll love it. Ricky has recently discovered girls, so that's gonna be fun." She smiled indulgently, aware that her complaints were received for what they were—expressions of love.

"I've been selling out of my soaps and lotions at the craft fairs," Quinn stated with a flourish. Her eyes were bright, revealing passion for her craft. "We've added ten more goats to the farm, so there's lots more to make! My latest goat milk soap 'flavor'. . ." She drummed dramatically on her kitchen table. "You'll love this. We're calling it Vanilla with a Cherry on Top!"

Chiara gave a jaunty thumbs-up sign. "Be sure to send us samples! Tess, what's going on with you?"

Tess tried to smile, but found it difficult. "Micah's graduating on Friday. I can hardly believe it."

"He must be so excited!" Quinn squeezed a lemon into her mug of tea. "And Eva?"

"Eva's best friend just moved to California so she's not a happy camper. No matter what I try to make her feel better, she pushes me away."

"Poor thing," murmured Chiara. "That's hard. I can't imagine if one of us had to move far away from each other when we were young."

"There's something else. I had a job interview on Saturday." She could see both women lean forward until their faces were taking up the whole screen.

"Tell us more!" "Say what?" Chiara and Quinn spoke at the same time.

She told them about it, ending with, "I don't know if I can make a move like this right now with Eva so upset, and Micah getting ready to leave for college in September."

Quinn held up her hand. "No, Tess. This is absolutely the *best* time to make a move. Eva's friend is gone. Moving to Seahaven would be a great distraction for her."

"That's what Aunt Kit said."

"I'm with Quinn." As usual, Chiara's voice was soft and serious. "We all know you're not happy at the Waverly office. You'd be moving farther away from me, but you'd be living near Kit. That's definitely a positive."

"Also, farther away from that annoying mother of yours." As Quinn spoke, she flung her arms wide. "You need to get out of the city; it's messing with your head. And your life."

Tess sighed. "I suppose you're right, but I can't picture it. Just thinking of packing and moving, starting a new job . . . makes me tired."

Chiara added, "Moving is a taxing venture, no way around it. But think of how happy you'd be in Seahaven. All that fresh air. A new start. You deserve to be happy, and the best part is you'll be farther away from your memories of Cameron." She waved a hand in the air, as if brushing off a swarm of pesky flies.

"There are memories in Seahaven too," Tess murmured, but the others didn't hear her.

At that moment, Eva pounded on the door. "Mom, Mom!" she cried. "Come quick! Micah's gone!"

# Chapter 6

Tess jumped up, almost knocking her chair over, and opened the door. She took in Eva's rumpled nightgown, messy hair, and the tears streaming down her pale face, then quickly turned back to the laptop screen. "Guys, I've got to go. Text you later." She blew a quick kiss to her concerned friends, then put her arms around Eva. "Tell me what's wrong."

Eva took her mother's hand and pulled her to the kitchen. She knelt shakily on a chair and pointed to a folded piece of notebook paper lying open on the table. Tess warily picked up the paper with one hand; her other arm around Eva's trembling shoulders.

*Dear Mom and Evie,*

*I wanted to tell you this in person but I couldn't figure out how. I joined the Army and am headed this morning to Fort Jackson in South Carolina. The recruiter gave permission to skip my graduation ceremony. I'm sorry. I know you want me to go to college and I promise I'm going to do that when my commitment is up. I want to see the world first, and do something good for my country. I'll be in Basic Training for ten weeks and then I'll come home before I go to my next assignment.*

*Will call tonight when I get settled in.*

*Mom, take care of Eva. Eva, take care of Mom. I love you both.*

*Micah*

Tess dropped the note and held her hand to her furiously-beating heart. What on earth had he done? Momentarily stunned, she dropped into the chair next to Eva.

Eva stared at her mom, wide-eyed. "He joined the Army," she whispered. "People *die* in the Army!" She grabbed a napkin to wipe away her tears.

"Honey, no! That's not what the Army is for."

"What's it for then?" Eva jumped off the chair and stood facing Tess, hands on her slim hips, tears replaced by a perplexed scowl.

Tess rubbed her forehead, searching for the right words. "The Army is for keeping our country safe." She tried to keep her voice low and steady, but it was harder than she expected. A grim headache began to scrape at her temples. "Hardly anyone dies nowadays in the Army." She had no idea if that was true, but it sure sounded good, and with all her heart, she wanted to believe it.

"I still don't understand. Why did he go?"

Tess grimaced and pulled her daughter close. "I don't know why he thought he couldn't tell us first, but remember how he loved watching *The Amazing Race*? He wanted to see the world and . . . well . . . joining a branch of the military is one way to do that."

Eva allowed the embrace for exactly one minute, leaning into her mother in a way she hadn't since she was seven. Then she pushed away from Tess.

"I'm sure he'll tell us more when he calls us tonight." Tess picked up the paper again, trying to read between the lines. What was Micah thinking? This was such a huge step for a young man. Had anyone helped him make this decision? More importantly, why hadn't he come to her? Pressing fingers to her temples, she had to admit that she knew exactly why he hadn't come to her: she was either working or at night classes; she was hardly ever home. He had taken on the responsibility of babysitting Eva for the past four years, whenever she'd needed him. She thought he'd done it gladly but now she wasn't sure. How was Eva supposed to get safely home from school, and who was going to stay with Eva this summer while Tess was at work?

Aggravated, she dropped the paper onto the table, then noticed something written on the back. "Eva, look. He wrote you a separate note."

She grabbed the paper from her mother's hands, almost ripping it in half as she read aloud, "Evie, I left you a present in the living room on the top shelf of the bookcase. Mom can reach it for you." She raced to the living room, pointing to the shelf which almost reached the ceiling. "Can you get it for me? Please?" Eva hopped nervously from one foot to the other, pointing at a brightly-wrapped package resting atop the entire set of Harry Potter books which she'd already read twice, thank you very much.

Tess stood on tiptoe to reach the package, then handed it to Eva who eagerly tore off the wrapping paper. "It's a book," she said eagerly, then frowned when she saw it was a children's book about the Army. "Why would I want to read this?" She tossed the book on the sofa and sank, dejected, into the cushions.

"Maybe he wanted you to understand what his life would be like." Tess picked up the book and flipped through the pages. Something fell out and she caught it before it hit the floor. "Looks like this is for you too." She handed Eva a shiny silver bookmark with a bright green tassel. A sticky note was attached to it.

Eva took the bookmark gently in her hands. It was made from a thin sheet of metal, cool and smooth to the touch. Two dolphins—one large and one small—were etched onto the surface. It was from Mystic Aquarium, where he had taken her last summer. "I know you love dolphins the most," the note said in Micah's messy scrawl. "Remember what I told you that day? I'm the big dolphin and you're the little dolphin. I'll always be your big brother, no matter where I am. I love you." He had drawn several swirly hearts under his name. Tears formed in Eva's hazel eyes as she carefully set the bookmark on top of the book. "I'm going to my room now." She stood slowly and—Tess thought—somewhat painfully, as if she were eighty years old instead of eleven.

"Hon, you need to get ready for school."

"I'm not going to school today." Her tears began in earnest and Tess handed her a tissue. "There's no one to pick me up at the end of the day." She wiped her eyes and looked at her mother. "And who's going to take care of me this summer now that he's . . . gone?"

Tess touched a tissue to her own eyes, then pulled Eva onto her lap for a moment, kissing the top of her head. Her daughter smelled like strawberry shampoo and sadness. "I will pick you up from school today, Evie."

"Please don't call me Evie," she said wearily.

"I'm going to stay home today to figure things out and I'll pick you up at 3:30. Let's go to Friendly's for an early supper and ice cream."

Eva shrugged and headed for her room to get dressed. "All right. But it won't be the same without Micah."

*Figure things out. Figure things out.* Tess sat alone at the kitchen table, a stone-cold mug of coffee next to a legal pad on which she was writing furiously. Make a list, Aunt Kit had advised—the pros and cons of moving to Maine. It always worked for Rory Gilmore, but Tess had never tried it herself. The more she wrote, the longer the "pros" list became. She paused, frowning. This was unexpected.

She got up and poured the stale coffee down the sink. The mug was decorated with the words "Best Mom" surrounded by multicolored hearts; Micah had given it to her for her birthday when he was ten. Micah. She sighed and set the coffee maker to brew another cup, leaning against the counter while she waited, inhaling the rich scent which always seemed to soothe her. But not today. Today, her anxiety was too big for a simple cup of coffee.

Gazing through the window which looked out on another brick apartment building, she felt a tightness in her throat that turned to a burning heat and then rose, stinging her eyes. The irrefutable fact was that Micah had left them. Sure, he was eighteen now. A man. He was *supposed* to leave, live his own life, learn to be on his own. She knew that. But . . . the Army? When he was all set to go to RISD on a full scholarship?

She warmed her hands with the fresh cup of coffee and swallowed back the tears. She wished he had talked about this decision with her first. Then a wave of guilt hit her as she remembered the last four years of running from the office to night school and back home again, studying on the weekends, hardly any time for the kids. She had been a horrible mother. Maybe she should have stayed in the dental assistant role. What if all that time away from her son and daughter had damaged them—and her—irreparably? If she had been a better mother, maybe Micah wouldn't have left.

There was no way she could frame Micah's leaving as a positive thing. Eva was heartbroken; Charli had left, and now Micah was gone too. Who knew where he would be sent after Basic Training? How safe would he be? How could she possibly keep her baby boy safe?

Tess felt abandoned. There had been a similar ache in her body on the day she realized that Cameron was never coming back. At least Micah had taken the time to leave a note.

How was she supposed to do all of this—comfort Eva, get her to and from school, keep her busy over the summer, and work fulltime—without being able to depend on Micah? An image of her mother floated through her mind. Cecilia lived in Wallingford, which wasn't that far. Tess knew that if asked, her mother would step up and take care of Eva this summer, but she didn't want to ask her. She didn't want to put Eva through Cecilia's constant negativity. It was bad enough that Tess had had to live with it for eighteen years. No. Her mother was not an option.

She needed to create a Plan B.

Sipping her black coffee, which tasted bitter instead of comforting, she sat down and surveyed her list:

## Moving to Maine: Pros

- ✓ change of scene
- ✓ fresh air
- ✓ near the ocean
- ✓ someone to watch Eva when I'm at work
- ✓ close to Aunt Kita
- ✓ a promotion
- ✓ getting to tell Justina "I quit"
- ✓ Max and Mimi Pearl- good bosses
- ✓ weekends off

## Moving to Maine: Cons

- ✓ having to pack everything up
- ✓ starting over
- ✓ memories of Luca

Tapping her pencil against the legal pad, she looked again at the smaller list. Yes, having to pack up this apartment was going to be a pain. Starting over? That was going to take major courage, but she had done difficult things before. As for the memories of Luca, they had faded, and she'd gotten adept at pushing them away when they did surface.

The pros outweighed the cons three to one. The thought of handing in her resignation to Justina made her smile briefly. That was definitely the biggest pro on her list. She picked up the phone and dialed the Pearly Whites office first. When Marilyn's cheerful voice answered, Tess took a deep breath. She felt like she was stepping off a towering cliff, and only hoped that the landing wouldn't be as painful as it seemed from the top.

# Chapter 7

Thursday June 9
To: charlib@webmail.com
From: evareads@newhavenmail.com

OMG Charli, I miss you so much!!! Mom says we can Face-Time on Sunday and she's letting me use her laptop to email you. You won't BELIEVE this. Micah joined the ARMY!!!! And if that's not enough, guess what? Mom and I are moving to MAINE. You at least got to move somewhere warm like California. I think the winters up north are going to be AWFUL but Mom says it'll be good for us. I can't think how but I don't get a vote. She's already got a job up there and we have a place to live.

How are you? What was it like flying in the airplane? Do you like your new house?

Love and hugs,
Eva xoxoxo

Friday June 10
To: evareads@newhavenmail.com
From: charlib@webmail.com

Thanks for writing. I miss you too. The plane was fun except for when the baby threw up. What a mess! The flight attendant was NOT happy.

Micah joined the ARMY??????? Why, why whhhhhyyyy? You must be so sad.

We're all fine but it's very strange here. We have nosy neighbors who keep bringing us vegetarian food that no one will eat. Mom's pulling her hair out trying to get us unpacked. Dad already started his new job so he's no help.

There aren't any kids my age on this street and I hate the idea of a new school. Maybe your mom can get a job in San Diego and you can move here instead of Maine.

Love forever,
Charli xoxoxo

Saturday June 11
To: charlib@webmail.com
From: evareads@newhavenmail.com

I sure wish we COULD move to California. Not gonna happen. Mom says Micah wants to see the world and that's why he joined the Army but he only went to South Carolina. That's not exactly THE WORLD! I think maybe he got tired of taking care of me. I'm still really sad and don't want to do anything or go anywhere. Mom quit her job and she is busy packing but I don't want to help. Jasper says MEOW. He misses you too.

Is there a library near you? Try to get the book Anastasia Again. It's about a girl who has to start over again in a new place. I think you'll like it. Maybe it'll help.

Love and hugs,
Eva xoxoxo

Saturday June 11
To: evareads@newhavenmail.com
From: charlib@webmail.com

Mom says she'll take us to the library when she finishes unpacking and that hopefully will be before September LOL. The book sounds good. I think YOU should read it again because you're going to be starting over at a new school too! Micah loves you. He would never get tired of taking care of you.

Love you forever,
Charli xoxoxo

# Chapter 8

A week later, as they drove north on Route 95, leaving behind New Haven, the only home Eva had ever known, Tess felt her shoulders relaxing for the first time in years. It hadn't been easy to get Eva out of bed every day and into a mindset of moving forward without Micah. *Micah.* She wondered what he was doing right now. How early were new trainees in the Army required to rise? Would he regret his decision? Would she regret hers? The clock on the dashboard read five o'clock exactly. The sky was still dark but she could see the faintest bit of light beginning to fade the stars.

A while later, Tess yawned and touched her daughter's arm. "Look," she said, pointing out the window. "Sunrise!"

Eva glanced up from the book she was reading and squinted at the crimson light edging its way through the sky. "What's the big deal about sunrises?" she grumbled, turning a page in her well-loved copy of *Nancy Drew and the Hidden Staircase*.

"They're all about new beginnings, right?"

"I guess."

Tess ratcheted up her enthusiasm, even though she knew that Eva was feeling anything but. "Well, we're off to a new beginning—"

"I hate new beginnings!" Eva slammed the book shut and rested the side of her head on the cool glass of the window.

"I know you're upset because—"

"Upset? You think I'm *upset?*" Eva picked up the book and tossed it in the backseat where it landed with a thwack against the side of Jasper's crate, eliciting a sleepy meow. "I'm more than upset!" Tears formed in her eyes. "Charli's in California. She's not coming back. Micah's in the Army. Also, not coming back. And now we're moving to *Maine* where I'm going to be all alone and totally bored for the whole entire summer!" She crossed her arms over her chest.

Tess glanced at Eva, who was blinking back tears. "It's going to be hard for me too. We'll just have to . . . figure out a way to get ourselves through the hard part."

Eva looked over at her mom and attempted a weak smile. "I still wish we didn't have to go."

Tess wondered if she should continue trying to convince Eva that living in Seahaven could be an amazing adventure for both of them. She wondered if she should continue trying to convince *herself* that this move was going to be an amazing adventure. There had been no adventures of any kind in her life for a very, very long time.

She swallowed hard and flipped the turn signal. So much of parenting was hit or miss; she'd realized this years ago after Cameron had left for the last time, but it seemed that lately there had been more misses than hits. "Let's get breakfast," she said now, pulling into the parking lot beside the golden arches at one of many look-alike rest stops on the highway.

"I'm not hungry," Eva said with a yawn, although Tess heard both of their stomachs rumbling.

"I'll get you a breakfast sandwich and hash browns just in case. You can always eat them later."

While Eva waited for her mom to come back, she released her seat belt and turned around to pet Jasper through the metal grating of his crate. Jasper purred into her touch. "I'll give you a piece of egg from my sandwich," she promised, then picked up her book and held the silver bookmark to her cheek as she turned back to the front seat. She remembered the day that she and Micah had seen the dolphins at the Aquarium, but the happiness faded quickly. Her big brother was *gone*. So much for the big dolphin always being there to take care of the little dolphin. Still, she inserted the bookmark gently at the beginning of chapter four.

When Tess returned, the salty smell of the hot sandwich was too much for Eva and she gratefully peeled off the wrapper and bit into it. "Thanks, Mom," she said in between mouthfuls.

Tess lifted the lid on her cardboard cup of coffee as the familiar, soothing smell invaded the car. She placed it in the cup holder and took a bite of her breakfast burrito, then put the key in the ignition and backed out of the parking space. "Aunt Kit texted me while I was getting breakfast. She's excited to see you again."

"Whatever," Eva crumpled up the wrapper and popped it back in the white paper bag after feeding Jasper a small piece of the egg. She wiped her hands on her shorts and opened the book again, solemnly tracing a finger over the two dolphins on the bookmark.

A while later, bored and restless, Eva shut the book, carefully enclosing the bookmark on chapter seven, and rubbed her eyes. "How much further?"

Tess glanced at the GPS. "About an hour, hon."

"Do you have to go to the office today?"

"Yes. I told the Pearls I'd come in this morning to meet the rest of the staff. Do you want to come with me? You'll love the exam rooms. There's even one designed around the Harry Potter books."

Eva's eyes widened in surprise and for a moment, a glimmer of excitement shone in her eyes. Then she remembered how mad she was at her mom for making them move, and how much she hated going to the dentist. "No thanks." She twisted a bunch of hair in her right hand and feathered it across her upper lip; the softness was soothing. "You don't have to work weekends, right?"

"Right."

"What am I going to do while you're working during the week?" She picked at the hem of her T-shirt.

"You can visit with Aunt Kit or help out at her store." Tess put on her sunglasses against the morning glare. "Also, there's a girl who lives across the hall from our apartment. Kalila, I think her name is. She's sixteen and you'll be spending time with her."

"You didn't tell me I was going to have a *babysitter*! I'm not a little kid anymore!"

Tess felt her earlier relaxation ebbing away, replaced by a familiar irritation. She took a breath. "I'll feel better knowing that you're not by yourself in the apartment. Kalila can take you to the beach or she can hang out with you at home. There's lots for kids to do in Seahaven in the summer. I think Aunt Kit mentioned a program at the theatre."

"No! I can take care of myself! I've never had a babysitter before and I don't need one now. I want to stay home while you're at work. I'll read and watch TV. It's my summer vacation. I shouldn't have to have a *babysitter*!" Eva looked out the window again, shoulders slumped in defeat.

Tess brushed her irritation aside—in hopes of not stirring the waters any more than they were already stirred—and made a heartful attempt at reasoning. "You've never had a babysitter because Micah has always been there, and you spent a lot of time at Charli's house with her family. I'm trying to do what's right for you. Try thinking of Kalila as an older friend instead of a babysitter."

Eva rolled her eyes. Right. An older friend. She sighed. Just the reminder of being at Charli's house made her sad. Charli and her big, happy, *real* family. So unlike Eva's disjointed family—mother, son, daughter. That was it; that was all the family Eva had. Well, there was Gram, but she wasn't much fun and was hardly ever around. Of course, she wasn't complaining about Micah; he was the best big brother ever. But Charli was the oldest of five children. She had three little brothers and one baby sister. Charli felt like the sister Eva had always wanted but never would have. She knew that families came in all shapes and sizes, but she didn't like the shape and size of her own family.

She was deciding one thing right now. Kallie or Kalipe or whatever her name was, wasn't going to come anywhere near *babysitting* her. She'd refuse to talk to her, let alone *like* her or spend time with her.

Eva must have fallen asleep, because the next thing she knew, her mom was pointing out the Seahaven sign.

*Welcome to Seahaven, A Harbor of Safety for All*

"We're here, hon! We'll be at our new house in just a few minutes."

As much as she didn't want to be there, Eva admired the friendly-looking sign and the way the illustration of the round sun contained the ocean waves and seagulls. "You mean we'll be at our new *apartment*."

"That's right," Tess replied, turning off of Route One and onto a tree-lined side street dotted with pastel cottages. "Either way, it's our new *home*."

Eva nodded and rolled down her window. Sunshine and fresh air poured into the car and she smiled in spite of herself. "Are we close to the ocean?"

"Yes. You can't see it from here, but it's only a short walk."

Tess turned right at street sign for Beach Blessing Way, then stopped in front of an enormous Victorian house that was painted a buttery shade of yellow. "This is it, Evie—" Her daughter scowled. "I mean *Eva*. Our new home. Let's get out and find Aunt Kit!"

Eva was happy to get out of the car and move around a bit. Also, Jasper was meowing plaintively from the back seat; she was anxious to get him into the house with his litter box and breakfast.

A tall, slender woman with long silvery hair appeared from around the side of the house, walking with a younger, stockier man. The woman appeared to be floating; her soft blue skirt swirled around her ankles.

"Aunt Kit!" called Tess.

"Tess!" Kit threw her arms around her niece, then held her at arm's length. "I'm so glad you decided to come." Next, Kit focused her warmth on Eva, who let herself be hugged. "I'm happy to see you both. Bright and early too!" Still holding Eva's hand, she turned to the man beside her. "Tess and Eva Gilmore, this is Jasper Goodman. He lives—" She halted mid-sentence on hearing Eva's delighted gasp. "What's wrong, dear?"

Eva looked shyly at Jasper, then back at Aunt Kit. "It's just that . . . my cat's name is Jasper too."

Jasper let out a boisterous laugh. "I've never had a cat named after me before!"

Eva looked uncertainly at the man who had bright blue eyes and reddish-gold hair peeking out from under a *Lion King* baseball hat. He was wearing white board shorts and a fire-engine-red T-shirt with the Sands of Time Theatre logo on it. "Um, I didn't know you when I named him, so how could—"

He reached for her hand and shook it heartily. "I'm just foolin' with ya! I'm really glad you're here, neighbor. To avoid confusion, call me Theatre Jasper, and your feline can be Just Jasper."

"What a lovely synchronicity," Kit murmured thoughtfully.

Eva frowned. Was Aunt Kit always going to use such big words? Suddenly, she spotted a pretty brown and white feather on the sidewalk and stooped to pick it up. "What's a sink . . . ron . . . city?"

"Synchronicity. It's like a coincidence but much more mean-ingful." Kit pointed to the feather. "What did you find?"

Eva twirled the feather between two fingers and held it out for them to admire.

Kit and Jasper exchanged a meaningful look while Eva bent down and ran her hands through the grass as if looking for more feathers. Jasper cleared his throat. "That feather is a great example of a synchronicity, and I'd bet anything that Aunt Kit will talk with you about synchronicities later."

"I will indeed," Kit replied cheerfully. "Is your cat in the car?"

"Yes." Eva tucked the feather behind one ear; it looked striking against her hair.

"Let's get him into your new place along with these boxes and bags. Theatre Jasper lives in the apartment above yours, so you'll be seeing him around. He's my resident handyman as well as the props guy at Sands of Time." Kit noticed the puzzled look on Eva's face. "Sands of Time is our theatre; actors come from all over the world to be in our shows. Do you like theatre, Eva?"

Eva looked shyly at the adults. "Mom took me and Micah to see *Cats* in New York when I was five. I really liked that one. We also went to *The Lion King.*"

"Those are great shows, kiddo," said Jasper. He hummed a few bars from "Hakuna Matata," then continued. "We've got *Hello, Dolly!* and *Seussical the Musical* coming up at the theatre this summer. I'll get you and your mom tickets."

Tess began moving toward the car and they all followed. "That's so nice of you," she murmured.

"No problem," he replied, taking the cat carrier from her and peering into the cage solemnly. "I'm happy to meet you, *Just* Jasper. I do love your name!"

After all the boxes and bags had been piled in the living room, and her mom had gone to Pearly Whites, Eva found herself sitting on a folding chair in the apartment's kitchen with Aunt Kit. The moving van with their furniture would arrive midafternoon.

Most adults, Eva knew from experience, would use questions to fill in awkward silences like this one. She was expecting to be asked about her classes, what her favorite subject was, and what she liked to do when she wasn't in school, but Aunt Kit seemed to be okay with the silence. She wasn't even looking at Eva expectantly, or any other way for that matter. She was gazing at a painting of sunflowers that hung on the wide white wall between the two kitchen windows.

Remembering her mother telling her that she looked like Kit when Kit was younger, Eva scanned her great-aunt's face for similarities but couldn't find any. She had a kind face that was almost wrinkle-free, unlike Gram's face. Eva wondered how a person could get to be that old without wrinkles. Aunt Kit's eyes were a light shade of gray; Eva thought they looked like a poufy cloud when the sun is right behind it. In some ways, Kit looked like Eva's mom. They both had similar oval faces, but her mom's eyes were definitely brown. What Eva liked best about Aunt Kit was her hair. It was the prettiest shade of silver—definitely not gray—very thick, and almost as long as Eva's. Today that long silver hair was pulled back into a loose braid.

There was something peaceful about Aunt Kit, Eva decided, sitting in the kitchen that late June morning. She remembered feeling the same way when she went to church with Charli and her family. Not during the Mass, but before it began—when people were silently walking down the aisle, kneeling in the pews, eyes closed. Perhaps they were praying; Eva wasn't sure. She only knew that she liked that feeling, and now she was feeling it again. Right here in Seahaven, Maine, where she hadn't wanted to go in the first place. Interesting. Very interesting.

Eva finally cleared her throat. "Are you always this quiet?" she asked shyly.

Aunt Kit turned toward her great-niece. "Not always, dear heart. I can talk up a storm, you'll see! I just wanted to give you a little time to adjust. It's not easy leaving one home behind and moving into another."

*Exactly*, Eva thought, but she didn't say it out loud.

"Theatre Jasper lives upstairs. Kalila and Samuel live across the hall with their Grandmother Glory. The fourth apartment is empty right now. It will be interesting to see who will live there next."

"Interesting?"

"Yes, I always find it interesting to see who's drawn to live in these apartments."

"What do you mean? Can't you just place an ad and interview people?"

"I don't need to do that," Kit replied. "I depend on synchronicity to lead the right people here." She noticed Eva's puzzled expression. "Yes, there's that word again. What I mean is, there's usually a reason that people rent one of these apartments. Take Jasper, for instance. I needed a handyman because I'm getting too old to be changing light bulbs and painting bathrooms." She paused. "Well, I'm not too old for that, obviously . . ." She chuckled. "But I decided I didn't want to do those things anymore, and that's when Jasper came along, looking for a place to rent."

"Sounds like good timing," Eva suggested.

Kit lightly slapped her elegant hands on her knees. "Exactly! Synchronicity is when two things happen, like a coincidence, that can't be explained any other way. A *meaningful* coincidence."

"I think I get it now. So . . ." Eva played with a section of her long hair. "Is it sink-ron-icity that Mom and I are moving in right now?

Kit looked at Eva thoughtfully. "I believe it is, sweetheart, I believe it is."

"But . . . how?"

"We'll just have to wait and see now, won't we? Time will tell. Time always tells us exactly what we need to know." Kit stood and brushed her hands over her skirt as several silver bracelets jingled on her wrists. "Come, let's look at your bedroom. Theatre Jasper said he would paint it any color you want."

Eva followed her down the long hallway. Her mother's bedroom was the first door on the right; Eva's was next to it. Across the hall was a bathroom and a smaller bedroom. She paused at the last bedroom. "Is that Micah's room?"

Aunt Kit put her arm around Eva's shoulder. "It is."

Eva felt a distinct warmth radiating through her body at her aunt's touch. She'd never felt anything like it before, but it was almost like when the priest at Charli's church shook her hand after the Mass, only better. "I miss Micah," she whispered. "I wish he was here with us."

"I know, dearie, I know."

She leaned into Kit's touch.

"It's a hard thing, to be separated from those we love," murmured Aunt Kit, and Eva was amazed that she didn't try to explain his absence or reassure her that everything would be all right. Nothing would be all right as long as Micah was away. It felt like nothing would be all right ever again.

# Chapter 9

The next morning, as Tess and Eva were unpacking boxes and moving their furniture around, Jasper stopped by. "Just poppin' in for a minute, on my way to the theatre." His profuse energy filled up the stagnant corners of the apartment as he looked around. "Heck yeah, it's lookin' good in here!" He tipped his plum-colored fedora to his new neighbors, then set it back on his head as he swiveled from side to side, taking in a sublime mixture of order and chaos. "Need any help?"

"No thanks," Tess replied tersely, wiping her forehead on the sleeve of her T-shirt.

"All right. Pound on the ceiling if you need anything at all." He pointed upward. "I'll be at Sands of Time 'til five, but let me know later if I can help with anything."

Eva and Tess exchanged a puzzled look; they weren't used to such friendliness. In New Haven, they had only seen their neighbors in the stairwell once in a while. At that moment, Just Jasper scrunched out from under the sofa and ran over to Theatre Jasper, rubbing against his bare legs and tennis shoes. The cat gave up several rounds of contented, rumbling purrs as he found himself lifted up and held in strong arms that were peppered in reddish-gold hair.

"I'll be darned!" Jasper cuddled the gray cat close to his chest. "This big guy must know we have the same name." He closed his eyes and hummed an unidentifiable tune, then noticed his new neighbors staring at him in bewilderment. "I'm here to invite you to my place." He pointed at the ceiling again and gently set Jasper on the floor. "Monday night. The theatre's dark which means it's my day off and I'm having a Backwards Dinner for everyone in the apartments!" He clasped his hands dramatically in front of his stomach as though begging for the right to live. "Please, *please*, say you'll come!"

Eva squatted down to pet Just Jasper. "What's a Backwards Dinner?"

Jasper held his palms to his face. "You've never heard of a Backwards Dinner?"

Tess and Eva shook their heads, perplexed but mesmerized by their new neighbor's intense joie de vivre.

He took another step into the apartment. "First off, you dress backwards! All your clothes or just one piece. Doesn't matter. Hat. Shirt. Pants. Shoes—"

Eva giggled, wiggling her bare toes. "How do you put shoes on backwards?"

"Where there's a will, there's a way! Now, what else? We turn the chairs backwards and straddle them instead of sitting the regular way. We eat dessert *first*!" He rubbed his hands cheerfully. "That's the best part. And of course, we say grace last. That's it. Whaddya think?" He looked from Tess to Eva and back again, raising his eyebrows, lifting his hefty body up on his toes and back down again several times.

"It sounds like fun! Can we, Mom?" Eva saw Tess hesitate. "Please?"

"You'll get to meet Glory, Kalila, and Samuel. Kit said she'd come too. I promise it'll be fun!" Jasper added.

Tess resignedly picked up a pile of books and walked to the built-in bookcase on the back wall. "That'll be okay, I guess. Can we bring something?"

"Nope," Jasper replied. "This time you'll be my guests. I'll be cooking my stupendous Chicken with Sticky Rice, and Glory is bringing her famous blueberry pie which we will, of course, be eating *first*!"

"Thank you, Jasper. It sounds delicious. Right, Eva?" Tess carefully placed the books into a straight line on the top shelf.

"Sure" Eva shrugged nonchalantly while hiding a smile.

Tess looked over her shoulder at Jasper. "We'll be there. What time?"

At six o'clock on Monday, Tess and Eva climbed the stairs and knocked on Jasper's door. It had been a tiring few days of unpacking and grocery shopping, all while fighting the disorienting feeling of doing everything without Micah. Tess was carrying the emotional exhaustion of so much transition, plus she had spent eight full hours at Pearly Whites today, getting a feel for the new computer system.

"You look cute," she said to Eva as they waited for Jasper to let them in. Eva was wearing a pair of green cotton shorts, a flowered top, and a Giants baseball cap, all on backwards. This was the first time Tess had seen her enthusiastic about something since they'd found Micah's note two weeks earlier.

"Thanks! I've always wanted to eat dessert first!"

Tess chuckled and stroked the waterfall of her daughter's hair that streamed from the cap.

"You look good too." Eva tugged at the navy linen blouse her mother had buttoned up the back instead of the front. Tess's capris were white, but they weren't on backwards.

"Welcome, welcome!" Jasper wore a backwards Hawaiian shirt and bright yellow board shorts. "What, no cat?" He acted dismayed.

Eva giggled. "Just Jasper couldn't figure out how to come backwards so we left him at home."

He high-fived Eva. "Good one! Please, have a seat. Glory and the kids will be here soon. Aunt Kit called to say she has to fill in at Coastal Soul tonight, so she'll catch up with you tomorrow."

"Aunt Kit stayed with me today," Eva volunteered, looking around the living room which was laid out like theirs. Jasper's couch and two matching chairs were covered in soft creamy leather which felt cool against her bare legs. "She helped me unpack the stuff in my room."

"I bet you're glad that's done! Tess, how are you doing? You're from New Haven, right?"

"That's right."

Jasper strode into the kitchen to check on the oven. They could see him from the sofa. "Wow, *New* Haven to *Sea*haven! How about that?"

"New Haven certainly wasn't new anymore, not for me anyway."

"And I bet New Haven doesn't have a great slogan like we have!"

"Slogan?" Eva asked.

"A harbor of safety . . . for all who pass through." Jasper sang the words slowly in a deep baritone and with huge emotion as he rummaged in the fridge.

Eva glanced at her mother. "We saw that sign on Saturday. Does New Haven have a slogan like that?"

"I'm not sure, but if they did, it wouldn't be as unique as this one," mused Tess. *Harbor of safety, indeed.* It had been exactly that the summer she was fifteen; she hoped it was a safe harbor again. "Jasper, have you always lived here?"

"Heavens no! I grew up in Iowa." He spoke to them from the doorway. "My dad was a rabbi; my mom stayed home. Big family—three sisters, two brothers."

Eva eagerly moved to the edge of the sofa. "Wow!" Her voice was tinged with awe. "I wish I was in a big family like yours."

Tess bumped her daughter's shoulder. "Eva! Don't say that!"

"It's true!" Eva insisted. "We used to be a family of three and that was bad enough but now Micah is gone, so it's just two."

Tess looked helplessly at Jasper. "Sorry about that. We don't mean to be glum. We're both missing Micah."

"I heard he joined the Army."

"That's right," Eva said, crossing her arms over her chest. "He's in South Carolina for eight more weeks!" She paused. "After Basic Training, he'll be sent somewhere else but we don't know where." She looked at Jasper who had returned to the matching recliner directly opposite her. "Have you ever been in the Army?"

"I sure haven't. But wait 'til you meet Glory. Her daughter's in the Air Force."

Eva straightened. "Really? Her *daughter*?"

"I guess I need to get my daughter up to date on women's options," Tess said wryly as a light knock sounded at the door.

Jasper chuckled and greeted his other downstairs neighbors, hugging them the way he'd hugged Tess and Eva, then made introductions all around. Glory Jones was a short, curvy woman with a short Afro peppered with gray. She had a warm smile and Tess liked her immediately. "Tess and Eva, I'm happy to meet you!" Glory said, shaking their hands heartily. "People must call you the Gilmore girls."

"Not if I can help it," Eva murmured, glancing quickly at her mother who frowned and looked away.

Kalila stood a little taller than her grandmother, with the same wide face and dimpled cheeks. Her shoulder length hair was studded with many tight braids that were tipped with an astounding array of lavender and purple beads. When she moved, a pleasant clicking sound met their ears. She wore a pair of jean shorts with a backwards belt and a gauzy white top that set off her dark skin.

"You must be Sam," Tess said, crouching down and offering her hand to the five-year-old boy who seemed strangely serious for one so young. Perhaps it was the gold-rimmed glasses that he wore along with the white button-up shirt and bow tie, both of which were on backwards.

"Don't call me *Sam*. I am Sam-u-el!" he announced, standing with his legs spread and arms raised up so that he looked like a little X.

"Please?" prompted Glory, gently touching his head.

"O-*kay*," he announced with a tinge of annoyance. *"Please* call me Sam-u-el. *That* is my name. I am *not* Sam!"

"I stand corrected," Tess replied, shaking his hand. "I'm happy to meet you, Samuel."

"Don't make that mistake again, Tess," Kalila said, her eyes bright with love for her brother. "Or you'll never hear the end of it!"

Eva liked the sound that the teen's beaded braids made, but her mind was made up. Mom might pay Kalila to stay with her, but she couldn't make Eva enjoy it.

They dug into Glory's blueberry pie that Jasper doused with generous scoops of vanilla ice cream. "This is simply divine, Glory!"

Tess agreed. It was almost as delicious as Chloe's Delight. "I've never seen such big blueberries. Where did you get them?"

Glory wiped a smear of blueberry juice from Samuel's chin. "We picked them ourselves."

"There's a great place in Wells," Kalila added. "Spiller Farm. I thought Eva and I could pick our own this week and make some blueberry crisp."

Eva squirmed in her seat. No way was she going blueberry picking with this stranger! It might be fun if Micah was with them, but that was impossible. She didn't want to be impolite so she shrugged and broke off a piece of pie crust, dragging it through the purplish red juice on her plate.

Tess decided to change the subject. "The ice cream tastes homemade, too."

"It's from Simply Sweets, downtown," Jasper replied. "You can get your daily fix on your way to work, because it's around the corner from Pearly Whites. But there's a catch." He leaned back in his chair which was already backwards and patted his stomach.

"What's the catch?" Tess scooped up the last spoonful of ice cream and savored the creamy sweetness. When was the last time she had dawdled over a family dinner like this?

Glory and the kids nodded as Jasper explained. "Simply Sweets is actually two shops in one. In the morning the sign on the door says 'Simply Coffee' and that's what they serve—good, strong coffee along with Scuffins—" He noticed Eva's perplexed expression. "A Scuffin is a magical amalgamation of a muffin and a scone. You have to try them to believe them. Now, where was I? Oh yeah . . . the catch! At two o'clock exactly, they put away the Scuffins—"

"And the coffee," Glory said, pointing her spoon at Tess.

"That's right. They put it all away and start serving ice cream and *only* ice cream. If you want coffee, you need to get there before two o'clock." He stood up and began taking their plates and spoons to the sink, waving away their offers to help. "And if you want ice cream, you have to wait until two when they change the sign."

"Fred Gustafson and Samuel Blinkens own it; they've lived together in Seahaven for thirty-five years," added Glory.

Kalila chimed in, "We call them Framuel."

Samuel clapped his hands. "They make the *best* ice cream in the *world*. And big Samuel has the same name as me!"

"Absolutely right, little man." Jasper patted Samuel's shoulder as he picked up his plate. "Fred makes the baked goods for the morning crowd and Samuel churns the ice cream."

Glory got up to help Jasper bring the main dishes to the table. "It was such a unique concept that *Yankee Magazine* did a two-page spread on the place three years ago, and ever since, we've had a huge influx of tourists from May through October." She looked meaningfully at Tess. "So . . . if you have a yen for homemade ice cream before two in the afternoon, you can either go ten miles up the coast to Waker's Beach, or resign yourself to hurry up and wait."

"If you want coffee or a melt-in-your-mouth scuffin in the afternoon, then you're split-out-of-luck," Jasper said. "The only thing to do is set your alarm for five the next morning."

"Because you just have to *wait*!" echoed little Samuel. They all laughed.

"Okay, everybody, dig in. This was my mom's special recipe. It's simple as pie—" Jasper glanced apologetically at Glory. "Not that your pie is simple." She chuckled. "When we were growing up, we called it Chicken with Sticky Rice."

"It's super easy to make," Kalila said, cutting off a piece of chicken and smearing it around in the oniony, mushroomy rice. "I make it sometimes when Grammie's working."

Tess looked at Glory. "Where do you work?" she asked politely.

"I'm the Assistant Props Master at Sands of Time. I work with Jasper."

"That sounds interesting. How long have you worked there?"

Glory leaned over Samuel's plate and cut up his chicken. "Twenty years this September. Had four bosses before ol' Jasper here."

"I'm the best, right?" Jasper winked at her.

Glory nodded. "He's the best. A joy to work with. Not perfect though."

"She's right about that," Jasper replied with a grin.

"How long have you been at the theatre, Jasper?" Tess asked. She found herself relaxing a bit in this pleasant company and with each bite of comforting food, although it was awkward straddling a backwards chair.

"This is my fifth season as props master. I was in a few of their shows before that, and when I heard they were looking to replace their props master, it sounded like the perfect job for me. Ten years of traveling all over God's creation for acting jobs . . ." He pressed his lips together. "It's not all it's cracked up to be. I was ready to settle down."

"I can imagine," Tess murmured.

"Anyway, I spoke with Grace and Will about it and they thought it was a great idea. But first I had to make sure that Glory didn't want the promotion."

"No way," Glory said, wiping her hands on a napkin and shifting in her seat. "I told Grace and Will that I was perfectly happy with the assistant's job. Gives me more time at home with these guys." She put a hand on each of her grandchildren's shoulders and they leaned into her touch. Tess stifled an envious sigh.

Eva cleared her throat and set down her fork. "Did you say *Grace and Will?* Like the TV show, only backwards?"

"That's right," Glory replied. "You'll meet them next week when Kalila takes you to *Imaginarium*—that's the kids' summer program at Sands of Time. Their real names are Graciela and William; they've been best friends since high school. Everyone called them Grace and Will after the TV characters—"

"Except Grace is gay and Will is straight." Kalila added.

"Also backwards," noted Eva happily.

"They run the theatre?" Tess asked.

Jasper took his plate to the sink. "Grace is Executive Producer and Will is Artistic Director. This is the theatre's fortieth anniversary so we're putting together a fundraiser gala and concert. It's on August eighteenth. You won't want to miss it."

"Mom, that's your birthday!"

Tess took her plate and Eva's to the kitchen counter where Jasper was busy scraping leftover chicken and rice into a glass container. She grimaced. "Forty-one, believe it or not. I'm older than the theatre!"

"Honey, you look great," Glory said, motioning Samuel to wash his hands. "I'm fifty-seven. Sometimes I feel like thirty-seven, and sometimes my bones tell me I'm seventy-seven, but I absolutely refuse to think any more about it. What matters is what's in here—" She patted her heart. "Isn't that right?" She didn't wait for anyone to answer. "The Gala will be an excellent way for you to celebrate your birthday, Tess."

"Plus," Jasper added, placing the leftovers in the fridge. "Ben Shepherd is going to be the featured performer and we all know how Kit looooves Ben Shepherd!"

"Who's Ben Shepherd?" Eva asked.

Jasper tapped his right palm against his forehead. "Who is *Ben Shepherd?*" he repeated in disbelief.

"Sweetie, don't ever ask Kit that!" Glory replied, shaking her head and chuckling. She inspected Samuel's now-clean hands and gave him a thumbs-up. "Ben is a phenomenal singer and songwriter. Have you heard his song, 'Your Smile, My Eyes?'"

"No."

"My stars, girl! That's his latest hit; he wrote it about his little boy. Tess, you must have her listen!"

Tess leaned against Jasper's stove and wiped her hands on a checkered dish towel. "To be honest, I haven't had much time to keep up with the latest music. But that's going to change now that we're here and starting fresh. Right, Eva?"

Eva looked out the window, her arms crossed over her backwards shirt. An uncomfortable silence followed.

Later, while Jasper was entertaining the children with a video of last season's production of *Mary Poppins*, Tess joined Glory on the front porch. Glory sipped from a glass of wine; Tess had her customary cup of coffee. The late June day had cooled a bit and there was a soft breeze rustling through the pine trees that lined the driveway. The murmur of the ocean nearby, along with the spicy floral scent of Kit's rose bushes reminded Tess of the summer she was fifteen.

"Kit tells me your son joined the Army recently." Glory gently rocked in the swing that hung from one end of the porch; her bare feet didn't touch the floor.

Tess felt her throat tighten as she set her mug down on a low wicker table. "That's right." She glanced at Glory who was listening patiently. "Eva's devastated, and I keep wondering if it's all my fault."

Glory raised her eyebrows.

"If I'd been a better mother, been around more often, he might've been able to talk about his decision with me first."

"Hush now," Glory replied, resting her wine glass on the porch railing. "It's not your fault, hear? He made a decision about his life."

"Sure, but . . . the Army?"

Glory leaned forward. "If it helps any, I understand what you're going through. My daughter, Aida—the kids' mother—is in the Air Force."

"How long?"

"Up and joined when she was seventeen. Granted, we talked about it first, but her mind was made up. She wanted to make a difference. This was in 2002, soon after the September 11 attacks that killed her father."

"I'm so sorry."

Glory closed her eyes, the horrific memory engraved on her mind. "He was a theatre producer, on his way from Boston to L.A. to meet with the backers for his latest project." She looked out over the yard for several long, unguarded moments, then continued. "Aida was a senior in high school and it affected her deeply. Until then, she was talking about studying engineering in college." She took another sip of wine. "After the attacks, she began to be interested in world history and politics. She was passionate about wanting to *do* something."

"So . . . the Air Force beckoned?"

"That's right. She's in Germany now, believe it or not, serving as a canine training specialist. She's made it her career. We're all proud of her but it's hard on the kids."

"I can imagine. How often is she able to come home?"

"She gets leave once or twice a year. Those are happy times, but when she gets back on that plane—" Glory stretched her legs out in front of her and flexed her bare feet. "Kalila's gotten used to it, but Samuel doesn't understand."

Tess's face darkened, thinking of the years that Micah would be separated from them. "What if Micah chooses to make a career of the military. . . like Aida did?"

Glory quickly drank the rest of her wine and looked pointedly at Tess. "I have a feeling that you're strong enough to handle that. . . if it happens."

Tess looked doubtful.

"My guess is that you've made the best of a whole lot of the foolishness that life has thrown at you, eh?"

"That's for sure. But I don't how to make the best of *this*."

"For one thing, Micah's decision prompted you to move up here."

Tess thought about this. Max and Mimi had offered her the office manager position before Micah had left, but she hadn't seriously contemplated accepting it until after he was gone. "You're right, it did."

"I'm right about a lot of things." Glory winked at Tess as she stood. "Now, come inside and I'll show you another way to make the best of this. There are online support groups—and a few in-person ones—that I want to share with you. I think you'll feel more hopeful about all of this once you realize you're not alone."

# Chapter 10

*E*va waited for her mother in Jasper's apartment after Kalila took Samuel downstairs. It hadn't been too bad of a night, she thought, looking around the cluttered living room. Glory was nice, and so was Jasper. Samuel was adorable and she guessed she could put up with Kalila if she had to. The backwards dinner had definitely been better than being stuck in the apartment with her mom who had been more tense and uptight than usual.

She wandered around the living room while Jasper played his electric keyboard. "Who's this?" she asked, pointing to a framed photo of Jasper with a handsome man on a sunny beach. They were leaning into each other in a way that made her think they were more than friends.

Jasper's fingers stilled as he noticed what Eva was looking at. "That's Jake," he said quietly. "About three years ago, on the island of St. John."

Eva waited but he didn't offer more information and her curiosity was piqued. "Is he your boyfriend? Does he live in Seahaven? What does he do?"

"Hey, new friend, that's a lot of questions!"

"Sorry. Micah liked it when I asked questions. He called me Curious Girl."

Jasper got up from the piano and stood beside the bookshelf with Eva. "No worries. Being curious and asking questions is a good thing, don't you forget that."

"Thanks." Eva pointed again at the photo of the two men.
"Jake is kind of my boyfriend."

"Kind of?" She wrinkled her nose and looked up at Jasper.

"Yeah. We met in college and fell in love. Both of us were theatre majors. Then we graduated and he went off to play leading-man roles all over the place. I was getting roles too, but only chorus and character parts, which is fine, but it's hard to keep a relationship going when you're only together a few times a year."

"I know what you mean," Eva said sadly, plopping down on the sofa. "Obviously, I'm not in love with Micah like you are with Jake because Micah's my brother, but I love him a lot and it's never gonna be the same again now that he's gone. I miss him so much."

Jasper sat next to her. "How could you not? But listen, you guys are related. You grew up together. You've got the same blood in you. Nothing is ever going to change that."

"Really?"

"Promise."

He pointed a pinky finger at her and she crooked hers around it. "Pinky swear." She giggled as they shook on it, feeling a little better already. "Do you think you and Jake will break up?"

Jasper stood, gazing longingly at the photo as he held it in his hands. "I don't want that to happen. I still love him."

"Where is he now?"

"He's wrapping up the lead in *Crazy for You* at the Starlight Theatre in Kansas City." He set the photo back on the shelf. "He'll be here for the Fourth of July so you'll get to meet him." His voice was uncharacteristically flat.

"You don't sound too happy about it."

Jasper gazed down at her thoughtfully. "You're mighty perceptive for eleven, young lady!" Eva shrugged—no one had ever called her perceptive before—then looked at him expectantly. "I'm happy enough," he finally said. "It's just . . . really hard when he leaves."

"He could do a show at Sands of Time and then maybe he could move here like you did. Isn't there a job at your theatre he'd be good at?"

"We've talked about him moving here and settling down. I would like that, but he's in demand. This fall he's playing the lead in the revival of *Oklahoma!* on Broadway, and he has other projects already lined up for the next few years. It's hard to compete with all of that."

"You must be sad because he's far away."

"I try to focus on what's happening in my life right here and now, instead of how much I miss him."

"Like what?"

"Like what's going on at the theatre, or sharing a backwards dinner with new friends like you!" He poked her arm with his elbow.

Eva grinned. "I get it. I'm trying to think of a book that might make you feel better, but all the books I know are for kids like me, not necessarily grownups." She studied him for a moment, her head tilted. "You look a little bit like Patrick on *Schitt's Creek*. Except your hair is redder . . . and longer." She frowned, studying Jasper some more. "That would be a good show for you to watch, since I can't think of a book. Have you seen it?"

Jasper's eyes widened. "Heck yeah, I've seen it, more than once. But girl, why on earth would *you* be watching *Schitt's Creek*?"

"Micah let me watch it with him."

He didn't have a chance to respond because Tess poked her head in the open living room door. "Eva, are you ready? Glory gave us some stationery so we can write Micah a real letter."

"A real letter? You said I could email him whenever I email Charli. Isn't that a real letter?"

"No, hon. A *real* letter is written with an actual pen on paper like this." She held the stationery in the air. "It goes into an envelope with a postage stamp and then is dropped off at the Seahaven Post Office. Glory told me about an online group called Soldiers Angels where volunteers write letters to service members who are away from home. We're going to be Micah's angels first, and after a while, we'll write letters to other service members too."

June 21 Tuesday
Dear Micah,

I hope you like this paper that Glory gave us. She lives next door and her daughter is in the Air Force so she writes her letters all the time with pen on paper just like this! It has American flags on it. Well, I guess you can see that.

I'm glad you're safe. I told Theatre Jasper about Schitt's Creek but he's already seen it. I loved it when you booped me like Alexis always booped David and everyone on that show. I miss you.

Seahaven isn't all that bad except you're not here. Aunt Kit is really nice and so is Theatre Jasper, just like you said. Kalila is Glory's granddaughter and yesterday we picked blueberries at a farm. It was so hot I almost fainted. But I didn't. Then I helped her make blueberry crisp. Did you know the secret ingredient is lemon?

On Saturday Aunt Kit is going with Mom and me to watch the sunrise and we have to get up when it's still DARK outside. Next week Kalila is taking me to a summer camp thing at the theatre. I guess I'll learn about acting and stu□, but I don't think I'll be good at it.

Love and hugs and kisses,
Evie

June 21 Tuesday
Dear Charli,

We are writing REAL letters to Micah so I decided to write a REAL letter to you too. I hope you like it. Micah FaceTimes with us every week. He said to say hi to you.

Next week I'm going to a theatre camp that you would be good at but I don't think I will be. I wish you were going with me because you'd make it fun.

Yesterday Mom and I got up wicked early to watch the sunrise with Aunt Kit on the beach. It was so early that it was totally dark out!!! But it was awesome!!! Aunt Kit reminded me that the sun isn't moving even though it looks like it is. It's actually the earth that's moving. We learned that in science last year, remember?

What are you doing? Do you live near the beach? Does your dad like his new job? What are you watching on TV? Mom keeps asking me to watch Gilmore Girls with her but I like watching it by myself. What season are you up to? I'm on the third and I like Jess better than Dean, do you?

I hope you can read my handwriting.

Love and hugs,
Eva xoxoxo

# Chapter 11

That Friday night at seven o'clock, Tess came out of her bedroom and found Eva sprawled on the living room sofa, watching an old *M\*A\*S\*H* rerun. The air conditioner was on full blast; Eva wore a yellow sweatshirt with two blankets piled on top of her. "Hon, I'm going out for the monthly dinner with people from the office. Remember? I told you yesterday."

Eva gave her a quick thumbs-up sign, but kept her eyes glued to the screen. Hawkeye and Trapper John were racing toward a helicopter transporting wounded soldiers. "I hope Micah doesn't get hurt."

Tess turned down the air conditioner to a more reasonable temperature, then sat on the end of the sofa and rubbed Eva's feet through the blanket. "This show took place during the Korean War, but we're not at war right now. Chances are good that Micah will never be in harm's way." She grabbed the remote from the coffee table and muted the sound, hoping beyond hope that what she'd said was true. "Kalila will be here soon."

"Okay." Eva stretched, then took the remote back. At least her mom hadn't said the dreaded word *babysit*. She watched as Tess picked up her purse from the small table by the door. "You look nice!" Eva offered, and it was the truth. Her mother rarely dressed up; she always wore boring clothes and hardly ever went shopping except at stupid thrift stores. Tonight, she wore a pale blue and white striped sun dress with white sandals. Her hair fell loose to her shoulders instead of being pushed back with a headband. The Mother's Day necklace gleamed at her throat.

Tess let herself savor the rare compliment. She was looking forward to an evening out with adults; more and more, she was liking the Pearls and her co-workers. "Thanks! Have fun with Kalila."

"As if," Eva murmured, turning the volume back up just in time for a commercial. Although the sun had been sweaty-hot, picking blueberries with Kalila and Samuel hadn't been too bad; Eva would admit that if she was forced to. However, tonight she was missing Micah in a big way, especially watching those soldiers on *M*A*S*H*. "Mom?"

"Yes?" Tess headed to the living room door.

"Now that Micah's gone, I need a cell phone."

Tess halted in her tracks and turned to face her daughter. "We talked about this when you turned eleven last month. You're too young—"

"Charli had one!" Eva crossed her arms over her chest.

"Charli is a little older than you, plus she sometimes had to stay at home with her brother and sisters. It was a necessary expense."

"But I—"

"I'll get you a GABB phone for texting and calling next year, for your twelfth birthday. You won't be here alone because—"

Kalila knocked and opened the door before Tess could say the teenager's name. "Hey, Ms. Gilmore, I'm not late, am I?"

Tess held the door open for her, admiring her purple jeans and lavender embroidered tunic. "Not at all, this is perfect timing. I'll be back around ten. Call if you need anything, okay?"

"Sure thing. Have fun!"

Tess said goodbye to Eva, and Kalila waited for the door to close behind Tess, then stood beside the couch, her arms crossed over her chest, brown eyes sparkling. Eva's unhappy eyes were now focused on Hawkeye and Hot Lips.

"Hey Eva, I can see you're really into this show." She raised her eyebrows at the on-screen antics, then turned her attention to Eva's disgruntled expression. "It looks exciting and all, but I know something we can do that'll be way more fun."

Eva didn't take her eyes off the screen. "What?" she said flatly, shifting slightly on the sofa.

Kalila perched beside Eva and tapped her on the head. "Let's go down to Sunrise Beach and make snow angels!"

Eva looked up from the television and blinked slowly. "Are you kidding? It's eighty degrees outside and guess what? There's *no snow.*"

"Not kidding, not even a teeny little bit," said Kalila brightly, extending her hand. "We'll be making sand angels instead of snow angels, but it's the same idea. Come on, I'll show you how. It'll be fun!"

In spite of herself, Eva was intrigued. "Can we come right back here when we're done?"

"Sure. It won't take long."

Eva hesitated, then clicked off the television and stood, dropping the blankets behind her. "Okay, but I'm not putting on a bathing suit."

"Nah, it's better to do this with regular clothes on. Put on long pants instead of shorts, okay?" The younger girl headed down the hall. "And hey, Eva?"

"What?"

"I was thinking about what you said about not liking the word *babysitter*. What do you think about calling me a *sitter* instead? Because obviously, you're not a baby."

Eva turned to face Kalila, hands on hips, mouth pursed in thought. "Okay. Thanks." Besides, she thought, *sitter* sounded an awful lot like *sister*, and since her brother wasn't here, she liked the idea of having a *sitter-sister.*

Tess paused awkwardly in the waiting area at Chloe's by the Sea and glanced at her watch. Was she early? Who was she kidding? She was always early. Perching on the edge of a crowded oak bench near the door, she smoothed her hands over her hair. She was eager to have a relaxing evening out, but couldn't help feeling disoriented. Part of her was still back in New Haven. Part of her was in South Carolina with Micah. And part of her was right here in Maine.

They say that when one door is shut—and she *had* firmly closed the New Haven door— the Universe opens another one. That may be true, but those times in between sure felt like hell. No doubt about it, she was still in the in-between.

Eva sat down gently in the sand at Sunrise Beach, the way Kalila had shown her. The sky was slowly darkening and stars were beginning to sparkle above. In the distance, the ocean hummed at low tide. There were few people around; the tourists usually scurried away as soon as the light began to fade.

Careful not to make a bigger indentation in the sand with her butt, she slowly laid back until her body was one straight line. "That's perfect," said Kalila, the purple beads at the end of her braids shining in the rising moonlight. "Now, open your arms out wide. That's right. Do the same thing with your legs. Good! Now, arms and legs together at the same time." She pulled her phone out of her shorts pocket and snapped several photos.

Eva beamed. "I'm doing it, I'm doing it!" She liked the soft swooshing sound the warm sand made against her body as she created the angel wings.

"Yes, you are," encouraged Kalila. "Now, this is hard part. You have to be really careful when you get up."

Eva lifted her head and looked around. "Uh oh. I see what you mean. How do I get off of this without ruining it?"

"Sit up slowly but don't use your hands." Eva did. "Now stand up without putting your hands down into the sand."

Eva stood up slowly. "Now what?"

"Take a leap with both feet together, as high and as far as you can." Eva looked doubtful. "Don't worry. It's just sand. If it gets messed up, we'll make another angel."

"Okay, here goes!" Eva held her breath, squinted her eyes shut, and leaped away from the sand angel, falling to her knees a short distance away.

"You did it, girlfriend!" Kalila helped her to her feet and they high-fived with satisfaction. She turned Eva toward the angel.

"Take a picture, take a picture," Eva exclaimed, hopping on one foot and then the other in delight. She posed next to the angel, then noticed something lying in the sand by one of the wings. "Hey, look what I found!" She picked up the feather and held it out to Kalila. "An angel feather!"

The older girl hesitated, unsure how to respond. "Um, I think that's a seagull feather, Eva," she said gently, gesturing toward the sky. "There are a lot of them around here."

Eva held the feather tightly to her chest. "No, it's definitely an *angel* feather. Mom and I joined Soldiers Angels and now I just made a sand angel, so it's like the angels paid attention and left me a feather. They want me to know that they'll keep Micah safe!" She smoothed the feather briefly over her top lip; tiny grains of sand drifted onto her shirt.

"Okay then, it's an angel feather," Kalila said agreeably, deciding to humor her. "Come on, let's make a few more and I'll treat you to a double scoop at Simply Sweets."

Eva tucked the feather behind her ear and plopped down in the sand again. "I'm ready!"

The next morning, Eva woke up with the sun, and the first thing she saw was the feather, smooth and white against her green and pink polka-dotted pillow. It was comforting to have it so close, right there next to a softly snoring Jasper who was curled up next to her head. Tess was asleep, so Eva quickly pulled on a pair of chartreuse shorts and a striped top, gently picked up the angel feather—she didn't care what Kalila had said, this wasn't an ordinary seagull feather—and tiptoed through the kitchen and out the back door. Standing on the solid concrete steps, she surveyed the yard.

Maybe she would find more feathers!

She carefully observed the large rectangular lawn, the colorful flower garden against the back fence, and Aunt Kit's cottage to the left of the garden. Aunt Kit and two women were seated at a round picnic table in front of the cottage. Their pleasant chatter floated across the lawn, sounding like sweet music to her ears. It had been a while since she'd been close to female camaraderie. The last time was when Chiara and Quinn had visited in December. Her mother had taken a whole day off from work which was a huge deal because Mom *never* took days off from work. Eva had come home from Charli's house to find the three of them—Mom, Quinn, and Chiara—sitting in the living room, drinking wine and laughing. They had hugged Eva and invited her to tell them about her day. No wine for her, though; the ginger ale with a splash of cherry juice had tasted divine.

Now she noticed Aunt Kit waving. "Eva, come over and meet my friends!" She made a beckoning motion with both of her hands.

Eva skipped across the lawn, eager to show Aunt Kit the angel feather. Halfway across, she spotted something blue in the grass, stopped and bent over to inspect it more closely. Another feather! She picked it up and ran as fast as she could the rest of the way.

Arriving at the patio, she held out the feathers to her aunt, who hugged her gently and kept one arm around her. "What have we here?"

"Angel feathers," Eva declared proudly.

"I see," Kit replied. She held the feathers up for the other women to see. "Are you sure these aren't bird feathers?" she asked gently. "From a seagull and a blue jay?"

"No. They're definitely *angel* feathers. Mom and I joined Soldiers Angels, remember? Also, Kalila and I made sand angels last night, and the white feather was on top of the angel's wing when I stood up. I found the blue one over there." She pointed behind her. "I think the angels are letting me know that Micah is safe."

Kit smoothed Eva's hair back from her forehead.

"What are you going to do with them?" asked one of the women at the table, both of whom had been listening intently to the conversation.

Eva looked in the direction of the voice; she had forgotten that Aunt Kit wasn't alone. The woman had a head full of sandy brown curls that were threaded with gray. She wore a lemony-yellow sun dress with a necklace of rainbow-colored beads that curved around her throat.

"I'm Olivia Mattheson, and this is Violet Dunbar. We come here at the crack of dawn now and then to watch the sunrise with your Aunt Kit."

"And then we harass her until she provides us with breakfast," chortled Violet, slapping her hands briskly on the table. Her hair was cropped short and stark white, like freshly fallen snow, except for several streaks of lavender that framed her slightly wrinkled face. Eva would love to put green streaks in her hair but she knew her mom would never allow it, although Glory might let Kalila have *purple* streaks!

Eva remembered her manners and stopped staring at Violet's hair. "It's nice to meet you." She turned back to Aunt Kit. "You have friends?"

The women laughed in varying measures of sound—Kit's was the softest, like a gentle caress; Violet's sounded like a honking goose; Olivia's was somewhere in between. Although their response was woven with kindness, Eva realized her mistake and clapped a hand over her mouth. "Oh! I didn't mean—"

Kit patted her arm. "It's okay, dear. I may be old, if you call sixty-four old . . ." Her friends chuckled. "But I do have good friends, and I'm glad you got up early today so you could meet them." She gestured to the table. "Are you hungry? Would you like a cup of tea and a muffin?"

"No, thanks," Eva replied, noticing the plate full of purple-studded muffins that were bigger than her hand. People in Maine sure loved blueberries.

"Olivia asked what you're going to do with the feathers." Kit handed them back to Eva.

She hadn't thought of what she might do with them. If Micah were here, he might put them into an art project. Wait! She suddenly remembered an art project that she had helped him with last year. There were feathers and famous words on it . . . something about hope. She frowned. Had Micah's project been about angels? "I don't know," she finally replied.

"Come with me; I have something to show you that I think you'll like." Aunt Kit stood, holding her hand out to Eva. "Excuse us, ladies."

Kit led Eva through her sunny kitchen and into a small living room. She stopped in front of a low bookcase in between two bay windows and pointed to the array of objects resting on top of a golden cloth. Eva admired the items—a carved wooden statue of a mother holding a baby, a small pottery bowl full of water, a large conch shell, several purple and white stones, and a pink heart-shaped paperweight. "It's beautiful," she said quietly, sensing something special about this display. "What is it?"

"It's an altar that I made. These things are special to me for one reason or another. Whenever I see it, I'm reminded to take a breath and give thanks for the beauty that's all around me."

Eva's forehead wrinkled in thought. "There was an altar in Charli's church, but it didn't look like this."

"Well, there are many kinds of altars. This one is more personal, but every altar is meant to be a reminder."

"So . . . the one in Charli's church is a reminder for people to think of God?"

"That's right. This one is a reminder to slow down and notice what's around me."

Eva touched one of the purple stones.

"Come, I'll show you another one." She led Eva out of the living room and into a sea-green wallpapered hallway that led to three closed doors. They entered the first one.

"Is this your bedroom?" Eva asked, looking around in wonder. The walls were painted the same soft green as the hallway; the comforter and pillows on the large bed were made up of swirls in many shades of turquoise, teal, and aqua. Across from the bed was a comfy window seat pillowed in the same fabric as the bed's comforter. A set of seashell wind chimes hung over the window and moved with the breeze that flowed through the white lace curtains.

"It is. Do you like it?"

Eva nodded solemnly. "I love it. When I grow up, I want a bedroom like this. In fact—" She looked around a bit more. "Can Jasper paint my room *this* color?"

"He sure can. I'll try to find you a comforter and pillows that are similar to mine. Would you like that?"

"Yes, please."

"Wonderful. Now, here's another altar that I made." She pointed to a small shelf that was mounted over an oak bureau, next to an oval mirror. She stood behind Eva, her hands on the young girl's shoulders. This shelf had only three things on it: a small cup of seashells, a clear glass heart, and a photo of a cheerful young man with curly brown hair. Eva could almost hear him laughing. The photo was tucked into a round gold frame.

Eva sensed something unusual about this altar, and she noticed that her aunt appeared more solemn and was standing a little straighter. She was curious about the man in the photo but didn't know if it was polite to ask, so she simply waited.

After a while, Kit spoke. "This is the altar I made to honor my Ollie."

"Ollie?"

Kit gently touched the frame. "Oliver Sean Mattheson. The love of my life. Everyone called him Ollie."

"What happened to him?"

"He died when we were twenty."

Eva gasped and turned to look up at her aunt whose face was wistfully gazing at the photo. "That's so young."

"You're right. It was. And I was very, *very* sad for a long time." She turned to Eva, smiling gently. "But you know what?"

Eva slowly shook her head.

"My friend Olivia, out there on the patio? She was Ollie's twin sister. She and their mother, Lillian, helped me through it."

"And you helped *them* through it too, right?"

Kit thoughtfully ran her fingers over Eva's long hair. "We did indeed help each other through the loss. That is a wise thing to say, dear heart."

No one had ever called Eva *wise* before. Just the other day, Jasper had called her *perceptive*. She stood up a little straighter. "Do you think I could use my feathers to make an altar for Micah?"

"That's a great idea!" Kit turned to leave the bedroom and Eva followed.

In the living room, Kit opened the drawer on a side table and pulled out a shimmery golden cloth similar to the one on the nearby altar. "Would you like to use this for your altar?"

"Wow, thank you! I have a picture of him that I can use, and the dolphin bookmark that he gave me. I'll put these feathers on the cloth, too."

"It will be an excellent reminder of your big brother."

Eva happily agreed.

# Chapter 12

Preparing for the fireworks display on the Fourth of July, Tess set up two low beach chairs for herself and Aunt Kit. Eva helped Jasper spread a large blanket over the gently sloping grass near Sunrise Harbor as he hummed the beginning of *America the Beautiful*. They all settled in, enjoying the lobster rolls and fries that Kit had picked up on the way over. "I've never eaten lobster before," Eva mumbled, her mouth full.

Jasper elbowed her. "Hey, if you're gonna live in Maine, you have to pronounce words properly." He held up his half-eaten roll. "For instance, this is lobstah, not lobster."

"I sure love this *lobstah*," Eva said, giggling as a hunk of the glistening white meat fell out of the roll and onto her shorts. She picked it up and chewed it quickly. "It's soooo good!"

"Heck yeah, it is! Now, let's try some other words. For example, *from away* means you weren't born here. Which means that you, Eva, are *from away.*" In between bites, he continued to give Eva an education in Maine slang and she eagerly paid attention.

"They're getting along, eh?" Aunt Kit said to Tess, passing her a tumbler of white wine.

"Yes, and I'm glad. Jasper's a good distraction for her. Micah's leaving hit her pretty hard."

"How has his leaving affected *you*?" Kit's voice was curious and kind.

Tess sipped the chilled beverage and looked out over the noisy crowd and across the horizon that was showing hints of darkness.

Truthfully, she couldn't believe how much she missed Micah. He was a trustworthy son who had always stepped up whenever she needed him, with nary a complaint. Good-natured, talented Micah. What she hadn't counted on was how lonely she felt without him. Had she been using him as a replacement for Cameron all these years? She certainly hoped not. "I'm okay, I guess" she said, setting the tumbler down in the grass and absent-mindedly picking up a few fries.

"It's okay to *not* be okay."

"I don't know about that. I have to show Eva that everything's all right."

"Do you think it might help her if she knew you missed him as much as she did?"

Tess munched on a crispy fry. "Maybe. I'll talk with her about it later."

"There they are!" Little Samuel shouted gleefully as he dashed up to them; Kalila and Glory followed close behind, carrying their own chairs. Glory was wearing a red, white and blue striped loose top with white jeans, and Kalila had on a purple sundress embroidered with white flowers; the skirt dragged through the sand as they made their way to where the Gilmores sat on the grass. Samuel settled himself on the blanket next to Eva.

"Come, we saved room for you." Kit motioned Glory to the space beside her chair.

"Why, thank you!" Glory said with a big smile. She glanced at Jasper as she settled into her beach chair. "Hey boss, where's Jake?"

He had been joking with Eva but stopped mid-sentence and looked up. "He texted last night. They changed the schedule; rehearsals for *Oklahoma!* started yesterday." He shrugged, trying to act nonchalant, even though they weren't fooled one bit. "Broadway waits for no man . . . or woman."

"I'm sorry. I know you miss him," Glory replied. "I was looking forward to getting a Jake-Hug again."

"What's a Jake-Hug?" Eva asked.

"Jasper's boyfriend gives the best bear hugs ever. Doesn't he, guys?"

"He sure does," Kalila responded, taking a tray of deviled eggs out of the cooler they had brought. "Anyone want one?" Eager hands reached for the eggs.

"Not me, I'm allergic," said Kit, standing and stretching. "Looks like it'll be another hour or so 'til it's fully dark. I'm going for a smoke break."

Puzzled, Eva looked up at Aunt Kit. "You *smoke*?"

"I'm not proud of it, but I do. It's an old, old habit that I've never been able to kick." She looked down at Eva's concerned expression. "I've heard all the warnings, dear, so please don't start. I'm as healthy as a horse, according to my doctor. I don't need a cigarette every day, just now and then."

Tess thought she might have to take up smoking herself. Having a son in the Army was no small matter. She didn't think she'd ever be unstressed again. Her head started to ache whenever she thought of him being sent overseas to a war zone. Even though America wasn't currently at war, one never knew what was going to happen.

Later, after the Red, White and Blueberry salad had been eaten along with Glory's Seven Layer Whammies, Samuel climbed into Eva's lap and rested his head against her shoulder. "Hey, little man, are you going to fall asleep before the fireworks?" Eva asked fondly. More and more, he seemed to gravitate toward her. Her own personal Admiration Society.

"Nope. I'm just resting," he murmured with a contented smile—and pink strawberry smudges—on his face.

Tess had gone with Glory and Kalila to the bathrooms, leaving Kit and Jasper with the kids. Jasper was tapping away on his phone, texting with Jake, humming quietly what sounded like the chorus of "Fools Fall in Love."

"Samuel is quite taken with you," Kit said, laying a hand on Eva's shoulder.

"Yeah. He already has a big sister, but I'm like a second big sister to Samuel, the way Micah was always a good brother to me."

"That's lovely, Eva. You know, Micah *is* still a good big brother."

"But he's not *here*."

"That's right. He's not here." Kit tapped the blanket. "But he is right *here*." She tapped Eva's chest lightly with one finger. "He's your brother. He'll always be your big brother, no matter what."

Eva held her hand over her heart and smiled briefly, remembering Theatre Jasper's words the other day.

"What you're doing with Samuel is actually a way of carrying Micah's light forward."

"His light?" Eva shifted the now sleeping Samuel in her arms so she could see Aunt Kit better.

"Yes, the same way that I carry Ollie's light forward as best as I can. That's why I try to watch the sunrise every day. It reminds me that I've been given a brand-new day, and it helps me remember that after every dark time comes a new morning. Does that make sense?"

Eva met Kit's eyes. "A little." She wasn't sure. "But what does that have to do with Ollie?"

"Several weeks after he died, his mother, Lillian, dragged me out of bed and took me with her to watch the sunrise. Right here on Sunrise Beach. It was February and I was terribly sad, as you can imagine." Eva nodded solemnly, her eyes wide. "Anyway, she forced me out of bed and brought me out here in the freezing cold. I'll always remember what she told me—that Oliver had touched our lives with his joyful way of living, and now it was our job to carry that forward in our own lives." She smiled down at Eva. "It was quite a lecture, let me tell you. We watched many, many sunrises together before I really understood."

"But Micah's not dead." Eva gently lifted the sleepy boy off her lap and settled him on the sun-warmed blanket.

"No, of course not. I'm telling you this so you can see that when the people we love go away, whether it's a short goodbye or a forever farewell, a part of them still lives inside of us." She placed her hands over her heart. "Right here." Eva put her hands over her heart too. "Our Micah is off now on a grand adventure, making his way in the world. He's doing a brave thing. Think of all the things you love about him." Eva nodded. "They're in you too, and you're already carrying them forward right here, with Samuel. You'll carry them forward with the new friends you make, and your teachers, too."

"I think I see. But I don't think I'll ever have another friend like Charli."

"No one will be like Charli, but I know that other good friends are in your future." Aunt Kit pointed at Eva as Tess and the others approached. "You're a thoughtful, wise spirit, like my Ollie was. Like your mom is."

"No, I'm not like her at all," Eva exclaimed, getting up on her knees just as her mother and Kalila joined them.

"You're not like who?" Tess asked cautiously, the fresh air and movement having eased her headache.

"No one, never mind," Eva replied guiltily, grabbing Kalila's hand and pulling her down beside her.

But Tess knew exactly who her daughter was referring to, and there was nothing she could do about it. If only . . . No, this wasn't the time or place to dwell on past mistakes. She blinked back tears as she sat down next to Kit, stretched her bare legs in the slowly cooling grass, and waited for the sky show to begin.

Later, after the brilliant display of fireworks and saying good night to a sleepy daughter who insisted on putting herself to bed, Tess sat alone on the front steps of the apartment building. Before Eva headed off to her newly-painted bedroom, Tess had attempted to connect with her. "I understand how much you miss Micah," she had said as they put away the leftover food and wiped the smelly bug spray from their arms and faces.

"He would've liked those fireworks," Eva agreed as she refilled Jasper's water bowl.

"You know, I really miss him, too."

"You do?"

"I do! He's my son. The two of you are my everything."

Eva straightened and stared at her mother, shaking her head slowly.

"It's true," Tess insisted, wiping her hands on a dish towel and crossing the kitchen to her daughter.

"It might be true that you miss him," Eva said. "But do you miss *Micah*, or do you miss all the ways he used to help you out, and how he took care of me when you weren't home?"

Tess stiffened. Although she recognized an element of truth in Eva's question, she also knew that her relationship with her son was grounded in love. "Eva," she had said, her voice trembling. "I love Micah and you . . . to the moon and the stars, to infinity and beyond." They used to say that to each other every day, but she hadn't said it, or heard them say it to her, in many years.

"Whatever, Mom." Eva replied wearily and headed down the hall, leaving her mother behind with an indescribable ache in her heart.

Now, in the humid evening, Tess could hear Jasper playing the piano; a sad melody drifted through the second-floor open window, accompanied by the comforting refrain of crickets in the dark, and the shushing of waves in the distance. These intricate sounds of summer had been profoundly absent in New Haven.

These *lonely* sounds of summer, Tess thought, hugging her knees to her chest and wiggling her bare toes in the warm salty air.

Yes, she was lonely. She hated to admit it, but she was. All those years of working and going to school, and then the last several months of trying to prove herself while working for Justina—she'd been so busy that she hadn't had time to be lonely. Now, here she was, in this beautiful seaside town, working in an office where people actually took the time to appreciate one another. Her weekends were free, but she no longer knew what to do with free weekends. Eva didn't want to spend time with her, didn't want to watch *Gilmore Girls* with her, didn't even want to *be* like her. What kind of a mother was she turning out to be?

The monthly Zooms with Chiara and Quinn were comforting, but she wanted . . . needed . . . something more.

She took off the patriotic striped headband that Kit had insisted she wear. Tossing it lightly from one hand to the other, she heard a commotion down the street. Holding her breath, she listened carefully, ready at any moment to run back inside. Now she could hear footsteps and heavy panting. A streak of white fur came into view. What the—

A large dog skidded up the sidewalk, a red leash trailing behind. It bolted through the grass and bounded into Tess's lap, knocking her sideways into the porch post for a moment. Tess righted herself and held onto the creature that was now licking her face and neck. She couldn't help laughing out loud at this unexpected interruption to her dreary thoughts. "Who *are* you?" she asked, trying unsuccessfully to remove the dog from her lap. Still panting heavily, it stopped licking Tess's face, grabbed the festive headband from her grasp, and started chewing.

"Rocky! ROCKY! Come back here right now!" shouted a woman around Tess's age who was sprinting down the sidewalk.

"He's right here!" Tess called, trying to stand and failing. Rocky was still weighing her down as he happily chewed the headband in half, his stomach and hind legs draped over her lap like a weighted blanket.

"For God's sake," the woman said as she stood in front of Tess, bent at the waist and panting almost as heavily as Rocky. She was wearing blue running shorts and a white T-shirt sporting the words *Boston Marathon 2019*. Her hair—the longest, reddest, and curliest hair that Tess had ever seen—was streaming around her neck and shoulders like a Superwoman cape. The woman stared at the sidewalk while catching her breath, then peered up at Tess with bright blue eyes and a face full of freckles. "I am so sorry about this. Rocky, get off of her! Now!" She straightened and slapped her thighs. Rocky paid no attention, continuing to gnaw on Tess's headband. She let out a frustrated groan along with a few choice swear words, then pushed her hair back. "I got him last weekend, and I swear to God, I'm either returning him or taking him to doggie obedience school. Rocky, come!"

At this command, Rocky paused his intense chewing, looked over at the red-haired woman, then back at Tess who noticed that the dog's eyes were the exact same vivid blue as the woman's. Rocky licked Tess's face and neck again. "I don't mind," she said, giggling, trying to remember the last time she had giggled. "Looks like he needed something to chew on. I'm Tess, by the way. Tess Gilmore. Come, sit." She tapped the empty space beside her on the top stair.

"I'm Carolina McDonald. And before you ask—I wasn't born in either state, North or South. My mom adored James Taylor and he has that song—"

"Carolina on My Mind."

"That's the one!" Carolina sat down next to Tess. "Thank you for being so understanding about Rocky. I'll replace the headband."

"No need. I have plenty." Tess tossed its soggy remains in the direction of the front door and Rocky settled onto the floor between the women. "His eyes are as blue as yours," Tess commented, placing her hands behind her on the porch and leaning back. "How old is he?"

"We're not sure. The Animal Rescue League found him wandering on Route One up in Wells. They brought him to Dr. Brightman, the vet over at Bright Lives Animal Clinic. That's where I work, by the way." She stroked Rocky under the chin and he lifted his head, leaning into her touch. "He's a border collie."

"I'm glad he found me tonight. I was feeling a little lonely. Do you live around here?" She glanced at Carolina's hands and noticed a gold band rimmed with tiny rubies on her left ring finger.

"Yep." Carolina pointed to the left. "One street over on Sugar Shores Road. My husband's in the Air Force. I got tired of moving every few years, so when he was stationed in Portsmouth six years ago, we bought a house in Seahaven to be near the water. The next time he deployed, I stayed here. What about you? I haven't seen you around."

"We've only been here a couple of weeks."

"We?"

"My daughter, Eva, and I. Do you know Kit Gilmore?"

"Sure." Carolina continued stroking Rocky's head.

"She's my aunt."

"You lucky duck! Kit's a beloved fixture in this town. Hey! The three of you should call yourselves the Gilmore girls, although I must say, Kit is nothing like Emily Gilmore."

Tess rolled her eyes. "I agree about Kit and Emily, but Eva wants nothing to do with calling ourselves *Gilmore Girls*. She's eleven."

"Tough age, I get it. By the way, have you been to Kit's gift store, Coastal Soul, yet?"

"We've been there a few times. Eva and I enjoyed wandering around, and it smells good too, like . . . I don't know, incense and magic. Does that make sense?

"Absolutely."

Tess groaned and leaned back, stretching her neck. "Aunt Kit is trying to get me to schedule a massage there."

"Samantha Stone's Coastal Soul massages are the best! You won't regret it."

Tess quirked one side of her mouth up uncertainly.

"Trust me, it's true. I go religiously every month. Sometimes more if Daniel—that's my husband—is overseas."

"What does he do?"

Carolina faced Tess, smoothing both hands over Rocky's drowsy body. "Daniel's in Air Force Intelligence which means he's at a high level of security, so whatever mission he's on, it's classified."

"Aren't you afraid something bad will happen to him?"

Carolina looked away for a moment. "Every. Single. Day." She looked back at Tess, her expression fierce. "But screw it, you know? I love him and this is what he loves to do. I've chosen to live with it."

"You make it sound so easy."

She shook her head adamantly and her abundant red curls flew every which way. "Not easy. Not easy at all." She looked at Tess intently. "Why did you ask that, about being afraid?"

Tess rubbed her forehead. Talking about it might lessen this slowly burgeoning headache. "I was thinking of my son, Micah. He recently joined the Army."

Carolina glanced at Tess. "Let me guess. You tried to talk him out of it."

"He didn't give me a chance." She rolled her eyes. "Left a note instead."

"That sucks. How long ago?"

"Last month."

"It's still new, then," she replied gently, scratching Rocky between the eyes. He rolled over, offering his snowy white belly to the women. "I know you won't believe me, but you'll get used to it."

"Have you?"

"Most days, my answer would be yes. Most days I'm able to go about my life, living it the best I can."

"And the other days?"

Carolina placed her hands behind her neck, stretching it from side to side. "Other days I go up to Waker's Beach at two in the morning and scream until I get it all out of me." She directed her gaze at Tess. "Next time either of us feels that way, let's go up there and scream together."

Tess couldn't picture herself doing that in a million years, but she smiled back.

"Other times when I can't stand it, I get a massage at Coastal Soul. Or I go for a really long run. Do you run?"

"Not if I can help it."

"A long walk would be just as good. There are excellent hiking trails around here, and of course, there's always the beach!" She glanced at Tess's left hand. "Not married?"

"No. Never married," Tess replied, taking a breath, and rubbing her upper arms. The ocean's gentle rumble was a little louder now. The tide must be rolling in, and with it, a slight breeze. "I should go in. It's late and I need to get up early for work." She stood and stretched, savoring the sensation of movement after sitting for so long.

"C'mon, Rocky, let's go." Carolina got up and nudged the dog, who blinked up at her for a moment, then closed his eyes again. She clapped her hands briskly. "Not kidding!" The two women bent over and lifted the dog to a standing position. Rocky promptly shook himself and tufts of white fur flew in their faces.

Tess stroked Rocky's back and he looked at her with what could only be called a doggie grin. "Thanks for introducing me to Carolina," she whispered loudly into his brown-spotted ear. As if he understood, he offered her a pure white paw.

"Hey, thank *you* for listening to me ramble on. Can we get together again? I can show you around the area."

"Sure, that'd be great," Tess replied. "What's your schedule like?"

Carolina headed down the steps, then turned. "I'm a receptionist at Bright Side Animal Clinic, and I'm also one of Dr. Brightman's fabulous vet techs. Monday through Thursday, nine to five, Fridays off, Saturdays ten to four. You?"

"I'm the new office manager over at Pearly Whites and I'm there nine to five, Monday to Friday. Weekends off."

Carolina reached into a pocket, pulled out her phone, and handed it to Tess. "Give me your number. I'll call or text this week."

"Sounds like a plan," Tess agreed gladly.

# Chapter 13

*E* va found another feather the next day as she and her mom headed for the car. It was perched precariously atop the hood, longer than the blue and shorter than the white. This one was a bright shade of green with white dots scattered over it. Eva quickly grabbed it and tucked it into her backpack. She wondered what kind of angel was green with white spots, then promptly forgot about it as she imagined what Imaginarium theatre camp would be like. She hoped it was the tiniest bit interesting, but she didn't expect to make any friends. Part of her still wished she was back at the apartment in New Haven, lying on the sofa watching *Schitt's Creek* for the third time with Micah, or playing *Minecraft* at Charli's house.

After following her mother into the rehearsal studio that jutted off the side of the main theatre building, they were met by Grace and Will who were warmly welcoming children and parents alike. Eva thought they looked like siblings—both were tall and had similar white blond hair, although Will's was short and bristly, and Grace's lay in two thick braids over her shoulders.

Tess signed Eva in, then led her to the stage area where the sixth and seventh graders were gathering. "Okay, hon. I'm heading to the office now," she said, glancing at her watch. "I'll come by at one o'clock on my lunch break to pick you up." She kissed Eva lightly on the top of her head. "Have fun. I want to hear all about it."

"All right." Reluctantly, she turned back to the group and was greeted by a familiar face.

"Hey there, Eva!" Kalila said, reaching out and pulling her closer to the group. "Everyone, listen up! This is my neighbor, Eva. Make her feel at home. I'm going to bop over to Grace and Will for the final roster, okay?"

A plump girl with frizzy brown hair and big green eyes hurried over to Eva. "Hi! I'm Poppy." She took Eva's hand and began introducing her to the others. There were thirteen kids, not counting Eva. "Last but not least, my best friend, Teo." Poppy stopped abruptly in front of a boy who was sitting on the floor, his head bent over a book. "Teo!" Poppy stomped her foot and he reluctantly looked up. "This is Eva. She's new."

"Hey." Teo squinted up at them with greenish-gold eyes almost hidden by a thick mop of messy dark hair. He didn't smile at her like the other kids had; he just blinked solemnly and went back to his book.

"Don't mind him," Poppy said. She took Eva by the arm and sat with her in two folding chairs nearby. "He's had a big heartache."

"A big *what*?" Eva took off her backpack and set it on the floor. It contained her lunch, an old shirt for when they did artwork, and a paperback copy of the same book that Teo had been reading. What was that thing Aunt Kit had told her about? Sink... ron... *Synchronicity*. Very interesting.

Also in her backpack: one green spotted feather.

Poppy rhythmically tapped the side of one hand with the palm of the other. "A big heartache. Teo is very sad." She put both hands over her heart dramatically. "His heart still hurts from—" She glanced at Teo. "It's a very big heartache that's not mine to share. He'll tell you if he wants to, and I'm sure he will, sooner or later."

Eva nodded. She knew something about a hurting heart.

Thursday July 7
Dear Charli,

I started Imaginarium Theatre Camp this week. Well, it's not really a camp. I mean, we aren't outside in tents or making campfires like when we went to Girl Scout camp. It's more like a bunch of activities to keep kids out of trouble in the summer. That's how Poppy explained it anyway. I met her on the first day! I like her BUT NOT AS MUCH AS YOU!

We got into groups to do acting exercises which I did NOT like at ALL but it was fun. Poppy invited me to be in her group with Teo who is her best friend. He's sad most of the time and I don't know why.

Here's a secret that I haven't told anyone else but Aunt Kit. I've been finding ANGEL FEATHERS all over the place!!! Seriously. I know you're thinking I've gone bananas, but I have six so far and here's where I found them:

1. A white feather in the sand when Kalila and I made sand angels
2. A blue feather in the grass behind our apartment
3. A green and white feather on top of our car
4. Another white feather ON THE SEAT OF OUR CAR!!!!!
5. A purple feather outside the door of our apartment
6. A metallic gold feather on the sink in our BATHROOM

Aunt Kit showed me how to make an altar so I put all the feathers on top of my bureau next to Micah's picture. Every time I find another feather, or see the feathers in my room, I remember that the angels are keeping him safe. Now I don't have to worry about him so much. I should probably show to Mom because she's still worried, but I don't think she'll believe me when I say the angels are leaving these feathers.

On Sunday, Mom and I are going hiking with this lady named Carolina. She has a cool dog named Rocky and he's going hiking with us so I guess it'll be okay.

Love, your friend,
Eva xoxoxo

Thursday July 7
To: micahcgilmore@usmil.com
From: tessagilmore@pearlywhitesseahaven.com
Dear Micah,

It was great to see you on FaceTime last weekend. I can't even imagine what it's like to be doing what you're doing, but I want you to know how proud Eva and I are of you

The other day I was telling Eva how much I missed you, and she suggested I was only missing you because of how much you always helped me around the apartment, and how you took care of her when I was working. I don't think I thanked you enough for the way you stepped up when I decided to get my business degree. The truth is, I couldn't have done it without you, and I hope you didn't join the Army just to get away from all the responsibility I handed over to you these last four years.

Eva seems to be enjoying Imaginarium camp at the theatre. She spends mornings there, and afternoons here with Kalila. On weekends, I have a hard time getting her out of her room to go anywhere or do anything, but this Sunday we're going hiking with my new friend Carolina and her dog Rocky.

I love you, my dearest son.

Mom

"Slow down and wait for us!" Tess called. She could see Eva and Rocky ahead of them on the trail.

"Kids and dogs! So much energy," Carolina said, striding along. Tess was doing her best to keep up with her.

"Are you and Daniel planning to have children?"

"Those few years he was stationed in New Hampshire? We tried. Man, we tried!" Carolina gazed into the distance. "It sure was fun trying, but it doesn't seem possible anymore. I'm almost forty and I don't want to go through a pregnancy and birth without him here." She lifted her yellow tank top to mop her sweaty neck, revealing a gray sports bra.

"Are you disappointed?"

"For sure, but I don't see any way around it. By the time he retires, we'll be forty-five, which is too old unless we adopt and I'm not sure how keen he is about that. What about you?"

"I've already got my two," Tess replied. They were walking the two-mile loop at Eastern Trail, south of Portland. The warm July day had gotten hotter the further from Seahaven they'd driven.

"Yes, but would you consider having more? If, for instance, their dad came back into the picture?" She pulled a water bottle from her knapsack, took a long drink, then offered it to Tess. "Do you see what I'm doing here?"

Tess took a swig and handed back the bottle. "Sure, you're fishing for information."

"You're onto me, girl." They laughed.

"The kids' father is long gone, not in the picture." Tess stopped walking as they came in view of a picturesque lake surrounded by evergreens. "Eva, come look at this!" She watched as Eva turned around and reluctantly began walking back to meet the women. "Cameron and I didn't marry because it never felt completely right. We were together and then not together so many times. Finally, a year after Eva was born, I woke up one morning and he was gone, along with all of his things. He called me the next day and said that he just couldn't do it anymore."

"It?"

Tess leaned against a nearby tree and pointed to herself. "Us. The kids. I guess he was as tired as I was of the way he kept leaving and coming back. He couldn't commit . . . and to be honest, I didn't want him to." She cupped her hands at the sides of her mouth and called Eva again.

"Mom, what do you *want*?" Eva asked impatiently as she came around the corner, Rocky prancing close behind.

Tess gestured at the stunning view.

"Yeah, so? It's a lake. I'd rather look at the ocean." She tugged at Rocky's leash. "C'mon, boy, let's go!"

Tess watched them jog away. What kind of a mother was she if her own daughter didn't want to take a simple walk with her? And how had it happened that Eva wasn't moved by the sight of such beauty?

"Kids," Carolina half snorted as they continued on the trail. "Give her time. She'll grow out of it."

"I don't know about that," Tess replied. "I haven't been the best mother. She won't even watch a simple TV show with me. Remember *Gilmore Girls*?"

"I loved that show! Watched it with my mom when I was—" She noticed the dejected look on Tess's face. "Sorry."

They walked in silence for a while, as Tess nervously tried to keep Eva in her line of sight.

"I know what you need!" Carolina said suddenly, as the parking lot came into view. Eva and Rocky were dancing around each other, and it looked like Eva was singing. Would wonders never cease?

"What?" Tess bent down to scratch a mosquito bite on her leg.

"You, my friend, need to get back out there."

"Out where?" Tess straightened and stretched.

"Into the dating world."

Tess put her hands on her hips and faced Carolina. "No. I'm done with all of that."

"Are you sure?"

"Absolutely sure."

Carolina leaned in. "Was Cameron your first love?"

Tess startled and took a step back. "What?" She took a breath. Carolina didn't answer. "No, he wasn't," she finally admitted.

"Okay, then. Do you remember what that first love was like? Don't you want to feel that again?"

"Definitely not." Tess shifted the weight of her backpack and began walking quickly toward the parking lot.

Carolina caught up with her. "Wait a minute, Tess! Tell me what you're thinking."

Tess waved her off and kept walking but slowed her pace. "It was good, that first love . . . until he broke off communication." They walked slowly. "His name was Luca," she added softly.

"Luca?"

"That's right. I was fifteen, he was two years older. We met in Seahaven. I was there on vacation with my mom, visiting Aunt Kit. Dad was working, as usual, and couldn't come with us. I have lots of special memories of that time with Luca. But my mom—"

Carolina touched Tess's elbow, forcing her to stop. "Let me guess. Your mom made you stop seeing him."

"Yeah, she cut our vacation short that summer, but Luca and I kept in touch . . . until his emails stopped coming. I knew he and his family were going back to Portugal, but I couldn't understand why he stopped writing."

"That sucks! Have you tried looking online for him? Search engines are much better now than they were back then."

Tess put her hands on top of her head, keeping her eyes on her daughter who was still playing with Rocky near their car. It looked like they were happily wearing each other out. "It's a common Portuguese name; there are hundreds of Luciano Silvas listed. No, that ship has sailed, and I'm okay with it."

Carolina raised an eyebrow as they headed toward Eva and Rocky again.

"Really, I am."

"If that's true—and that's a big if, I'm just sayin'—why don't you start dating? Go out and have some fun."

Tess looked away. "I'm trying to have a better relationship with Eva. There's not enough time for dating, and—"

"Get the Zoosk dating app. It's how I met Daniel! You don't have to be up for it, trust me."

"Up for what?" Eva danced over to them, curiosity shining in her hazel eyes. For once, Rocky stood still, panting heavily, looking up at the women expectantly.

Tess reached out to pull Eva close but she stepped away. "Just an idea that Carolina had. We'll see."

In the back seat, stroking Rocky's head, Eva wondered why—after spending all afternoon in the woods and hearing thousands of birds singing in the trees—she hadn't found a single feather. Except for the first white feather in the sand when she was with Kalila, all of the feathers on her altar had appeared around—and inside—the apartment building. She stroked Rocky's head and decided she didn't care where the feathers were coming from, only that she knew they meant that Micah was, and always would be, safe.

# Chapter 14

After a few weeks of Imaginarium Camp, Eva had learned some interesting facts about herself. For one thing, she didn't like acting, even the tiniest bit. For another, she was incredibly bad at singing, even though she loved it. She was just so-so at art, nothing compared to the special talent that Micah had. But this day, what she was learning about herself made an excited bubble of happiness rise up inside: she was really, *really* good at writing plays.

She had become close with Poppy and Teo throughout the month of July; whenever Kalila had invited the middle schoolers into small groups, the three of them always chose each other. Teo had warmed up to her a bit. He was brilliant at acting and they often talked about the books they had read. Although Teo wasn't familiar with Nancy Drew, he was a Hardy Boys expert, and they agreed to try each other's books after Imaginarium ended. Poppy was her usual happy-go-lucky self, and she was the best singer of the three of them. What Eva and Poppy had in common was that neither girl had a relationship with her biological father. Poppy's parents divorced when she was five and her dad had moved to western Canada with his new girlfriend. Last year her mom had married Steve, whom Poppy described as "wicked cool."

"Guys and gals!" Kalila called from the stage, holding a clipboard in her hand. Her purple tee with the theatre's logo was tucked neatly into a pair of jean shorts. Lavender nail polish gleamed on her toes which looked striking against her white flip flops. The children quieted down and looked up at her. "I need someone from each group to shout out the name of your play. Grace and Will are working on the program for the final performance event which is next Friday."

Several hands shot up in the air. "Do we really have to perform these plays in front of *everyone*?" a slender girl with strawberry-blonde hair and a smattering of freckles called out.

"Yes, Jen, you really do," Kalila replied firmly. "Today is Wednesday, which means you have nine more days to practice."

There was much murmuring among the children, and Eva felt a few newly-hatched pesky butterflies flitting around in her stomach. She glanced at Teo and Poppy. Would they be ready? She knew her play was good, and Kalila had suggested ways to make it even better, but to perform in front of a real audience? She wasn't sure about that.

"Okay, now. Quiet down! I'm ready for your titles." Kalila checked her clipboard. "Jasmine, Miranda, and Sue?"

"The Last Time Machine," Jasmine called tentatively.

Kalila continued to jot down play titles. Finally, she got to Eva's group. "Poppy Peterson, Teo Silva, Eva Gilmore?"

"The Boy Who Said Goodbye," Eva called out.

Kalila wrote it on her clipboard. "Okay, thanks everyone! Keep working. I'll run this up to the office and be back in a few minutes."

Poppy nudged Eva excitedly. "I didn't know your last name was Gilmore."

"I didn't know yours was Peterson."

"Ugh. Poppy Peterson. It's so . . . What's that word for when all the letters of the words begin the same?"

"Alliterative," Teo said, pushing his hair out of his eyes. "But your *middle* name doesn't begin with a P."

"No, it's Belle," she replied, rolling her eyes. "My mom was really into fairies when she was a little girl and that's why I'm Poppy Belle Peterson."

"I think your name is pretty," Eva insisted.

Poppy groaned as if her stomach hurt. "It's not as nice as your name. Eva Gilmore. I bet you have a cool middle name too."

"It's just Katharine."

Poppy leaned back on her hands and tried out the name, rolling it out slowly on her tongue. "Eva Katharine Gilmore. Yes, that's the best name ever! When I turn eighteen, I'm going to change my name."

Teo rolled his eyes. "By then you'll probably actually like it." He set the notebook down with a thud. "Let's get back to work."

"Wait!" Poppy laid a hand on Eva's arm. "Please, *please* tell me you've watched *Gilmore Girls*! Oh. My. God. It's such a great show. I tried to get Teo to watch it with me but he's not interested. Boys!" She rolled her eyes.

"Sure, I watch *Gilmore Girls* all the time."

"What's your favorite episode?"

Completely bored, Teo drummed his fingers on his crossed legs and looked around the room to see what the other groups were doing while Eva and Poppy prattled on in the background about dance contests, double birthday parties and the critical differences between some dudes named Dean and Jess.

Teo finally interrupted them. "Enough! We need to get back to work or we'll never get this finished. We still need to practice, remember?"

"Sure." Poppy clasped her hands in front of her dramatically, then turned back to Eva. "I like to watch *Gilmore Girls* with my mom. I bet you and *your* mom have fun watching it together, because you and your mom literally are *Gilmore girls*!"

"Yeah, like Eva hasn't heard that before," Teo mumbled, tapping his hand on his notebook.

Eva picked up her green pen. "I don't watch the show with my mom," she said quietly, drawing small circles on the final page of the script.

"Why not?"

She thought for a moment, then lazily lifted one shoulder. "Because she wants me to."

Poppy looked perplexed. "Isn't that a *good* thing?"

"No," Eva replied slowly. "I don't want to start it with her because she might not have time to finish it with me. There are one hundred and fifty-three episodes, plus the four *A Year in the Life* movies! One day last year we were watching *Whale Rider*, and then she got a call about work and had to leave. She never even offered to finish it with me! It's actually better if I watch *Gilmore Girls* alone, although Micah sometimes watched it with me."

Poppy sighed. "You're so lucky to have a big brother."

"Yeah, I know."

Before Tess had a chance to download the dating app, Mimi Pearl offered to set her up on a blind date with one of their office's medical supply reps. "Blake Greene is the coolest guy," Mimi assured her after Tess reluctantly agreed. Mimi quickly typed in a text before heading down to the Narnia exam room, then turned to Tess. "He's down to earth, grounded, and successful. He has two boys, both in high school." Looking extremely pleased with herself, she headed down the hallway, calling over her shoulder, "You can thank me later."

All things considered, the date with Blake—lunch at The Artist's Table on the other side of town—was okay. Nothing special. They found each other in the colorful waiting area and stumbled through introductions as the hostess led them to their table. Tess noticed that Blake raised his eyebrows when she ordered an iced espresso instead of herbal tea. He was taller, with thinning sandy hair and brown eyes. Tess had brushed her hair and worn it loose, leaving behind her usual headband. The tiny spark of hope that she allowed herself to feel while driving across town fizzled and died as soon as Blake started complaining about his ex-wife. It seemed he was expecting her to commiserate, but Cameron had been gone so long, she was way past the misery phase.

As they said goodbye under the restaurant's awning on Beech Street, Blake shook her hand politely and said he'd call. "Let's take in a movie and dinner this weekend."

What Tess wanted to say was *don't bother*, but the manners instilled in her by Cecilia didn't allow for such a blatant dismissal. Instead, she replied, "That won't work for me. A few friends are driving up this weekend to check out my new place." She left off the requisite "Maybe another time" and hoped he'd get the hint.

It turned out that Mimi wasn't upset at all. "You gave it the old college try," she said cheerfully. "Max and I will think of someone else for you." She patted Tess on the shoulder.

When Jasper found out she was dating, he fixed her up with Gerry, the marketing guy from Sands of Time. "He may not be perfect for you, Tess, but he'll be fun—I can promise you that."

Tess had to admit, Gerry was fun. He was in his late forties, never married, and quite handsome, with full lips and a head of wavy brown hair. On Friday night they went dancing at a club in Ogunquit that only played music from the sixties and seventies. Tess had worn a pretty, full-skirted lavender dress that she'd found at a nearby thrift shop.

The fast dances were loud and fun, and Tess found herself letting loose—just a little bit—after a glass of Riesling. But when the music slowed down to Eric Clapton's *Wonderful Tonight*, and Gerry held his arms out to her, she flashed back to the one time she'd danced with Luca—under "their" tree—to this very song playing softly from Luca's iPod, surrounded by the silvery stars overhead and the lulling sound of the ocean in the background. It had been the last time she'd seen him, although she hadn't known it at the time.

Shaking the memory away, she smiled briefly at Gerry. "I'm sorry, I'm all danced out. Besides, it's getting late and I should get home to Eva." She went to collect her purse and sweater from the coat check area.

Arriving home, she found Eva and Kalila sharing a bowl of popcorn on the sofa facing the TV. "Hey guys, what are you watching?"

"Nothing, Mom." Eva sat up quickly and hit the OFF button on the remote, but not before Tess heard the voices of Lorelai and Sookie laughing about something in the Dragonfly Inn kitchen.

Eva looked hesitantly at Tess after Kalila left. "How was your . . . um . . . date?" She perched on the edge of the sofa as if ready to leap up at any wrong word, her hands tucked under her thighs. Just Jasper snoozed at her feet, oblivious to the tension in the room.

Tess looked uncertainly at her daughter. "It was okay, I guess. We went dancing."

Eva tried, but couldn't picture her mother—*her mother* — dancing. She slid to the floor and Jasper opened his eyes sleepily as she settled beside him. "Are you going to see him again?"

"No, hon. I'm not."

Eva looked relieved and Tess reached for the remote. "It sounded like you were watching *Gilmore Girls* with Kalila. Do you want to finish the episode? I'll watch it with you."

"No thanks," Eva said breezily as she stood and headed to the hallway.

"Don't forget," Tess called, unable to hide her disappointment. "Quinn and Chiara are coming tomorrow."

Eva turned. "Oh."

"We're going to show them around Seahaven, walk on the beach, and have supper at Chloe's by the Sea. They'll want to hear all about what you've been doing at Imaginarium."

Eva tapped her foot impatiently. "Okay." She turned to go, then looked back at Tess. "A week from tonight is the final performance for parents. I wrote a play and my new friends, Poppy and Teo, will be performing it with me that night. Could I invite them over one night next week so we can practice?"

Tess's heart lit up; Eva had made friends already. "Sure! We'll use the grill and picnic table on the back deck. How does that sound?"

"Good, but we won't have much time to eat because we'll be practicing."

"I understand. Good night, Eva. I love you."

"'Night, Mom."

Tess turned on the television and lost herself for a while in the fictional world of Stars Hollow, where one special mother and daughter actually enjoyed spending time together.

Chiara and Quinn arrived within ten minutes of each other late the next morning. After exclaiming over the new apartment, saying hello to Kit, and being given a quick tour of Seahaven, they settled on the old Victorian's front porch with tall glasses of iced coffee and crabmeat sandwiches from King's Deli. Aunt Kit joined them for lunch, then took Eva's hand and announced that she had a special treat for her at Coastal Soul.

"I loved hearing Eva talk about theatre camp. She seems to be adjusting," Chiara said as they watched great-aunt and grand-niece strolling down the sidewalk, chatting away, their hair flowing behind them in the humid breeze.

Tess took a deep breath. "At camp, yes. At home, not so much."

"What do you mean?" Quinn took another bite of her sandwich, crabmeat oozing out from two thick slices of multigrain bread. She leaned back in the rocking chair, chewing thoughtfully.

Tess sipped her iced coffee. "She keeps pushing me away, won't let me into her room. And the strangest thing of all—she isn't worried about Micah anymore. Which is okay, I guess, because I'm worried enough for the both of us."

"You've heard from him, right?" Chiara asked, sweeping her bangs aside.

"He video chats with us once a week. Eva and I send an email or a real letter almost every day, just to stay connected."

"That's good, right?" Quinn put her feet up on the swing and settled back against the turquoise pillows.

"I don't know. It still seems so . . . wrong . . . that he's *there* while we're *here*."

"It's understandable, Tess," Quinn said. "When Braden went to California for college, it took me months to get used to it."

"But you could book a flight and see him in less than a day if you needed to. The Army frowns on such spontaneous visits, I'm sure."

"It's got to be hard, Tess," said Chiara, her voice soft and soothing. "Now, tell us about your new job. How's that going?"

Tess tore little pieces off the edge of her napkin and watched them float into her lap. "It's the best thing about Seahaven right now. The Pearls like me and they're easy to work for. Nothing like Justina." She shuddered slightly. "I just wish I could be closer to Eva." She looked at her two friends. "You guys are close to your kids. And I used to be close to mine, but . . ." She looked across the porch toward Aunt Kit's garden and the house next door. "Not anymore."

"Hello?" Quinn waved her hand. "It takes time and energy to create close relationships with kids."

"And you've been in short supply of both," Chiara added agreeably, setting down what was left of her sandwich—the crispy brown crusts—and brushing the crumbs from her fingers. "Those four years are behind you now, and the two of you are making a fresh new start. Do you remember when Matt . . .?"

Chiara's husband had died five years ago from an inoperable brain tumor. Tess nodded soberly.

"I pushed everyone away. My mom had to take the kids for a while, remember? I just couldn't cope. The grief . . . it was too much for me. But you guys . . . you stuck by me even when I didn't think I wanted you to. What Eva's going through isn't the same, of course, but she's still going through a loss. She needs you to keep trying, even if it doesn't seem that way."

Tess plucked an ice cube from her coffee, crunching it with more pressure than necessary. "You're right. I'll try to think of it that way from now on."

"I'm gonna pop in and use the bathroom, okay?" Chiara headed inside.

Quinn started to ask a question about Seahaven when Tess's phone chimed. She plucked it out of her pocket and looked at the screen, then sighed. "It's my mother." She looked helplessly at Quinn for a moment before answering. "Mom, hi. What's up?" She rubbed her forehead with her free hand. Quinn quietly excused herself and left the porch for a walk around the yard.

The phone reception wasn't the best, but she heard her mother mention Micah. "Can you say that again, please? I didn't hear you."

"I'm asking about my grandson. I haven't heard from him yet."

"He's doing fine, don't worry."

"I'm not worried, Teresa Marie. I simply asked how he was. I was expecting a call or a letter from him by now. It's been almost a month."

Tess closed her eyes. "It's not summer camp, Mom. He's in Army Basic Training! There's not a lot of free time."

"Don't get snippy with me! I deserve to know how he is."

"I told you, he's fine." She couldn't keep the irritation out of her voice. Why didn't her mother ask how Eva and Tess were doing too?

Cecilia sighed dramatically. "That's all I wanted to hear. The next time you write to him, please tell him to call me."

"I will."

Perturbed, Tess disconnected the call and shoved the phone back in her pocket.

Chiara returned from the bathroom to find Quinn standing on the top step looking worriedly at Tess who was pacing back and forth, murmuring to herself.

"Her mom called," Quinn informed Chiara. They both grimaced, then Quinn stepped forward and put her hand on Tess's arm, stopping her in her tracks. "Sit down and tell us about it." The three sat close together on the wide porch swing, with Tess in the middle.

"She didn't ask once how I'm doing, or what Eva is up to. This is the first time she's called since we moved up here."

Quinn put her arm around Tess; Chiara did the same. "Cecilia is not the best mother in the world. You know that, right?"

Tess leaned into her friends.

"You're a thousand times better mother than she is." Chiara added gently.

"A million trillion times!" said Quinn, stroking Tess's arm.

"Come on, let's not talk about that witchy woman anymore!" Quinn stood and grabbed Tess's hands and Chiara joined them in a circle. They touched palms with the woman on either side of them, then pressed their hands to their hearts, and made eye contact with one another, basking in the familiarity of their friendship.

Tess immediately felt better. "Let's walk over to Coastal Soul," she said, shaking off the critical residue left over from the conversation with her mother. "Later, we're all going to Chloe's by the Sea for dinner. Aunt Kit is treating us."

"Eva too?" asked Chiara, gathering up the paper plates and napkins.

"Eva too," Tess agreed.

# Chapter 15

Monday August 1
To: charlib@webmail.com
From: evareads@newhavenmail.com
Dear Charli,

Why aren't you emailing me anymore? I miss you a lot.

Poppy and Teo and I are writing a play for the final show on Friday. Actually, I wrote the play and I suck at acting, so I'm the narrator. Guess what? I really like writing plays and Kalila says I'm good at it.

Here's a very sad thing. Teo's mom died two years ago. They lived in Portugal. That's near Spain, I think. Last year Teo moved here with his dad. It's just the two of them. He speaks really good English because he had to learn it in school over there. I'm letting him borrow my copy of Bridge to Terabithia because I think it will help him. Did you get the book I told you about, The Girl Who Drank the Moon? It's magical and mysterious. Kalila took me to the Seahaven Library twice already and now I'm reading The Last Dragon Chronicles. I love it!!!!!

Mom's friends came up this weekend. They stayed at Aunt Kit's big house near Seahaven Harbor. Aunt Kit took me to her store so Mom could spend the afternoon with her friends, and she gave me a little pouch that has flowers on it. The words on it say "Beautiful girl, you can do hard things." She told me she was proud of me for how I'm handling moving to a whole new place without my brother. I told her I wasn't worried anymore about Micah because I know he's safe.

Did I tell you I found more feathers? They are definitely not bird feathers. The last three that I found were bright pink, do you believe it? One was on our kitchen floor and another one was stuck in the windshield wiper of Mom's car. I don't remember where the other one was. They HAVE to be angel feathers!

I miss you a hundred times a zillion.

Love, your friend,
Eva xoxoxo

"Okay, kiddos," Grace and Will called in unison from the front of the rehearsal area bright and early on Monday morning.

"We're getting excited about the big show Friday night, and your parents are looking forward to it too," Will said. He had grown a thin blonde moustache in the last few weeks and was stroking it thoughtfully. "Any questions?"

Poppy cupped her hands around her mouth and shouted a bit louder than necessary. "Are we doing the plays in the rehearsal studio here or in the big theatre?"

"Mon cheri," Will responded in an outrageously fake French accent. "We will be in zee *big* theatre, of course."

Poppy's eyes widened. "Did you hear that?" she whispered to Teo and Eva. "The *real* theatre!"

Kalila then checked in with each group to see how they were doing. When she got to Eva's group, Teo said, "We're *almost* ready."

"That's great, guys," Kalila replied with a satisfied nod.. She leaned forward and whispered, "Don't tell anyone, but I think your play is the best. We're saving it for last." She high-fived each of them, then moved to the next group.

Eva sat up a little straighter. She was happy to finally be good at something. Micah had been the one in the family with all the talent, and Charli was so athletic. Eva had always been the one cheering them on; she had never imagined what *she* might be good at. But now she knew.

During the break, Poppy skipped off to talk with friends in another group, while Eva and Teo walked outside and sat at a picnic table. Eva sipped from her apple juice box; Teo set down a bottle of pineapple juice. "It reminds me of Portugal," he said.

"I like pineapples," Eva said agreeably. "It must be sunny and warm in Portugal."

"It is." He twisted off the top of the colorful bottle.

"I bet I'd like it there. I've only ever lived in Connecticut and it was only sunny and warm in the summer. Do you like Seahaven?"

"It's okay, I guess." He gulped his juice.

They sat in companionable silence, looking around at the deep stretch of pines behind the theatre, listening to the myriad sounds of birds and the distant hum of the ocean. "I've never been inside the big theatre," Eva finally said. "Have you?"

"Yeah, my dad and I went to all the shows last summer. It was cool." He set down the nearly empty bottle and began playing with a chain around his neck. They both were wearing the Imaginarium T-shirts that Kalila had given them the first week.

"What's that?" Eva asked, pointing to the silver chain.

Teo's already tan skin darkened with a blush. "Oh, it's . . ." He looked up at Eva. "My mom gave it to me before she . . . before she died." He slipped the chain off his neck and handed it to her.

Eva turned the solid silver medal over in her hands. There were words on it in another language, and a raised image of what looked like an old man with a baby on his back. "What does it mean?"

"It's a Saint Christopher medal. He's the patron saint of travelers. It says 'Saint Christopher, protect us' in Portuguese."

"What's a patron saint?" She handed the medal back to him carefully.

"We're Catholic, so we have saints for everything," Teo replied. "Saint Christopher is the one who's supposed to protect us when we travel. It didn't seem to help my mom, though, so I'm not sure it's going to protect me."

"But you wear it because she gave it to you."

"All the time. I don't even take it off in the shower, or when I sleep."

"Micah gave me a bookmark when he left." Eva looked down at the ground. Poppy and Teo knew all about Micah. "It reminds me of him, so I keep it in my bedroom on a little altar that Aunt Kit showed me how to make."

"An altar, like in a church?" Teo drained the last bit of juice from his bottle.

"Exactly. She said the purpose of an altar is to honor God or someone special to us, so I made an altar for Micah and—"

She was interrupted by Poppy who plopped down on the bench across from them. "Grabbed these from the snack table," she said, tossing three small bags of pretzels in front of them. "Help yourself, and you're welcome!" She looked at her friends and noticed their intent faces. "Were you seriously talking about *altars*? We should be talking about our play!"

"I was telling Teo about making an altar to honor Micah. It's to keep him safe."

"That's interesting." Poppy leaned forward, her green eyes alive with curiosity.

"It's on the bureau in my bedroom with a picture of Micah, and the bookmark he gave me and some . . ." She hesitated. Should she tell?

"Some what?" Teo prompted.

So far Eva had told no one but Aunt Kit and Charli about the feathers, but who knew if Charli was even reading her letters and emails? She took a breath and replied in a rush. "I keep finding all these feathers so I put them on the altar too."

"Feathers?" asked Poppy. "What kind of feathers?"

"Different kinds, all different colors. One was orange and a few were pink; there was even a purple one."

"That's strange," mused Teo, tossing his medal from hand to hand. "There aren't any birds around here with those colors."

Eva jumped up, excited. "That's just it! They're not bird feathers. They show up in the strangest places, like the car, and in our kitchen. There was even one in the bathroom by my toothbrush! I'm sure they're angel feathers and that the angels are letting me know that Micah is safe so I don't have to worry about him anymore."

Teo and Poppy looked at her doubtfully.

"Hey, Teo believes in Saint Christopher. I guess I can believe in angels! Look, I'll prove it. My mom said you could both come over one night this week for supper so we can practice. I can show you the feathers then. Will you ask your dad?" She looked at Teo hopefully. "And your mom?" She looked at Poppy.

"That'll be fun!" Poppy exclaimed. "We could use some extra practice and I'd love to see your feathers."

"Okay," Teo agreed. He pointed at the rehearsal studio entrance. "They're calling us back, let's go." He looped the Saint Christopher medal over his neck and the three of them ran back to the theatre.

Tuesday August 2
Dear Micah,

Thank you for emailing and reassuring me that you didn't join the Army because of your responsibilities at home. I miss you but I do understand that you need to be on your own and that traveling and serving your country is important to you. I'm so proud of you.

Eva and I went to a stationery store last week in Portland to buy special paper for our letters, and for some reason, Eva chose the one with feathers, so you'll be getting a letter from her soon. She said she was looking for paper with angels on it but they didn't have any, so she settled for feathers. I don't know why she's suddenly so interested in angels.

Remember when you guys were little and halfway through summer, I'd let you stay up as late as you wanted? The other day I was looking at one of our family scrapbooks and I saw the photos that I took of you both, with notes about how late you were able to stay up each year. We stopped that when you were fourteen and Eva was seven. I suggested that she and I stay up all night this Friday, after the show, and she agreed! Do you believe it? I'm probably more excited than she is.

Gram called while Quinn and Chiara were here. She wants you to call or email her soon. I think she misses you more than she misses me and Eva.

Love, Mom

On Wednesday afternoon, Tess came home from work early to fix supper for Eva and her friends. "Their parents are dropping them off at five," Eva said anxiously, looking at the clock on the kitchen wall. "We'll be ready by then, right?"

"Sure thing, hon," Tess replied, dropping two bags of groceries on the kitchen table. "I'll get the burgers ready while you set the table on the back deck. Sound like a plan?"

Eva nodded and got to work.

Tess proceeded to mix the ground beef with bread crumbs, barbeque sauce, and a little ground mustard, then formed several thick patties for the grill. Eva set the table with paper plates, sunshine-yellow napkins and the silverware from the kitchen drawer. "Hey Mom," Eva said as Tess came outside. "The forks and knives have seashells on them. They're cool!"

"I found them at a thrift store on Route One the other day. New silverware for our new home by the ocean."

Glory strode around the side of the house and headed toward them. "Eva! Tess!" She held a wicker basket covered with a red and white checkered cloth. "I made something for your special supper." She set the basket on the table and looked at Eva. "Jasper told me your friends from camp are coming over tonight."

Eva hopped on one foot, then the other. "Is it those Seven Layer Whammies from the Fourth of July? I hope it is!"

"No, these are my famous Whoopie pies," Glory announced, removing the cloth with a flourish. Eva and Tess peered down at the thick, round chocolate cakes with creamy white filling. The heavenly scent of rich, dark cocoa filled the air.

"Famous is right," Jasper said, jogging over from Aunt Kit's cottage where he had been power washing the patio. He took the porch steps two at a time, shouting "whoopie" at the top of his lungs. Today he was wearing a Portland Sea Dogs baseball cap and a matching tank top with black jogging shorts.

"What's a Whoopie pie?" Eva asked innocently.

Glory chuckled and Jasper dramatically fell to his knees. "Dear child, don't tell me you've never had a Whoopie pie?"

Eva giggled at Jasper's theatrics. "Never."

"You're in for a treat, and once you have one of Glory's, you'll never want another kind."

"There are other kinds?"

"Heck, yeah! There are Whoopie pies all over the place up here. Other brands and other flavors."

"Just be sure that the filling uses Marshmallow Fluff along with the butter," Glory added. "That's how my Mama taught me."

"She's right," Jasper agreed, rising to a full standing position and rubbing his knees. "I salute these Whoopie pies!" He smacked his forehead with the edge of his right hand. "And maybe I'll steal one for my own supper . . . if it's okay with you, m'lady." Eva laughed.

"Take two, there are plenty," Tess said, setting them on a paper plate and handing them over.

Jasper began to sing as though he were on stage giving a star performance. "Thank you very much, thank you very much, that's the nicest thing that anyone's ever *done* for me!"

"I think you should thank Glory," Eva said with a giggle.

"Then thank you, my most *glory-ous* assistant," he said solemnly, kissing her hand.

She waved him away, shaking her head and smiling.

"Glory and I are heading over to the theatre now to start setting up for the Friday night event. And guess what else! Jake is coming tomorrow and he'll be here all weekend!" Jasper literally danced off the porch and around the side of the house waving and singing, "I'm so excited, and I can't deny it. I'm about to see my Jake and I think I like it!"

Tess and Eva burst out laughing as he and Glory waved goodbye.

"Now, what else do we need?" Tess asked, surveying the table.

"Can I pick some flowers from Aunt Kit's garden for the center of the table?" Eva asked.

"Good idea! You do that while I put the rest of the food out."

At five o'clock, Tess and Eva waited in the living room. Tess had changed out of her work clothes and into white capris with a rose-colored cotton top, another thrift shop treasure. "You look nice, Mom," Eva said. "I'm just wearing what I wore to camp." She pointed her Imaginarium T-shirt and flowered shorts.

"Thank you, and you look lovely too," Tess replied, happily savoring another rare compliment from her daughter.

Poppy arrived first with her mother, Rosa. The girls ran into the living room as the two adults talked on the porch. "Where's Teo?" Poppy asked.

"He said they might be a little late because his dad's boat comes in at four-thirty and he has to get cleaned up first. Mom's not gonna put the burgers on the grill until you're all here. Aunt Kit's coming too. And Glory—that's Kalila's grandmother—made something called Whoopie pies for dessert."

"Oh boy! I've had Glory's Whoopie pies. She's famous for them around here!"

"Really?" Eva was surprised.

"Absolutely! Anytime there's a fundraiser or something where everyone in Seahaven gets together, Glory brings the best stuff. Moose Tracks cookies, Whoopie pies, blueberry pie. I'm getting hungry just thinking about Glory's desserts. She should open a bakery."

Eva thought about this for a moment. Maybe small-town life wasn't so bad after all. It seemed like people really got to know each other here; everyone was much friendlier than in the city. "Let's sit on the porch while we wait, it's cooler out there." The girls sat together on the swing, pushing themselves back and forth with their feet.

"I'll pick Poppy up at nine o'clock, okay?" Rosa said to Tess as she headed down the sidewalk. Tess agreed with a wave.

As Rosa drove away in her SUV, a silver pickup truck pulled in to take its place.

Teo opened the passenger door and jumped out, holding a small bouquet of flowers in one hand, and clutching a paper bag with the other. "Hi, Ms. Gilmore," he said politely as he climbed the porch steps. "These are for you. Dad said it's always polite to bring the hostess a gift."

"Thank you," Tess murmured, burying her nose in the wild-flowers, not noticing the tall, attractive man who had finally exited the truck and was heading up the walkway.

"Mrs. Gilmore?" he said, carefully walking up the first two steps. The woman was obviously enjoying Teo's flowers, even though he couldn't see her face. "I'm—"

Tess looked up from the bouquet, prepared to politely intro-duce herself, but she gasped and dropped the flowers instead, clapping trembling hands to her suddenly-hot cheeks. "Luca?" she whispered in wonderment. "Luca, is it really you?"

The man stopped between the second and third step, and gazed at Tess in astonishment. Teo was standing next to the girls on the porch swing which had abruptly come to a halt as the three of them stared at the adults.

"Tessa?" A hopeful question graced the man's dark eyes.

# Chapter 16

The two adults stood, as still as statues—Tess on the top step, Luca on the next step down. Even so, he was taller than Tess. They stared at each other in a strange mixture of surprise and confusion.

"Mom?" Tess heard Eva speaking as if from very far away.

Teo walked over to the adults and tugged on his dad's bare forearm. "Dad?" Luca gazed into Tess's eyes a little longer. "Dad!" Teo raised his voice and repeated himself a few times until Luca finally blinked and looked down at Teo.

"Do you guys *know* each other?" Eva demanded, leaving Poppy so she could stand next to Teo. No one had ever called her mom *Tessa* before. If anyone tried, her mom always stopped them. Now this man—Teo's father—was calling her *Tessa* and it was *okay*?

Luca cleared his throat and focused on the children. "You must be Eva," he said kindly, holding out his right hand. "I'm Luca, Teo's dad."

Eva hesitantly shook his hand. Obviously, he was Teo's dad. But how did Teo's dad know her mother? This was totally bizarre.

Tess finally came out of what felt like a hypnotic trance. "Luca, this is my daughter Eva, and this is Poppy." Poppy came over to say hello, then looked questioningly at Eva and Teo, whose expressions were as clueless as her own.

"Mom? What's going on?" Eva demanded.

Tess looked down at Eva and touched her shoulder. "Luca and I met the summer I was fifteen when Gram and I came to Seahaven to visit Aunt Kit. We were . . ." She looked at him again. "We were friends."

Eva rolled her eyes. *Friends.* She had a feeling they had been way more than that. They were looking at each other the way that Luke and Lorelai were looking at each other now that she was up to season four of *Gilmore Girls.* "You haven't seen each other since then?"

"That's right," Luca replied. "Your mom went home to New Haven, and my family and I went back to Portugal. It's been twenty-five years, I think."

"Twenty-six," Tess corrected.

Teo interrupted with an intentional frown. "I'm hungry."

"Of course, of course! I've got burgers ready for the grill, and everything else is on the table." Tess bent down and picked up the flowers that Teo had brought. "Thank you for these, Teo, they're beautiful. Eva, why don't you put them in the vase that Quinn brought us last weekend?"

Luca rubbed his hands together. "I'm getting hungry too."

Eva paused on her way into the apartment with the flowers. "Is Teo's dad staying for supper? You didn't invite Poppy's *mom.*"

Tess blushed. "I didn't think to invite the parents, but you're welcome to stay, Luca . . . I mean . . . if you don't have other plans. We have plenty of food. I didn't mean to assume—"

Luca lightly touched her hand which was nervously fidgeting with her headband. Tess paused and looked up at him. "I would love to stay," he reassured her, his eyes offering only curiosity and gladness.

"Okay, I'll set another place at the table," Eva said reluctantly. She motioned to Teo and Poppy with her free hand. "C'mon, you can help me, then we'll walk down to the beach. After we eat, I can show you the—" She glanced at her mother who was still talking with Teo's dad, then lowered her voice to a whisper. "You know." Her friends nodded conspiratorially and followed her to the kitchen.

Tess showed Luca the apartment, then handed him the platter of raw burgers and led him to the grill. She found herself unusually chatty, hopefully covering up how nervous she felt. Luca had grown out of adolescence and into an attractive man. His skin was as tan as she remembered, but his hair was darker and a bit longer now. As a teenager, he had been slightly thin and awkward in his gait, but now . . . he seemed confident and comfortable in his own skin. Her mind was positively bursting with questions. *What happened when he went back to Portugal? Why had he stopped emailing her? Where was his wife? What was he doing in Seahaven?* But this wasn't the time to ask. In her confusion over seeing Luca again, she didn't want to forget her daughter. This evening was meant to be about Eva and her friends.

They stood side by side in front of the grill, watching the meat sizzle and turn from burgundy red to toasty brown. She stared at the meat and felt her mouth water as the savory smoke reached her nose. Across the back yard, she saw Aunt Kit reading as she lit a cigarette on her patio.

"She still smokes, eh?" Luca said, gesturing toward Kit's cottage. "I thought she might have stopped by now."

"We've all stopped trying to get her to quit. Although she doesn't light up as much as she did when you knew her."

He turned to her. "Tessa," he began, reaching out to touch her arm. "There's so much I want to—"

Eva, Teo, and Poppy suddenly appeared beside them, looking a bit disheveled and out of breath. "You're lucky to live so close to the beach!" Poppy rocked back on her heels, hands clasped behind her back.

"Is it time to eat?" Eva looked from one adult to the other. She didn't like the way he was touching her mom's arm.

Luca picked up the spatula and flipped the burgers again. "Just another minute or two, I think."

The children took their seats at the table and an awkward silence ensued.

As soon as the burgers were ready, Tess called to Kit across the yard. "Supper's ready! Come and join us!"

The conversation got livelier as soon as Kit arrived, although when she first saw Luca, she paused and looked at Tess, eyebrows raised.

"Aunt Kit, you remember Luca Silva," Tess said, looking around the table to make sure that the children had what they needed.

"Long time, no see," Kit said happily, giving him a thorough hug and a pat on the back. "Now, what on earth are you doing here? Are you part of the Imaginarium program too?"

"He's my dad," Teo announced flatly, biting into his juicy hamburger which he'd placed between two halves of a fluffy roll and slathered with ketchup.

"Oh, my stars and garters!" Kit laughed out loud, then stopped abruptly when she realized that no one else was smiling. "Well then," she said, carefully taking a seat and looking at Eva's friends. "You must be Teo and Poppy."

Mouths full, they nodded politely.

"I'm Tess's Aunt Kit, which makes me Eva's great-aunt."

Poppy swallowed the slice of tomato she'd been chewing and took a sip of lemonade. "I have a great aunt too. My mom's sister, Marigold, but we call her Aunt Mari instead. She's—"

"I know everyone thinks I'm a *great* aunt," Kit said, winking at Eva. "But there's another way to use that term. I'm actually *Tess's* aunt because I'm her father's sister. See? That makes me, not Eva's *aunt*, but her *great*-aunt."

"Cool!" Poppy processed this information as she crunched thoughtfully on a chip. "I get it now. Anywho, my Aunt Mari is a regular aunt, but she's also really *great*. We go on a trip together every summer, just the two of us. Right before school starts, we're going to Nova Scotia. That's where the house from *Anne of Green Gables* is."

Eva's eyes widened. "I love those books! Mom, can we go there?"

"Maybe we can go next summer or on spring vacation. How does that sound?" Tess was determined—within reason—to be agreeable.

Eva smiled for the first time since Luca had appeared on the front steps. She took a handful of chips and placed them neatly on her plate. "Micah might want to come too. Do people in the Army get vacations?"

Luca looked up from his plate which now held only a bit of salad. "Who's Micah?"

"My son," Tess replied as Eva said, "My brother."

He set down his napkin. "Ah. Eva, you have a brother!"

"He was going to go to RISD, that's the Rhode Island School of Design. It's the best school for artists, because that's what Micah is, an artist." She dragged a fork through her salad. "But he decided to join the Army instead."

"You must miss him," Luca said kindly, swirling the ice in his water glass.

"I do," Eva replied. "But it's okay. I know he's safe."

Luca looked uncertainly to Tess and Kit, then back at Eva. "Well, that is a very good thing," he finally said.

After Glory's fabulous Whoopie pies, the children headed to Eva's bedroom, and Aunt Kit said goodbye. "I've got letters to write for Soldiers Angels." Luca looked at her as if to ask a question. "It's a volunteer group online. We write letters to service members who are deployed."

"Like Micah?" he asked.

"I do owe Micah a letter, but I also write to deployed soldiers. There are many overseas now, and letters brighten their time away from home."

"That is an incredible thing," Luca replied. "But you do not have to leave—"

"I'm sure you two have a lot to catch up on." Kit smiled knowingly at Tess as she carried some dishes to the kitchen, then waved goodbye.

Tess watched her aunt's slim figure disappear into the cottage. She wasn't sure she wanted to be alone with Luca. Or maybe she did. It was quite confusing.

"I will help you clean up." Luca stood and picked up the remaining plates and silverware.

Tess put her hand on his arm to stop him, then pulled it back immediately. "You don't have to do that; you're our guest."

"I insist." He helped her clear the table, then carried the two vases of flowers into the kitchen and set them by the sink. "I am going to call Poppy's mother and tell her what she missed," he teased, leaning against the counter.

Tess busied herself putting away the chips and condiments. "I didn't even think to invite her." Her tone was serious and self-deprecating. "I hope she isn't upset when she finds out."

"I understand," Luca replied. "It was meant for the children."

"Yes, it was . . . until you showed up." She managed a smile. "The kids are rehearsing their play in Eva's room and the weather's cooled off a bit. Would you like to sit on the front porch until they're done?"

"I would like that very much."

"This is my altar, and these are all the feathers," Eva said proudly once Teo and Poppy were in her bedroom. She shut the door quietly and led them to her dresser.

"Wow!" exclaimed Poppy. Her mouth fell open at the sight of the colorful feathers displayed on the shimmery cloth. "You *found* all of these?"

"Around *here*?" Teo asked, shaking his head in wonder.

"I did," Eva said as she picked up the framed photo of Micah. "This is my brother."

Poppy touched the glass that covered Micah's face. "He sure is cute."

"Don't get any ideas." Eva set the photo back down. "He's gay."

The three were silent for a moment, then Eva spoke. "Teo, what's up with your dad and my mom?"

He looked away. "No idea." His voice was hushed to a whisper.

"It's strange, isn't it?" Eva picked up the dolphin bookmark and rubbed it between her hands. "They haven't seen each other in twenty-six years. That's a really long time."

"It was weird how they looked at each other," Teo commented, flopping down on Eva's bed and gazing at the ceiling.

Eva set the bookmark next to Micah's photo. "I don't like it."

"Me either," Teo replied, pulling a polka-dotted pillow over his head.

"It might be romantic, though." Poppy said hopefully.

Teo suddenly sat up and threw the pillow across the room, narrowly missing a sleeping Jasper who sprang off the window sill with a startled meow. "Romantic? I don't *think* so!"

Eva ran to Jasper who was clawing at the door. She picked him up and nuzzled him under her chin, then said to Poppy, "I sure hope not."

"But why?" Poppy responded with a little pout as she picked up a fuchsia feather and twirled it over her head. "Think about it. They obviously were more than friends a long time ago. Now they've found each other again and it *is* romantic. My mom and stepdad found each other after a long time and it worked out for them. It could work out for your mom." She pointed to Eva with the feather, then faced Teo. "And your dad." Poppy dropped the feather back onto the altar.

"It's a good thing, trust me," Poppy continued confidently, then seated herself on Eva's desk chair and crossed her legs. "My stepdad is a better dad than my real dad ever was." She watched as Eva finally set Jasper down and opened the door to let him out. "You said you hardly knew your father, so this could be good for you. Your mom could get a husband and you could get a new dad."

Eva frowned. "What if I don't *want* a new dad? I hardly even have a *mom* right now."

"I already have a mother!" Teo said, pure misery soaking his words. "She was a good mom." He covered his eyes with his hands. "I don't need another one!"

Poppy looked from Teo to Eva. Obviously, her friends weren't ready to hear about the upside of having a stepparent. "Okay, I get it," she finally said. "Maybe it's not what I think it is." She picked up the paper bag that Teo had brought, opened it, and took out their props along with the script. "Let's just practice and forget about them for a while."

"I still have no idea how you can drink that stuff at night," Luca said, indicating Tess's steaming coffee mug. He held a sweating glass of ice water in his hands. They were sitting on the porch—Tess in the rocking chair, Luca on the wicker loveseat.

She blew the fragrant steam away before taking a tiny sip. "It never bothered me, even when I was a teenager."

"Me, on the other hand . . ."

"I remember."

The sky was slowly fading from a brilliant summery blue to the faintest shade of lilac. Nearby, crickets were beginning their evening serenade.

Luca set his ice water on the wicker table beside him. "Tell me more about yourself. You said you recently moved here and are managing the office at Pearly Whites."

"That's right."

"Eva is eleven and your son is in the Army. You are divorced?"

"Cameron and I never married. We met when I was in college, both of us working part time at the same coffee shop." She took another sip of coffee. "It was an on-again, off-again relationship that wasn't built to last. He's actually married now and has two kids. Doesn't see Micah and Eva anymore."

"I'm sorry."

She shrugged. The grief about her relationship with Cameron had long since ebbed away. "All I know about you so far is that Teo is your son, and your fishing charter business keeps you very busy."

"They both keep me busy."

"Is there a Mrs. Silva?"

The corners of Luca's mouth turned down. "Madalena. She died two years ago. Congestive heart failure. It runs in her family. I . . . have to keep an eye on Teo's health."

Tess set her coffee down. "I'm so sorry, Luca."

He gazed over the front walkway just as the streetlights flickered on. "We met in Uni. I was studying business and Madalena was in the nursing program. She worked as a nurse in Lisbon right up until Teo was born."

Part of Tess wanted to sit next to him on the loveseat and put her arm around him, offer comfort to this man who had once been a kindred spirit. But she stayed where she was. Too many years had passed. He was different now, and so was she. "When did you move back to the States?"

"About a year ago. The memories in Portugal were too difficult. I was beginning to move on, but Teo . . ." He sighed. "We needed a change of scenery, so I decided to come back to Seahaven, where I had once been very happy." He looked at Tess meaningfully; she looked away. "I had no idea that you were here. I thought of searching for you online, but Teo and the business have kept me busy, and I wasn't sure if you were still in Connecticut. When I saw you tonight, standing on these steps—"

"Yes." Tess shifted in the rocker until she was perched on the end of the seat, then hugged a striped pillow to her chest. "I guess we were both shocked."

Luca also leaned forward. "Tessa, I—"

"Please don't call me that again!" she said sharply. "You lost the right to call me that when you . . ." She looked away for a moment, then turned back to him. "Why did you stop emailing me?" Her voice had sunk to a hoarse whisper and her hands felt clammy. "It hurt so much when I couldn't reach you anymore."

"What?" Luca looked surprised. "I did not *want* to stop emailing you or talking on the phone!"

Tess's eyes widened. "You didn't? Then why—"

Luca quickly moved to the straight-backed chair that was next to her rocker. He gently removed the pillow from her grasp and took one of her hands in his. "Your mother emailed me. She told me you had a new boyfriend, that you were in love with him, and that there was no place for me in your life anymore." He searched her eyes. "Surely, you remember."

Astonished, Tess held onto his hand tightly, her voice trembling. She sat up straighter and spoke more firmly. "It wasn't true."

"There was no boyfriend?"

"No," she repeated. "I didn't start dating again until college. When I met Cameron, we were in love for a little while, but then . . . over the years, it was too hard. I mean, I'm no saint, but he had more than the usual shortcomings. Fear of commitment being number one."

Luca stood and began pacing the length of the porch, running his fingers through his tousled dark hair. "I cannot believe Cecilia did this!"

"I can," Tess replied flatly. "She's the reason we left Seahaven early that summer. Her excuse was one of her incessant fundraisers, but I knew it was because she didn't like you. She's got a thing against people who are different, including Micah."

He turned to face her. "What about Micah?"

"He's gay. It took her a long time to come to terms with that, but it was rough going for a while."

Luca scratched his neck. "I am glad that you have moved away from her."

"Not as glad as me," Tess replied emphatically. "She's only called me once, but even then, it wasn't to ask how Eva's doing, or if I like my new job. It was to demand that I ask Micah to contact her." She picked up her coffee mug, warming her suddenly cold hands.

"Tessa . . . I mean, Tess. I am sorry that I believed your mother all those years ago. To tell you the truth, she frightened me. She threatened to call the Polícia in Lisbon if I continued to email you. She said she would tell them I was harassing you."

"She would have done that too." Tess drank the last of her coffee, then set the mug down.

"That is the only reason I shut down my email account." He moved his hands to his heart. "I am sorry. I never wanted to hurt you. I thought you had found someone else."

"It wasn't your fault." She suddenly felt a startling tenderness toward this man she no longer knew but was beginning to remember, along with a slow-burning anger that focused on her mother. It was an anger that had been present for many years, but she'd been too much of a "good girl" to express it. She wondered if it was time to fan the flames a bit.

They sat in silence for a while, letting their conversation—and the feelings that were beginning to stir—settle. As the sky darkened to indigo and stars appeared like brilliant pinpoints of light, the two old friends—now new friends—began to talk more easily. The conversation roamed from Luca's business, to Tess's new job, to the children, to what they were reading.

Finally, Luca looked at his watch. "It is almost nine. I should get going. My first charter goes out at seven, and Teo needs to get some sleep before camp tomorrow."

They both stood. "Of course. I'll tell the kids it's time to stop rehearsing." She turned to leave but Luca stopped her.

"Wait. Would you like to have dinner with me tomorrow night? There is a great new fish place down by the harbor. I remember how much you liked scallops and theirs are very good. He smiled hopefully, his brown eyes rimmed with the thinnest band of gold. Tess remembered getting lost in those eyes once.

She rubbed the palm of one hand against the back of the other. "Eva and Teo too?"

"No, just us." He took one of her hands in his. "We still have much to learn about each other. You and me first, then the kids."

This sounded perfect to her. "I'd like that," she replied. "But I have to see if Kalila—she lives across the hall—can stay with Eva. I don't want to leave her too long."

Luca raised his eyebrows.

"I've been away so much with work and night school the last four years. Eva and I haven't had much time together."

"I understand." He raised her hand to his lips and kissed it playfully. "I can pick you up at six and have you back with Eva by eight. If Kalila cannot help you out, we will choose another day."

"I'd like that." They exchanged phone numbers.

After everyone had left, Tess finished putting things away in the kitchen while Eva fed Jasper who had evidently forgiven her for letting Teo throw a pillow at him. "How did your play practice go?" Tess asked, wiping down the counter.

"Okay, I guess. Teo and Poppy are so good at acting."

"What about you?"

"Actually, I stink at it, so I'm the narrator." Eva sat on the floor and watched Jasper crunch his food. "But I wrote the whole script and Kalila says it's really good."

"That's great, Eva!" Tess replied, pausing a moment to look down at her daughter. For once, she noticed, everything seemed right in the world. Her job was better than she had dared to hope; Eva finally seemed happy. And now there was Luca, who had suddenly appeared at her door. Was his synchronistic presence in their lives the final stroke of happiness? She rubbed her temples as if to send that thought far away. There was too much water under the proverbial bridge. Wasn't there?

"Kalila told us that everyone can't be good at everything," Eva said, getting to her knees and picking up Jasper's bowl. He meowed plaintively at her. "More? You want more?" He meowed again and she shook some more food from the crinkled bag into his bowl. "But at least I'm good at *something* now."

Tess leaned against the counter. "You may have just discovered that you're a good writer, but you've always been a good friend, and a good sister, and you always know the exact right book to suggest to people."

Eva paused. "I never thought of that before. I wanted to be good at swimming and soccer like Charli, or good at art like Micah, but that's never gonna happen in a zillion years."

"Well, now you've discovered something you love that you *are* good at." Tess wiped her hands on a dish towel and folded it carefully next to the sink. "We're still on for Friday night, right? After the final performance, we're going to pull an all-nighter like we used to?"

"Just you and me, right?" Eva looked up shyly.

"Just you and me. I wonder how late you can stay up this time," Tess teased. She opened her arms and Eva moved in for a quick hug.

"I bet I can make it 'til sunrise." Eva's voice was muffled against Tess's side. "And Mom?"

"Yes, hon?" Tess savored this rare hug and unusually normal conversation with her daughter.

Eva pulled away but stayed close. "Are you and Luca going to get married?"

"What?"

"You had these funny expressions on your face, the way Luke and Lorelai look at each other in season four." Noticing Tess's surprised and somewhat hurt expression, Eva quickly continued. "I mean, you and Luca were friends a long time ago, and Poppy said that's how she got a stepfather."

Tess bent down and looked Eva in the eye. "Luca and I don't know each other anymore. We're not going to get married."

"But I heard you ask Kalila to stay with me when you go to dinner with him tomorrow night. That's a date, and after people date for a while, they usually get married, right?"

Tess hugged her daughter again, overwhelmed with love. "It's not a date, Eva. It's dinner at a fish shack. Luca and I are going to talk about old times and I'll be home by eight so you and I will have time together before bed."

Eva looked doubtful as she bent down to pick up Jasper's bowl again. "If you say so."

"I'll come tuck you in in a minute, okay?"

She rolled her eyes. "Mom. I'm *eleven*. I don't need you to tuck me in."

Tess smiled as she turned out the lights and headed to her bedroom. Life felt good right now. Eva had hugged her for the first time in ages and they were planning a whole night together, just the two of them. Maybe there was hope for them as Gilmore girls after all. Luca's unexpected reappearance felt like icing on the proverbial cake, or the sweet frosting in the middle of those delectable Whoopie pies. But how long could the sweetness last?

.

# Chapter 17

The next night at quarter to six, Tess was nervously getting ready for dinner with Luca. As teenagers, they had never officially had a "date," so she was inclined to think that this was not a date either. Back then, they had walked the beach at sunset, ridden bikes all the way up to Kennebunkport and back. They'd strolled through town holding hands and treated each other to ice cream at the shop that now was Simply Coffee / Simply Sweets. They had talked nonstop, and they had kissed. Boy, had they kissed. Tess hummed softly now, remembering how special their time together had been. Could that connection still exist? It seemed improbable.

She chose the blue and white sundress that she'd worn to Chloe's with the gang from work—was that only a month ago—and stepped into a pair of new open-toed sandals with a little heel. Caressing the Mother's Day necklace at her throat, she remembered the day not long ago when Micah had clasped the seashell necklace around her neck. Filled with a sudden urge to find it, she opened the bottom drawer of her dresser and pulled out the Seahaven box as the scent of musty cedar filled her nose. Looking in the mirror, she slipped the long necklace over her head and felt the sensuous weight of the shells and sea glass against her chest. "There," she said aloud with satisfaction as she ran a brush through her hair. She wondered if Luca would remember the necklace.

Pushing her hair back from her face with a white headband, Tess turned to pick up her purse and saw Eva leaning against the door jamb. "Hi, hon! Is Kalila here yet?"

"Not yet Are you *sure* it's not a date?"

"It's not a date, I promise." They walked to the living room together.

"Whatever." Eva plopped on the sofa and picked up the remote.

"I'll be back by eight so we can read together, okay? We haven't done that in a long time."

Eva nodded agreeably, then pointed to the seashell necklace. "I never saw you wear that before."

Tess's cheeks flushed. "This is just an old necklace I found in my drawer. I thought it would brighten up my dress."

"But the only jewelry you ever wear is the necklace that Micah and I gave you."

"I'm still wearing it, see?" She touched her throat. "I only take it off in the shower, and I promise I'll always wear it." A soft knock sounded at the door and Tess hurried to let Kalila in. "Thanks for coming," she said as the teen settled next to Eva on the sofa, resting her bare feet on the coffee table. Today, her fingernails were painted with the same lavender polish as her toes and both middle toes sported a silver spiral toe ring.

Eva admired Kalila's feet, then squinted one more time at her mom's long necklace. "Are those real emeralds?"

"Oh no, just bits of sea glass." Tess kissed Eva on top of her head. "I'm going to wait out front for Luca and I'll see you at eight. Have fun!" She blew a kiss as she headed out the door.

Waiting on the porch in the humid evening, Tess couldn't sit still. She sat in the rocker, moved to the loveseat, then gave up and stood at the back end of the porch, looking across the driveway to Kit's garden. She glanced at her watch. Ten minutes 'til the hour. Butterflies danced in her stomach; she hoped she'd be able to digest those scallops. She hoped—what did she hope? That she and Luca would find the connection they'd once had? That they might fall in love for real this time? Could she possibly dare to hope for that?

It seemed too crazy to be real. She had been alone for so long; it hardly seemed possible for love to find its way to her again.

"Howdy, neighbor," called Carolina, interrupting Tess's jumbled thoughts as she jogged around the corner with an energetic Rocky by her side. She stopped in front of the porch, but continued to jog in place.

"Carolina, hi!" Tess walked quickly to the top of the stairs.

"Pretty dress!" She slowed her pace and reined the panting Rocky in on his leash.

"I'm going out—"

"Hooray and hallelujah!" Carolina grinned, bringing her jogging to a standstill. "You found someone on the Zoosk app!"

"No, I'm seeing an old friend. He owns the Sea Dove Charter over at the Pier."

"Ah, an old friend," she teased, making air quotes with her fingers.

"It's not like that," Tess insisted, although she wondered if it *was* exactly like that. "I told you about him, remember? We met here on vacation when I was fifteen. We're going to eat a meal together and talk about old times."

"I see." Carolina raised her eyebrows and slowly walked to the steps; Rocky trotted beside her. "And where might you be going on this not-a-date?"

"Pete's Fish Shack."

"Mmmm . . ." Carolina mused, lifting her heavy ponytail off her neck for a moment and brushing several strands of flyaway hair from her sweaty forehead. "That's a pretty necklace you're wearing. I've never seen you wear any jewelry at all except for the Mother's Day necklace."

"Yes, I . . . I found it in my dresser. Luca gave it to me the summer that we met."

The words were no sooner out of her mouth than Tess heard a dismayed gasp from the doorway. She whirled around. Eva stood there, one hand over her mouth, her eyes wide. "You told me it was just an old necklace that you found!" Her words seeped indignation and betrayal.

Tess moved toward her daughter but Eva ran back into the apartment and slammed the door. Tess followed. Eva had curled herself into the far end of the sofa. "What's happening?" Kalila asked, standing quickly as she looked between mother and daughter.

"I'm not sure, Kalila. Please give me a minute with Eva." Kalila moved quietly into the kitchen and Tess sat down next to Eva. "Hon, listen—"

"No. You *lied* to me." Eva folded her arms tightly across her chest and turned away.

"I shouldn't have lied. I didn't want you to think the necklace means anything more than it does."

"What does that mean?" Eva wiped her eyes.

"It means that it's just an old necklace. And yes, Luca is the one who gave it to me, but it was twenty-six years ago. It doesn't mean anything now."

"It must mean *something*," Eva grumbled. "Because you kept it all this time and you're wearing it tonight which means you want him to see it."

Momentarily stunned by her daughter's perception, Tess replied, "I honestly don't think Luca will even remember that he gave it to me. So much has happened in our lives since then." She smoothed Eva's hair off her forehead. "I'll take it off and throw it away if you want me to." As soon as she said it, she found herself hoping beyond hope that Eva wouldn't ask her to do that.

Eva's brow puckered in thought. "No. It's too pretty to throw away and it looks good with that dress."

"Thank you." Tess touched her daughter's hand and stood. "Luca's probably waiting so I'm going to leave. Call me on Kalila's phone if you need anything. I'll be back by eight."

As Tess quietly closed the door behind her, she found Luca chatting with Carolina on the front walkway. Squatting down, he was being licked frantically all over his face and hands by an exuberant Rocky. As soon as Luca saw Tess, he stood and smoothed down his neatly pressed khakis. Carolina handed him a tissue from her back pocket and he gladly wiped the remaining doggie-drool off his face. "Tess!" He pocketed the damp tissue and headed to the porch. "You look beautiful!"

Tess felt her cheeks redden. "Thanks, you look nice too." The dark green button-down shirt he was wearing set off his eyes and sun-darkened skin. "I didn't mean to be late, but Eva—"

"Carolina filled me in; it is not a problem. By the way, I like your necklace." He touched the strands of shells near her neck and she shivered slightly at his touch. "I can't believe you kept it all these years."

"You remember?" Tess's surprise filled the air between them as Luca stepped down to the sidewalk again.

"Of course! It took me hours to pick that out from one of those souvenir shops on Route One, and when I gave it to you, you said you would never take it off. Did you think I would forget?"

Carolina cleared her throat to get their attention and started jogging in place again. "I'm off now to finish my run. You two have fun!" She pulled on Rocky's red leash, mischievously wiggled her eyebrows at Tess, then took off, a happy Rocky running ahead as far as his leash would stretch.

Luca took Tess's hand and led her to his truck. "Seriously. That was a special night for me. I'd never given a girl anything before, much less a necklace." He opened the passenger door for her. "And I see you kept your promise because you are still wearing it!"

Chuckling, Tess settled herself in her seat. "I did keep the promise, until . . ." She looked over at him as he started the engine. "Until you stopped writing." She touched the necklace. "But that's all in the past, right?"

He turned the key in the ignition, then pulled away from the curb. "It is."

"I'm glad I kept it, though. It reminded me how special that time was with you . . . how special I felt that summer."

Luca kept his eyes on the road but reached over and took her hand. "From what I see, you are still pretty special."

Tess gazed up at the darkening sky. They were close to the harbor now, and Pete's Fish Shack appeared on the right—bright lights blazing, parking lot overflowing, faint music floating on the sea breeze. "I don't know about that," she replied. "The kids' father left me, my son joined the Army without even telling me, and my daughter is mad at me ninety percent of the time."

"Hey," Luca pulled into the one remaining parking spot at Pete's and cut the ignition. He turned to face her. "All of that? It is only one piece of who you are."

"Is it?" She looked away. "It feels like all of me right now."

"That is not how I see it." He hopped out of the truck and before she knew it, he was opening the door for her.

The restaurant was jam-packed with tourists and locals alike. Wait staff scurried about, and a country band played—quite loudly—from a small stage in the corner. Rough-hewn tables and benches were scattered about and colorful mosaic fish sculptures hung haphazardly from the ceiling. Tess ordered the baked stuffed scallops and Luca ordered the Caldeirada, a Portuguese fish stew with wild cod, mussels and shrimp. "So that's why you like to come here," Tess teased when the steaming stew arrived. "Portuguese comfort food."

Luca agreed as he took a sip of the broth and closed his eyes. "Just like Mãe used to make."

"The Portuguese language still baffles me, but I remember that the word for mother is mãe."

"That's right."

"When you introduced me to her, she asked me to call her Paloma. I always liked that name. How is she?" Tess dug into her scallops, savoring the salty scent.

"She is well. It was good to have her nearby after Madalena died. For Teo." He looked up at her. "And for me."

"I can only imagine," murmured Tess, scooping up some spicy rice.

"What did you say?" Luca gestured toward the band and grimaced. "It's so loud in here!"

Tess raised her voice. "I can imagine your Mãe being a comfort to have around after . . . such a loss." *Unlike my own mother*.

"She knew the right way to explain . . . things to Teo."

"Explaining the unexplainable."

"Yes."

It was difficult to talk with the loud music, the noisy chatter, and the clanging of dishes coming from the open kitchen, so they mostly ate in silence, glancing up at one another every so often and exchanging a smile.

After Luca insisted on paying the bill, he chatted for a moment with the owner in Portuguese, then they walked, side by side, a short distance to the pier. "Thank you for dinner," Tess said as they leaned on the weathered gray railing overlooking the harbor.

"Thank *you*," Luca replied, gazing out at the three boats that remained tethered to the dock. The rest of the boats were still out on the water somewhere, enjoying a cloudy but warm summer evening.

"For what?"

"For the excellent company, of course."

She looked away from him, down into the dark water where wavering streams of moonlight had managed to skip through the layers of clouds.

Luca turned and tipped her chin until her eyes met his. "Tessa," he said softly. "May I call you that now?"

She nodded, her heart thudding, her world growing suddenly brighter.

"Tessa, you are more lovely now than all those years ago when we were best friends. No, not best friends. What was it that you called us? From that book you loved as a little girl—Anne of the Gables. Was that it?"

"Anne of *Green* Gables," Tess corrected. "It was *kindred spirits*. That's what I said we were. Back then."

"Ah, yes. Kindred spirits. I remember now." He put one arm around her shoulders and they leaned, hip to hip at the railing. "I wonder if that can still be true for us."

"I . . . I don't know." That was what the fearful side of Tess's brain was telling her to say. Her heart was stubbornly insisting on something else altogether.

"What does your friend, Anne of the green gables, have to say about it?" he asked into the darkness.

"Anne Shirley would say that kindred spirits are forever," Tess replied reluctantly. Her brain couldn't quite figure out how it might possibly be true for her and Luca.

"And you? What would you say?"

"I would say that Anne didn't run into Gilbert twenty-six years later, so she couldn't really know for sure that kindred spirits are forever."

Luca bowed his head for a moment. He didn't necessarily agree with Tess, but he could see where she was coming from. "Only time will tell," he finally said, and he felt her relax a bit against his side. "Can we do that, Tessa? Can we give it time? I would like to see if our connection is still there."

She looked into his familiar face and wondered. Could she give it some time? Could she give him . . . them . . . a chance? What if the connection was still there? What if it was there in an even deeper way? He certainly was different from Cameron, not to mention Blake and Gerry. What would it be like to be able to start over with Luca? How different was he from when they were teenagers? How much time would it take to test their kindred spirits factor?

"Tessa?" he prompted hopefully.

Tess remembered loving the sound of her name in his soothing European accent, the sensation of his lips against hers, and the sensual feelings that their kissing had evoked. When she had been with him—laughing, sharing ice cream, fishing, biking, talking— she had felt more like herself than she ever had before that summer, except when she'd been with Quinn and Chiara. She was feeling that way again right now: more like herself, glad to be who she was, faults and all.

She took a deep breath, the warmth of the summer night clinging to her like a second skin, and let her heart respond instead of her head. "Yes. Let's give it some time." She wondered what it would be like to kiss him again, but she didn't have to wonder long. Luca leaned down, a question in his eyes. She nodded, and as his lips touched hers for the first time in twenty-six years, she remembered what it was like to feel lovable. It was such a strange but welcome feeling that she suddenly stopped thinking and put her arms around him, inviting the kiss to go deeper.

"Wow," he said softly a few minutes later, keeping his arms around her, but inhaling a lazy breath of the salty air.

"Double wow," she replied, touching her hair and realizing that she'd lost her headband. "Look!" She pointed at the white band floating amidst the seaweed in the moon-stroked water.

Luca leaned against her, arm to arm. "Would you like me to jump in and get it for you?" He pretended to climb onto the railing.

Tess playfully tugged on his arm. "Don't you dare jump in and leave me here alone!"

He stood beside her, his voice thick with emotion. "I have no intention of doing that."

At exactly five minutes before eight, Luca pulled up to the curb in front of Tess's apartment building. "Right on time . . ." he said, pointing to his watch. ". . . as promised."

"Thank you for that." Tess kissed him lightly on the lips, then paused and sat back in her seat. "And for everything else."

"I thank you as well." He took both of her hands in his as she turned to face him. "Tomorrow night is the kids' big performance. Would you like us go together?"

"I'd love that," Tess agreed. "But Eva and I are going to spend the rest of the night together. I promised—"

"Teo and I are going to stay up late and watch movies, like we do every Friday night. You and I will go out together another time . . . Hopefully, many more times."

Tess looked at the apartment building, observing Kalila's and Eva's shadows in the faint light from the television screen. "What about Eva and Teo?" she asked thoughtfully.

"They will be fine. Teo asked me the other day if I was going to start dating."

Tess reached for the door handle. "Eva asked me the same thing, but she didn't seem too keen about it."

"Hey." He touched her shoulder, and the warmth of his hand seeped through the chilled air conditioning and through her dress, heating her skin right down to her core. "We are going to give it time, remember?" He kissed her again, and the heat built until Tess thought she would melt with longing. All her worries about Micah, Eva, Teo . . . Everything melted away with the delicious closeness of this newly-familiar man.

"Yes, you're right. This will take time," she replied slowly as she eased herself out of the truck. "I'll see you at the theatre tomorrow. I'm going to drop Eva off at five-thirty and stay. I'll save you a seat."

"I will be there." Luca put his hands to his heart and then opened his palms out to Tess. She smiled in wonder as she mirrored his motions, realizing how similar it was to the blessing that she, Quinn, and Chiara always shared during their Zoom calls.

# Chapter 18

Thursday August 4
Dear Micah,

Glory gave me some new paper to write letters on today. I hope you like it. There are snow angels on it and I know it's not winter, but it reminds me of when Kalila took me to the beach and showed me how to make sand angels. It was fun. When you come home, we'll do double angels in the sand together!!!

Tomorrow night is the final Imaginarium performance. Guess what? I WROTE A PLAY and Teo and Poppy are going to act it out in front of a real live audience while I narrate it. They are good actors and I am a good writer so we make a good team. The play is a little bit about Teo whose mom died two years ago.

You're not going to believe this. Mom went on a DATE tonight. With Teo's father. His name is Luca. They knew each other when they were teenagers. Isn't that weird? Mom says it wasn't a date but she was so happy! We read Anne of Avonlea together when she came home. We haven't read together in a long time.

What do you think about Mom going out with Teo's dad? I liked seeing her happy and it was like some of her happy fell onto me, but I still think it's weird, don't you?

Love, your sister,
Eva

Eva, Teo, and Poppy stood in a tight circle, nervously holding hands in one of the backstage dressing rooms. The second to last group of kids was performing their original song, and soon it would be time for their short play, *The Boy Who Said Goodbye*. Eva's mouth was dry so she kept licking her lips. Teo's hand in hers was clammy; Poppy's fingers were buzzing as if a current of electricity was running through them.

"Hey guys, you ready?" Jasper came around the corner, wearing jeans, a pressed white shirt, a bright red bow tie and a khaki Stetson hat. He was holding the hand of a tall, handsome blond man. Eva recognized him from the photo in Jasper's apartment as his boyfriend Jake.

Eva dropped her friends' hands. "As ready as we'll ever be," she quipped, showing more confidence than she was feeling. She took a breath and introduced Teo and Poppy.

"Nice to meetcha, Teo and Poppy!" Jasper happily shook their hands. "I've seen you both at Imaginarium. I'm the props guy and this is my . . ." He looked at Jake, who shrugged evasively. "This is Jake," Jasper finally said. "He's a singer, actor, and dancer extraordinaire!" His fake British accent made the introduction sound especially important.

"Hi Jake," the kids said in unison. Eva thought he looked older—and more somber—than the photo in Jasper's apartment. She remembered Glory talking about Jake's wonderful hugs, but he was preoccupied with his phone which seemed permanently attached to his left hand.

"Do you work here too?" Poppy asked, moving closer to the doorway so they'd be sure to hear Kalila's two-minute warning.

"No," Jake replied, looking up from his phone and flashing a practiced, megawatt smile. "I live in New York City and from there I travel around doing shows." His voice was measured, deep, and mesmerizing.

"He's in rehearsals now to star as Curly in *Oklahoma* on Broadway," Jasper announced proudly.

"Wow," said Teo. He knew what a big deal Broadway was. Someday he wanted to star in a show there too, but who would want to play a guy named Curly? Jake pocketed his phone. "I can see you're all nervous, but did you practice as much as possible?"

They nodded, fascinated by his theatrical presence and deep blue eyes.

"Then you have nothing to worry about. The more you've practiced, the more ready you are, and the fact that you're anxious tells me that you really care about this play. Is that right?"

They nodded again, transfixed.

"Nervousness is simply excitement that's gotten a little out of control. But it will help you once you get onstage."

Jasper clapped Jake on the shoulder. "Pay attention, guys; he's an expert!"

"Two minutes, kiddos," called Kalila, sticking her head in the doorway.

Immediately released from Jake's spell, the three friends followed Kalila into the hallway. "Goodbye!" Eva called, tightly grasping her narrator's folder in her hands.

The men skirted around stage left to take a seat in the audience. "It's gonna be great," Jasper whispered to Eva, tipping his hat slightly. "Break a leg."

"Break a *leg*?" she whispered back, perplexed.

Poppy shushed her, saying under her breath, "That's how actors wish each other good luck."

Eva, Poppy, and Teo stood near the edge of the stage, behind the curtain. The current act was at the end of their song—one more chorus and they'd be done.

Teo peeked around the curtain and gave a small gasp. "Eva!" he whispered, pulling on her sleeve.

"Shhh!"

"Sorry." He lowered his voice. "Your *mom* is sitting with my *dad* out there."

Eva started to look around the curtain, but Poppy moved both friends aside to peek. "So what?" Poppy whispered, one hand on her hip.

Eva edged Poppy away from the curtain. Yes, there was her mother, leaning into Luca. They were both laughing uproariously along with the rest of the audience at the antics of the singers onstage. She had to admit, she liked seeing her mother so happy.

"So what?" Teo repeated, drawing out the words indignantly. "Look. He's holding her hand."

Eva double checked. Her mom and Luca were indeed holding hands, and as the singers finished, right before the audience broke into applause, she saw Luca bring her mom's hand to his lips briefly. Eva blinked. She wasn't sure if she liked what she was seeing or if she hated it, but she certainly wasn't going to mention that little kiss to Teo.

"So romantic! What did I tell you?" Poppy nudged Teo and Eva as the audience began to applaud.

Teo frowned and Eva swallowed hard. There was too much going on; she needed to focus on their performance. "Let's concentrate on our play right now. We can deal with that . . ." She gestured toward the audience. ". . . later." As the clapping died down and the curtain closed, the three friends made their way onstage and took their places, holding their collective breath until the curtain opened again.

Jasper had been right. In spite of their nerves, Eva's ten-minute play was a huge success. Jake had also been right: they had practiced so much that—as soon as they got going—their nervousness changed back to excitement and it helped their performance enormously.

After several curtain calls for the entire Imaginarium ensemble, and announcements from Grace and Will, the three children joined the crowd in the lobby. Poppy left them to meet up with her mother and stepfather.

"You guys, that was amazing!" Tess called, running up to them and gathering Eva in her arms. Eva, giddy with the exhilarating buzz of success, let herself be hugged.

Luca was close behind Tess; he grasped Teo in an equally tight embrace. "Teo, my main man," he murmured against his son's dark hair. "That was well done. Your Mãe would be so proud of you."

Teo pulled away, a little embarrassed by all the attention, and flustered by Tess's presence.

"Tessa, you remember my son, Teo," Luca said happily.

"Yes, of course. What a great job you did. I was crying at the end. We all were." Tess held out her hand, but Teo crossed his arms and backed away, shaking his head slowly.

Watching in semi-shock at her friend's blatant display of rejection, Eva moved closer to Teo and touched his arm. She understood. It was too weird, seeing their parents together like this.

"I'm sorry—" Tess began, straightening up anxiously.

Luca interrupted. "Teo, manners!" Teo looked down at the floor, his eyes brimming with tears.

"It's okay," Tess said quietly. Part of her knew exactly what he was feeling. How strange it was, even to her, to be together with Luca after all this time.

Luca took a breath and consciously chose to let his son's behavior slide. "Teo, you and Poppy did such a great job acting. Eva, you wrote the script, right?"

She nodded shyly.

"I think you all have brilliant careers ahead of you!" He clapped his hands once. "Let's get ice cream at Simply Sweets."

Teo looked uncertain. "You and me, right?"

"No, son. All of us. All four of us."

Teo looked surprised, then angry. "No! You go ahead," he said, loudly enough that several people in the lobby turned to stare at him. "Eva and I will hang out here."

Tess was also a little surprised and glanced at Luca warily. What had happened to *just us* and *taking some time*?

Luca caught Tess's raised eyebrows. "I see," he said slowly. Perhaps just the four of them together right now was not a good idea. "I will ask Poppy and her parents if they would like to join us."

"Join you?" asked Rosa who suddenly appeared at the edge of the uneasy little group. Poppy was beside her, bouncing up and down like a certain famous battery-powered rabbit.

"Hi ladies!" Tess exclaimed brightly, relieved to have this awkward moment interrupted. "Poppy, you were so great in Eva's play!" She ruffled Poppy's curls.

Poppy attempted a curtsy. "Thanks, Ms. Gilmore! It was fun!" She joyfully high-fived Eva, then Teo. "We did great, guys!"

"We are going to Simply Sweets for ice cream. Would you like to join us?" Luca asked after introducing himself to Rosa. "Your husband too?"

"Daddy has to get up super early tomorrow," Poppy explained.

"He's a surgeon at Portsmouth General, but we'd love to go, wouldn't we, Poppy?"

"You bet!" Poppy replied enthusiastically.

"Did I hear someone mention Simply Sweets?" Jasper joined them with Jake following slightly behind, thumbing a text message on his phone.

Eva spoke up hopefully. "We're all going for ice cream. Will you come too?" She understood that the more people there were in the group, the less upset Teo might be.

Jasper glanced at Jake who looked up from his phone briefly and nodded. "Heck yeah, wouldn't miss it!" Jasper agreed. "Hey, you guys were AA up there!"

"AA?" Eva asked, wrinkling her nose in confusion.

"Absolutely Awesome!" Jasper responded while whipping off his hat and offering a low bow. The kids giggled while thanking him.

"He's right," Jake added, holding his phone behind his back and making eye contact with each of the children. "I would sign up to be onstage with you, any day of the week. And Eva, kudos to you for writing a compelling script. There wasn't a dry eye in the house."

"Wow, thanks!" Eva blushed.

"What do you say, Teo?" prompted Luca.

"Thank you," Teo said, gazing up at the tall actor as they all headed out the front door and into the parking lot.

At Simply Sweets, there was only one table left so they all crowded around it. Teo dragged his father to seats on the opposite side from where Tess had settled. Luca lifted his shoulders and mouthed "I'm sorry" to her across the long table. Tess wasn't sure what to think; Teo obviously didn't want her around, but she missed the nearness of Luca.

Eva was sitting between Poppy and Teo; Rosa was on Tess's left, and Jake was on her right, next to Jasper. After dipping into her dish of Blueberry Bliss ice cream, Tess took several photos of the children who hammed it up for the camera, although it was obvious that Teo was faking it.

"We can send these to Micah!" Eva said happily, taking a big spoonful of her butterscotch sundae that overflowed with chocolate chip ice cream and several extra cherries.

"Excellent idea!" said Jasper, licking his black raspberry chip cone.

Eva scooted her chair back and ran to her mother's side of the table. "Can I take some pictures, too?"

Tess used her napkin to wipe a smudge of butterscotch sauce from Eva's cheek, then handed over the phone.

As Eva walked around the table, she took photos of various combinations of people. Poppy with her mom. Poppy and Teo. Luca and Teo. Finally, she turned the camera toward Jasper and Jake. She'd just had an idea for a present that Jasper would appreciate. "Smile, guys!" she said, and they did, each intent on their own Simply Sweets dessert. "No, no!" Eva exclaimed, holding the phone by her side for a moment. "I want you to really *smile*." They sat up straighter and smiled at the camera. "At each *other*," Eva insisted, tapping her foot. Jasper put his arm around the back of Jake's chair and leaned into him, then turned his head slightly as Jake did the same. Eva clicked several more photos. "These are good," she said, after skimming through them. She handed the phone back to Tess and went back to her seat.

After more conversation, the group stood up to leave and Luca found his way to Tess's side, taking her hand. He whispered in her ear, "Have fun tonight with Eva. I will miss you."

Jake noticed something special passing between Luca and Tess. "Eva, you didn't get a picture of your mom with Teo's dad!" He grabbed Tess's phone from the table and snapped a photo of them.

As Teo watched his father whisper in Tess's ear, he felt a clear, distinct anger starting to crackle inside him, starting at the pit of his stomach. Eva's mom was not his mother. His mother was dead, dead, *dead*. How could his father be whispering in another woman's ear? As he watched Jake take a picture of his dad and Tess, fury boiled up inside, propelling him around the table breathlessly. He knocked the phone out of Jake's hands, then kicked it angrily, tears streaming down his face. All conversation halted as Jake discreetly retrieved the phone from under the next table, apologizing quietly to the customers who were sitting there. Jasper watched all of this in dismay.

"Teo!" Luca cried, rushing to kneel at his son's side. "What are you doing?" Teo was now crouched on the floor, sobbing. Luca laid a hand on his son's shoulder, but Teo stood angrily, shaking him off.

"I don't like her," Teo said, pointing at Tess. "She's not my Mãe and she never will be!"

Rosa coughed lightly and put her arm around Poppy. "Let's go home, dear. Teo and his daddy need to talk." They said their goodbyes and quickly left.

Jake handed the phone back to Tess, saying quietly, "It's not damaged, and I saved the photos for you." Then he and Jasper hurried away.

Eva stood very still as she watched Luca apologetically lead Teo out of the shop. "Mom?" She looked at her mother uncertainly.

Tess held unsteady hands to her flushed cheeks as she stared after Luca and Teo. Her heart might be trying to insist otherwise, but she knew now that she and Luca weren't meant to be together. Teo had made that perfectly clear. This brought up a strange mixture of sadness and relief. There was sorrow because she wouldn't have a chance to get close to Luca again, and relief because she wouldn't have to worry about when or if Teo would ever be able to accept her. Also, she'd never have to think about what would happen if she and Luca got close but it didn't last.

The sound of her daughter's voice brought her back into the room. Eva. Yes, this was the time to be focusing on her precious daughter, not on an old love story that refused to bring itself into the present day. "Let's go," she said as steadily as she could, tugging tenderly on Eva's long ponytail. "We've got a long night ahead of us and a sunrise to get ready for!"

# Chapter 19

As Eva got into her watermelon-print pajamas, she found another feather sitting on her pillow. This was even bigger than the other feathers. A peacock feather! She jumped on the bed and gazed at the feather reverently before picking it up and turning it over and over in her hands. "Thank you, Angels," she whispered, laying it gently on her altar among the others.

This had been *almost* a perfect day! The play had gone better than expected, and having ice cream with everyone afterward had been fun . . . until Teo had freaked out. Now she and Mom were going to stay up all night watching movies and reading stories. Of course, when she was little, she had never stayed awake the whole night, but she was sure she could do it now that she was eleven.

As for Teo, Eva couldn't imagine in a million years how she would feel if her mother died. She didn't mind that Luca and her mom had held hands, or that they each seemed to shine with a little more happiness when they were together, but she was waiting to hear what Micah thought. He was older; he would know if it was okay.

She picked up a sleepy Jasper who curled contentedly into her arms, and headed down the hallway toward the living room. Eva paused outside her mother's bedroom when she heard Tess talking loudly on the phone.

"Luca, I enjoyed our time together last night, but I just can't do this." Then, a long pause. Eva could imagine her mother rubbing her forehead with the hand that wasn't holding the phone. "I know that we said—" More silence. Eva held her breath. "Look, it's obvious that Teo isn't ready for you to . . . for me to be part of . . ." Tess let out a breath that sounded like harsh cough. "I can't discuss this anymore." Eva noticed her mother's voice losing strength and volume. "Teo is the one who needs time, not you and me."

Eva heard her mother say goodbye, then the thuds and clatter of drawers opening and closing more loudly than usual. Eva hurried to the living room before her mother discovered her at the door. She didn't need to wait for Micah's opinion about Mom-and-Luca anymore because there was no more Mom-and-Luca, and she wasn't sure whether to be disappointed or happy about it.

Tess, also wearing summery pajamas, joined Eva in the living room. "Here we are, hon!" She sat on the other end of the sofa and propped her feet up on the coffee table. "It's ten-thirty. Are you sure you're going to make it until sunrise?" Her tone was teasing but her eyes were focused on her lap—one palm smoothing the back of the other hand.

Eva perched on the edge of the sofa. She looked at her mother uncertainly and picked up a cushion, hugging it to her chest. Tess's eyes were lightly tinged with sadness. "I can if you can," Eva replied hesitantly.

"Hey, why don't we get some snacks from the kitchen? If you're not too full from all that ice cream!"

Eva ran to the kitchen, returning with a big bag of pretzels, two glasses of lemonade, a bowl of Skittles, and a box of chocolate nonpareils from Perkins Cove Candies over in Ogunquit. "Here you go, Mom. All your favorites!" She dropped them on the coffee table.

"A few of your favorites too, I see," Tess teased as she reached for the lemonade, holding the icy glass to her cheek for a moment. She drank thirstily, then set it down on one of their new Seahaven coasters. "That hit the spot. What do you want to watch? How about Lorelai and Rory?"

Eva picked up the remote but didn't push any buttons. "Are you okay, Mom?"

"I'm fine." Tess munched on a pretzel, enjoying the way the salt stung her tongue.

"But tonight, at Simply Sweets . . ." Eva took a handful of Skittles and popped a few in her mouth. "Teo was mean to you."

Tess swallowed the last bite of pretzel and gazed at her daughter thoughtfully. "Yes, he was."

"Aren't you . . . mad or something?"

She took her feet off the coffee table and scooted over to the middle of the sofa so she could pull Eva close to her side. "I'm not mad." She sighed. "Teo's had a huge loss."

"But what about you and Luca? You were so happy when you came back from dinner last night."

Tess sat back and took the remote from Eva's hands, then turned on the TV and clicked over to Netflix. "I told him I can't see him anymore," she replied, intently gazing at the screen.

"But—"

"It's over, that's all there is to it. I want to spend more time with you, Eva. That's what's most important right now." She ran her fingers through Eva's long, messy hair. "See? It's all working out for the best. Now, how about we watch the first episode of *Gilmore Girls*? I bet we could watch six whole episodes before sunrise!" She gazed hopefully at her daughter.

Eva hesitated. She was almost at the end of Season Four on her own. It might be more fun to watch it with her mom, now that she was home more and actually paying attention. But she wasn't sure. Not yet. Eva took the remote from Tess and clicked on *One Day at a Time* instead. "Let's watch this. Kalila and I started it the other night. I think you'll like it."

Disappointed—once again—Tess took another sip of lemonade while Jasper curled up between them. She supposed it shouldn't matter what show they were watching. Could she set aside her hope to share *Gilmore Girls* with Eva? She had begun watching the series when she was pregnant with Micah; that was when she fell in love with the mother-daughter duo of Lorelai and Rory. Then Kit had sent her the DVD set when she was pregnant with Eva. There was a certain wistfulness in her heart every time she watched, because she had never had a close relationship with her own mother. In fact, Lorelai's mom, Emily, reminded Tess of Cecilia—the same bristling attitude and condescending comments. As Tess watched the episodes while expecting Eva, she set in motion an expectation that they would be just as close as the fictional *Gilmore Girls*. But it hadn't worked out that way. It hadn't worked out that way at all.

After several episodes of *One Day at a Time,* a movie, more snacks, and a few bathroom breaks, they moved to the kitchen table and wrote "real" letters to Micah. Eva also wrote another letter to Charli. "Mom, I can't believe she isn't writing back. Do you think Charli's okay?"

"They're probably busy settling in," Tess replied, pressing a postage stamp onto her latest letter to Micah. She sat back, yawned, then glanced at her phone. Luca had texted several times and called twice. She frowned, hoping that Eva hadn't noticed. "It's almost four o'clock. We'll leave in half an hour, okay?"

"Okay!" Eva had gotten another burst of energy and was busy drawing a picture to add to Charli's letter. "I sure hope Micah and Charli like getting *real* letters! Eva bit her lip in concentration while adding extra strokes of violet to a rainbow. "I almost forgot!" She looked up at Tess. "Can you print one of the pictures of Jasper and Jake? I want to give it to Jasper."

"Sure, hon. I'll do that before we leave." Tess yawned again and got up to make a pot of coffee. It had been years since she'd attempted an all-nighter, but it was now Saturday morning and they could both sleep as long as they wanted to . . . after the sunrise.

Sitting side by side with Eva in the cool darkness on the beach was both thrilling and sobering for Tess. A sleepy Eva leaned against Tess's side and let herself be held. Tess couldn't remember the last time Eva had snuggled into her like this. Wait . . . she did remember. It was four years ago; Eva was seven and Tess hadn't started the night classes yet. That summer she'd had two weeks off from work and they'd rented a small cottage in nearby Clinton for one of the weeks. It had felt like heaven, worth all the scrimping and saving she'd done to make it happen. She was too tired for sunrises at that point in her life, but she and the kids had spent many happy hours in the water, building sand castles, collecting shells, eating fried clams, and playing board games. At fourteen, Micah had spent the evenings on his own, texting with friends, sketching, and reading, but Tess and Eva snuggled together on the sofa each night, reading or playing word games.

Yes, she thought now, as the evening star shone brightly over their heads and the first band of pale light claimed its space on the horizon, she was right to have broken it off with Luca. This was her time to get close to Eva again. Who was she to think she could have both? Eva was growing up so fast . . . who knew how many chances she'd have like this with her daughter?

"Mom?" Eva sat up a little straighter and snapped her fingers in front of Tess's eyes. "Mom! The sky's getting brighter."

Tess blinked. "Sorry. I was thinking of the time we rented that little cottage in Clinton. Do you remember?"

"Yeah, that was fun." More alert now, she pointed to the curved yolk of a sun that was beginning to peek through the thin layer of clouds striping the horizon. "It's so cloudy today. Maybe it won't be a pretty sunrise."

"Oh, it will be. I guarantee it. The clouds will make it even better."

"No way!"

"Just watch," Tess replied, and her sadness started to fade with the night sky.

The striated clouds softened the rising sun's brilliance and the sky melted into a series of stunning corals, pinks, and violets that left both Eva and Tess wide-eyed. They were both silent as the sky lightened with color. At one point, Eva reached for Tess's hand and Tess held it gladly. Was there anything in the world more important than this? She thought not.

After taking several photos of the sky, and a selfie of both of them with the sunrise in the background, Tess stood and offered her hand to a sleepy Eva. "Come on, hon, let's go home."

"Okay," Eva agreed, stifling a yawn. "But can we come back and see the earthmove again, just you and me?"

Tess shook out the blanket they had been sitting on and collected their containers of coffee and hot chocolate. "See the what?" They headed up the slight hill to the parking lot.

"The sun is always in one place." Eva got in the car and adjusted her seat belt. "It isn't moving; the *earth* is moving. So, it's not actually a *sunrise*, right? It's an *earthmove*!"

Tess chuckled as the started the car. "Right you are. And we will definitely watch another sunr— I mean *earthmove* soon."

For the first time since Theatre Jasper had painted Eva's bedroom, she didn't protest when her mother came in to help her get ready for bed. It was six o'clock in the morning and sunlight was streaming in through Eva's curtains. Tess gently pulled them closed while Eva took off her sandals and flopped onto the bed, already half asleep. She debated asking Eva to change back into her pajamas, then tossed that idea out. They were both tired. Tess could do with a nap herself right now.

After kissing Eva on the forehead and pulling the sheet over her, something bright and colorful caught her eye on Eva's dresser. She moved a little closer and discovered a shimmery gold cloth that held Micah's photo, the dolphin bookmark, and over a dozen brightly colored feathers—all different sizes and colors. "Eva?" she whispered, lightly touching her daughter's shoulder. "What's all this?"

"What?" Her voice already thickened with the beginning of slumber, Eva blinked slowly and raised her head a few inches.

"These feathers on your bureau next to Micah's picture."

Her head dropped back to the pillow and she closed her eyes again. "Oh, yeah. Those are angel feathers. For Micah."

Tess kept her hand on Eva's warm shoulder. "What do you mean?"

From the edge of dreamland, Eva replied in a voice so soft that Tess had to lean in to hear. "I found them. One at a time. The angels left them for me. That's how I know that Micah is safe."

Confused, but not wanting to wake Eva any further, Tess slowly stood and gazed down at her daughter whose long hair fanned across the pillow. "Good night, hon," she said gently. "You can tell me more when you wake up." She stood for a long time in the small bedroom, breathing in the comforting scent of her daughter mixed with the tang of fresh paint.

Tess brushed her fingers over the feathers on Eva's dresser for a moment. All these feathers, so interesting and bright. Did Eva actually believe they were from angels? Where would she have gotten that idea? She frowned and turned off the dolphin-shaped lamp before shutting the door behind her. She had been thinking about taking a nap, but now all she wanted was coffee. And answers.

# Chapter 20

Tess carried her coffee mug onto the back deck. The clouds that had created such a stunning sunrise had dispersed, leaving a perfect Saturday sky, inviting a day that promised to be hot and clear. She intended to sit outside, breathe the fresh sea air, and ponder the events of the past few days until her busy mind stilled and she could make sense of everything—kissing Luca, Teo's anger, a tentative renewed closeness with Eva. And now . . . angel feathers? Sensing the beginning of a headache, she rubbed her right temple as she set her mug down and eased into one of the cushioned chairs.

Taking a sip of coffee, she quickly turned when Aunt Kit called across the back yard, "Come and join us!" Theatre Jasper was seated on Kit's patio, his head resting in his hands. *Sure, why not?* thought Tess. Maybe they could help her make sense of Eva's feathers.

"I saw you and Eva heading out before dawn this morning, so I took in the sunrise at the Marginal Way instead," Kit said as Tess took a seat next to Jasper. Kit sat across from them and placed a mug in front of Jasper. "Here you go. Peppermint. It will cheer you right up."

Jasper raised his head and gripped the mug's handle, moving it back and forth in a distracted manner. "Thanks." He was wearing a pair of old jeans and a T-shirt that had seen better days. His reddish-gold hair looked like he hadn't taken a comb to it yet, and his eyes were rimmed with red. For the first time since Tess had met him, he wasn't wearing a hat or humming a jaunty tune.

"Is Jake still asleep?" Tess asked.

Jasper sat up a little straighter and held the mug to his nose, inhaling the minty steam. "No," he said, setting down the mug without drinking from it. "He's gone."

"Gone? But I thought—"

He ran his fingers over the mug. "He had to leave early. I dropped him off at the airport a little while ago."

"I'm so sorry. I know how much you were looking forward to his visit." Tess had never seen him so subdued.

Jasper shrugged. "It is what it is, I guess. Jake's pretty much a celebrity now, and when the director changes rehearsal days and times at the last minute . . ." He shrugged again and stuck his finger in his tea. "Ow!" He yanked his finger out and blew on it. "At least we had a day and a half together."

"Did Eva enjoy the sunrise?" Kit asked, intentionally changing the subject as she sipped her tea.

Tess savored the scent of spicy citrus that wafted across the table from Kit's mug. "Yes, and thanks for giving us some privacy. Eva and I . . . We haven't had much together-time in a long while."

"Anything special planned for today?" Kit wore a pale pink cotton shawl over a gauzy white sundress, but let the shawl fall against the back of the chair as the sun climbed a little higher in the sky.

"Eva's asleep and I'm going in for a nap soon, but I thought we'd stop by Coastal Soul this afternoon. Would you two like to join us for supper later?"

"I'd like that, dear. Maybe we'll head over to Kennebunkport. I've been craving the seafood risotto from Alisson's. Jasper?"

Jasper seemed to brighten a little and took a sip of tea. "You know what? I'm tired of sitting around feeling sorry for myself, and I'd love to join you all for dinner."

Kit leaned forward. "You have every right to feel sorry for yourself. Just don't wallow in it for too long."

He raised his mug and softly sang a few lines about love from "Both Sides Now." The women reached out and patted his arm. "Thanks for cheering me up. I'm heading over to the theatre later this morning, but I'll be back by six, no worries. We're starting to get things ready for the big anniversary gala fundraiser."

"It's coming up soon, and on your birthday." Kit looked meaningfully at Tess. "I purchased a table for the gala and I'm saving two chairs for you and Luca."

Tess felt her face heat up. "Thank you, but Luca and I . . . We're not . . ."

Kit sat back, surprised. "You're not together? But you went out with him the other night and I thought—"

"We did go out, but it's . . ." She cleared her throat. "It's bad timing, that's all. Luca's wife died two years ago and his son is still grieving. The fact is, I want to spend more time with Eva." She looked into Kit's kind gray eyes. "I'm happy to come to the fundraiser but I'd like to bring Eva instead. Is there an extra seat for Carolina? I bet she'd like to get dressed up and join us."

"Of course. I'd like to get to know her better." Kit held the mug to her lips and sipped slowly before speaking again. "One of my favorite singers is the featured performer at the Gala. I'm on the Board of Directors there, and I suggested him as a possibility, but I can't fathom how Grace and Will were actually able to book Ben Shepherd."

Jasper stretched and glanced at his phone. "I'll tell you how. Grace has connections in New York and she knew someone who knew someone who knows his agent. It turns out that Ben's wife grew up in Portsmouth, right down Route One, and they were eager to come to New England for a little vacation."

"Is his wife coming too?" Kit asked eagerly. "I think her name is Savannah. Their little one must be two years old now."

Jasper chuckled. "She sure is. We actually hired Savannah's business, *Life Celebrations*, to run the Gala for us. Catering. Decorations. The works." He took several swallows of tea and patted his belly in satisfaction. The peppermint, as well as the women's friendship, was lifting his spirits. "She asked us to recommend someone to babysit their son while she and her team get everything ready."

"You asked Kalila?" asked Kit hopefully.

"We did, indeed."

They sat in companionable silence, enjoying the murmur of a sea breeze and the sounds of a neighbor's lawn mower right up against the cheep-cheeping of the birds at Kit's feeder.

After a while, Tess noticed that the birds at the feeder were mostly of the brown variety, with the exceptional blue jay and cardinal squawking in between. Definitely *not* the rainbow colors of the feathers on Eva's dresser. Her curiosity rose again. "Do either of you know anything about the feathers that Eva's been finding? She's got over a dozen of them spread out on her bureau next to Micah's photo."

Kit and Jasper exchanged a surprised look, which Tess noticed immediately. "You *do* know something! Look, those feathers can't be from birds; the colors are too bright. She told me that angels are leaving them for her to find so she knows Micah is safe." Tess raised both hands in exasperation. "I don't know what to make of it."

Jasper glanced at Kit for a moment; she nodded slightly. He turned to face Tess. "It was Micah's idea," he said eagerly.

"Micah?" Tess pushed her seat back in surprise. "But we've never been the type to believe in angels or even talk about them! She went to church once in a while with Charli's family, but—"

Jasper interrupted her. "That wasn't the plan. Micah was worried that Eva would feel lonely up here, so he had this idea of leaving feathers for her to find, and he asked me to do it."

Kit pushed aside the mug and clasped her hands on the table. "He wanted . . . We all wanted to inspire her curiosity. We thought she'd wonder who was leaving the feathers for her, and it would give her something to look forward to."

"Right. It was supposed to take her mind off of missing her big brother. There was never any talk of angels. Eva helped him with an art project once that she especially liked. He built it around that quote about hope and feathers . . . you know, from Emily Dickinson."

Tess looked from Kit to Jasper and back again. "You were in on this too?"

Kit tapped the fingers of both hands together. "Right after you moved in, Eva showed me the first two feathers she'd found. They appeared to be from actual birds, a seagull and a blue jay, but she insisted they were from angels who were keeping Micah safe. You had just joined Soldiers Angels, and Kalila had showed her how to make sand angels down at the beach, so I guess she had angels on her mind. That's when I showed her how to make an altar to honor Micah. I showed her the altar that I dedicated to Ollie and gave her the gold cloth."

"Wow." Tess scratched her forehead. "Just . . . Wow."

"What's the harm of letting her think they're angel feathers?" Kit asked gently.

Tess looked around the yard, trying to find words to convey her muddled thoughts. "For one thing, it worries me that she thinks angels are actually keeping Micah safe."

"Maybe they are." said Jasper. "My dad was a rabbi, so I'm familiar with Old Testament theology. Our faith believes that angels are everywhere. Messengers from God, to be exact."

Tess removed her headband and smoothed back her hair. "Okay. I understand that. I don't mind if she believes in angels, but Eva is certain that Micah is completely and utterly safe right now, and I . . ." She looked at Kit uncertainly. "I'm not sure that it's okay for her to believe that. Anything could happen . . . he's in the Army!" Her eyes filled with tears and her upper lip trembled slightly.

"Oh, sweetie," Kit stood and quickly moved behind Tess, rubbing her shoulders from behind. "As a mother, you're always going to have some degree of worry about your children. It's part of the job description, from what I've heard."

Tess reached back to clasp Kit's hands.

"Eva is still a child." Kit continued. "If believing in angels is minimizing her worry, can there be harm in that?"

"I suppose not," Tess replied, wiping her eyes with the paper napkin that Jasper kindly handed to her.

"Why don't you leave her a feather too?" Jasper asked. "I've left them on or near your car, and on the steps and on the porch. Kit has even gone into your place and left them in the kitchen, the bathroom, and on Eva's bed! It's great fun."

Tess brightened at Jasper's words. "I could definitely do that. It might bring us closer because now that she's shared the feathers with me, she might want to talk more about . . . about everything."

"When you come to Coastal Soul later," said Kit. "I'll show you our section on angels." She moved back to her seat, picked up her mug and walked to the back door of the cottage. "I need to head over to the store now. You two stay as long as you like."

"Thanks, Aunt Kit." Tess blew a kiss.

As the door closed behind Kit, Tess turned to Jasper. "You and Micah have been in cahoots all this time?"

"Absolutely," Jasper replied good-naturedly. "He's a good kid."

"I remember the summer he came up to help you paint Kit's house."

"He was going through all that stuff with Leo then, and I could relate. I think I helped him through it. I hope I did anyway. That's the summer he was debating about coming out."

"I'm glad you helped him with that too. He needed a male role model."

Jasper nodded. "I'm glad I was there." He pushed the mug away, then stretched and yawned. "I'm gonna take a nap before heading to the theatre."

They walked across the lawn together, and before going their separate ways into the apartment building, Tess paused. He was humming a sad song from *The Lion King*. "Jasper?"

"Yeah?"

"Where did you get the bright-colored feathers?"

"We're preparing to stage *Seussical the Musical* next month. Some of the characters' costumes are adorned with bright feathers, so I've got a few bags of them in my apartment. Feel free to borrow some any time."

"Okay, I will, thanks."

After a lazy lunch of tuna sandwiches and watermelon, Tess and Eva walked downtown to Coastal Soul. Tess was savoring the sheer luxury of moving her body briskly on a warm summer afternoon. A free weekend, just her and Eva. They were holding hands, walking side by side.

The second time Eva had visited Coastal Soul, Aunt Kit had seen her admiring a shell necklace, similar to the one Luca had given her mom. Kit had wandered over to where Eva stood. "Let's see what it looks like on you." She had slipped the necklace over Eva's neck and walked her to a stand-up mirror framed with smooth pieces of sea glass. Eva's eyes had widened when Kit told her to keep it.

Now, walking with her mother, Eva wished she had worn the necklace. If Mom wore the one from Luca too, she and her mom would be even more alike. But no, Mom probably wasn't ever going to wear that necklace again. Besides, she didn't want to be more like her mom; she wanted to be more like Aunt Kit . . . and maybe Kalila, except she'd never wear *that* much purple. She also thought it would be cool to be like Rory Gilmore—she certainly loved to read as much as Eva did— even though Tess was nothing like Lorelai.

Approaching Coastal Soul, they stopped to admire the sign swinging above the shop. The words *Coastal Soul* were spelled out in swooping blue and green letters, surrounded by a bright mandala design in shades of sunny yellow, warm orange and fiery red. The chimes hanging on the door rang softly as they entered. "My two favorite people!" Aunt Kit greeted them with a hug as they entered the shop, the scent of light incense and lavender wafting over them like a soothing blanket along with the slight chill of the cool indoor air.

"Come with me, Tess," said Kit, taking her niece's elbow. "I'll have Samantha Stone show you what we were talking about earlier." She called to a young woman with jet black hair piled on top of her head like a fountain. When they had gone, Kit turned to Eva. "Now, what are you interested in today?" Kit asked.

Eva walked to the shelf that held an assortment of unique hair accessories, then wandered to a wooden cupboard full of picture frames. "I want to get one of these," she said, bending down to study the selection. "But I want to pay for it myself." She patted her pocket. I've been saving my allowance."

"Fiddlesticks!" exclaimed Kit. "What's mine is most definitely yours. Now, which frame would you like?"

Eva frowned. She'd been saving her allowance and wanted to buy this with her own money. Jasper had painted her bedroom; he had helped her with the script. Plus, he was fun to be around. "I have a photo of Jasper with Jake. I'm going to frame it and give it to him."

"How thoughtful!" Kit gestured to the display. "Go ahead, then. Choose one and I'll—"

She was interrupted by an elegant woman who strode up to them. "Excuse me," she said briskly. "I'm looking for the owner." Kit and Eva turned toward her. She was dressed in a trim gray suit with a white silk blouse, and her silver-streaked hair was lifted away from her face in a stylish chignon. An overly sweet scent wafted from her, making Eva wrinkle her nose in displeasure as she turned back to the picture frames. The woman definitely wasn't from Seahaven. People in Seahaven, especially on a Saturday, wore shorts with lightweight tops and sandals. Bare legs, bare arms, relaxed smiles. Unlike this woman.

"I'm the owner," Kit said, giving the woman's hand a firm shake. "Kit Gilmore. What can I do for you?"

"My name is Isabella Franklin. A few years ago, when I was here on vacation, I purchased an original piece of art by a young man. Maybe you recall?" She opened a sleek leather purse and pulled out a photograph.

"Yes, of course!" Kit's eyes widened in recognition. "That was created by my niece's son, Micah Gilmore."

Eva straightened at the sound of her brother's name but didn't turn around. She listened carefully.

"That's it!" Isabella's shoulders relaxed. "Micah Gilmore."

"I remember that piece," Kit continued. "He brought several to sell when he came to stay with me that summer, and that one was my favorite. Now, what was the name of it? A line from Emily Dickinson, right?"

Isabella's strident tone mellowed. "Hope is the thing with feathers that perches in the soul, and sings the tune without words—"

"And never stops at all," Kit finished, smiling.

Eva's heart gave a flutter at the phrase about feathers. She remembered working on that art project with Micah several afternoons after school. There had been so many feathers! He had entrusted her with gluing them down, one at a time. She gave up an entire Saturday afternoon to help him finish. It was a three-dimensional piece that also contained driftwood, several birds that he had shaped out of modeling clay, and a small bush created from one of Gram's house plants. He made one tiny pink tissue paper flower and attached it to the bush. His art teacher said it was good enough to sell, so he'd brought it to Aunt Kit's store where it had sold for almost a thousand dollars. Eva could hardly believe it when Micah had told her; he had given her fifty whole dollars for helping him!

Isabella smoothed her hair which did not need fixing since not a strand was out of place. "I was going through a hard time that summer, and Micah's collage helped me get through it. I'd like to see any other pieces he has for sale." She looked around at the cases and display tables, none of which held any trace of Micah.

Eva caught her breath and picked up one of the frames, pretending to examine it more closely. She hadn't thought about how a piece of art could help someone get through a hard time.

"I'm sorry," Aunt Kit replied, shaking her head. "Micah is away right now. We won't have any more of his art to sell for quite a while."

Isabella tapped an elegantly-heeled foot in dismay. "I can't believe this. I came all the way from Philadelphia!" She looked around the store again, then turned and left without another word. Kit sighed. She wished she had more of Micah's art to sell, but that was simply not possible at the moment.

Tess appeared from behind a book stack with a paper bag tucked under her arm. "Eva, did you find a frame?"

Eva pointed to a bright red frame covered with colorful hearts. "I think Jasper will like this one." She looked at her mom's package. "What did you get?"

"A couple of books. Do you want to choose a book too?"

"No, I'm ready to go as soon as I pay for this." She picked up the red frame and walked to the counter where Samantha rang up the sale, giving her a generous family discount, per Aunt Kit's direction.

"Thank you, Samantha," Eva said as she handed the money over and received her change.

"No probs, little one," Samantha replied serenely. "And you—" she gestured to Tess who was almost at the door. "Promise me you'll come in for a massage soon. You won't regret it."

"She gives the best massages," Kit agreed.

Tess glanced over her shoulder and waved them off. "Maybe," she called lightly as she and Eva headed out, but as the door clinked shut behind them, she muttered under her breath, "More like never."

# Chapter 21

Before heading home, Tess and Eva stopped at Simply Sweets. "But Mom, it's after two o'clock; they won't have coffee!" Eva exclaimed as they stepped up to the counter.

"That's okay. I'll make a fresh pot when we get home. What flavor ice cream do you want to try today?"

Eva took her time studying the massive chalk board behind the counter. It must be a miracle; Mom was letting her have Simply Sweets two days in a row! She had loved the chocolate chip ice cream she'd had here with Kalila the day they made the sand angels, and she'd had it again last night in her sundae, but Micah had always encouraged her not to get stuck in a rut. "You never know until you try," he would tell her whenever she hesitated over a new flavor or type of food.

The tourist in line behind them impatiently cleared his throat. "I'll have Sunrise Strawberry," Tess said quickly to the teen behind the counter. He had straw-blond hair and an anchor tattoo on his left forearm. "And my daughter will have . . ."

"It's so hard to choose," Eva moaned. "I guess I'll try the Cocoa Confetti. It's chocolate ice cream with bits of gumdrops!" The teen busied himself scooping the ice cream for them.

"And colored sprinkles on mine too, please." Eva stood on tiptoe, eagerly watching the young man. "I'm adding more confetti, Mom, isn't that cool?" Tess's heart lit up at her daughter's creativity.

"You got it!" the teen replied cheerfully, handing over the cones.

"Mmm, this is even better than what I had last night," Eva said, happily licking her cone from bottom to top as they left the shop. She abruptly stopped walking and looked up at her mother. "Sorry. I didn't mean to remind you about Teo—"

Tess's eyes clouded over as she remembered that awful scene and her conversation later with Luca. It was over between them, and she really wanted to blame Teo. She had blamed Luca all those years ago when he'd stopped emailing, only to find out it had been her mother who'd made that separation happen. But what about *this* situation? Yes, Teo had been disruptive; he had pushed her away. And now? Luca was the one who brought the kids into their relationship so quickly after reassuring her that it would be just the two of them for a while. So, who was to blame now? Teo? Luca? No. She had to take responsibility. Instead of talking it out with Luca, she had shut him out. She was the one who had chosen not to give them a chance, and she would choose that again if she had to, she thought, looking down at Eva. Her beautiful daughter. Her beautiful, happy daughter.

Tess put her arm around Eva's shoulder, steering them onto the sidewalk. "I'm okay." She tasted the fresh strawberries and sweet cream on her tongue and allowed herself to feel the pleasure of it. "*We're* okay. We don't need Luca and Teo." But the words felt wrong in her mouth even as she said them.

"I still want Teo to be my friend, though. Is that okay?" As Eva looked up at her mother, she narrowly missed bumping into a curly-haired woman pushing a stroller. They all stopped abruptly. "Oops, sorry!" Eva said anxiously. Then she noticed that Kalila was standing behind the woman, and a large golden dog was connected to the teen by a short leash that matched her purple tank top. "Kalila!" Eva excitedly stooped down to pet the dog who promptly knocked the ice cream cone out of her hand and gobbled it up quickly.

"Zannah, what are we going to do with you!" exclaimed the woman with a lighthearted chuckle as both she and Tess reached down to wipe up the remains from the sidewalk. "I'm so sorry. I'll buy you another cone."

"You don't have to; it's okay," Eva replied, totally enthralled with the pinkish hue of the dog's nose and the sunshine color of its fur.

"Is this the girl you were telling me about?" asked the woman as she patted Zannah's head and slowly stood. She was tall, Eva noticed, and her eyes were like that goldish-brown gemstone she'd once admired in Aunt Kit's shop.

"Yes," Kalila replied. "Eva and Tess Gilmore, this is Savannah Adams. She's Ben Shepherd's wife and she runs the *Life Celebrations* company that's in charge of the Anniversary Gala at the theatre."

"I'm pleased to meet you both," Savannah said, shaking their hands. "This is JJ." She pointed to the little boy in the stroller. He clapped his hands and tilted his head up at them; chocolate was smeared at the corners of his mouth. He sported a mop of dark auburn ringlets and big green eyes.

"Hi JJ," Eva cooed, bending down to reach out a finger. He happily grabbed it and didn't let go.

"His name is Joshua John, but that's a mouthful, so we call him JJ."

Tess gazed at the little boy and murmured, "He's adorable." She was remembering Micah at that age. Such fond memories. She cleared her throat, bringing herself back to the present and bit into the cone for another burst of strawberry sweetness. "Is Kalila showing you around Seahaven?"

"She is," Savannah replied. "Ben is over at the theatre right now meeting with Grace and Will about his set list. I met with them this morning about the dinner. I actually grew up in Portsmouth, not too far from here. My dad ran the music theatre there."

"I love theatre!" Eva stood. "Guess what? I wrote a play and my friends and I performed it at the theatre camp."

"This girl has real talent," added Kalila. She bent down and handed JJ a musical rattle, disentangled his fingers from her beaded braids, then looked up at Eva. "Guess what? Savannah hired me to babysit JJ the day of the Gala so she and her colleagues can get everything set up."

"That's awesome!"

Kalila continued. "She also wants someone who'll look after Zannah while I'm taking care of JJ."

"If it's okay with your mom, of course," added Savannah.

Eva was so excited, she didn't even care that she hadn't gotten to finish her cone. "Can I, Mom? Please? Pretty please with strawberries and espresso and pretzels and nonpareils on top?" She was hoping that naming her mother's favorite snacks would make her say yes.

Tess looked from Savannah to Eva and back again. It would be good for Eva to have something to look forward to besides the feathers, especially now that Imaginarium was over. "Sure, I think that would be splendid!"

Savannah caught her breath and swiftly moved her hand to an elegant silver dragonfly pendant nestled at her throat.

"Are you okay?" Tess asked, concerned.

Savannah rubbed the necklace between her fingers for a moment, then looked at Tess. "I don't tell many people this but my mom died when I was fifteen and right before she died, she told me I was going to have a splendid life. I don't hear the word *splendid* very much these days, so when you just said it, I was remembering her."

"Did she give you the necklace?"

"No, I bought this myself because . . . it's a long story, but dragonflies always remind me of her."

Eva had been listening to this exchange and watching the expressions on the women's faces. She thought of Teo whose mother had died when he was young, and it made her sad. Now, watching Savannah's animated face as she continued to talk with Tess, she realized something important and the words burst out of her mouth before she could even process them. "Savannah, your mother was right!"

The women looked at Eva curiously.

"She said you were going to have a splendid life, and that's exactly what happened!" Eva hopped from one foot to the other, beaming up at Savannah. "You're married to a superstar and you've got JJ and a beautiful dog, *and* you own your own business! See? It *is* splendid! *Splendid* is now my most favorite word!"

Savannah laughed out loud and cupped her palm briefly on the back of Eva's head. "You're absolutely right, Eva. Thank you for reminding me." She glanced at Tess. "I bet the two of you are having a splendid life right here in Seahaven, along with Kalila and her family."

Eva and Tess exchanged a tentative look. "We're trying," Tess said. "We just moved here, so—" She paused to look at Eva. "We're definitely trying. We even stayed up all night together and watched the sunrise this morning."

"You mean the earthmove," Eva corrected. She knelt on the sidewalk again to pet Zannah. "It's actually the *earth* that's moving, not the sun, so I call it an earthmove instead of a sunrise."

The women chuckled and Tess held out her hand to Eva. "I stand corrected. This morning we watched an earthmove! Come on, now, let's head home. Savannah, are you sure that you want Eva to dog-sit the day of the Gala?"

"Absolutely! I think it'll work out perfectly."

"Thank you thank you thank you!" Eva kissed her mom's shoulder three times, then bent down and hugged Zannah who licked her face agreeably.

"I think she likes you, Eva!" said Savannah, getting a grip on the stroller's handles. They moved along the sidewalk slowly as Tess and Eva stepped out of the way while waving goodbye.

A few seconds later, Savannah called over her shoulder. "Eva, I'll pay you the same amount that I'm paying Kalila, okay?"

Eva's eyes widened in astonishment as she stopped and turned, staring at Savannah. "Mom?" she whispered. "She's going to *pay* me? For playing with a dog all day?"

Tess smiled indulgently as she called to Savannah. "That'll be fine, and thank you!" She nudged Eva's elbow.

"Yes, thank you!" Eva called, still blinking in disbelief.

They walked in silence for a while, the summer sun shining through striated clouds. "By the way," said Tess as they turned the corner of Bright Blessing Way. "I didn't get a chance to answer you."

"What?"

"Before we bumped into Kalila and Savannah, you asked about being friends with Teo."

"It's okay, right?" Eva was swinging her mother's hand. She thought they looked like a younger version of the famous Gilmore Girls—a mother and daughter walking side by side in a small town. Both brunettes with straight hair and fair skin. Exactly like Lorelai and Rory. Well, not *exactly*. More like their own personal version of the *Gilmore Girls*. She felt happy, but she wasn't quite certain it would last.

"It's definitely all right. Luca and I are adults. We can handle seeing each other when you and Teo get together." She hoped so, anyway.

"Good. Because I really like Teo. Not like a boyfriend, *obviously*. Just as a friend."

"Well, I think Teo and Poppy are lucky to have you for a friend," Tess said.

As they strolled up their front walkway, Eva suddenly said, "Hey Mom, know what?"

"What?" Tess asked as they climbed the steps to the front porch.

"I'm glad we moved here. Seahaven is actually turning out to be splendid! My new favorite *word* describes my new favorite *town*!"

Tess's heart lit up; she never thought she'd hear those words coming out of Eva's mouth. She smiled at her daughter as they entered their apartment, but she couldn't quite bring herself to say the same words back to her.

Saturday August 6
TO: micahcgilmore@usmil.com
FROM: evareads@newhavenmail.com

You won't believe this, but I'm going to tell you anyway. I got a job! It's just for one day but I'm going to get paid and everything. I'm going to take care of Ben Shepherd's dog at the theatre Gala thing on August 18 which is also Mom's birthday in case you forgot which you might have because you're so busy. Do you know who Ben Shepherd is? Aunt Kit loooooves him.

Also, did Mom tell you that she and Luca aren't going on any more dates? She says she's okay but she won't talk about it. Can you ask Mom about it if you have time?

I miss you lots and lots and lots. There's no one here to BOOP me so I'm going to boop you instead. Boop!

Love, your Li'l Sis,
Eva

The following week on a rainy Thursday afternoon, Kalila took Eva and Samuel to see *The Secret Garden*, a children's play at Sands of Time.

"I'm excited about this show," Eva said as they got in a long line that led to the theatre entrance. "It's one of my favorite stories!"

"Is there really a garden?" Samuel asked.

"There is! The story is a little sad at first," Eva added. "But it doesn't stay sad."

Samuel popped his thumb in his mouth thoughtfully and put his other hand in Eva's. "That's good. I don't like sad very much."

The line moved closer to the wide doors that led into the darkened theatre. Bored, Eva stood on tiptoe and looked around the overcrowded theatre lobby. As Eva slowly turned around, she waved at several kids from Imaginarium and smiled when they waved back.

"Look! There's Teo and his dad!" There were at least a fifty people between her and her new friend, but she cupped her hands around her mouth and shouted, "Teo! Teo!" Kalila, who had the advantage of height, also called to Teo, who finally turned around. When he saw Eva, he frowned, crossed his arms firmly over his chest and turned away.

Eva couldn't believe it. Her body sagged and Kalila pulled her in for a quick one-armed hug. "I know he doesn't like my mom," Eva murmured. "But why doesn't he like *me* anymore?"

"What happened with Teo and your mom?" Kalila asked, inching the three of them a bit closer to the door. The usher was getting ready to scan tickets.

Eva fidgeted with her hair. "Mom and Teo's dad started dating and he didn't like seeing my mom with his dad. Teo's mom died when he was ten."

Kalila took Eva's hand again and squeezed it lightly. "Poor kid. He probably needs time to get used to them being together."

"I guess." Eva sighed. Poppy was her only friend in Seahaven now, but what if Poppy sided with Teo? Then she'd have no friends . . . again. Charli wasn't answering her letters, so maybe she *really* had no friends.

"C'mon, guys!" Kalila led them down the aisle to their seats in the fourth row. As she handed out the bags of caramel corn that they'd made in Glory's kitchen, she whispered in Eva's ear. "It's going to be all right, I promise. Let's enjoy the show for now and think about Teo later."

Eva nodded, but she couldn't stop thinking about Teo as the show began: poor little motherless Colin, locked away in the manor. She held Samuel's hand at the beginning so he wouldn't be sad while they munched on the buttery-sweet popcorn. Watching the story unfold on the stage as Mary started making friends with the reluctant Colin, Eva began to understand a bit more about Teo's reluctance to let a woman into his dad's life. That's when she came up with a plan to get Teo to like her again.

# Chapter 22

"What are you doing, hon?" Tess asked the following Tuesday after work, standing in Eva's doorway. She had changed into khaki shorts and a flowered top, hoping to relax a bit before dinner.

"Hi Mom," Eva replied, twisting around in her desk chair until she was facing the door. "I'm making a secret garden for Teo!"

Tess sat on the edge of the bed, disrupting a sleeping Jasper who meowed plaintively before lumbering over to Eva's pillow and curling up in a velvety gray ball. She gazed in admiration at the large glass bowl on Eva's desk.

"Actually, it's a terrarium. Aunt Kit gave me the dirt and the plants. Kalila gave me the ceramic frog because Teo's mom collected them which means he loves them too. Do you like it? Do you think Teo will like it?" Her voice was edged with worry.

"It's wonderful!" Tess leaned in to get a closer look at the bowl. It contained brown dirt and several small leafy plants, one of which had blossomed with a yellow flower. In the center of the bowl sat a green, warty frog figurine; a feather was stuck into the dirt on either side of it, standing stiffly like tall sentinels. "I'm sure he'll love this! Why on earth wouldn't he?"

Eva took her hands out of the dirt, then pushed her hair out of her eyes, leaving a streak of earthy brown across her forehead. Tess plucked a tissue from the box on the nightstand and gently wiped off the dirt. "He doesn't want to be my friend anymore."

"Why would you say that?"

"Last week when I was at the theatre with Kalila and Samuel, Teo was there with his dad. I waved and called to him, but he turned away."

"Maybe he didn't see you. I bet it was crowded—"

"He saw me all right." Eva stared at the floor, then turned back to the terrarium and adjusted some of the greenery.

"What about Poppy? Was she there too?"

"Poppy's on vacation with her family. She won't be back 'til after the Gala and then she's going on that trip with her aunt." Eva walked to the dresser. "Do you think I should put more of my feathers in?" She picked up one that was a bright shade of turquoise. "This is my favorite. If I put more feathers in his secret garden, the angels might take more of his sadness away."

Tess's heart widened with love at her daughter's thoughtfulness. "I love this color, too." She reverently touched the feather in Eva's hand. Should she tell Eva that she was the one who left it on the front porch rocker this morning before leaving for work? She had taken Theatre Jasper up on his offer to share his *Seussical* feathers. No, this wasn't the right time; she didn't want to destroy her daughter's innocence just yet. It was bad enough that Santa Claus and the tooth fairy illusions were all in the past. "But the two feathers that are already in the garden—"

"*Secret* garden," Eva reminded Tess as she put the turquoise feather back on the altar and settled into her chair again.

"I stand corrected. The *secret* garden." Tess paused for a moment, studying her daughter. "I think the feathers you've already placed in the secret garden are perfect just as they are. Sometimes less is more."

Eva wrinkled her nose in thought. "Less is more? Does that mean that the less people there are in a family, the better it is? Like it should just be Teo and his dad? And it should just be you and me and Micah? And no one else? Less . . . instead of . . . more?"

Tess looked startled. "No, I was referring to when you're creating something. Like Micah's art—many times I'd see him put something into one of his mixed media pieces and then later take it out. It seemed to me that the piece he was working on was usually more effective with less 'stuff' in it."

"Yeah, I remember Micah doing that too." Eva picked up the glass container. "Okay." She took a deep breath and let it go. "I won't add anything else, but I'm going to write a letter to go with it, to tell Teo I'm sorry."

Tess took the container from Eva's hands. "This sure is heavy. Let's put it on your dresser to keep it safe." She set it carefully next to the feathers and Micah's picture. "What are you sorry about? You didn't do anything wrong."

"I'm sorry that we're not friends any more. I'm sorry that his mom died and that you and Luca can't be friends."

Tess put her hand over her heart; Eva was growing into such a thoughtful person. "You know, when you write that letter, it might be better not to remind him about me and his dad."

Eva stuck another finger in the dirt. It felt thick and cool, with exactly right amount of damp. "Yeah. Good idea."

"I'm going to get supper ready. How does Chicken and Sticky Rice sound?"

"Great. I'm hungry! Did Theatre Jasper give you the recipe?"

"He did, and it's so easy, you won't believe it!"

Eva lightly touched the secret garden container and Micah's picture on the way out of her room. She felt comforted, knowing that the angels were doing their job—for her brother and now also for Teo. "Can I help?"

"Sure," Tess replied as Just Jasper scooted through the bedroom door ahead of them. "When are you going to give Teo the secret garden?"

"At the Gala."

They washed their hands side by side in the kitchen sink, then Tess took the chicken thighs out of the fridge. She glanced at the magnetic white board attached to the freezer door, noticing her to-do list carefully printed in blue marker, as neat as ever. Tess wouldn't have it any other way, but she noticed that the list was a whole lot shorter than the lists that had been on the fridge in New Haven. She smiled at the photos of Eva and Micah that hung beside the white board list. Yes, the to-do list was getting shorter, and her connection with Eva was getting stronger. Exactly as it should be. She smiled again and set the package of chicken on the counter. "That sounds like a good time to give the gift to Teo, but aren't you supposed to be dog sitting that night?" She turned on the oven.

Eva took the red and white box of rice from the cupboard. "Kalila and I will be with JJ and Zannah during the *day*. But Savannah will be at the Gala."

"She's taking JJ and the dog to the Gala?" Tess sprayed the baking dish with olive oil, then measured the rice and sprinkled it over the bottom. "Can you get me the soup please?"

"She's taking JJ, but she's gonna leave Zannah at the Sea Gem hotel. The owner will look in on Zannah." Eva handed her mother the can of mushroom soup. "That way I can go to the Gala with you!"

"I'm glad." Tess finished preparing the chicken and placed it in the oven. "Carolina will be at our table and two of Aunt Kit's friends too."

"Olivia and Violet?"

"You met them already?"

"One day I got up early and they were having breakfast on Aunt Kit's patio. That's the day she showed me her altars."

"Ah. I see."

"Mom? What do people wear to a Gala?"

"It's a special event, so everyone gets dressed up."

Eva frowned. "We never get dressed up. What will we wear?"

Momentarily stymied by what sounded like criticism, Tess paused and rubbed her forehead, then decided to shake it off. "We'll go shopping on Friday night and find new dresses, okay?" Her voice was uncertain, but hopeful. She and Eva hadn't been clothes shopping together in a long time. "I'll ask Carolina to come with us. I bet she likes shopping."

"You mean shopping at a thrift store?" Eva said skeptically, pouring Jasper's food into his bowl.

"Of course not!" Tess said brightly, although that was exactly what she'd been thinking. "We'll go to the Maine Mall in Portland and find something so pretty that Teo won't be able to ignore you when you give him the terrarium."

"And something pretty for *you* that will make Luca ask you out again!" Eva added cheerfully, kneeling on the floor next to Jasper who was completely oblivious to his number one fan.

Tess felt her face heat up and turned away from Eva to look out the kitchen window. "He's not going to ask me out again, and even if he did—"

"What?" Eva looked up curiously. "What would you do if he did?"

Tess turned from the window and studied her daughter. What would she do? She knew what her heart wanted to do, but life was never that simple. Luca had called and texted several times. He had shown up at Pearly Whites but she'd refused to see him. Marilyn wasn't happy about this turn of events—Tess could see it in the receptionist's romantically-hopeful eyes—but Luca hadn't tried again. Just as well, she told herself, even though that thought made her incredibly sad.

"Mom?" Eva picked up Jasper who had finally stopped eating. She cradled his hefty body to her chest.

At that moment, Tess's phone rang and she breathed a sigh of relief. Saved by the smartphone. How could she possibly answer Eva's question? "Just a minute, hon." She held up a finger, then frowned at the unfamiliar number on her phone. "Hello?"

# Chapter 23

*E*va watched as her mother slowly turned away, holding her free hand to her head as she absent-mindedly bunched up her hair. A man's gruff voice could be heard through the phone but Eva couldn't make out the words. Tess walked in slow motion toward the living room, then gasped and clutched at the door frame in order to steady herself.

"Mom?" Eva set Jasper down and moved to Tess, who stood frozen in the doorway. Little ripples of anxiety cascaded from Eva's brain and landed—plonk—in her stomach. She had never-ever seen her mom like this. "Mom!" She impatiently pulled on the bottom of Tess's shirt.

"Shhh!" Tess looked down at Eva briefly with tears in her eyes but Eva felt invisible.

"What? What is it?" whispered Eva.

"Yes. Yes, I understand. Thank you for calling," her mother finally said in a strange, wooden voice that Eva had never heard before. Tess mechanically returned the phone to her pocket and stared off across the room.

Eva waited, her heart racing. Something was very, very wrong. What if Gram had died? She hadn't been sick, but . . . why else would Mom be acting like this? It couldn't be about Micah because the angels were keeping him safe and she had the feathers to prove it. Not knowing what else to do, she tentatively guided her mother into the living room and onto the sofa.

Tess put her head in her hands. "I can't believe it. I can't believe that Micah—" Her words turned to gut-wrenching sobs that hurt Eva's ears like shards of broken glass tearing at soft skin.

Eva decided in an instant that her questions could wait. Mom needed help, right now. "I'll get Aunt Kit." She raced to the back door and across the lawn to Kit's cottage.

Eva had never seen a grown woman move as fast as Aunt Kit was running right now—so fast, it was impossible to keep up with her. She trailed behind the older woman, watching Kit's yellow gauzy skirt and flowered shawl flapping in the air behind her. Even Carolina didn't sprint that fast on her daily runs.

When Eva arrived in the living room, she paused to catch her breath. Her mother was still sitting on the sofa, bent over like an old woman. Her hands were folded over the top of her head which rested almost in her lap. Aunt Kit sat hip to hip with Tess, one arm around her, speaking in a low, soothing voice. Eva's heart felt as if it would jump out of her throat. "Aunt Kit? Mom? What's going on?" Her voice was a whisper but the words thundered in her heart.

Kit looked up and beckoned Eva to sit beside her. Eva cautiously sat on the edge of the cushion, tears and fear muddled in her eyes. Kit put one arm around Eva and kept the other firmly anchored around Tess. "That was Micah's C.O. on the phone and—"

"What's a C.O.?"

Tess finally took her hands off her head and straightened up a bit. She reached across Kit for Eva's hand. "It stands for Commanding Officer. His name is Terrell Hawkins. Micah told us about him, remember? He's in charge of Micah's training unit."

Eva stared at her mother blankly; she was having a hard time remembering anything. "Why did he call?"

"There was an accident . . ." Tess began, then bent her head again. "I should never have let him join the Army."

"Tess, sweet girl. You couldn't have stopped him. He left on his own, remember?" Kit's voice was controlled and calm. She rubbed slow circles on Tess's back the way Micah had sometimes comforted Eva after a bad dream.

"An accident?" Eva's mouth was suddenly dry and her words sounded like they were coming from far away even as they escaped her lips. "What do you mean? What happened?"

Eva literally held her breath until her mother finally spoke, her voice shaking a little. "Officer Hawkins said that during a training session a few hours ago, one of the unit's utility vehicles was involved in an accident. Three service members were injured, including Micah."

"Injured? How?" Eva demanded, looking from her mother to Aunt Kit. She felt like she was underwater. This couldn't be happening. Micah *couldn't* be hurt. The angels were supposed to be keeping him safe. All those feathers . . .

"They all have broken bones and internal injuries. Micah sustained the worst of it and is in surgery right now." Tess looked away.

Eva stood, hugging herself tightly as if to stop her entire body from trembling. She knew how serious internal injuries could be because she and Micah had watched every season of *New Amsterdam*. "Tell me he's going to be okay," she said fiercely. "He *has* to be okay."

Tess reached for her daughter and pulled her onto her lap. "They don't know much right now. Commander Hawkins said he'd call when Micah is out of surgery."

"Waiting is the hardest part," said Kit, reaching for a box of tissues on the coffee table and handing them to Tess and Eva. "I'll stay right here with you while we wait for the call." She folded her hands in her lap. Thinking it best to change the subject, at least for a moment, she said, "What is that delicious smell coming from the kitchen?"

"We made Theatre Jasper's Chicken and Sticky Rice," Eva offered, blowing her nose.

"That sounds—"

Kit was interrupted by a loud moan from Tess who lifted Eva from her lap and stood abruptly. Tess pressed the palms of her hands to her temples, trying to silence an even larger moan that was building in her heart. Micah was seriously injured. *Her son.* How could she sit around and wait for a stranger to call her back? She had to get to Micah. "Aunt Kit? Would you go online and book me the next flight to South Carolina? Columbia Airport."

"Maybe you should wait for—"

"I am going to go to the hospital to be with him," she replied slowly and emphatically, as if in a daze. "Please get me a flight. I can't focus right now. I just—"

"Of course, I understand," Kit replied softly as she stood, touching Tess's hunched shoulder. "Eva, will you please bring me your mom's laptop? We'll take care of this in the kitchen."

Eva ran down the hall and was back lickety-split. "I'm going too, right?" she asked tentatively, handing the computer to Kit who immediately sat down at the kitchen table and busied herself by logging onto a travel site.

"No, of course not," Tess snapped, pacing back and forth. "You'll stay right here. We have no idea what shape he's in. He might be. . . I don't want you to see him if . . . I'm going alone."

Stunned, Eva shrank back against the wall. "But I want to be with him too. He's my brother!" Tears streamed down her face.

"I know he's your brother, Eva, but this is serious. He wouldn't want you to see him like this." Tess glanced at Aunt Kit who was intentionally minding her own business as she scrolled through screens on the laptop. Then she looked at Eva, who had lowered her body to the floor and was rocking back and forth.

"You don't *know* what Micah would want. You don't know him like I do!" Eva's words filtered through her sobs. Tess heard them as if from a faraway planet.

In spite of her disconcerted, fearful thoughts, Tess had to admit that Eva was at least partially right. She didn't know Micah like she used to. Yes, they FaceTimed every week, but how much could a mother ever really understand? She crouched next to Eva and tried to still her daughter's shaking body, but Eva turned away. Tess took a breath and tried to calm her own anxiety. "I have to do this alone. I promise to call you as soon as I get there. I'll call you every hour."

Eva sniffed indignantly. "I don't have a phone, remember?"

Tess got to her feet stiffly, as if every bone in her body ached. "I'll call Aunt Kit; she'll be with you the whole time."

Kit regarded Eva seriously. "I'll take good care of you, don't you worry." She took a phone out of her skirt pocket and held it up for Eva. "This will be our best friend." Eva attempted a smile, then looked away. Her brother needed her and she couldn't go to him. This wasn't right. But what could she do—hijack a plane? She felt completely powerless. As if sensing emotional distress, Just Jasper wandered into the kitchen, and with laser focus, headed straight for Eva's lap. "Come here, beautiful boy," Eva whispered into his soft gray fur. "Micah is hurt and it's all my fault. I should have found more feathers. I should have looked for more feathers so he would be safer." No one heard her but the cat.

# Chapter 24

"This looks delicious," Glory said an hour later, rubbing her hands as she sat in her kitchen with Eva and Samuel. Kit had carried the casserole to Glory's apartment, then taken Tess to the airport.

"I like the sticky rice best!" announced Samuel brightly. Eva tried to match his smile but failed.

"Let's say grace," said Glory, taking one of their hands in each of hers.

Samuel reached across the table to hold Eva's hand, completing the circle. "Your hand is cold," he whispered.

"Sorry," Eva murmured as Glory began the short prayer. It was the middle of summer but her whole body was cold, inside and out. Micah was far away, in a hospital; she was here in Maine with these strangers. Wait . . . that didn't sound right. She glanced at Glory, whose dark head was bowed, then at Samuel whose eyes were scrunched in concentration behind his glasses. Last month they had been strangers; now they were friends. Her head told her she was lucky, but her heart wanted only to be with Micah.

"Where's Kalila?" Eva asked as Glory began dishing out the chicken.

"She's on a date." Samuel announced. His glasses had slipped down his nose, and he pushed them back up with a chubby thumb.

Eva took a small bite of the sticky rice even though she wasn't hungry. How could she possibly eat when her brother was in a hospital, so far away? Her stomach was tied in knots. Even Glory's carrot coins simmered in lemon butter—Eva's favorite—tasted bland.

After loading the dishwasher, Glory turned to Eva. "It's okay to feel worried, darlin'. This waiting time isn't easy, but we'll do our best to help you through it. Your mom will call as soon as she gets to the hospital and talks with the doctors."

Eva blinked back tears. "Glory?" She looked up at the older woman who was wiping her hands on a terry cloth apron embroidered with cherries. Glory would understand what Eva was feeling because her daughter was deployed overseas and they rarely got to see each other.

"Yes, dear?"

"What if . . ." Her words caught in her throat for a moment, but she forced them out. "What if Micah dies?"

Glory bent down and looked into Eva's eyes, then placed her palms on either side of the girl's face. "I don't think he's going to die, honey. Your mom said his C.O. was pretty sure the surgery would fix him although it would take a while to heal."

"But what if it doesn't fix him?" Eva whispered.

"If that happens, Sugar, and I'm almost certain that it won't, we'll all get through it together, hear? You won't be alone. Your mom will be here for you and so will your Aunt Kit and me and Kalila and Samuel right along with Jasper and the fine folks at the theatre. You're a part of Seahaven now. We all take care of each other; that's what we do here. We celebrate together when life is good . . . and when it isn't, we help each other through to the other side."

Eva rocked back on her heels, trying to understand how life could ever be good again if Micah wasn't alive.

Glory patted Eva kindly on the head and stood up straight as she rubbed her lower back. "Do you know what my mama taught me to do whenever I'm anxious and the waiting is hard?"

Eva shook her head and looked shyly at the floor.

"I try to do something thoughtful for someone else. That usually takes my mind off my own troubles."

"That's a good idea, but what could we do?"

"Well, Jasper has been feeling down lately because Jake had to leave early last weekend so maybe—"

Eva's face brightened. "I know!" she said, allowing the tiniest bit of excitement to warm her thoughts again. "I bought a frame for the photo I took of Jasper and Jake. Can we go to my apartment and put that together now?"

"That's a great idea!" Glory was happy to see some color return to Eva's cheeks. "I've got wrapping paper and bows that you can use. Let me grab them while you get Samuel from his room, and we'll head over to your place."

Eva loved getting presents, but she also loved giving them, especially when she had thought of the gift idea herself, and this was such an occasion. She wrapped the framed photo in Glory's colorful wrapping paper, then stuck a shiny red bow on top.

"I'm going to put Samuel to bed while you go upstairs. I'll leave both of our apartment doors open until Aunt Kit comes back from the airport, and I want you to holler if you need anything." Arms folded in satisfaction, Glory stood in the doorway; she had successfully kept Eva's mind off of Micah for exactly fourteen minutes. Raising her eyes heavenward, she silently sent up a prayer that all would be well for Eva's family.

"Okay!" Eva stood on tiptoe and kissed Glory's cheek. "Thank you for helping me wrap it. I hope Jasper likes it." She started up the stairs, but turned on the third step. "In case you're worried, my bedroom door is shut. That way my cat won't go over to your place. I know Samuel is allergic."

"Thank you, dear." Glory watched as Eva climbed the stairs and knocked on Jasper's door, then she took Samuel's hand and walked him back to his bedroom.

A surprised Jasper opened the door just wide enough to peer out. When he saw it was Eva holding a colorful package, he hesitated, then opened the door all the way and let her in.

Eva noticed that his living room was messier than usual, and he was wearing pajama bottoms with a stained gray T-shirt. His hair was mussed up, no hat in sight. Something was definitely wrong with this picture.

"What's happening? My birthday isn't until October."

She held the gift out to him proudly. "It's not a birthday present. It's a Just Because."

"Just because?" Bleary-eyed, Jasper took the package and stared at it in confusion.

"Yeah. When you give someone a present and there's no real reason for it, it's called a Just Because."

He stared at Eva for a moment, then blinked rapidly, as if to bring himself out of his thoughts and back to the room. "Where are my manners? Please sit down. Should I open this now?"

"Yes, please," she replied hopefully, sitting on the edge of the sofa and leaning forward, her hands under her thighs. The best part of giving a Just Because was about to happen—the expression on the other person's face when they opened it.

Jasper sat next to her on the sofa and carefully unwrapped the package. Staring at the framed photo of himself and Jake, he gasped in surprise, then frowned.

"What's wrong?" Eva asked, concerned. This was not the reaction she was expecting. "Don't you like it?"

"I love it," Jasper insisted. He stood quickly and walked to the bookcase, then placed the new photo next to the one that Eva had seen the first day she'd visited. She joined him as he looked back and forth between the two pictures. "Thank you, Eva. This is such a great gift." His words said one thing, but his expression said otherwise.

Eva looked up at him in concern. "You're welcome, but why are you so sad?"

Jasper traced the outline of Jake's face in the first photo, then pointed to the new one. "He's different in this picture. Do you see? *We're* different."

Eva stepped closer, looking back and forth at the two photos. "I think so," she replied. You're smiling at each other in the first one, and in the new one, he's fake-smiling and looking away. Even though I told you twice to move closer."

"That about sums it up," Jasper said sadly. "I've known for a long time that Jake and I weren't meant to be together for the long haul. I just didn't want to admit it, and now the proof is literally staring me in the face." He sadly touched each of the photos.

Eva stepped back, uncertain. "I'm sorry. I shouldn't have—"

"It's perfectly okay. I'm just remembering the fact that no matter how much we love a person, sometimes we have to let them go." He hummed a bit of a sad song that Eva didn't recognize, then put his hand on her shoulder. "You know what? I love that you took this picture and gave it to me. It's a thoughtful gift."

"But—"

"This picture woke me up to something I was afraid to see." He touched the frame thoughtfully.

"Okay, but why do we have to let go of people we love?" She frowned. "I sure don't want to let go of Micah."

"Hey, let's go in the kitchen. I've got a new flavor of ice cream from Simply Sweets." He led the way and asked over his shoulder, "Why would you have to let go of your brother?"

Eva leaned against the door jamb, watching Jasper take two bowls out of the cupboard next to the sink. She rubbed her thumb over her upper lip and took a breath. "There was an accident and he's in the hospital having surgery."

The bowls clattered to the countertop as Jasper spun around. "Oh, sweetie! What happened?" Eyes wide, he guided her to the kitchen table and urged her to sit.

"I don't know exactly. It had something to do with an Army car or truck . . ."

"A utility vehicle?"

"I think that's what it was." She looked at her bare legs, goose-pimply from the air conditioning, or maybe from this inner shiver that wouldn't go away.

"I'm so sorry. Is he going to be all right?"

"No one knows." She began to cry and he squatted in front of her, placing his hands on her knees in an effort to steady her.

"It's okay, it's going to be okay," he murmured, swallowing hard. "Is your mom on the way to see him?"

"Yes, and she wouldn't take me with her."

"Oh dear. You want to be with him too, don't you?"

She nodded, then stood and wiped her eyes. She had to say this out loud or she would burst. "Jasper, I think it's all my fault."

"Micah's accident?" What on earth could this child be thinking? How could it possibly be her fault?

"Yes," she replied mournfully, hanging her head. "I didn't find enough feathers. The angels were supposed to be keeping him safe. If I had found more—"

Jasper knelt beside her and took her icy hands in his. "There is no way on God's beautiful green earth that you caused Micah's accident."

"But I started finding angel feathers as soon as I got here."

"Angel feathers?" Jasper repeated as nonchalantly as he could, biting his lower lip.

"Yes. I was sure they were angel feathers and that the angels were telling me they were keeping Micah safe so I shouldn't worry about him. But now—" Her voice broke into a sob and she fell silent.

"Now you're worried about him again."

She took her hands out of his and rubbed her eyes. "Yes."

Jasper sat next to her at the table. "My daddy is a rabbi. Did I ever tell you that?"

"Yes, I remember."

"We believe that angels are everywhere, always watching over us. There are many stories in the Torah about angels helping people. I'll find them and read them to you next time I see you, okay?" He sang a few bars of a soothing song in Hebrew.

"What are you singing?" Eva asked, her mind finally starting to quiet.

"It's called "The Angel Song" or "B'shem Hashem" in Hebrew. The English words go something like this: *In the name of God, the God of Israel, on my right is Michael, on my left is Gabriel, in front of me is Uriel, behind me Raphael, and all around, surrounding me, Shekhinat-El.* Michael, Gabriel, Uriel and Raphael are the archangels and their names basically mean "Who is Like God?" "God's Strength," "Light of God," and "It is God Who Heals."

"I like that." She repeated the angels' names as best she could. They felt soothing to her whole body, and her mind calmed as the words formed on her lips. "What about the last one? Shek-in...?"

"Ah, yes." Jasper held one hand to his heart. "Shekhinat-El. The dwelling place of God." He lightly laid his other hand on Eva's head. "It means *the love of our God is around us at all times.*"

"*All* times?" murmured Eva.

"Yes. Even the hard times. Especially the hard times."

She took a deep breath in and let it out slowly, as Aunt Kit had taught her one day at Coastal Soul. Maybe Micah would be okay after all. "Thank you."

"Anytime, and thank *you* for the gift. I will treasure it always." Jasper stood and held out his hand. She stood beside him.

"But you and Jake aren't going to be together anymore, right?"

"Right. But he will always be a M.I.P."

Eva furrowed her eyebrows. "What's that?"

"M.I.P? It stands for Most Important Person, and Jake is one of mine. This picture will remind me of the love we shared . . . when things were good."

"I get it," Eva said, yawning. She was suddenly tired, but couldn't imagine actually sleeping until she heard from her mother. And if Micah *wasn't* okay . . . she might never sleep again.

"Now, how about that ice cream?" Jasper studied her intently. "The new flavor is Mainiac Maple Walnut, and I have Simply Sweets Simply Superior Fudge Sauce to go with it. Whaddya say?"

"I say okay," Eva said quietly. She hadn't eaten much supper and her stomach was beginning to grumble. "Can I use your bathroom first?"

"Sure thing, right down the hall." He took a tub of ice cream from the freezer and busied himself at the counter, quietly singing "The Angel Song" again.

In Jasper's black and white bathroom, Eva turned on the faucet and looked at her pale face in the mirror. Her hands were shaking slightly as she splashed cool water on her cheeks and forehead. The angel feathers *had* to keep Micah safe. No, not the feathers . . . the actual *angels*! Eva liked that they had names. She whispered them now as she dried her hands on a striped towel. *Michael, Gabriel, Uriel and Raphael.* Saying the names out loud felt like a prayer, but she still wanted to *do* something. She still wanted to be with Micah.

Making her way down the hall on her way back to the kitchen, Eva stopped at an open doorway. There were Broadway musical posters on the walls, and a large computer monitor stood on a metal desk, flanked by a hard drive and speakers. This must be Jasper's study.

Standing at attention in the back corner was a life-size shiny suit of armor. Eva had been fascinated with stories of the Knights of the Round Table in history class last year. Their teacher had even shown them a movie about it. This suit of armor must have been from the theatre's production of *Camelot*. Lucky Jasper; he got to keep it!

Walking across the room, entranced by the thought of actually touching the shiny silver armor, Eva didn't notice the two big plastic bags that blocked her path. She tripped and fell into one of them and it burst wide open, covering her with a flurry of multi-colored feathers. "Oh!" she cried, at first from the shock of standing upright one moment and finding herself on the floor the next. She uttered a second—much louder—cry when she realized that she was lying among *feathers*. Not just any feathers, though. These feathers were the same bright colors as the angel feathers on her dresser. Completely baffled, she looked around.

Finally, everything began to slowly click into place. *There were no angel feathers. There were no angels.* A sickening feeling swept over her as she struggled to stand. She seriously thought she might throw up.

Jasper called from the kitchen, "Eva? You okay?" When she didn't answer, he ran toward the bathroom, then stopped when he saw her standing in the middle of his study.

They looked at each other in dismay.

Eva stared at Jasper as she brushed feathers from her shorts and plucked one out of her hair. "It was you?" she asked in bewilderment. "*You* left me all those feathers?"

"I can explain. They're from the show we're mounting next month, *Seussical*—" Jasper reached out his hand, but she raced past him, through the kitchen, and down the stairs. "Eva!" he called, sharp worry tracking through his voice. "It wasn't my idea. Micah—"

But she didn't hear him as she thundered down the stairs, anger coursing through her. Fresh sobs rose from her belly, burned her throat and erupted from her mouth harshly, "They're not angel feathers at all and they never were!"

Jasper started to follow her down the stairs, but realized he was still barefoot and in his pajamas. "Don't go anywhere, Eva! I'll be right there," he shouted, hurrying back to his apartment to change clothes.

"What on earth is going on?" Glory ran to the hallway, just in time to see Eva rushing into her own apartment. "Honey, stop! Tell me what's wrong!"

Eva paid no attention. She had to find a way to get to Micah. There were no angels watching over him. There never were. It was all in her imagination. Her stupid imagination. She flung open the door to her bedroom, startling Just Jasper who meowed plaintively and watched his mistress furiously grab her backpack from the closet and haphazardly stuff clothes into it. Then she spun around and gazed mournfully at the feathers on her dresser. She didn't need them anymore. They weren't real. *Obviously.* How could she have been so stupid?

She picked up Micah's picture and dropped it into the backpack, then yanked the golden cloth as hard as she could, sending the feathers soaring all over the room. Because it was partially resting on the altar cloth, Teo's terrarium also flew, landing on the floor with a loud thud as it broke into several pieces. Eva surveyed the mess, her eyes clouded with tears, then grabbed her backpack. She didn't have time to clean it up right now, and besides, Teo wasn't her friend anymore. He had made that perfectly clear.

Just Jasper meowed happily as he batted a bright yellow feather across the floor. Eva bent down and kissed the top of his head, her tears soaking into his gray fur. "I love you, Jasper. Micah needs me now, but I promise I'll be back."

She slung the backpack over her shoulder, then raced down the hall and out her apartment door, not bothering to close it behind her. A wide-eyed Glory watched from her own doorway. "What on earth—"

Eva abruptly halted and faced Glory, hands on hips. "Did you know about the feathers too?" she demanded.

"Feathers? What's this about feathers?" Glory's confusion was written plainly on her face.

"Never mind," Eva shouted, the words exploding from her mouth like an angry volcano. "I'm so stupid. I bet *everyone* knew except me!" She flung open the apartment building's front door so hard that it smacked the hallway wall with a thud and remained open.

Glory turned to Theatre Jasper who was hurrying down the stairs. "Please tell me what's going on!"

As he began to explain, neither of them noticed that Just Jasper had trotted after Eva onto the porch, down the front steps, and into the night.

# Chapter 25

Tess's shaky hands clutched the cold bed rail as she stared down at Micah's body, motionless against sterile white sheets. She was still wearing the shorts and flowered top that she'd changed into after work. The drive to the airport with Kit, the flight, the Uber ride to the hospital—it was all a cloudy blur. Her fingers felt automatically for the Mother's Day necklace at her throat as she took a deep breath. This was her son—her vibrant, easy-going son—lying bruised and broken in a strange hospital more than a thousand miles from home. Her eyes blurred with tears; she felt a physical ache in her chest.

Still grasping the necklace, she studied the room. A pale light shining from the wall fixture illuminated her son's bruised face. Steady, rhythmic beeping came in tandem from two machines to which Micah was attached, one of which was a ventilator. He wasn't even breathing on his own. She gripped the bed rail tighter, then laid an unsteady hand on his forehead. "I'm here now, Micah." Could he hear her? She had no idea.

His left arm was encased in a cast from wrist to elbow. She tenderly traced the stitches on his left cheek and other arm.

"Mrs. Gilmore?" A solemn doctor with thinning hair the color of tar and a matching trim mustache entered the room quietly and reached out his hand.

"Tess," she replied simply, too weary to explain why it was Miss instead of Mrs.

"I'm Doctor Mullings." His handshake was firm and brief; his warm, lilting voice called to mind a sunny Caribbean beach. "Your young man made it through the surgery. He has a lengthy recovery ahead of him, but he is strong and he is going to be fine."

Tess let out a long exhale and sank onto the vinyl chair that was next to the bed. She rubbed her forehead, fighting back tears of exhaustion and relief. "When . . . when is he going to wake up?"

Dr. Mullings moved efficiently around Micah's body, checking the readouts on the machines, and lifting each of the patient's eyelids. "We've placed him in a medically-induced coma—"

Tess gasped and sat bolt upright. "He's in a coma?"

"It is quite common in cases like this. His body needs time to heal. It is not just the outer injuries that you can see." He indicated the broken arm, bruises, and various stitches. "We also repaired internal damage to his spleen." He made a few notes on his tablet, then looked up at her. "Trust me. This is best for him."

She looked into the doctor's steady brown eyes which were set a little too close together. Deciding to trust him, she felt her body relax the tiniest bit.

"You must be tired." He headed briskly to the door. "I'll be back again in the morning to check on him. In the meantime, try to get some rest so you can be here for him when he does wake up."

"Thank you, Doctor." She sank back into the uncomfortable chair and was about to call Aunt Kit when the door opened again and a balding Black man in his early sixties walked in. He was of average size, but his full-dress Army uniform and erect posture made him seem taller. His round face and strong physique reminded her of a more mature Wayne Brady. Tess immediately stood, and although she felt a surprising urge to salute, she kept her hands at her sides.

"You must be Micah's mother," he said quietly, shaking her hand. "It's good to meet you, Mrs. Gilmore, although I wish it were under different circumstances. I'm Lieutenant Colonel Hawkins, but please call me Terrell. We talked on the phone this afternoon." She nodded, captivated by his Southern accent. "Your boy's been through a difficult time," he continued. "But the doc says he'll make a full recovery."

"Please call me Tess," she replied, steadied by his firm handshake. "Micah's in a coma, though. That doesn't sound good to me." She tucked her hair behind her ears. Somewhere along the way she'd lost her headband.

Terrell moved to the other side of the bed and laid a hand on Micah's shoulder. "The doctor assured me that placing a patient in a medically-induced coma is common practice. Your son needs a bit of time to heal. I'm not worried, nor should you be." He closed his eyes and clasped his hands as if he were praying. Perhaps he was. He was silent for several long moments. Tess decided to close her eyes and offer up a prayer herself. Were Eva's angels real? If so, one of them ought to come down here right now and—

"We are all tremendously proud of your son."

Terrell's imposing voice startled Tess and she opened her eyes. "What do you mean?"

He took his time moving to her side of the bed, then balanced himself on the edge of a matching chair that stood parallel to hers. "Micah saved the two recruits who were in the utility vehicle that crashed into the gully." Nodding briskly at Tess's surprised expression, he continued. "Micah and his training partner were in the vehicle behind the one that went off course. As soon as they saw what happened, Micah climbed down into the gully while his partner radioed to camp for help." He paused and scratched his head. "Privates Aubree Smith and Marcus Ziegler were trapped under their vehicle. It was Micah who moved the vehicle off their bodies. By the time we got there with Medivac, he was already holding pressure on their wounds even though he had broken an arm and sustained internal injuries in the process."

Tess's mouth fell open in amazement. She took a breath and let it out slowly. "Are Aubree and Marcus going to be all right?"

"Affirmative." Terrell's voice was crisp and clear. "They'll be in the hospital several days also. The doctors told me that if Micah hadn't done what he did, it would have been too late for Aubree and Marcus by the time our medics arrived." He stood and moved closer to the bed, then saluted Micah. "Your son is a hero."

She joined him at the bed and gazed down at her son. Her motherly pride was so fierce, it was almost unbearable. Now, if he would just wake up and smile the Micah-smile she so loved. "What happens now? If he wakes up—"

"*When* he wakes up," Terrell corrected.

"When he wakes up, he won't be able to finish Basic Training . . . like this." She gestured to Micah's broken arm. "Will he?"

"After he's released from the hospital, he'll be in Physical Therapy, most likely for a few months. Once he's completely healed, he'll need to pass a physical exam and then he'll join the next band of recruits at their eighth week of Training. He'll complete his commitment with them, along with Marcus and Aubree."

Tess fingered the thin white blanket that rested against Micah's collarbone. "It's just that . . . I live so far away. I've got a job . . . and my daughter. "I don't see how I can—"

His voice softened. "Yes, your life is up north, and Micah is beginning a new life right here. You'll visit him on weekends, or whenever you can." He laid a warm hand on hers.

His sincerity was comforting, but Tess didn't see how she could go back to Maine and leave Micah alone like this.

"I understand," Terrell continued, observing the fear and hesitation in Tess's silence. "I've got three of my own." She looked into his kind eyes. "That's right. Had to let them go, one at a time. Wasn't easy, not by a long shot."

"Did they join the Army?" Tess asked ruefully.

He stifled a yawn. "My oldest did. She's overseas right now on her second deployment. The other two own a popular restaurant in Chattanooga. The wife and I go down there once a year to visit."

Tess glanced at Micah again—her brave, responsible, artistic son. She would love to see Micah with children of his own one day. He had always been so good with Eva, even when he was seven and she was a baby. *Eva!* She needed to call Aunt Kit with an update, but how was she going to tell Eva that her beloved brother was in a coma?

Terrell shook her hand again. "One of the nurses will be in soon. She'll give you my assistant's phone number. You're to call him for a ride to the closest Marriott. He'll drive you back and forth and he'll get you anything you need."

"Thank you, Terrell. I'm glad that Micah has been under your watch."

"I'll see you soon." He backed out of the room with a little wave as Tess said goodbye.

She sank down into the chair again, feeling twice her age. It was after midnight of a very long day which had been full of unexpected—and not very pleasant—surprises. Waiting for the nurse, she reached for her phone which she'd powered off when boarding the plane. Eva would be so worried.

As the screen lit up, she prepared to call her aunt, but was stopped by a stream of cascading text messages from Jasper, Glory, and Kit, all of them saying the same thing. "Call home now. Eva is missing."

# Chapter 26

*E*va made it as far as downtown Seahaven before she slowed down. It was getting dark but the air was still warm and humid. She was tired and sweaty. What to do now? She couldn't go back to the apartment; Mom had gone to South Carolina. Jasper was probably worried, but why should she care? Jasper had been the one who had left the feathers for her to find. Angel feathers? Ha! He had tricked her. She knew for a fact, now, that there was no such thing as angels, because if there were, then Micah wouldn't be in the hospital. Hot tears filled her eyes as the desperate reality of the past few hours began to sink in: Micah was seriously hurt, Mom had left her behind, and there were no angels.

She rubbed her eyes and looked around. A few people were still strolling the Main Street sidewalks, looking into shop windows, biting into cones from Simply Sweets. She was sure she looked a mess as she hurried down Main Street carrying a bulging backpack on a random Tuesday night. Plastering on a pretend smile for the next tourists who walked by, she decided to where no one would notice her—Sunrise Beach. She could be alone there; she would come up with a plan. A plan that would take her to Micah.

The sky was almost completely dark when she finally sat down in the sand. She was right, this was a smart choice. No one else was here, just the wide night sky, and the shushing sound of the nearby low tide.

She dropped her backpack and looked around. Could she actually stay out here all night? She didn't even have a phone!

Seahaven seemed like a safe place, but things could change in an instant—she knew that now. She had to get to Micah. But what was she going to do . . . walk all the way to South Carolina? She stared miserably at her sneakers. This whole situation was impossible; she had run away and now she had no place to go.

Salty tears formed again, but she swallowed them away. If only Charli lived in Seahaven. Charli's mom would figure out how to help her, but Charli's family might as well be on the other side of the world. Eva stared out at the foaming shallow waves, thinking of her other Seahaven friend. Poppy was on vacation with her family. That's right, Charli and Poppy were with their *families*. Eva had never felt so alone. Where was *her* family? Not with her.

But what about Teo?

The thought popped into Eva's head abruptly and she looked around. It was almost as if someone had spoken. *What about Teo?* Her heart beat more quickly, fueled by hope, but just as quickly, the hope faded. Teo didn't want to have anything to do with her. Besides, he lived on the other side of town, near the harbor. She knew she couldn't walk that far, especially not after the running she'd already done tonight.

As she stared at the water which was briefly tinged with moonlight that looked like smears of sparkly vanilla icing, her stomach rumbled and she wished she had eaten more of the Chicken and Sticky Rice at supper. Why hadn't she at least packed a granola bar? The minutes turned into an hour—maybe more, she couldn't tell. Bereft and lonely, she finally stood, feeling the need to move.

Suddenly, she heard the sharp intrusion of a car door slamming shut. Her heart beat furiously when she became aware of the plodding sound of heavy footsteps crossing the small bridge that led from the parking lot to this section of Sunrise Beach.

Heart pounding, Eva grabbed her backpack and turned to run, but halted again at the sound of her name. "Eva? Eva, is that you?" It sounded like Luca. But what was Luca doing here?

She cautiously turned, then breathed a sigh of relief. It was Luca. She raised a hand in a weak gesture. "Hi."

He took a few steps toward her, but she backed away and he stopped, raising his palms to her in a gesture of safety. "Why are you here by yourself?" His slight European accent reminded her of the day he had brought Teo for the cookout and been reunited with her mom. She watched him survey the quiet beach as if looking for clues, then noticed his expression change the moment his gaze landed on her lime green backpack which glowed against the dark sand like a cartoon sea creature.

Eva studied him for a moment, assessing the situation. She knew she couldn't get to Micah by herself. Jasper had tricked her by leaving what she'd thought were angel feathers everywhere, and Glory was probably in on it. Aunt Kit was following her mom's orders even though she didn't agree, and Kalila didn't have her license yet.

However . . . it was a definite possibility that Luca might help her. She took in his calm demeanor and handsome face, his kind eyes. He was gazing at her intently, the way Micah often looked at her, in a way that signaled he was paying attention. She decided to trust him but had a question first. "What are *you* doing here by yourself?" She echoed his question back to him defiantly, hands on her hips, backpack tucked between her feet.

"Fair question," he replied thoughtfully, rubbing his fingers against his throat. "See this? The ocean?" He gestured toward the water, the small waves lapping white foam against the moonlit sand. Eva nodded and kept her gaze on him. "It is peace to me. It reminds me of my birthplace, Cascais in Portugal. I come here when I need to think."

Eva wondered what he needed to think about, but instead asked hopefully, "Does that mean that Teo stays home alone?"

Luca chuckled. "Definitely not. He is at a friend's house. They are watching a different *Star Wars* movie every night this week."

"Oh," Eva replied sadly, twisting her sneakered foot in the sand. Of course, Teo had other friends. *They* probably didn't have mothers who wanted to date his father.

He waited a moment, then asked again. "It is not right for you to be here alone, Querida." He gestured toward her backpack. "Do you need a ride home?"

She shook her head adamantly, but allowed curiosity to overcome her false bravado. "What's *care-ee-da*?"

"It means 'dear one' in Portuguese. Like when your mom calls you 'honey' or 'sweetheart.'"

Eva liked the sound of that. *Querida.*

Luca tried again. "Please tell me where your mom is."

She crossed her arms over her chest, the anger flaring up again. "Mom went to South Carolina to be with Micah. There was an accident and . . ." It all came pouring out as she sank to her knees in the soft sand, sobbing. Luca was beside her in a flash, one arm around her, carefully listening to every word.

When she was done, she leaned against him, inadvertently wiping her eyes on his gray T-shirt. He smelled of salt water and something like a forest full of warm sunlight. She had no idea what it felt like to be comforted by an actual father, but she imagined it would feel exactly like this.

"So, Querida . . ." Eva loved the way he rolled his r's. "It sounds like you need help getting to your brother." He tipped her chin up and made eye contact. "You do not have your pilot's license, I suppose?" He smiled when she croaked out a short laugh. "I cannot take you to South Carolina; that would not be right. I understand that Kit has to do what Tessa asked her to do. Is there someone else I can call for you? Maybe your pai?"

"My *pie*?" Eva asked, repeating his pronunciation exactly as she'd heard it. He raised his eyebrows kindly as he waited for her to get the meaning. "You mean . . . my father?"

"Yes. It is pronounced like the dessert, but it is spelled p-a-i. I will call him and he will take you to see Micah. He will want to know about the accident, yes?"

"Trust me, he won't care."

"Meu deus! How can that be? If anything happened to my son, I would be there as quickly as possible."

"That's because you love Teo and Teo loves you. Cameron left right after my first birthday. He has a new family now." She paused, taking in Luca's sad expression. It was suddenly clear to her that *this* man was one who wouldn't leave, a man who would be there through the good times as well as the not-so-good times.

"I am sorry that your pai is so . . . distant." He feathered his fingers through the sand.

"I never missed him because I never really knew him." Eva took a breath and made a decision that brought her hope for the first time since that afternoon's dreadful phone call. "I don't even know Cameron's number, but I just thought of someone you *can* call.

# Chapter 21

Aunt Kit was going out of her mind with worry. She'd come back from the airport to find Theatre Jasper and Glory pacing the front lawn. Carolina had joined them while on her evening run, and the four of them—along with Rocky—were now sitting on the edges of various seats on the front porch. Except for Rocky. No sitting for him. He was straining against the limits of the leash that tethered him to Carolina.

Seahaven police cars were now actively searching for Eva. The four adults sat silently in the meek glow of the single porch light, swatting mosquitos and awaiting word . . . any word.

Theatre Jasper had claimed the wicker chair closest to the steps, repeatedly kicking his feet against the railing. Kit knew he was blaming himself, but there truly was no one to blame. Eva had run away, plain and simple, and was it any wonder? Kit covered her eyes in frustration. What was Tess thinking, leaving Eva behind, when they all knew how close she was to her brother? But that was Tess, wasn't it? Trying so hard, in so many different ways, to be a good mother, yet sometimes missing the most obvious action, right under her nose. Eva must have felt scared and abandoned. Kit hadn't been surprised that Eva had fled, but where on earth could she have gone?

Glory was perched on the porch swing, still as stone, staring off into the night as if she were listening for an answer to a question or offering a prayer. Perhaps both. Carolina sat on the top porch step, attempting to rein her feisty dog in.

It appeared that Eva wasn't the only one missing. Her cat had also disappeared. When Kit heard that Eva had left in such a hurry, she immediately went into Eva's room to look for clues, gasping at the mess. Clothes were strewn all over, along with the colorful feathers from Eva's altar. The terrarium lay smashed and forlorn by Eva's desk. Just Jasper wasn't in any of his usual sleeping spots, and Kit had noticed that the apartment door and the door to the building were both wide open. She'd tried shaking Jasper's food bowl and she'd tried opening a can of tuna, either of which would ordinarily have brought Jasper out of a deep, settled sleep, but he was nowhere to be found.

Kit tried to calm her breathing, but it was difficult. Her heart was skittering and lurching in her chest and she wrapped her sweater closer, even though the night air was humid. Where was Eva? Where was that cat?

She tapped another text to Tess into her phone. Surely her niece's flight had landed and she was at the hospital by now. Kit badly wanted a cigarette but she didn't dare leave the front porch in case Eva or the cat showed up.

At that moment, her phone rang and the others rushed to her side, staring at the phone. "Eva? Is that you?" She paused, then sagged with relief against the rocking chair. "Luca! I can't thank you enough for . . . What?" Kit sat up again and exhaled loudly. "Yes, you can tell her that I knew about the feathers." She looked up at the others and mouthed the words *she's safe*, then continued listening to Luca. "Okay. I think that's probably the best idea at this point. Thank you for taking care of her." She listened. "I'll talk with you in the morning. Godspeed."

She clicked off the phone, checking once more for a message from Tess. Nothing. She relaxed into the chair and rubbed her hands on the yellow skirt that covered her legs and flowed almost to the floor. "Eva is with Luca."

"Luca?" Glory asked, her eyes wide. "How on earth—?"

"He was heading to Sunrise Beach where he sometimes goes at night to think." Kit nodded emphatically. "Thanks be to Spirit, because that's where Eva was. She told him what had happened."

Jasper frowned. "I wish I had—"

Kit shushed him. "It's okay, Jasper, you didn't do anything wrong."

"But she found the feathers and she didn't let me explain that it was all Micah's idea."

Glory patted Jasper's hand. "I was right there too, and I wasn't able to stop her either. I'm sure that once Eva calms down, she'll be ready to listen."

"I just wish Micah and I had thought the whole thing through. We were so excited about surprising Eva with the feathers that we didn't think about how to tell her the truth. If Micah knew how he wanted to handle that, he didn't tell me."

"That's on all of us, Jasper," Kit replied. "Sometimes we get inspired to help someone, but we don't think of the consequences."

"She's right," said Glory. "I'm sure it will all work out." Jasper looked doubtful.

Carolina had no idea what feathers they were talking about, and she was getting tired of struggling with her feisty dog, so she attempted to change the subject as she stood. "Is Luca bringing Eva home now that he's found her?" Rocky stood beside her, impatiently eyeing the sidewalk.

"No, she's going to stay with him and Teo for a while, until we get more news about Micah. She's still pretty upset. I'll text Luca as soon as I hear from Tess."

Jasper ran his hands through his hair. "She's safe; that's what's important. Now, what do we do about the missing cat?"

# Chapter 28

Tess tossed and turned in the surprisingly comfortable hotel bed. Eva had discovered the truth about the feathers and run away, but Luca had found her. Her heart ached for her daughter. Maybe she should have brought her to South Carolina, but how would Eva have reacted to seeing Micah so terribly wounded and in a coma? It was hard enough to see Micah like that herself. She and Eva had been getting along so well . . . and now this. Would she ever be able to have a close relationship with her daughter?

Tossing and turning was getting her nowhere; sleep was as elusive as the happiness she so longed for. Tess fretfully tossed the covers aside and sat up. Her heart was racing and her body was filled to the brim with conflicting emotion. Suddenly she remembered what Carolina had told her about going to Waker's Beach in the middle of the night and screaming at the top of her lungs. She had dismissed the idea as childish at the time, but right now? It seemed like the smartest idea in the world.

She looked around. Columbia was nowhere near a beach, and if she screamed out loud, whoever was in the next room would surely call the police. But she needed to scream or she thought she'd go crazy with the intense anxiety that was clogging her veins, so she flung herself face down on the bed, buried her face in a pillow, shoved the other one over her head and let it all out. She pounded the bed with tightly clenched fists and soaked the pillow with long-bottled-up tears. She could no longer hold back the guttural moans and screams of a woman—a mother—who felt alone and helpless and afraid.

Finally, weary and spent, Tess pushed herself back up to a seated position and blew her nose. She finally understood what Carolina had meant about such a cathartic release, even though Carolina's fears were about her husband, and Tess's worries concerned her wounded son and the daughter she'd thoughtlessly left behind.

Feeling the need to stand on her own two feet, she walked to the wall of windows and drew back the heavy drapes. Pressing her warm forehead against the cool glass, she gazed at a thin slice of moon arched perfectly over the adjacent shopping center. There was the North Star, peeking bravely through a delicate mass of southern clouds. The moon hung there, seemingly suspended on nothing but God's will—a sliver of pure brightness, defying the surrounding clouds. The tiniest wave of hope flowed over Tess now as she stared at the moon. It felt like a promise—from where or from whom, she had no idea—a promise that lightened the sadness in her heart even as it brightened the night sky.

She closed the drapes, sank back down on the edge of the bed and peered at her phone which sat vigil on the night table. 3:20 a.m. The numbers silently glowed against the screensaver which showed herself with Micah and Eva at his birthday party. She wished she could go back in time and do things differently. She would have asked more questions, spent more time talking with Micah about what was going on in his life. She wouldn't have taken so many night classes all at once. She would have slowed down, not been in so much of a rush.

A few more tears silently trickled down her cheeks as she lay on her back, staring at the ceiling. She had to stop clutching the guilt; she had to stop hanging onto her mistakes as though they defined her. She had to let it all go, for her own sake as well as Eva's.

She would create a new definition of herself. It wasn't too late to pay attention. It wasn't too late to make it right with Eva. The tears slowly ceased, but these new thoughts kept Tess awake for another hour, and then she fell into a light, dreamless sleep.

As Tess opened her eyes to the new day, bright sunshine leaked through the crevice between the stiff burgundy drape panels. She squinted at the thin beams of light penetrating the dark room, rose on her elbows and reached for her phone. How was it possible that she had slept until almost noon? She couldn't remember the last time she had slept this late.

*Micah.* She had to get to the hospital. On her way to the bathroom, she glanced at herself in the mirror and grimaced, quite certain that she couldn't show up at the hospital looking—or smelling—like this. She would take time for a quick shower and then check in with Eva.

*Eva.* Thank God and all of Eva's angels that her girl was safe. Because of Luca.

*Luca.* She should have reached out to Luca last night when Aunt Kit had called her, but she'd told herself it was too late. It had been well after midnight, but the issue was that it was too late for her and Luca; Teo had made that perfectly clear. Her priorities were straight now—Micah and Eva were the most important things in her life. It was too late for the love story that might have belonged to her and Luca; Cecilia had seen to that twenty-six years ago. At the thought of her mother, Tess cringed, then shoved the unwelcome resentment to the back of her mind. Today she was choosing to focus on her children, and only her children.

Tess stared at herself in the bathroom mirror now, taking note of her flat hair and haggard eyes, the faint wrinkles that were beginning to show around her mouth. No, she wasn't ready to talk to Luca yet. It would be better to simply call Aunt Kit . . . as soon as she showered and washed her hair. As soon as she felt more like herself again. Whenever that might be.

In spite of her determination to push Luca to the back of her mind, images of him continued to invade her worried thoughts as she rinsed the lemony hotel shampoo out of her hair. Teenage Luca intently reading the Stephen Hawking book under her aunt's tree at Seahaven Harbor. Riding bikes together on the Eastern Trail. And oh . . . the sweet surprise of their first kiss, and all the kisses after that. The day he gave her the seashell necklace. The year of emails and letters postmarked from Portugal with his slanted, practically illegible handwriting. The years of memories fading, but never forgotten. And then . . . finding him on her doorstep after so many years of feeling rejected. Learning the truth. Anger toward her mother for keeping Luca away. Dinner at Pete's Fish Shack. Laughter. Talking at the pier. A simmering connection. *Reconnection.* And the heated, familiar-but-better pleasure of more kisses. The hope that had filled her heart that night and the next day as they'd sat together watching their children on the Sands of Time stage.

Tess dried herself with the plush white towel and combed her hair. She desperately wished that things had been different. She wished Teo had given her a chance the other night instead of pushing her away. She wished Luca hadn't introduced her to his son quite so quickly. She wished—

A knock at the door jolted her mind back to the present. Time to stop daydreaming; she had to get to the hospital. But who on earth was knocking? She hurriedly put on the robe that hung on the bathroom door and tugged the belt tight as she called out,

"Who is it?" then stopped in her tracks and gasped when she heard a familiar, beloved voice.

"Eva?" Tess flung open the hotel door and sank to her knees in front of her daughter. "What are you . . . How did you . . .?" She attempted to pull Eva into a hug but she stiffened and pulled away.

Only then did Tess notice the figure standing behind Eva. "Mom?" Tess rose uncertainly, and clutched the door frame for support. "I can't believe you're . . . How did you even—"

Cecilia frowned and pushed past Tess into the room which smelled of lemon shampoo and something vaguely antiseptic. "Come along, Eva," Cecilia instructed, dragging a small overnight case behind her. She settled herself on the edge of the second double bed and pointed at Tess. Her words were more weary than harsh. "I've come all this way with your daughter who *ran away* because you wouldn't bring her with you to see her brother."

Tess shut the door firmly behind her, and leaned against it, staring at her mother. Cecilia's supposedly wrinkle-free Alfred Dunner pastel slacks and matching top looked disheveled. Even the pearl earrings from great-grandmother Evelyn looked dull and worn. "I don't understand . . ." She looked at Eva. "I thought you were with Luca."

Eva stood quietly, facing the mirror that hung over the standard-issue hotel desk, her back to the room. "Don't be mad, Mom," she pleaded quietly into the mirror, not quite meeting Tess's eyes. "When Luca found me, I asked him to call Gram. We met her on the highway in Massachusetts and she and I stayed in a hotel so we could get on a plane this morning in Hartford." She took a breath, still staring into the mirror where her mother's reflection eyed her in disbelief. "Don't be mad," she repeated, more resolutely this time.

"I don't know what to say," Tess replied, trying to get over the shock of seeing her daughter and her mother in her hotel room. She had been alone. And now, she was not.

"You could at least say thank you," Cecilia grumbled. "I had to cancel my book club, a manicure appointment, and a Humane Society committee meeting to bring Eva here." She looked meaningfully at her granddaughter. "By the way, I think it's high time Eva had a cell phone."

Tess caught Eva's surprised expression at the mention of the phone, then gazed at Cecilia, trying to assimilate this information. Her mother had made a sacrifice for her and for Eva. Her mother, who didn't make a habit of stepping up to the plate when needed, had not only stepped up to the plate, but picked up the plate and brought it all the way to South Carolina with her. "Thank you," she said sincerely, making eye contact with her mother. Then she turned to Eva. "But I'm disappointed in you."

Tears filled Eva's eyes as she turned to face her mother, but she didn't speak. Did she care that her mother was disappointed in her? A little, yes. But she cared more, right now, about her brother who was lying injured in a hospital near here. "You're disappointed in *me*?" she finally said, raising her voice an octave or two. "You knew about the feathers, didn't you?" She pointed at Tess as if identifying a criminal in a line-up.

"The feathers?" Tess seemed baffled. "Yes, of course. Jasper told me about the feathers last week. I even left one for you—"

Eva stomped to the window, pushed back the heavy drapes and let the bright noon sun stream over her long hair. "You should have *told* me they weren't angel feathers!"

"What does that have to do with anything?" Tess asked, her fingers automatically moving to her temples.

"It has *everything* to do with it!" She sank down on her mother's unmade, rumpled bed.

Tess moved toward Eva, but Cecilia stopped her. "Tess," she whispered, urgently gripping Tess's shoulder. "Leave her be. Poor girl. She misses her brother."

"I know that, Mom," Tess hissed.

"If you knew that, why didn't you bring her with you to see him?"

Tess removed her mother's hand from her robed shoulder. "I didn't think she should see Micah like that."

Cecilia stared at her, then gestured toward the unmade bed as they both realized that Eva was carefully observing her mother and grandmother. "Well, now that we've come all this way, are you going to leave her here while you visit him in the hospital?"

Tess heard Eva take in a small breath and hold it, waiting. This was it, then. There wasn't much of a choice. She would take Eva and her mother to the hospital; they would see Micah together. She looked at Cecilia now, feeling overwhelmed with the strangest mixture of gratitude and hostility. Yes, Cecilia had chosen to bring Eva here, but she couldn't forget one fact: it was her mother's fault that she and Luca had fallen out of touch. Then Tess remembered her middle-of-the-night revelation. This wasn't the time or place for placing blame; this was a time for trying on her new self-definition. "I'm not going to leave either of you here," she said decisively. "Give me ten minutes to get dressed and we'll go."

A tremulous wave of fear and anxiety simmered through Eva's young body. She didn't just want to see her brother; she *needed* to see him. But what would he look like? What if he was dying?

# Chapter 29

*E*arly the next morning, Theatre Jasper awoke in an uncomfortable position on his living room sofa. A patter of light rain streaked the windows. He'd fallen asleep after repeated attempts to check his Facebook page, where he'd posted a photo of Eva's missing cat along with a plea for help.

Now he paced the length of his apartment, kitchen to bedroom to living room and back again, frantically squeezing his brain in an attempt to figure out how to find Just Jasper. In the living room the tenth time through, he paused in front of the framed photo of himself and Jake on the beach in St. John; their happiness was an obvious aura around them. Next to it was the picture that Eva had taken last week—his own hopeful expression; Jake's distracted smile.

Jasper bit his bottom lip now as he studied the difference between the two pictures. He had looked at these photos with Eva—just yesterday—and realized again now with painful clarity that Jake was not the one for him. It may have been true at one time, but that time was past. They had spent too much time apart, and Jake was not ready to settle down in Seahaven or anywhere else. Jasper was ready to let go. He would call Jake tonight. But first, he would find Eva's cat.

He quickly changed into clean clothes, shrugged into his pale blue windbreaker and matching fishing cap, then grabbed an umbrella before rushing out to his car. As he turned the key in the ignition, Carolina rapped on the roof of the car. He lowered the window and squinted up at her. Her long hair was tucked haphazardly into the hood of her jacket, but strands of it lay wet and curled around her cheeks. "What's up? No Rocky today?"

"Nah, he doesn't like the rain," she replied, jogging in place. "Any word from Tess?"

"She's been in touch with Kit. Micah is in a medically-induced coma but they expect him to wake soon."

"That's great news! And Eva?"

Jasper flipped on the windshield wipers. "I assume she's still with Luca. I'm going to drive around looking for her cat. Any ideas?"

Carolina slowed her pace, then stopped altogether. "If someone finds him, I imagine they'll take him to Dr. Brightman."

"That's a great idea . . . I'll start there!" He put the car in reverse, then stepped on the brake when Carolina started talking.

"The clinic doesn't open 'til eight," she said, tapping on her waterproof sports watch. "I'll text you when I get there, okay?"

"All right," Jasper said miserably, rubbing his eyes for a moment. "I'll feel so much better if we can find him before Eva gets home."

"Me too." Carolina resumed her effortless jogging in place. "Hey, what was all that talk about feathers last night, anyway?"

"We were leaving feathers for Eva to find, thinking it would take her mind off of Micah being so far away. For some reason, she started to think they were angel feathers and that the angels were leaving her signs that her brother was safe . . ."

"And now she's learned that he wasn't so safe after all." She looked into the distance, thinking of her husband. Was he safe? Were service members ever actually safe? She wished an angel would leave *her* a feather so she could be sure.

"Right." Jasper nodded miserably. "She ran away because she found out I was the one leaving most of the feathers. Most of them were props from *Seussical the Musical*."

Carolina abruptly stopped jogging and leaned in the car window until her face was so close he could smell the wintergreen toothpaste she'd used that morning. "Maybe it's not just about the feathers. Maybe Eva ran away because she was mad at Tess for leaving her behind."

"Oh, I don't—"

"Think about it." Carolina straightened. "Finding out about the feathers was probably the metaphorical straw that broke the proverbial camel's back."

Jasper stared at Carolina. "Maybe," he finally replied, turning on the window defogger. "But that doesn't change the fact that Just Jasper is missing. I can't stop thinking about that darned cat. After all, we share the same name, and it's my fault that he got out that night."

"Go ahead and look for the cat, but stop blaming yourself. You're not the one who left all the doors open! I'm going to run home, hop in the shower, and head to work early. Even if Dr. Brightman's not there, Carlos will be."

"Carlos?"

"Carlos Fuentes. He's the other vet tech. If there was a message about a cat found overnight, he'll be the one taking care of it." She attempted a high five, which Jasper unenthusiastically returned.

Eva held her breath as she and Gram followed Tess into Micah's hospital room. Her mom had told her about his injuries; he was in a medically-induced coma to give his body a chance to heal. She shivered as they approached his bed now, still unsure of what to expect.

"Micah, look who I brought to see you," Tess said cheerfully, but Eva could hear the faint tremor of worry underneath the words. "Eva and Gram are here, and you're going to be all right."

Eva's eyes filled with tears when she saw her beloved brother laid flat—bruises and swelling all over, an oxygen mask over his mouth, and who-knows-what being pumped into his body from plastic bags strung up on metal poles near his shoulder. But she steadied herself because she instinctively knew that it was still *Micah* underneath the wounds and the stiff hospital sheets. She took the cold fingers of his left hand in one of hers, trying not to disturb the IV line. "Hi Micah," she whispered. "You probably can't hear me, but I love you."

"Dr. Mullings told me that he can hear us," Tess reassured her. "It's good for you to talk to him."

Cecilia had been standing by the door to give them privacy, but now she moved to the bed and gazed down at her grandson, placing one hand over her mouth to stifle a cry. Then she turned to Tess and embraced her. Eva watched, wide-eyed.

Startled, Tess patted her mother on the back but didn't fully return the hug. "Mom? Are you okay?"

"Seeing him like this reminds me of your father," Cecilia murmured. "His last hours were in a hospital and I haven't been in one since. I can't believe it's been seven years." Cecilia let go of Tess and rested her hand on Micah's bruised forehead for a moment, tears clouding her eyes.

Tess tentatively touched Cecilia's shoulder. She had never seen her mother like this.

"You weren't there," Cecilia replied quietly, all abrasiveness suddenly drained from her voice like sand gone quickly through an unassuming sieve. "You were at work. He had a heart attack at the office and then a few hours later he was gone."

Tess kept her hand on her mother's shoulder.

"It was so fast, but I got to be with him. The doctor called me and I got to the hospital in time. I'm so grateful that I got to be with him when he died." She lifted her gaze to the window beside Micah's bed, but she wasn't seeing the view of the parking lot.

Hearing Eva's shocked gasp, Tess rushed to the other side of the bed and hugged her daughter. "Mom!" She raised her voice, in spite of the hushed atmosphere surrounding Micah and all the machines. "Stop talking like this! Micah isn't going to die!"

Cecilia's memory-informed gaze found its way back to the present moment. She covered her mouth with both hands and backed away from the bed. "I'm sorry, girls. I . . . I wasn't thinking." Her voice lowered to a hoarse whisper. She looked directly at Eva and reached across the bed to take her hand. "Of course, our Micah isn't going to die." She pointed at the machines that beeped steadily next to the intravenous stands. "Eva, look. His vital signs are all good. I watch *New Amsterdam* too." She patted her neat blonde hairdo, then turned to leave. "There's a waiting room down the hall. I'll stay there until you're done with your visit."

"You don't have to go," Tess called after her uncertainly, but Cecilia waved a hand behind her and was gone.

"Wow," Eva said quietly. "Gram was so . . ."

"I know." Tess held on to Micah's bedrail. She was almost dizzy from the bizarre way that this day was unfolding.

"If you want to talk with Gram, I can stay here with Micah. The button to call the nurse is right here." She pointed to the table beside the bed.

Tess looked thoughtfully at her daughter, then at the closed door. Maybe this was a good time to finally confront Cecilia. Her mother seemed softer somehow . . . and slightly unfamiliar. "Are you sure?"

Eva nodded, not taking her eyes from her brother.

"Okay. When Dr. Mullings shows up, will you come and get me?"

Eva took a deep breath. "I will, don't worry. I'm okay now, Mom. Really."

Theatre Jasper sat outside the Bright Side Animal Clinic, attempting to wait patiently for the home screen on his phone to display the time as eight o'clock. Ten minutes to go. He tapped his thumbs nervously on the steering wheel in time with the steady patter of the rain.

After knocking on all the doors on Bright Blessing Way, plus the two adjacent streets, he had driven around Seahaven, all to no avail. It would be difficult enough looking for a dark gray cat on the sunniest of days, but today it was so foggy and rainy that it would be hard to find a ginger cat, much less a gray one. This was his last-ditch effort before heading to the theatre. Rehearsals for *Seussical the Musical* were in full swing and the anniversary Gala was fast approaching.

He tried to think of a song to hum that would cheer him up but the only one that came to mind was *Rainy Days and Mondays,* so in desperation he turned on the radio. *I Have Found Me a Home* by Jimmy Buffett was playing, and it almost made him smile. Many years ago, that was the song that he and Jake had slow-danced to on one of their first dates. But now, it only strummed a bittersweet melody in his heart. He turned off the radio and jumped out of the car as Carolina pulled up in her bright blue jeep.

"Hey!" he called, opening his umbrella to shelter them both as they ran together to the clinic. The front door was painted a cheery yellow and adorned with the red and black Bright Side Clinic logo. She jiggled the key in the lock, then pushed the door open to the sound of a lone dog barking in a back room, and a lively male voice belting out the words to "I Don't Know How to Love Him." Off key. Way, way off key. Jasper's heart skipped a beat. He had loved this song from the first time he'd seen *Jesus Christ Superstar* at a community theatre when he was a teen. The words always seemed so full of longing and love. He knew it was about Mary Magdalene and Jesus, but in his mind, it was about the desire to truly love someone. He thought he'd gotten it right with Jake, and he had . . . for a time. But not any more.

Carolina shook out her cloud of red hair and hung her jacket on the coat rack by a gigantic fish tank, then noted Jasper's curious expression. "The singing? That's Carlos." She put her fingers in her ears for a moment and grinned playfully. "He'll stop once he sees us."

"He doesn't have to stop. I love that song."

"You may love that song . . ." She opened the door to the receptionist's area and beckoned him to follow. "But I'm sure you can hear a better version of it elsewhere." She dropped her purse on the counter, then hollered, "Hey Carlos, concert's over!"

The singing and the barking ceased immediately, leaving heartbeats of silence.

A good-looking man about Jasper's age stuck his head around a door that led to the back of the clinic. His dark wavy hair was mostly hidden by a green surgical cap. "Good morning, Carolina," he said cheerfully. Noticing Jasper, he smiled even brighter and walked fully into the receptionist's area as he reached out a hand. "And good morning to you, too—" He looked at Carolina, who made the introductions.

Jasper was captivated by Carlos's enthusiasm and felt his own spirits lifting considerably. Carolina explained about the missing cat. "There were no messages on this morning's voicemail, but give me your number and I'll call you as soon as I hear something."

Jasper was grateful that Carlos hadn't said *if I hear something.* "Thanks. Um, Carolina has my number; you can get it from her."

She looked between the two men for a moment, then scribbled Jasper's number on a sticky note and placed it in Carlos's hands. "Here," she said brightly. "In case I'm not here when Eva's cat turns up."

Carlos thanked her, then turned to Jasper. "I'll send this info around to the vets in the surrounding towns, and we'll post it on our social media pages too. If you can get me his photo, that'll help."

Jasper quickly scrolled through the pictures on his phone and found one.

"What a handsome dude! Text it to me now and I'll take care of this for you." He gave Jasper his number.

"Thanks. I need to head over to the theatre now, so—"

"Wait!" Carlos hurried over to Jasper and laid a hand on his arm almost reverently. "You work at Sands of Time?"

"Yeah, I'm the props guy."

"I love your theatre! Bought season tickets as soon as I moved here five years ago. You've done such great shows!"

Jasper looked pleased. "Glad to hear it. It's a great place to work." He glanced at Carolina who was studying the two of them with a bemused expression, then headed for the door, his mind vacillating between worry over Just Jasper and wonder about Carlos, who had just lifted his spirits without even trying.

# Chapter 30

Checking her phone on the way to the waiting room, Tess saw a relieved message from Kit in response to Tess's earlier text about Cecilia and Eva's arrival. There was also a sad-faced cat emoji from Jasper with the words "Not found yet but spreading the word. Will keep you posted." Tess immediately deleted both texts. She had no intention of telling Eva that her cat was missing; they'd had enough drama for one day. Hopefully Just Jasper would show up soon. It sounded like the whole town of Seahaven was looking for Eva's lovable cat.

Tess found her mother sitting on a brown tweed sofa staring with a glazed expression at a flatscreen TV that was mounted on the wall. A rerun of *Gilmore Girls* was playing; Lorelai and Rory were eating junk food and watching a movie. Tess's heart caught. There had never been moments like that with Cecilia. In fact, Tess had never been quite sure if Cecilia had even enjoyed being a mother.

"Mom?" Tess reached for the remote and turned down the volume so that it was a whisper in the background. Tess and Cecilia were Gilmore girls too. Maybe they would never be close like Rory and Lorelai; but what if they could be just a tiny bit more connected than they were right now? She had rarely seen her mother show a genuine display of emotion the way she had several minutes ago at Micah's bedside. Even at her husband's funeral, Cecilia had been stoic and unwavering. Tess had cried copious tears, but her mother had never once offered to comfort her.

Tess's heart softened as a new realization occurred—Cecilia had needed comforting too.

Sitting in this hospital waiting room, Micah's condition still uncertain, Tess felt a slight yet tender wave of compassion for her mother begin to rise. Despite how Cecilia had squashed her budding relationship with Luca so many years ago, Tess decided to reach out to her mother now. She was creating a new definition of herself; perhaps it was time to redefine her relationship with Cecilia as well.

"Mom?" she repeated gently, peering more closely into Cecilia's stoic face.

Cecilia blinked. "I've been watching the girls." Her voice sounded as if she had carried a heavy sack twenty miles uphill and had little energy left for words.

"I see." Tess clicked the OFF button on the remote, sending the chattering mother-daughter duo and their junk food into darkness. She smiled ruefully. "It's one of my favorite shows. I wasn't aware that you liked it too."

Cecilia was silent. Tess could see that she was struggling to hold back tears, so she handed her mom the box of tissues that lay on the table between them. "It's okay. Go ahead and cry. I certainly did my share last night."

"I'm worried about Micah. And Eva. And you . . . all of you." Cecilia's voice broke as she pulled out a tissue and patted her eyes.

"Of course. It's not easy seeing him lying there like that. So still. All those tubes." Tess reached for a tissue and wearily blew her nose.

"What if he doesn't wake up?" Cecilia whispered, looking away.

"Doctor Mullings said they'll bring him out of the coma as soon as he shows signs of waking up. He's strong. He'll be okay."

Cecilia raised an eyebrow and made eye contact with Tess. "Do you honestly believe that?"

Tess took a breath. It was up to her now. She knew she had to be strong for Eva, but she could suddenly see that she needed to be strong for her mother too. Her mother needed her. This realization startled her and it took her a moment to fully absorb it. *Her mother needed her.* She nodded to herself as if agreeing with a best friend, then spoke firmly. "Yes, I do." She moved to the sofa and tentatively put an arm around Cecilia who leaned into her daughter slightly.

A crisp, static-filled announcement over the hospital intercom system jolted them out of their thoughts. "Dr. Zoa report to Emergency. Dr. Zoa to Emergency." The static disappeared; an awkward silence followed.

Cecilia finally spoke, her voice low. "Tess, I'm worried about all of you. Ever since Cameron left, I've watched you struggling."

Tess was taken aback. She'd had no idea that her mother worried about them. Cecilia had given no indication of this. Ever. "Mom, I'm okay. We're okay." She shifted her body so they were knee to knee and took Cecilia's hands in hers.

Cecilia looked down at their hands and then back up at Tess. "I don't see how you can be. You've got a new job; Eva will be in a different school. You're so far away now. And Micah's even further."

Tess blinked. Cecilia had been so critical when Tess told her they were moving to Maine, but it appeared that her mother actually missed them. Another revelation. With this in mind, she attempted a reassuring tone. "I love my new job; the Pearls are easy to work for and I'm finally able to put money into savings every month. Aunt Kit has been generous and Eva has already made friends—"

"That's all good, but what about you?" Cecilia interrupted.

"What about me?"

"Have you made friends too?"

Tess smoothed back her hair as she thought of her new life in Seahaven. "Yes. My friend Carolina lives down the street. She manages the vet clinic. Jasper lives upstairs and Glory is across the hall. Do you remember Quinn and Chiara? We're still close even though they don't live nearby."

"But are you seeing anyone? A man?"

The words sounded strange coming from her mother's mouth. When had her mother ever asked about her love life? She couldn't remember one time, not even during the summer she was fifteen. Cecilia had never invited confidences. Tess settled against the sofa but angled her body toward her mother. "No," she began, then hesitated. Was this really the best time to bring up the subject of Luca? She took a deep breath and exhaled slowly. *Never or now.* She could do this. "But I did run into Luca a few weeks ago. Remember Luca Silva? He's living in Seahaven again."

Cecilia's eyes widened and she dropped the crumpled tissue in her lap. Tess noticed her mother's cheeks redden slightly. "I remember Luca," she said quietly, looking uneasily around the room, her eyes settling on a coffee maker against the opposite wall. "I'm going to get a cup." She pointed to the machine. "Would you like one?"

What Tess would have liked was to force her mother to admit that she had lied to Luca twenty-six year ago, but coffee seemed necessary first. She hadn't had a cup since her flight last night. It seemed like a week had gone by, not mere hours. "Sure. No cream or sugar."

Her back to Tess, Cecilia busied herself at the machine in an undisguised effort to compose herself. "So, Luca left Portugal and moved back to the States?" She handed her daughter a cardboard cup printed with the hospital logo, then sat on the edge of the rocking chair. She absentmindedly stirred her coffee with a plastic spoon.

Tess inhaled the heady aroma of strong coffee. It was too hot to drink so she cupped it in her hands. "Yes. His wife died two years ago and he came back last year. He has a son who's a year older than Eva."

"I didn't know."

Tess stood and walked to the counter where the coffee paraphernalia was and poured a little cold water into her cup, then took a sip. "It's cool enough to drink now." She raised the cup in her mother's direction as if they were toasting the occasion, then took another sip. "It's actually not bad . . . for hospital coffee."

Gazing intently into her cup, Cecilia didn't acknowledge the attempted levity. "I remember how much you liked him, the last summer we visited Kit."

"Yes," Tess replied simply, sitting back down on the sofa. "And he liked me." She hesitated, then decided to pursue what had been on her mind for years. "I understand why you made me leave early that week. I was young; Luca and I were getting close. I have a daughter now; I get it. But Luca and I were emailing and writing letters, and then he just . . . stopped." She looked expectantly at Cecilia, waiting patiently.

Cecilia met Tess's eyes. "He told you," she said flatly.

"Yes." Tess sipped more coffee as she continued to study her mother.

"I'm sorry," Cecilia said slowly. She ran a manicured finger around the rim of her coffee cup and stared into it, seeing only the past. "I didn't want you to get hurt."

"I might have gotten hurt, but that was my choice to make, not yours."

"I see that now." Cecilia's voice was threaded with sadness. "I shouldn't have lied to Luca like I did. Your dad and I . . . We weren't getting along back then. He was burying himself in his work and was hardly ever home. It hurt my heart to see you so happy, getting so close to that young man." She set her coffee on the low table and frowned. "I had the feeling all along that Luca's family was going to go back to Portugal. Then they did exactly that, and I saw how happy his letters made you, but I didn't believe that it could work. You were only fifteen, Tess, and he was so far away. I felt so alone; your father didn't understand. He expected me to make all the decisions about you." She closed her eyes. "I didn't want you to get hurt. Honestly, that's all it was. I thought I was doing the right thing." She met Tess's eyes and Tess could see the regret written there. "I hope you can forgive me."

Tess couldn't believe that her mother had just apologized. Twice in the last few minutes. "Thank you," she said simply. What else was there to say? It was all in the past, and letting go of it now was easier because her mother had acknowledged how wrong she had been.

"You're welcome," Cecilia replied quietly, and the two women rested in the silence of a tentative forgiveness. "So . . . how is Luca now?" Cecilia asked, finally sipping her coffee. "Are the two of you dating?"

"He's built up his father's business. Remember Sea Dove Charters?" Cecilia nodded. Tess paused and looked away. "But no, we're not dating."

"Because . . . ?" Cecilia leaned forward.

Tess noticed a subtle change in her mother. She actually seemed softer around the edges; she was showing genuine interest instead of harsh disdain. "Because his son isn't ready to see his father with another woman."

"He's comparing you to his dead mother."

"Yes." She soothed the back of one hand with the palm of the other. "Anyway, it's not the best timing."

Cecilia raised her eyebrows as she drained the last of her coffee, then patted her lips with the small paper napkin.

"It's time for me to be spending time with Eva. I haven't been around much these last four years, but that's changing. It's just the two of us now. She'll be going off to college soon. I'll have time for dating then."

Cecilia shook her head adamantly. "You have seven years until Eva finishes high school! I thought I had many years left with your dad, but I was so, so wrong. If you think you still have a connection with Luca, you should spend more time with him. Now. Not when Eva leaves for college. Not when Luca's son decides he's ready. Now."

Tess had never heard her mother speak so passionately. "You don't understand. There aren't enough hours in the day. I can't—"

The door to the waiting room swung open just then and an excited Eva leaned in, shouting "Mom! Gram! Micah's awake!"

They were thrilled to discover that Micah was indeed awake. Both eyes were open—the blue one and the brown one—and he was attempting a smile, although it was crooked because of several dark, crusty stitches on his left cheek. A nurse was fussing over him. "Our hero is back," she said brightly to the women as they entered with Eva. "He was showing signs of waking up, so I called Dr. Mullings and he brought him out of the coma. He's slowly coming back, thank heavens." The nurse's name badge read "Paloma Dixon" and her springy curls reminded Eva of Ben Shepherd's wife, Savannah.

For Tess, the name "Paloma" held another meaning and she was startled at this surprising synchronicity. Luca's mother's name was Paloma, and his fishing charter company was named *Sea Dove* because the Portuguese word for dove is paloma. Remembering Luca, Tess's face heated briefly, then she pressed those thoughts out of her mind and willed her breathing to slow down.

"Micah, we're here for you," Tess said softly. She laid one hand on his shoulder and the other on her heart. "Micah."

"Mom." Micah's voice was hoarse, but he was speaking.

Eva was bouncing on her toes. "I was standing right here! I was telling him all about Seahaven and the play I wrote and then the machine started beeping and I didn't know if it was a good beep or a bad beep so I yelled for help and Nurse Paloma came in with the doctor and he did something to the machine and then Micah opened his eyes!" She took a breath and swallowed hard.

Tess kissed the top of her daughter's head. "I guess he wanted to see his little sister," she said, her voice full of emotion.

"Li'l sis," Micah said fondly, then coughed and winced at the pain.

"We don't want you coughing just yet," Nurse Paloma said. "I'll page the doctor for some medicine to clear your lungs. In the meantime, put this oxygen mask over your face before and after you speak, hear?" Her southern accent was warm, her blue eyes alight with concern.

Micah obediently placed the mask over his nose and mouth, breathing in lightly, eyes closed.

The women were silent as the nurse typed onto the tablet that rested at the foot of the bed. "Please don't tire him out," she said kindly. "He needs lots of rest. The doctor will be here soon."

Micah slowly removed the mask and pointed to Cecilia. "Gram," he whispered.

"Hello, dear." Cecilia moved to the other side of the bed, tears glistening in her eyes. "You're going to be all right." Relief caressed her words.

His gaze roamed around the room and landed on two vases of flowers and a bunch of bright-colored balloons with gold streamers on the windowsill. "Flowers?" He looked at his mother, then carefully replaced the oxygen mask.

Tess inspected the card next to each bouquet. "This one's from Aunt Kit. And this one's from Commander Hawkins and your whole company. Jasper sent the balloons. We've all been so worried about you."

"Why did Jasper send you balloons?" Eva asked suspiciously.

Micah closed his eyes for a moment, then took off the mask. "We're friends, remember?" he reassured Eva. "Painted . . ." He licked his lips. "Kit's house . . ."

Eva nodded slowly.

He took a shallow breath and swallowed, then his eyes met Tess's. "Didn't mean to scare. Anybody." His voice was halting and faint but his eyes were clear.

"It's all right," Tess murmured, leaning in and placing a kiss on his forehead. "I hear you were very brave." He tried to shake his head, but it was too painful. Then his eyes found his sister. "Hey, Evie." He wrinkled his nose as if it itched, then attempted a wink but found it difficult because of the stitches on his cheek. "Find any . . . nice feathers in . . . Seahaven?"

"How do you know about the feathers?" she squealed, astonished.

He put the mask back on and took several slow breaths. They watched and waited.

"My idea," he finally said, once the mask was off again.

"*Your* idea?" Eva was stunned.

Tess put an arm around Eva. "That's right, hon. He and Theatre Jasper cooked the whole thing up before he left."

"But I thought they were angel feathers."

Micah raised an eyebrow.

Eva looked at her feet. "I thought the angels were telling me they were keeping you safe."

"Sweetie, I don't think he meant for you to think they were from angels," Cecilia began.

"No," Micah whispered. He licked his lips, then gestured weakly to the cup of water. Tess leaned in and held the straw to his lips. "Evie. The feathers. I wanted you to be . . . hopeful. Remember that . . . art project? Hope . . . is the thing…" Breathless, he put the mask back on and closed his eyes.

"Hope is the thing with feathers that perches in the soul, and sings the tune without the words, and never stops at all," finished Cecilia, nodding her head in satisfaction. "Emily Dickinson."

"I remember," Eva said thoughtfully, sliding a section of her hair over her upper lip.

"That's all it was, hon." Tess laid a hand on Eva's head. "He wanted you to have something to look forward to, see? Something to take your mind off of missing him, to remind you to be hopeful."

"Was going to surprise you," Micah said, taking off the oxygen mask. "After Basic Training . . . Wanted to bring you a big . . . bouquet of feathers when I came home . . . so you'd know . . . it was my idea." He looked at the water cup and Tess held the straw to his lips again. "Thanks, Mom." He turned back to Eva. "Busted, huh? But you're right . . . I was safe. The whole time." He put the mask back on.

"No, you *weren't*. You got hurt!"

"He was safe, very safe indeed," said Colonel Hawkins, taking off his hat and walking briskly to Micah's bed. "Not only was he safe, young lady, he also saved the lives of two other soldiers! Nice to see you again, Tess." He gave a little wave to Cecilia and Eva as Tess introduced them.

"What do you mean?" Eva demanded as Hawkins saluted her brother.

Hawkins crouched beside her. "Your brother saw an accident happen and he ran down a steep hill to get two solders out from under the wreckage."

Her eyes widened and she looked to Micah for verification. He attempted a modest shrug—a bit difficult with a broken arm— and lifted off the mask. "Wow." She stared at her brother, then turned to Hawkins. "Are they okay now? The two soldiers?"

Hawkins straightened and scratched his bald head. "They're pretty banged up too, but they'll be on their feet in no time, just like our Micah here."

"So, Micah was safe the whole time? How could that be?" She gazed up at the imposing C.O. expectantly.

"Eva, I don't think you should—"

Hawkins raised a hand to stop Cecilia. "It's okay." He looked down at Eva. "We keep our soldiers as safe as possible. Always. But sometimes, things happen. Life intervenes."

"Like the accident that Micah saw?"

"That's right. Accidents. Bad weather. Sickness. Now and then, life has a way of interrupting and surprising us."

Eva frowned. "And that's when we're not safe anymore."

Hawkins bent down again and looked her in the eye. "We train our soldiers to look out for one another and we do the best we can for each other. That's the best kind of safety there is. That's how we protect one another in the United States Army."

"We keep each other safe," Tess murmured thoughtfully, while Eva struggled to understand.

"Angels too," Micah added from the bed, meeting Hawkins' gaze first, then Eva's.

"What do you mean?" Eva gripped the bedrail and studied her brother as he breathed into the oxygen mask again for a minute.

"Angels were there too," he finally said taking a short breath in between phrases. "I couldn't have gotten Aubree and Marcus out by myself. No way. I wasn't alone." His family looked at him in wonder. Eva started to tell him the names of the archangels but they were interrupted by Dr. Mullings.

"Excuse me, folks. I'm glad to see you all here." Mullings briskly addressed the group as he checked his watch. "Family is important to the healing process, but I need to examine this young man now, and then he needs time to rest, so please come back again later this afternoon."

"All right," Tess agreed, beginning to steer Eva and Cecilia toward the door. "Micah, we'll be back later."

"Wait," Micah rasped, weakly reaching out the hand that wasn't encased in the cast. "Evie. Come here."

Eva rushed back to his side and he lifted his unbroken arm to touch her nose briefly, although they could see that it hurt him to do so. "Boop!" Eva clapped a hand over her mouth in delight, then booped him back—ever so gently—on his forehead.

"What on earth was that all about?" Tess asked as they hustled out of the room. "You were always booping each other at home too."

"It's a brother-sister thing on the Netflix show *Schitt's Creek*," Cecilia replied, winking at Eva who gladly took her grandmother's hand. Cecilia nudged her daughter's elbow and teased, "Tess, don't you watch good television anymore?"

Eva's eyes widened. Whoever would have thought that Gram watched *Schitt's Creek?*

Tess was wondering the same thing. She'd observed her mother's homophobia for many years and found it appalling, especially after Micah had come out to all of them a few years ago. Evidently, people could change, even Cecilia. Perhaps *Schitt's Creek* had helped in some way to bring about that change.

"Eva, how do you even know about that show?" Tess admonished. She had overheard the staff talking about it in the Pearly Whites break room one day and it didn't sound like a show that an eleven-year-old should be watching.

"Micah and I used to watch it together," Eva replied, beaming one last grin at her brother before following her mother and Gram out the door.

# Chapter 31

On the back deck of the apartment building, Theatre Jasper obediently picked up a fork and speared a chunk of Glory's potato salad that was smeared with egg and mustardy mayo. He turned the fork this way and that, studying it as if it might tell him where Just Jasper had gone, then popped it into his mouth when he didn't get an answer. In spite of himself, he welcomed the pungent, oniony taste. "This is good," he said reluctantly, then checked his phone again. Nothing there but his screensaver—a photo of him and Jake right after they'd met. It was time to change that picture.

"I'm glad you like it," Glory murmured. "There's cold chicken in my kitchen too, if you feel like more protein."

"No thanks," he replied, still staring at his uncooperative phone. He turned it over in disgust. What was he expecting, a text from the cat?

"Tess said Cecilia is actually being quite helpful," Kit said, noticing Jasper's frustration and tactfully changing the subject. "I'm glad. Those two have had a hard time of it over the years. Seems like this whole thing with Micah may have finally brought them together." She chewed thoughtfully and took a sip of ice water. "Cecilia is going to stay in South Carolina for a while. Tess and Eva are coming back tomorrow."

Jasper was staring into the back yard and literally jumped in his seat when his phone rang. "Who is it?" asked Glory eagerly.

He held up a finger and took the call. "Hi Carlos! Have you heard anything—?" He set down his fork and listened intently. "Okay. Thanks. Yeah, I'm all right . . . They're okay too, thanks for asking." He glanced at Glory and Kit who were watching him intently. "Hey, thanks for checking in. Sure, I'll text you if. . . Okay, right." He laughed out loud and the women looked at each other, surprised but amused. "Thanks again."

"Was that the nice young man you met at Doc Brightman's this morning?" Glory asked as Jasper ate another forkful of salad, this time more enthusiastically.

Kit raised her eyebrows and leaned back in her chair. "A nice young man?" she teased. "Do tell!"

Jasper touched the brim of his suede fedora—found on his last foray through the theatre's costume department—and his fair cheeks pinkened up a bit. "Tell her," Glory said, sipping her iced tea and grinning.

"Carlos is a vet tech at the animal clinic. Carolina and I went there this morning to see if anyone had found Eva's cat. He said he'd stay in touch."

"And . . .?" Kit prompted, setting down her fork.

"He hasn't heard anything," Jasper replied.

"I'm glad that he stayed in touch with you," Glory said. "I'm going to bring out some watermelon. Are you game?"

"You bet!" Kit said, stretching her back.

"Jasper?"

"Sure." His shoulders relaxed a bit.

On Glory's way back to the patio, she almost dropped the platter of watermelon slices when they heard tires screeching in front of the house as a vehicle came to a sudden stop.

"What on earth—?" Kit was up in a flash, hurrying around the side of the house; Jasper and Glory were close behind.

There on the street, its motor idling, was Luca's silver truck. Teo stood on the front lawn, holding a bedraggled cat in his arms . . . a dark gray cat with white whiskers.

"You found him!" cried Theatre Jasper, rushing over to the boy.

Luca got out of the truck. "We were going out for ice cream and Teo saw this little guy limping along in the brush out on Purple Pelican Drive. He knew it was Eva's cat and—"

Teo had a firm grip on the furry creature; he wasn't going to let go of the cat for anything. "Look, his paw is hurt. Can you help him?"

Jasper moved closer to the boy and the cat. It was true. Its left front paw was bleeding. He crouched down and stroked the cat's head lightly, offering up a silent prayer of thanks.

"The Bright Side Clinic is closed, so we weren't sure what to do," Luca explained. He palmed the back of his head and looked at the others. "Any ideas?"

"Call Carlos back," Kit urged Jasper. "He'll help us."

Ten minutes later, they were at the clinic and Carlos was examining Jasper's paw while the adults hovered around. "Good timing. I was just cleaning up and getting ready to lock up for the night. Let me have a look-see, and if I can patch this up myself, I will. Otherwise, Doc Brightman will take care of ol' Jasper here." He glanced up at the group and smiled. "The cat, not the man." He winked at Theatre Jasper.

Kit chuckled, then said to the others. "Let's go to the waiting room now, okay?"

"I want to stay," Teo whispered.

"It's okay," Carlos said, glancing up at Luca while gently brushing out the cat's matted fur. "Your son can stay."

"I'll text Tess," Kit called over her shoulder.

Jasper nodded thankfully, then took off his hat and wiped the sweat from his forehead. "Thank you for doing this," he said, noticing how gentle Carlos was with the cat who was purring loudly as Teo scratched behind its ears.

"No probs," Carlos replied, setting down the brush and taking a closer look at the cat's paw. "What a good cat you are," he murmured, then glanced up at Teo. "Are you the hero who found him?"

"Yes." Teo replied excitedly. "This is my friend Eva's cat."

"Well, Eva is lucky to have a friend like you. You did the exact right thing by taking him to Jasper because he's a man with connections at the vet's office." Carlos smiled directly at Jasper, who blushed. The cat meowed plaintively when Carlos poured a little alcohol onto a cotton ball and cleaned the paw as tenderly as possible. "Hey, you're a theatre guy." He looked up at Jasper. "I think this cat looks like Mister Mistoffelees, am I right?"

Teo giggled as Carlos began to sing the song from *CATS* under his breath. It was out of tune, but Theatre Jasper was entranced, and Just Jasper didn't seem to notice. Carlos dried Jasper's paw, then secured the small wound with a dab of smelly ointment and a clean white bandage. "All done." He washed his hands in the metal sink next to the examining table. "No need for Doc Brightman tonight. This little guy will be just fine in a week, but you'll need to change the dressing twice a day." He handed Jasper a small bag containing a tube and several bandages.

Teo raced out to tell his dad the news.

"Thank you so much," Jasper said, picking the heavy cat up in his arms. "I'll give you my credit card."

Carlos waved his hand in the air. "Don't worry about it."

"But—"

"No buts, man. You did the right thing and I'm glad to help. That paw would have gotten infected if you'd waited any longer."

"Thank you again," Jasper replied uncertainly. He knew he should be taking Eva's cat back to the safety of Tess's apartment and a locked door, but he was held in place by the warmth in Carlos's gaze. He cleared his throat. What was happening? Why was he noticing Carlos's eyes? He paused as the cat snuggled into his neck. "I don't know what I would have done if we hadn't found this guy, or if anything bad had happened to him." He kissed the top of Just Jasper's head. "If you ever need anything, anything at all . . ." He swallowed hard.

"Thank you. Maybe we can grab a drink sometime?" He dried his hands on a paper towel, then tossed it over his head and behind him. It landed perfectly in the wastebasket by the door. "I'd love a backstage tour of your theatre if you ever have time."

"Sure thing, I'll call you tomorrow." But first . . . first he would call Jake. And then he would delete that outdated screensaver on his phone.

# Chapter 32

"Mom?" Eva scooted up on one elbow and held onto Tess's shoulder. They were sharing one double bed in the hotel room; Cecilia was sound asleep in the other. They had all watched *While You Were Sleeping* on the hotel's movie channel after having supper and visiting Micah again. Gram had fallen asleep halfway through the movie, but Eva and Tess had stayed up until the end. It was now after midnight and Eva had woken up, disoriented. "Mom!" She shook Tess's shoulder harder.

"What is it?" Tess sat up abruptly and looked down at her daughter.

"I had a bad dream." Tears filled Eva's eyes and she snuggled in to Tess who put her arm around her daughter and pulled her close.

Tess stifled a yawn. "Want to tell me about it?" She looked over at Cecilia, sound asleep on her back, both arms by her side. Her mother looked older and frailer. Had the two of them ever snuggled in bed like this when she was young? Had she ever, even once, been able to go to her mother for comfort from a bad dream? She turned back to Eva and kissed the top of her head.

"Micah was gone and we didn't know where he was, and you weren't anywhere. I was all alone."

"That sounds horrible." She held her close until Eva's tears stopped, then handed her a tissue. They scooted up so their backs were against the headboard. "Let's take three slow, easy breaths, okay?"

Eva slowly nodded.

"Follow me. One breath in . . . and out . . ." They closed their eyes as they fell into the rhythm of the breathing. When they were done, she lifted Eva's long hair off of her neck and curved it around her shoulder. "How do you feel now?"

"Better," Eva whispered, fingers smoothing the wrinkled sheet. She hesitated, then spoke again. "The dream is almost gone, but . . . can we maybe do that thing?"

"What thing?"

"That thing where we do the thankfuls back and forth."

"The Gratitude Game? We haven't played that in a long time."

"I always liked that game."

"Me too."

"Should we wake up Gram so she can play?" Eva asked eagerly, throwing off the covers playfully and sitting up on her knees.

"She's had a long, hard day, Eva. Let's try to be extra quiet so we don't wake her up."

"Okay." Eva lowered her voice and sat cross-legged next to Tess. "Who goes first?"

"The youngest always goes first. That's you." She tapped Eva's knee.

"I'm thankful that Micah is gonna be okay."

"Me too. I'm especially thankful that Luca found you and took you to Gram."

"I'm thankful that Micah loves me so much that he made a plan for leaving me all those feathers. Although I wish I hadn't thought they were angel feathers. That was so stupid."

"Hey," Tess replied, tilting Eva's chin up so their eyes met. "There's nothing wrong with thinking they were angel feathers."

"There's not?"

"Who knows? Maybe angels are watching over us all the time. Maybe an angel sent Luca to find you. Maybe an angel helped Micah save those two soldiers."

Eva told Tess about the four archangels and they sat silently together for a moment. "It's your turn, Mom."

"Okay." Tess drank some water from the glass beside the bed and offered it to Eva who finished it in one long gulp. "I'm grateful that my mother brought my daughter all the way to South Carolina."

Eva yawned. "I'm getting sleepy again, and I'm thankful that you played this game with me." She flopped onto her side, facing Tess, and hugged the pillow to her chest.

"I'll play this game with you any time." Tess eased herself back under the covers. "Micah is going to be okay. You know that, right?"

Eva nodded as her eyelids drifted shut.

"And you know that you'll never be alone?"

"Yes, 'cause even if something did happen to you and Micah, I'd still have Gram. And Aunt Kit."

"And both of the Jaspers, and Glory and her family."

"I forgot to say I'm thankful for Jasper the cat *and* Jasper the man." She opened her eyes and looked at Tess. "And Aunt Kit, too. Your turn."

"Okay, since we're still playing, I'll add that I'm thankful for Glory, Samuel, Kalila, Quinn and Chiara, and my bosses, the Pearls."

"I'm thankful for Charli even though she stopped writing to me. And Teo and Poppy, even though Teo might not like me anymore." She remembered the secret garden terrarium lying in pieces on her bedroom floor and frowned. That could be fixed, couldn't it? "Also, I'm really thankful for Luca. It was so dark last night, and I was running out of ideas for what to do next and I didn't want to go back to the apartment because you weren't there. Luca didn't tell me I was wrong for crying or for wanting to be with my brother."

"I'm glad he found you too." Tess smiled into the dark, noticing that her heart was beating a little faster as she thought of him.

Eva sleepily lifted herself onto one elbow again, still facing her mother. "No," she insisted, rubbing her eyes in an attempt to stay awake. "I'm thankful for *him*, not just for what he did to help me. I really like him." She rested her head against Tess's shoulder. "You like him too, don't you?" Eva whispered hopefully.

"Yes, I like him. Luca is a good person. He's a good father and—"

"No! I mean, do you like him the way you used to like him when you knew him before?"

Tess started to speak, then stopped and sighed.

"Mom?" Eva's voice held much more than a question.

"It's not about me liking him the way I used to, Eva. It's about whether the timing is right. And it isn't, not right now."

"That's not what Gram said."

Tess blinked at her sleepy daughter. "What did Gram say exactly?" she challenged.

"Er . . . nothing," Eva mumbled and rolled onto her back, squeezing her eyes shut. Tess rubbed her shoulder expectantly. "Okay, all right. She said that we have to love each other now because life is unpre . . . un . . ." She scrunched her nose, trying to remember the word.

"Unpredictable."

"Yes. And that she wished you would find someone who really loved you."

Tess was momentarily stunned—her mother wanted her to be happy. Remembering the conversation she'd had with Cecilia in the hospital that afternoon, she was actually starting to believe it.

"Also, on the plane, we talked about how I was so angry at you, and how I probably shouldn't have left the apartment the way I did. I'm sorry that I ran away, Mom. I wasn't thinking about how upset everyone would be."

Tess caught Eva's hand in hers and held it tight. "Thank you for saying that. I hope if you get angry like that again, you'll tell someone about it instead of leaving."

"I will."

"And Eva?"

"Yes, Mom?"

"I'm sorry that I didn't bring you with me yesterday when I flew down here. I won't ever leave you behind again."

Eva buried her head in her pillow and squeezed Tess's hand.

Close by, on the other bed, Cecilia smiled in the dark.

# Chapter 33

"Welcome home!" Glory and Kalila hurried down the porch steps to greet Tess and Eva as soon as Aunt Kit pulled into the driveway late the next afternoon. Glory, wearing a bright yellow flowered tunic and jeans, hugged Tess as she opened the car door before she even had a chance to get out. "We're so glad you're back!"

Tess gladly received Glory's embrace, then looked around at the front yard, the porch, and a visibly tired Aunt Kit. Home. This felt like home. Even with Micah so far away, it was home now.

Kalila hugged Eva tightly. "I missed you, kiddo! For a while there, I was worried you weren't going to be back for our baby and dog-sitting gig on Saturday."

"Evie!" Samuel cried as he raced down the porch steps. Eva cringed—but only a little—at the nickname she only allowed Micah to use. The name "Evie" sounded sweet coming from the little boy as he hugged her waist. "You'll never guess what happened to—"

"Come inside," Glory interrupted loudly, exchanging a pointed look with Kit as she briskly took Samuel's hand, lifted Tess's suitcase with her other hand, then headed purposefully for the porch. "Tess and Eva, put away your things, then come over to my place. I made seafood pie and corn on the cob!"

"There's another big surprise too," Samuel exclaimed, excitement peppering his voice.

"Hush now!" Kalila hustled him away, whispering in his ear, "Don't spoil the secret."

As she put her clothes away in her silent bedroom, Eva noticed two peculiar things. One was the secret garden terrarium she had made for Teo. It stood proudly on her desk, all in one piece, although she distinctly remembered it falling to the floor and smashing to pieces when she had flung the altar aside. Was that only two days ago? Who had fixed it? Also, all of the feathers were now arranged in a circle on her dresser with a different photo of Micah in the center.

Eva peered into the terrarium and inhaled the rich scent of earth and growing things. She touched the ceramic frog which miraculously hadn't broken. Then she walked to the dresser and stared at the photo of Micah, now surrounded by the feathers she had collected. She remembered earlier this week when she had been certain they were angel feathers. Now she knew better, but she touched them reverently anyway. "They're just as good as angel feathers," she whispered. "Because my brother sent them to me."

She also knew it wasn't angels who had fixed the terrarium and arranged the feathers in a circle, but she felt happy because she understood that only someone who loved her would have taken the time to do this. What Colonel Hawkins had said about people being angels for one another was starting to make sense.

As she entered the living room, she noticed another peculiar thing. Just Jasper was lying in his usual place on top of the comfy chair by the window. When she had come into the apartment, she had kissed him on the head and he had meowed politely, then promptly gone back to sleep. But now, as she waited for her mother, she could see that Jasper had uncurled himself and was stretched out full length with his front paws in the air. But! There was a bandage on one of those paws.

Eva kneeled on the chair so she could inspect his leg. "What happened to you?" she said plaintively, stroking his head. The cat yawned, then hopped down onto the chair on three legs and rubbed his sturdy gray head against Eva's thigh.

Tess came into the room, rubbing lotion on her hands and arms. "Mom!" Eva scrambled off the chair and Jasper followed her, limping slightly. "Something happened to Jasper while we were gone! Look!"

They both knelt on the floor and the cat rubbed up against them, purring mightily. "Glory will tell us," Tess said, scratching Jasper's tummy as he rolled onto his back, eyes closed in bliss. "Let's have supper, then we both need to get ready for bed. The Pearls have been understanding, but there's a lot of work to catch up on."

Carolina was knocking on Glory's apartment door just as Eva and Tess opened theirs to leave. "Hey guys!" Carolina happily hugged Tess and high-fived Eva. "Welcome back!"

Samuel flung open the door to let them in and immediately raced toward through the apartment.

Eva followed him into the kitchen where Glory and Kalila were placing a fragrant seafood pie and golden ears of hot corn on the table. "What happened to Jasper?" Eva asked, halting at one of the straight-backed kitchen chairs that had been painted bright yellow.

"Jasper's still at the theatre, sweetie," Glory replied, taking a tub of butter from the fridge. "He won't be here for supper."

"I think she's referring to our cat," said Tess, entering the kitchen arm in arm with Carolina.

Glory looked at Carolina and raised her eyebrows.

Carolina sat in the yellow chair and turned to face the worried girl. "When you ran out of the house on Thursday night, your cat ran out after you and—"

Eva covered her mouth with both hands, her eyes wide. "What happened to him? How did he get back? Who found him?"

Carolina replied with a hint of mischief, "We'll never know exactly where he went or what happened to him, because the silly cat won't tell us." They chuckled. "But the good news is that Teo found—"

"Teo?" Tess interrupted. "How on earth—"

The others took turns telling the story of the wayward cat. Aunt Kit, entering from the back door, told the final bit. "Jasper has been putting medicine on your cat's paw and changing the bandage."

Eva blinked away tears. She knew it was her fault that Jasper had run away because she must have left all the doors open in her hurry to leave. She quickly said a silent thank-full to Who-ever-Up-There might be listening. The fact was that Teo had recognized her cat and decided to save him; she hoped this meant Teo still wanted to be her friend. Maybe what Colonel Hawkins had said was true—that friends and family, and sometimes even strangers, are all angels because it's up to everyone to do the best they can to keep each other safe. Teo might be an angel. In fact, she might be an angel herself! It was definitely something worth thinking about.

"Grammie, don't forget the big SURPRISE," shouted Samuel, bouncing up and down in his seat.

"I haven't forgotten, love," Glory replied, wiping her hands on her apron. She came to the table and rested her hands on the boy's shoulders. Everyone fell silent, looking expectantly at Eva who suddenly realized she was the center of attention. "Eva, an old friend of yours stopped by for a visit yesterday, and I invited her for supper once I knew you were coming home." Glory turned toward the back hallway where the bedrooms were and called out, "You can join us in the kitchen now, sweetie."

Suddenly, there was Charli! She was standing shyly in the doorway, hopefully grinning at Eva.

Eva jumped out of her chair and ran to her friend. "I can't believe you're here!"

"I told you it was a BIG surprise!" shouted Samuel, who practically fell off his chair in his excitement.

The girls hugged each other for a long time while everyone applauded. Eva squeezed Charli's hands when they finally separated. "I still can't believe it! How did you . . . Why didn't you . . .?" She paused and hugged her friend again.

"Girls, sit down, sit down!" Glory bustled around, leading the girls back to the table.

"My mom had business to take care of in New Haven. Something about the house, I think." Charli rolled her eyes. "Anyway, I begged her to drive up here before we fly back to California."

"But you didn't—"

"I'm sorry that I stopped sending you emails. Once Mom and I knew we were coming back east, I stopped writing because I was afraid I'd spoil the surprise."

"But I wrote you letters, too. *Real* letters, with paper envelopes and stamps and everything."

"I didn't get any letters in the mail." Charli replied. "Maybe I gave you the wrong address. I'll ask Mom to write it down for you this time."

"Is your mother hiding in the back hallway too?" Tess asked, looking over her shoulder.

"No, she went back to our bed and breakfast downtown, but she's got a rental car and will pick me up later. Our plane leaves from Portland tomorrow. I'm so glad you guys got back to Seahaven before we had to leave!"

Eva, happily bumping shoulders with Charli, looked around the table as Glory invited the group to hold hands while she said a blessing over the food. Aunt Kit's head was bowed and she was smiling, her silver hair pushed back from her face with a green and yellow ribbon. Tess was staring into her empty plate, also smiling. Carolina sat between Kalila and Samuel on the other side of the table. Their heads were also bowed, except for Samuel's. He was looking right at Eva, his mouth turned upward in a mischievous grin. Eva smiled back, then put one finger to her lips. Glory was at the head of the table, her dark skin radiant as she said words of praise and blessing.

Eva's stomach rumbled, but she held tight to her mother's hand on one side and Charli's hand on the other. The only people missing were Jasper and Micah. Even so, Eva thought, this was what it felt like to be part of a big family, even though she was only related to two of them. She waited happily for the blessing to end, then bit eagerly into a warm, buttery ear of corn. They'd never had a meal like this in New Haven.

Glory dished out the rest of the food, and Eva took in the way that Kalila, Samuel and their grandmother interacted. They were a real family even though Glory didn't have a husband anymore and the kids' mom was far away serving the country. Maybe families were all about love and not about who was actually in them. Maybe she didn't need to have the same kind of family that Charli had, with two parents and a bunch of siblings. If what made a real family was all about the loving, then she and Micah and Mom were perfect already, no changes necessary. She giggled out loud and almost choked on her next bite of corn.

"Easy, hon." Tess patted Eva's back.

"I'm okay, Mom." And she meant that in more ways than one.

Eva dug into the seafood pie with gusto. Back in New Haven, there hadn't been much in the way of home cooking, much less food bursting with flavors of the sea like this pie. "Mom, let's get this recipe. We can make it the next time Quinn and Chiara come to visit."

Later, after Carolina had zoomed away in her jeep, Charli left with her mother, promising to meet Eva and Tess for breakfast before their flight the next morning. Kalila led Samuel to his room for a bedtime story, and Eva stood at the kitchen sink, helping Glory with the dishes. Kit and Tess were on the back patio—Kit with her tea, Tess with her coffee. The window over Glory's sink was wide open, so they could hear bits and pieces of the women's friendly conversation. At one point, Eva heard Aunt Kit say, "You owe Luca a phone call."

"I know," Tess replied wearily. "I was going to call him when we were in South Carolina, but when Mom showed up with Eva, it got complicated."

"I understand, but you're home now. No more excuses." Kit's voice was firm.

Tess sighed and Eva heard her scraping back her chair, preparing to come inside.

Kit spoke. "Glory thought about inviting Luca and Teo to your welcome-home supper tonight but I didn't think that was wise. You need to talk to Luca first."

Eva looked up at Glory who rinsed the last soapy dish and set it in the drainer for Eva to dry. Glory had heard the conversation too. "I wish you *had* invited them," Eva said sadly. "I want to see them again."

"I know, darlin'. But Kit is right. This probably wasn't the best time for Tess and Luca to meet again."

"When *will* be the best time?" Eva impatiently dried the last dish and set it in the cupboard. She laid the damp dish towel over the faucet and expectantly leaned against the sink while Glory lowered herself into a kitchen chair.

"I sure don't know, baby girl. My heart tells me that Luca and your mama belong together." She tapped her nose. "But sometimes people can't see what's right in front of them."

Eva's forehead wrinkled in thought. "I wish I could find a way to make them see."

Glory shook her head doubtfully. "I've found it best not to meddle in other people's business."

Eva didn't hear her; she had just had a splendid idea.

"Thank you for supper," she said politely, giving Glory a quick hug as Tess came in and they headed back to their apartment.

Eva gathered Just Jasper in her arms and headed for her bedroom after saying a speedy good night to Tess. "I'll come in later so we can play a little bit of the Gratitude Game again, okay?" Tess called after her.

Eva heard the hope in her mother's voice and almost agreed to the game to make her happy, when she suddenly realized that she actually wanted to play the game again. "Okay! I'll be ready in half an hour." In her room, she carefully shut the door and set Jasper down on the bed. He looked up at her, his fern-green eyes studying her intensely. Whenever he observed her this way, she thought he was about to open his mouth and say something wise. "Now, Jasper," she said seriously, grabbing a notebook and a green marker from her desk. "I've got a plan. Listen, and tell me what you think."

Tess surveyed her bedroom with weary eyes. She had left in such a hurry on Tuesday; clothes, books, and work papers were scattered everywhere. It didn't feel quite like her room, so she spent several minutes tidying up, then sat on the bed and reached for her phone. She took a deep breath, then directed Siri to call Luca. Best to get this over with. As Siri confirmed her request, the photo of Luca and Teo at Simply Sweets flashed onto the screen to remind her who she was calling . . . as if she could forget. He answered after one ring. "Tessa! How are you? Is Micah okay?"

A warm rush of happiness settled in her heart as she heard his familiar voice with the faint foreign accent. She tried to ignore it. "We're all fine. Eva and I are back in Seahaven and I'm calling to thank you for—"

"Graças a Deus," he said, and she could picture him standing there with the phone in one hand and the other behind his head, staring up at the ceiling . . . or the sky. Was he in his house or was he outside? As she imagined him in both places, she felt streams of delight whispering through her body, but reluctantly pushed them away. "I was so worried about you and Eva, and Teo was worried about Eva's cat." His words rushed over her like a cool waterfall. "Kit says his paw is healing, yes?"

He paused for a breath and Tess broke in. "Luca." Her voice was tense, strained. She spoke slowly, so as not to betray her rapidly beating heart. "I'm glad that Teo found Jasper. Please thank him for me. And thank *you* for keeping Eva safe. It means the world to us."

Luca was quiet for a long time and Tess thought he had put the phone down until he said, "You are welcome, and I will thank Teo for you. But I would like it if you would thank him in person. Would you come over one night this week for supper? You and Eva?"

"Thank you, but . . . that's a bad idea."

The silence stretched out again and Tess swallowed nervously. His disappointment widened the space between them as she heard him murmur reluctantly, "Okay."

Tess remembered how happy she had felt with him last week at Pete's Fish Shack and then at Eva's play. Then she remembered how happy she was with Eva last night, playing the Gratitude Game. She was realizing that there were different kinds of happiness, and it wasn't possible to have them all.

Luca's voice broke through her thoughts. "I have been thinking of moving Sea Dove Charters to New Bedford. One of my cousins bought a house there this spring. Seahaven is . . . I thought we could . . . but now there is no reason to stay."

The silence widened and Tess knew he was waiting for her to respond. Tears came to her eyes. This was it then. There really was no more hope for her and Luca. Their love story was over. No turning back. "I'm sorry, Luca. I'm . . . I'm really sorry." She ended the call and wiped her eyes with the hem of her T-shirt. Oh, she was sorry all right, but she had made the right choice. She couldn't afford to spend time falling in love with Luca all over again when things were finally starting to feel right with Eva. It was time to make the effort to keep Eva at the top of her priority list instead of the bottom where her children had been for the last four years. She just couldn't see how it was possible for Luca and Teo to be a part of that list too.

# Chapter 34

The next morning, Eva woke up bright and early. She had showered and dried her hair long before Tess's alarm went off. "You sure look ready to greet the day," Tess said with a yawn as she entered the kitchen and headed for the coffee maker.

"Sit down, Mom," Eva directed. "*I'm* making breakfast today. One English muffin, lightly toasted, comin' right up!"

Tess looked surprised. When was the last time Eva had been thoughtful enough to get breakfast ready? "Thanks, hon. I have about ten minutes before Kalila gets here to baby— I mean, to *sit* with you."

Eva chuckled as she peered into the toaster to check on the muffin's progress. Her mom didn't like her toast too dark. "Believe me, we're not going to *sit* today."

"You're not?" Tess took a long swallow of coffee from her Best Mom mug and sat at the table, watching Eva busy herself at the counter.

"Nope. We're going to—" She hesitated as she set the perfectly-toasted English muffin and a jar of Glory's blueberry jam in front of her mother.

"What?" Tess spread the jam on one half of the muffin, attempting to meet Eva's evasive eyes.

Eva smiled shyly and looked away. "There's a lot to do to get ready for tomorrow night."

Tess raised her eyebrows as she swallowed more coffee. "Tomorrow night?"

"For one thing, it's your birthday," Eva stated, staring at her mother in disbelief. "For another thing, it's the Sands of Time Anniversary Gala. Remember? Fancy dinner? The Ben Shepherd concert?"

"I remember. We're going to sit at Aunt Kit's table." Tess attempted enthusiasm but it was waning fast; her mind was otherwise occupied and her heart was heavy. A Gala Celebration was the last place she wanted to be tomorrow.

"Yes!" Eva sounded exasperated. "And tonight, we're going shopping with Carolina. For special dresses to wear!"

"That's right. I'm sorry, hon. This whole week has been . . ."

Eva joined her mother at the table with her own on-the-verge-of-burnt English muffin. "I know," she agreed, adding a spoonful of blueberry jam before taking the first bite.

Tess took a final gulp of coffee and set her mug in the sink along with the now empty plate. She turned to Eva who was diligently shaking food into Jasper's bowl and crunching her muffin at the same time. "What do you and Kalila need to do to get ready for the Gala?"

Eva began to answer but was interrupted by Kalila as she entered the apartment. "Hey Gilmore girls, I'm here!"

Tess blinked and glanced at Eva hopefully. No response. Of course. "We're in the kitchen." She brightened as the energetic teen appeared in the doorway. The beads on her multiple braids were all different colors today. Tess picked up her purse from the kitchen counter and headed out the back door. "You two have a good time today."

Eva ran to the living room window and waited until she saw her mother's car pull away. Kalila put her hands on Eva's shoulders. "So, kiddo, are you tired from your trip? Want to watch movies all day?" She headed for the sofa and the remote, kicking off her new purple flip flops. "It's hot outside and cool in here. If you want, we can write a letter to Micah later."

"No way!" Eva grabbed the remote from Kalila's hand and tossed it back on the couch. "We have work to do." She proceeded to explain her plan.

Kalila raised her eyebrows as she listened, then eagerly leaned in closer.

"I don't see the point of going to the Gala tonight," Tess said to Aunt Kit the next morning as they walked to Sunrise Beach.

"I'm sure you're tired from all that's happened in the last few days, Tess, but think of the Gala as a fun night out. You deserve to have a little fun!" The morning was slightly cool; the mist hovering over the horizon hadn't quite burned off yet. Kit wore white capris and a colorful batik tunic that flowed gracefully over her slim hips. "It's the perfect way to celebrate your birthday." Tess looked doubtful.

They arrived at the beach where both women kicked off their flip flops and walked toward the water which was ebbing and flowing in the low tide shallows. The sand was gritty yet soft under their bare feet. "Mom sure did step up this time," Tess said. "She's making my life easier. Eva and I will go down every other weekend to give Mom a break."

"I'm glad Cecilia's helping out. Now, I would love for you to be at my table at the Gala tonight; it might help to take your mind off of Micah. Olivia and Violet are looking forward to seeing you again, and I don't want you to miss Ben Shepherd!"

Tess turned her face away from the sunrise and studied Kit's eager face which was suffused with the soft morning light. Her aunt found a way to cherish each sunrise, the same way that she cherished each day of her life, even though she had lost her fiancé when she was twenty years old. Tess inhaled the vibrant ocean air. Maybe it would be good to get out and meet people at the Gala, even though those people wouldn't be Luca. She lifted her shoulders up to her ears, purposely tensing them, then let them drop with a short sigh. She could at least try to enjoy dinner and the concert, but she would forget about celebrating her birthday. "Okay, I'll go. I promised Eva, and we're going shopping tonight for new dresses."

They faced the sunrise again and Kit put her arm around Tess. "Is there anything else on your mind? Besides Micah?" She noticed her niece's anxious expression. "Is it Luca?" Tess abruptly turned around and headed back toward their flip flops. "Wait! You called Luca, didn't you?" Kit caught up with Tess who was rubbing her forehead with both hands.

"I did, last night. I called him to say thank you for taking care of Eva and for rescuing her cat."

"And . . ."

"He wanted Eva and me to go over there for dinner next week."

"That's wonderful!" Kit said as they slipped their sandy feet back into flip flops and headed back to the street. No response. "Isn't it?" Her niece was silent. "Tess?"

She looked away and shrugged as if it didn't matter. But it did. It mattered a great deal. She just had no idea what to do about it. "I told him no."

"Why on earth would you do that? He obviously is smitten with you. You didn't see him the night he and Teo brought Eva's cat back."

"No, I didn't. But—"

Kit walked a little faster and caught up with Tess as they reached Beach Blessing Way. "Be honest with me, Tess." They stopped as they reached Kit's driveway. "What are your feelings for him?"

Tess squeezed her eyes shut.

"The truth." Kit laid a hand on Tess's arm. "From your heart."

Tess shuffled her feet in the cool grass and sighed. Her aunt had a way of making people feel safe in her presence. "All right, you win. I still have feelings for him."

"Try to be more specific, dear."

"Feelings like . . ." Tess closed her eyes and gave in to a half-smile. ". . .like when we were kids. Only better." She paused, gazing into Kit's kind eyes. "But—"

"Let's sit on the porch," Kit said, making her way to the love-seat. She brushed the sand from her feet, then stretched her legs onto the flowered cushion.

Tess settled into the rocker and cleared her throat. "Thanks for waking me up for the sunrise," she said nervously. There was probably a lecture coming from Aunt Kit and she wasn't sure she was ready to hear it.

"Don't change the subject," Kit gently admonished.

"Okay, then. Let me have it." Tess tucked her hands under her thighs.

"Have what?"

"The speech you're going to give about why I should see Luca again."

Kit chuckled and began weaving her long hair into a loose braid. "Oh, Tess."

"Go ahead. I'm ready for the speech."

"I don't have a speech this time, dear. What I do have is a suggestion. I want you to tell me all of your *buts*."

"All of my *what?*"

"I'll say 'You should see Luca again' and you counter with 'But. . .' until you run out of objections. Think of it like a game. Sound like a plan?"

Leave it to Aunt Kit to try to make this into a fun activity. She pulled her hands from under her legs and inspected her nails.

They were looking a bit ragged. If she was going to the Gala, she should probably polish them. It had been a long time since she'd had a manicure.

"Tess?"

"All right, why not?" She would humor Aunt Kit and then eat breakfast. This little game wasn't going to change anything.

"Good." Kit rested her loose braid over one shoulder and leaned forward. "You should see Luca again."

"But there's not enough hours in the week. There's my new job, and Micah's in the hospital, and I want to be spending time with Eva. Where would I fit in time with Luca too?"

"You should see Luca again."

"But . . . Teo is still grieving the loss of his mother. He doesn't want me around."

"You should see Luca again."

Some game! It felt like Kit wasn't listening to her. "But Eva is finally starting to let me get close again and I don't want to ruin that."

"You should see Luca again." Kit's voice was low and calm; she kept her eyes on Tess.

"But . . ." Tess glanced at Kit, lowering her voice to a whisper. "But what if I start seeing him again and it doesn't last?"

Kit nodded thoughtfully. "You should start seeing Luca again."

"If it doesn't last, I don't think I could stand the heartache again."

"You should see Luca again."

"But what if he doesn't really love me? Cameron never—"

Kit swung her legs to the floor and scooted over on the loveseat so she was closer to Tess's rocker. "This isn't about Cameron, honey. Cameron is long gone and he didn't deserve you. He didn't deserve any of you!"

"I know that." Tess stood abruptly and began pacing the length of the porch. "But not all love stories are meant to last."

"Now it's time for me to add a *but*," Kit replied. "You're right. Every love story isn't meant to last, but many are. The only way to know which kind of love story you're in is to take a chance."

Tess looked away from Kit and up at the cloudy sky.

"We have to take chances in life, Tess. Otherwise, what's the point?" A small pesky fly buzzed around Kit's face and she waved it away.

"Okay, I hear you. But if Luca and I start seeing each other and it doesn't work out, I honestly don't think I could stand it."

Kit stood and stretched languorously. "You may think that, dear, but the truth is you're a strong, resilient woman."

Tess raised her eyebrows doubtfully.

"Look at all you've accomplished in your life!" Kit admonished. "You've raised two creative, kind, intelligent children. You've made lifelong friends in Chiara and Quinn. And on top of that, you've worked hard, educated yourself, and provided for your family. *You.* You did all that, Tess."

Tears came to Tess's eyes and she quickly wiped them away. What Kit was saying was true, but she had never thought of herself that way before. Looking back on her life with this new perspective, she could see that she had much to be proud of. Sure, Micah hadn't told her he was joining the Army, but what about all the things he *had* told her? She was the first one he'd come out to when he was sixteen. She was the first one to hear about his relationship with Leo, including all the ups and downs of that fragile time. And yes, Eva had become distant, but they were connecting beautifully now; things were better in her life than they had been in a very long time. Her relationship with Cecilia was also improving, amazingly enough. As for Cameron, she had tried—against all odds and for many years—to make it work, for the kids' sake. She had loved him, once upon a time—before she got pregnant, before the children. But she had never felt with Cameron what she had felt with Luca . . . what she still felt for Luca now.

Kit motioned Tess to join her at the porch railing. "I'm certain you'll be able to handle anything . . . *anything* that comes your way. Look at how you're handling Micah's accident."

Tess dabbed her eyes with the hem of her new T-shirt, emblazoned with the Seahaven logo and slogan: *A Harbor of Safety for All Who Pass Through.*

Kit bumped her arm against Tess's. "You're aware of this already but I'm going to tell you again—"

They were interrupted by Jasper's little red Nissan as it turned into their driveway. He got out and headed for the porch, whistling the first few bars of Nina Simone's "Feeling Good," then halted on the steps when he saw the two women standing there. "Hey there!" He glanced at his smartwatch nervously.

"Nice to see you, Jasper."

He took off his *Phantom of the Opera* baseball cap and smacked it against the railing, then placed it carefully back on his head. "I know it's early; I was—"

"You don't owe us an explanation, young man," Kit teased. "Even though it's 7 a.m. and the sun is already up."

Jasper's fair skin turned a mottled pink as he stammered. "I was . . . I was with Carlos. We went out for drinks and then back to his place for coffee and we ending up talking all night. Then we drove out to the Marginal Way in Ogunquit and watched the sun rise." He paused to take a breath.

Kit beamed at him. "I'm glad you've found someone new!"

Jasper climbed the three steps slowly until he was at eye level with them. "Oh, I—"

"Tess can take a lesson from you."

"Tess can . . . what?"

Kit leaned toward Jasper conspiratorially and whispered, "She's thinking of seeing Luca again."

"How exciting!" Jasper exclaimed. "Luca's a good guy." He tossed his hat in the air and caught it, then plopped it back on his head. "I'm heading in to shower and take a quick nap before work. We're gearing up for the Gala tonight."

"See you there!" Kit called after him, then turned back to Tess. "Good for Jasper, eh?"

"Yes," Tess mused. "Good for him."

"Now, I need to get ready for my day," Kit continued. "Olivia and I are going to the Farmer's Market in Wells and then we're going shopping in Kennebunkport; I'm going to treat myself to a new dress too. I've been meaning to tell you that my agent—Marshall Sorenson—is coming to the Gala and he'll be at our table. He's driving up from the city this afternoon." She ran her fingers lightly up and down her throat. "I want you and Eva to meet him."

Tess studied her aunt's face for a moment, her curiosity piqued. "Marshall? I remember hearing you talk about him from time to time. Is he coming here on business?"

"I'm not sure," Kit said hesitantly. "He and I have always been friends. Since the day he 'discovered' me waitressing at the Driftwood Inn when I was twenty-two and he was thirty-one. His wife died last year. Pancreatic cancer. It was difficult to lose her that way. The three of us used to hang out in New York whenever I was in the city. She was a good friend right up until the day she died. I miss her."

"I'm sorry," Tess murmured.

"Thank you, dear. She was special. Marshall and I still talk and email frequently. When I mentioned the Gala, and how excited I was about meeting Ben Shepherd, Marshall asked if he could join me."

Tess raised her eyebrows. This was getting more interesting by the minute. "So, what you're telling me is . . . you have a date for the Gala and he's special enough that you're going shopping for a new dress?"

"I guess you could say that," Kit said lightly as she undid the heavy braid and let her hair fall over her shoulders again.

"That's wonderful!" Tess hugged her aunt. "It's been a long time since Ollie."

"Of course, there have been other men along the way."

"Really?"

"Don't look so surprised, dear! I'm a sensual woman and I have needs like everyone else. But none of those men will ever compare to my first love."

"Even Marshall?" Tess asked.

"Even Marshall," Kit agreed. She paused and touched Tess's hair where it met her shoulder.

"The first time you told me about Ollie, I remember hoping that I would meet someone just like him."

"I think you already have."

Tess's heart thudded in her chest. Maybe it was true. What if Luca was her Ollie? She hugged herself. It suddenly seemed possible.

"Now. What I was beginning to tell you before Jasper showed up is that when Ollie died, I thought my world had ended. I didn't think I was strong enough to even go on living. For a while, I was barely existing. But the fact is, I *was* strong enough. I got through it."

"You did, didn't you?" Tess met her aunt's eyes.

"I did, but what I want to impress upon you is that I didn't do it alone. Ollie's mom and sister made the hugest difference. Also, it took a long time."

"I can only imagine."

Kit made her way to the porch steps. "My point is that if you were to let go of all these *buts* and start seeing Luca again, and it didn't work out, you are more than strong and resilient enough to come out on the other side with your heart and soul intact. I promise."

Tess pondered Kit's words.

"We become stronger at our broken places, Tess. Focus on that, and all of your *buts* might just disappear." She hugged Tess briefly and strode down the steps and back to her cottage.

# Chapter 35

Tess thought about Kit's words as she showered and dressed for work—she was working nine to three even though it was Saturday, to make up for the time she'd lost visiting Micah—and as she ate breakfast with Eva who was bubbling over with excitement about the Gala. Tess pondered the possibility of calling Luca and accepting his invitation for dinner at his house, but then she remembered he was probably going to move to New Bedford. Her stomach fluttered at the thought of telling him she'd changed her mind. Aunt Kit thought she was strong enough to handle a broken heart, but was she brave enough to start a new relationship, or to restart an old one? Did Luca care enough about her to stay in Seahaven now?

All of this whirled around in her mind as she drove to work, parked her car, and messaged Micah and Cecilia that she was thinking of them. Distracted, Tess said a hurried hello to Marilyn instead of stopping for the usual five minutes of good-natured Seahaven gossip. She did her work, but her mind and body were restless. At noon, she realized she'd forgotten to pack a sandwich, so she took lunch orders from the staff members and headed to King's Deli a few blocks away.

On her way out of King's, a large takeout box in her hands, she bumped into Luca who was on his way in. He had been on her mind all morning, so she blinked in surprise as she stared at him. Was it possible that she had actually summoned him with her thoughts? *Ridiculous.* Or was it another gift of synchronicity from the universe? *Possibly.* "Hi, Luca," she said, her mouth suddenly dry. She was grateful that her hands had the deli box to hold onto.

"Tessa!" He leaned in to kiss her cheek, then changed his mind and pulled away. "How are you?" He held the door as she stepped down to the sidewalk.

"I'm fine." She looked up at him. His brown eyes were subdued, his gaze intent. She glanced at his lips, then cleared her throat. "And you?"

"I am . . . okay," he replied cautiously.

Tess took a breath. This was it. He had shown up seemingly out of nowhere; maybe the universe was giving her a chance to make things right. "Luca, I'd like to—"

"Luca? Are you coming in?" A petite woman with a mass of honey-blonde hair joined Luca at the door; she appeared to be in her twenties. "Oh, hi there!" She turned her radiant smile on Tess for a second, then focused her attention back to Luca. "Sorry for the interruption, but I already ordered for both of us and—"

"Thank you." Luca rubbed his chin and glanced awkwardly from the young woman to Tess and back again.

Confused, Tess stood on the sidewalk as carefree, casually-dressed tourists walked by, completely oblivious to how hard her shattered heart was pounding. She pressed her lips together and tried to think clearly. *Where are my manners?* She would be perfectly polite, then head back to the safety of Pearly Whites. Where she belonged. It was obvious she didn't belong here. "Hello, I'm Tess Gilmore."

"Nice to meet you; I'm Madison Montgomery," the other woman replied cheerfully. "Hurry up, Luca," she said, hinting at an implied familiarity. "Don't let your grilled turkey sandwich get cold. We have a lot to talk about!"

"Yes, we do," Luca replied. "I will be right there." Madison disappeared into the deli, leaving a lingering scent of jasmine in the air. He turned around to speak to Tess again, but she was gone.

# Chapter 36

"I sn't it beautiful?" Eva stood with Tess at the entrance to the Gala that evening, her mouth slightly open in wonder. The large, high-ceilinged restaurant behind the theatre had been transformed into a summer wonderland. Thousands of incandescent white fairy lights were strung around the branches of potted evergreens that surrounded the space. Twelve large round tables were covered with alternating cloths of red and gold, each with a stunning centerpiece of fresh white flowers.

"It is," Tess agreed, adjusting the thin straps of her new periwinkle dress as she looked around. "I've never been to the theatre restaurant, but I'm guessing it didn't look like this yesterday." If she had to be here, she might as well admire the beauty that Savannah's *Life Celebrations* team had created.

"Tess! Eva!" Aunt Kit was on the other side of the restaurant, beckoning them to join her. The place was beginning to fill up. "Don't you look lovely!" she exclaimed as they made their way to one of the tables that was closest to the stage. Kit wore an exquisite sleeveless white dress embroidered with bold-colored flowers, all of which set off her silver hair. She looked regal yet openhearted, like a kind, benevolent queen.

"These are great seats!" Eva said, bouncing on her gold-sandaled toes and swishing the skirt of her new emerald-green dress with delight. "I wanted to be close to the stage, but I didn't think we'd be *this* close! Thank you, Aunt Kit!"

"You're very welcome, dear." Kit blew her a kiss, then turned to the distinguished gray-haired man who rose as she introduced him. "Marshall, I'd like you to meet my niece Tess Gilmore and her daughter Eva. Ladies, this is my agent, Marshall Sorenson."

"Pleased to meet you both," he said, shaking each of their hands heartily in turn.

"We've heard a lot about you." Tess felt warmed by his touch. He reminded her of the handsome actor Colin Firth, minus the British accent.

"And I, you," Marshall replied. Then he looked pointedly at Kit. "But I'd like them to know that I'm not just your agent."

Baffled, Eva looked between Kit and Marshall. "You have a *boyfriend?*"

"Don't sound so surprised, dear," Kit said, chuckling. "I'm not dead yet!"

"Wow," said Eva under her breath as she settled into her seat. "That's an extra surprise that I didn't see coming."

"Extra surprise?" asked Tess, placing her sweater on the back of the chair.

Eva's face flushed and she quickly said, "Never mind, it's nothing," then immediately started up a conversation with Kit.

The others soon joined them. Carolina was in a shockingly short red silk dress that almost matched her fiery hair. Olivia wore a casual yellow and white striped sundress, and Violet had on a silky pair of palazzo pants and sleeveless top that were varying shades of her name.

As the meal was served, Tess felt as if she were going through the motions. Eating. Smiling. Pretending to be interested in the lively conversation flowing around her. Nodding to give the appearance of joining in. She was glad she had come, but only for Eva's sake. The rest of her wished she was at home in her comfy pajamas.

"Weren't you able to fill the other seats at our table?" Olivia asked as she speared a slender stalk of broccoli.

Tess noticed as Kit and Eva exchanged a secretive look.

"The seats are filled," Kit replied, looking quickly at Tess. "But their occupants won't be here until later."

"Who on earth did you—" began Violet, but she was shushed loudly by Eva who put one finger to her lips, imploring Violet to end the conversation. Violet looked puzzled, but turned her attention back to her salmon.

"Oh boy, strawberry cheesecake!" Eva declared as dessert was served. She dug in as soon as the plate was set in front of her by one of the female servers. Marshall excused himself, saying he was allergic to strawberries and headed to the men's room.

As Eva was enjoying her dessert, Savannah Adams approached their table and crouched beside her. JJ sucked his thumb and hid behind his mother, clutching her hand. Savannah wore a slim black skirt and white blouse with the colorful *Life Celebrations* logo embroidered on the pocket. A simple dragonfly charm rested at her throat on a silver chain.

"Thank you again for staying with Zannah this afternoon," Savannah said after Eva had introduced her to the table. "I have no idea what you did with that dog, but she was tuckered out and is sound asleep right now! If we get invited back to Seahaven, I will definitely hire you and Kalila again." Savannah placed a pale pink envelope beside Eva's plate. "Here's the payment that we agreed on when I first met you." Eva started to protest then clapped a hand over her mouth as Savannah continued. "I didn't forget; we made a deal yesterday. Ben and I are keeping that deal, but we want you to have this anyway."

Eva blushed as she thanked Savannah. Tess looked confused. What a strange conversation. She looked at Kit who was whispering in Marshall's ear and then gesturing toward the stage. Marshall grinned back at Kit conspiratorially, then turned to Olivia and Violet.

Tess started to ask a question but was interrupted by Savannah picking up her son. "We've got to hustle backstage to wish Daddy luck!" JJ reached for the bright silver dragonfly and Savannah smiled as they headed to the side exit.

The chicken piccata was delicious, but Tess had only half finished it. The world seemed flat and dull, even though she was surrounded by happy chatter and all the colors of the rainbow. She wanted to enjoy the cheesecake slathered with fresh sliced strawberries, but found that she couldn't stomach the thought of it. She would sit through the entertainment; she would enjoy the rapture on Aunt Kit's face when Ben Shepherd took the stage. Then she was going to go home, attempt sleep, and get up on Sunday morning, determined to find a way to enjoy her life again. Without Luca, who had evidently found someone else.

"Look who I found!" exclaimed Marshall heartily.

Tess turned and her jaw dropped. "Mom! What are you doing here?" She stood quickly and embraced Cecilia cautiously. They had parted two days ago on good terms but she was a little worried that it might not have lasted.

"Happy birthday!" Cecilia held onto her daughter longer than usual. She was wearing black capris and a simple blue blouse with long matching beaded earrings. Tess could smell the rosewood perfume that she usually wore. In the past, the scent had seemed to push Tess away; today she felt comforted by it.

Eva jumped up and entered her grandmother's embrace. "Gram! You came!"

"You knew she was coming?" Tess asked as everyone sat back down and introductions were made.

Eva scraped up the last of the strawberry sauce with her spoon and licked it thoroughly. "It was her idea. She wanted to surprise you!"

"What about Micah?" Tess asked nervously. "Is it okay to leave him . . . alone in the hospital?"

Cecilia waved away a server who appeared with a plate of food. "No thank you, Miss. I ate on the plane." She reached across Eva and patted Tess's arm. "It's perfectly okay. He's in good hands."

Relieved, Tess sat back in her seat and glanced at her watch; the entertainment was due to start soon and then she could escape. She startled as Theatre Jasper rushed up to Eva and spoke to her quietly, his hand at the side of his mouth so no one would hear. Eva flashed a semi-guilty look at Tess. "Mom, I've got to . . . um . . . I'll be back soon. Just keep your eyes on the stage!" She wiped her mouth with a napkin and took a long gulp of water, then scurried off behind Jasper.

Tess turned to watch them go and her eyes landed on Luca a few tables away. She caught her breath. He looked devastatingly handsome in a black tux and red bow tie. Then she noticed the younger blonde woman sitting beside him. Madison was laughing and had her arm around the back of Luca's chair, somewhat possessively, Tess thought. Curiously enough, Teo's seat was empty. She turned away quickly and rubbed her palm against her forehead, eyes squeezed shut.

"Are you okay, Tess?" Carolina asked from across the table.

Tess felt grateful for her friend's concern but simply nodded and turned her attention to the stage where Grace and Will were tapping the microphone, patiently waiting for the audience to quiet down. They thanked everyone for attending, then made several announcements about the coming season. Finally, Grace introduced Ben Shepherd to thunderous applause.

"Greetings, Seahaven!" Ben grabbed the microphone from the stand and waited for the applause to die down. He looked suave in pressed black jeans and a pristine white T-shirt. Auburn curls fell over his forehead and ears. "I'm looking forward to singing my favorite Broadway tunes tonight but first, I'd like to introduce you all to my wife Savannah and my son JJ. Savannah owns *Life Celebrations*, the company that has arranged this Gala celebration for your theatre. Savannah?"

The audience clapped loudly again as Savannah walked onstage with JJ in her arms. "Thank you!" She leaned in to share Ben's microphone. "I'm glad you're all having such a great time tonight. I grew up not far from here in Portsmouth; my dad managed the theatre there and I've been a theatre geek all my life." Scattered applause interrupted her for a moment. "I'd like to thank my co-conspirators at *Life Celebrations*, Andi and Jeremy, who helped make all of this possible, and also our Seahaven temporary staff." She waved to the side of the dining area where her partners and employees waved back to more applause. "Now it's time to let Ben Shepherd do what he does best!"

Savannah and JJ took one of the remaining seats at Kit's table and smiled at everyone while settling the little boy on her lap. Her carryall tote occupied the extra chair. Kit held Marshall's hand as Ben sang three Broadway favorites, encouraging the crowd to sing along during each chorus.

"You're a great audience," Ben said, rising from the piano bench after the last number. He took a long swallow from the water bottle that rested nearby. "I was so happy when Grace and Will told me they wanted me to *only* sing Broadway songs. That doesn't usually happen!" He set the water bottle down and looked directly at Aunt Kit. "I've been asked to dedicate my next song to this beautiful woman here." He pointed two fingers at her. "Kit Gilmore, this one's for you."

Kit turned a delightful shade of pink and clapped one hand over her mouth. "Yes, Kit," Ben continued from the stage. "I have it on the best authority that you are one of this theatre's biggest and brightest supporters, and that you are one of my biggest and brightest fans. Is that right?"

"It is!" she replied happily. Marshall put his arm around her as Ben proceeded to sing "You'll Never Walk Alone" from the musical *Carousel.* Kit closed her eyes, savoring the music. Ben had no way of knowing this, but Lillian, Ollie's mother, had sung this at Ollie's memorial service; the words had offered comfort then that she still felt now, and a truth that she still believed to this day. When it was over, she ran to the edge of the low stage and reached up to take Ben's hand. "Thank you so much!" she said under the noise of the applause, grateful tears glistening in her eyes.

He smiled and squeezed her hand. After wiping his brow with a handkerchief from his pocket, he took another sip of water, then raised his hand to slow the applause. "I'm glad you enjoyed that, Kit! Our next scheduled act is our own Jasper Goodman and Glory Jones. I heard them rehearsing this afternoon, so prepare to be amazed. But I've had a very special request, so before they sing, I'm giving the stage over now to . . . Let me get this right." He pulled a small piece of paper from his jeans pocket and squinted for a moment. ". . . Eva Gilmore and Teo Silva. They have a short act prepared for you that I think you're going to love, and it's dedicated to . . ." He looked down at the paper again. "Their parents, Tess and Luca!"

Startled almost out of her seat, Tess's jaw dropped for the second time that evening. As Eva and Teo walked onstage holding hands, she blinked rapidly. The last she'd heard, Teo wasn't speaking to her daughter. She quickly looked over her shoulder and made eye contact with Luca who seemed equally surprised. He raised his eyebrows in confusion and she did the same. Madison was leaning forward eagerly, her elbows on the table, hands clasped, eyes focused on the stage.

Tess turned her gaze to Kit, who was also excitedly leaning forward, as were Cecilia and the others. No one made eye contact with her, not even Carolina. This was feeling stranger by the minute. Were they purposely ignoring her? There were two older teenagers on the stage with Eva and Teo: a boy and a girl. She watched in amazement as the four of them acted out the love story of Tess and Luca. A love story in the past, to be sure, but a love story all the same. She was glad they left out the bit about the fearful mother who brought that story to an end. Tess had to keep reminding herself Eva had written this short play with her and Luca in mind. Was this Eva's way of bringing them back together? She shook her head slightly, still in awe of the scene unfolding before her eyes. Eva was going to be so disappointed when she found out about Madison.

The spectators gave a thunderous standing ovation to the foursome on the stage. Tess found herself standing with the crowd, her hands clapping automatically, but all she could hear was her heart thudding in her chest and an ocean of cautious love roaring in her ears.

Grace and Will ran onto the stage, congratulating the performers on a job well done. "Ladies and gentlemen, we're going to take a fifteen-minute break." Will placed the microphone back on its shiny silver stand and the six of them left the stage.

As Eva made her way back to the table, Tess noticed a smiling Teo being embraced by both Luca and Madison. Her heart caught as Luca made eye contact with her, but she quickly looked away. Here was her brilliant, talented daughter, standing right in front of her. "Eva, you were amazing!" Tess enveloped the girl in a hug and refused to let go for several long moments, only releasing her grasp when Cecilia and Kit tapped her on the shoulder for a turn.

"Am I correct in understanding that you wrote the script yourself?" Marshall asked as they all settled back into their seats.

"Teo helped me with the idea at the beginning. But yeah, I'm the one who wrote it."

"Young lady, you are quite the writer!" exclaimed Olivia. "I've got a short story due soon for the creative writing class I'm taking at the Community Center. Can you help me with it?"

Eva opened her mouth to reply, then realized that Olivia was teasing and giggled instead. Teo suddenly appeared behind Eva. He jokingly covered her eyes with his hands and said, "Guess who?"

She flung his hands away, turned and playfully smacked his upper arm. "Everybody, this is Teo. Teo, this is . . . my family!"

Teo waved shyly, then said to Eva, "Are you ready? Is it time?"

"Yes," she replied emphatically. "Mom, you have to come with us. Right now, let's go!" She tugged her mother's arm.

Confused, Tess quickly stood beside Eva. "I didn't think you guys were friends anymore."

"We made up," Eva explained impatiently. "It happens all the time . . . people *making up*." She fixed her mom with a meaningful stare, then continued. "Aunt Kit and Glory put the secret garden terrarium back together; I gave it to Teo yesterday and we're friends again."

"Okaaaaay . . ." Tess looked curiously at Teo who smiled up at her with no hesitation whatsoever. Things were getting stranger by the minute.

"I love the terrarium," Teo said. "But we were always gonna be friends anyway."

She looked around the table. Aunt Kit and the others were eagerly urging her to go with the children. These were undoubtedly the faces of people who knew something that she was not privy to. She turned back to Eva. "But the concert isn't over. I don't want to miss Jasper and Glory—"

"Come *on*!" Eva insisted. "You can hear them sing any time; they live in our apartment building!" She grabbed Tess's hand in her right and Teo's hand in her left, and headed for the side exit. Tess reluctantly followed, noticing with dismay that Luca and Madison were no longer at their table.

# Chapter 31

The children led Tess outside the restaurant to a wide patio that overlooked the theatre. The sky was darkening past sunset and a sliver of moon shone overhead. The sounds coming from the theatre were muted and seemed far away. She inhaled the fresh air that carried a sweet, tangy reminder of the sea as she admired the view. "Isn't it beautiful?" She turned when she heard no response; the children were gone. "Eva? Teo?" she called, folding her bare arms across her chest and rubbing her upper arms. She headed back to the side entrance but stiffened at the sound of her name.

"Tessa?" She would recognize that voice anywhere. Luca was slowly climbing the back stairs to the patio in the semi-darkness. His expression was unreadable.

She kept her arms folded over her chest as he stepped nearer to her. Her heart thudded in her chest like the bass drum from one of Ben Shepherd's backup players. What on earth was Luca doing here?

"The kids said that you wanted to see me," he explained, looking at her expectantly.

"They said *what*? Eva and Teo dragged me out here and then left me all alone. I don't understand. I'm going back—"

Luca cleared his throat and took a step closer. "You are no longer alone."

Tess looked over at the side entrance and listened to the faint chatter and laughter of happy theatre-goers. She could easily leave

Luca here and go right back inside, but was that what she really wanted? She turned her attention back to the man who could have been hers. What she wanted now was a life that echoed with laughter and happiness, but how could she have that with him if Madison was in the picture? "I'm so confused."

He tapped the side of his head twice with three tanned fingers. "I understand now," he said, laugh lines wrinkling out from his eyes.

"Understand what?" She couldn't help admiring those golden-brown eyes and the sheer solidity of his body in that tux.

"They arranged this—your Eva, my Teo. "

Tess clapped a hand over her open mouth. "Oh my God, you're right!" Things suddenly shifted into focus. "They performed that play, then brought me out here . . . and they also lied to you." She clasped her hands behind her back, remembering Madison. "I'm so sorry, Luca. They interrupted your evening and—"

"I am not sorry," he replied quietly, gazing at her steadily and moving closer. "I am glad. I wanted to see you again, to ask if you would reconsider coming for dinner, with the children, or to let me take you out again, without them."

She lowered her gaze, then walked slowly to the whitewashed railing and leaned her elbows on it.

Luca followed her. "Tessa?" He stood beside her, only a sliver of moonlight between their bodies.

Tess inhaled sharply. Just this morning—thanks to her talk with Kit—she had been eager to accept Luca's invitation; she had been ready to try again. But that had all changed when she'd seen him at King's Deli with Madison. Now . . . here he was . . . standing beside her, and he was asking again. "I would like to, Luca. But what about Madison?"

Luca looked at her with genuine curiosity. "What about Madison?"

Tess continued to look away from him and into the night, rubbing her suddenly clammy hands together. "I saw you with her at King's Deli today, remember? And tonight she was sitting—"

Luca quickly turned her to face him, his hands warm and sure on her upper arms. "Madison is Teo's new nanny. Which is another way of saying babysitter, but she is older than most sitters and more experienced, so we refer to her as a nanny."

Tess looked up at him and shakily smoothed back her hair. "I thought . . ." She clasped his arms with her trembling hands.

"I am flattered you would think this, but the new nanny is eighteen years younger than me." Luca smiled gently and placed his right palm on Tess's cheek.

She leaned into his touch, then pulled away as she remembered their last phone conversation. "What about New Bedford? You're moving at the end of the summer."

Luca took her hands in his. "New Bedford was Plan B, as they say. You know about Plan Bs, right?" She nodded slowly. "I thought Seahaven would be our home for many years to come, because we were here together. When you pushed me away, I didn't want to stay."

"And now?" Tess looked down at their clasped hands.

He lifted one of her hands to his mouth and kissed it lightly. "If you would give our love story another try, I will gladly stay in Seahaven. I do not want to live anywhere else but where you are."

"What about Teo? He didn't want—"

The children interrupted them, whooping and clapping loud enough for the whole county to hear as they raced around the corner of the patio.

"Hold it, guys!" Luca held up both hands to slow them down. "Tess and I are having a private moment here. What is going on?" His expression held an endearing blend of puzzlement and love.

"I knew she would ask about Teo!" Eva exclaimed breathlessly. "He has something to say." She poked Teo's arm and lowered her voice. "Go ahead, *tell* her."

"I'm sorry, Tess," the boy said quietly. He bowed his head, then shyly looked up at her. "Eva and Madison . . ." He swallowed hard and glanced at Luca for a moment. His father nodded reassuringly, and Teo continued. "They made me see that I don't have to . . . I don't have to stop loving my Mãe if Dad wants to be with you." He shuffled his feet and looked down for a moment. "I mean, I know Dad wants to be with you. It's about whether *you* want to be with *Dad*." He touched the Saint Christopher medal that gleamed in the dim light against his collared shirt. "Madison's mother died a few years ago, so she understands what I'm going through. I just want Dad to be happy." There were tears in his eyes but the corners of his mouth were beginning to turn up.

Luca knelt on the cement patio floor and hugged his son tightly. "I will never stop loving your mother either," he reassured Teo. "I have enough love in my heart for all of you." He pulled Tess and Eva down until they were all sitting on the hard ground, leaning against each other, fancy clothes and all.

"Thank you Teo," Tess was finally able to whisper. "I'm glad that Madison and Eva have helped you. I want you to know that, if it's okay with you and Eva, your dad and I are going to start seeing each other again."

Luca looked at her across Eva and Teo's heads. "We are?"

"Yes," she said with a bright confidence that had eluded her for many years in every area of her life that didn't pertain to her work. "I'm ready." They smiled at each other and it seemed as if the sliver of the rising moon shone a bit brighter. She was absolutely certain this time. No *buts* whatsoever.

Eva clapped her hands, then high-fived with Teo. "It worked!" Her voice was full of happy relief. She hugged her mother; Tess was speechless. "Okay, Mom," Eva said as she jumped up. She tugged Tess's hand until she was standing and began to pull her toward the restaurant's side entrance. "Time to leave!"

"Leave?" Tess looked helplessly over her shoulder at Luca who grinned mysteriously at her and began to follow, Teo at his side. "The Gala's not over yet, is it? Jasper and Glory still have to—"

"The Gala's over, as far as we're concerned," Eva replied. "We're actually going *home* now."

Eva led the small procession back into the restaurant where chimes were sounding, indicating that intermission was almost over. Olivia and Violet remained at their table. "We should really go back, Eva. Where are Aunt Kit and Gram?"

Luca edged up beside Tess as Eva led them through the crowded space and out to the parking lot. "Tessa," he murmured. "It's okay. Your daughter has a surprise for you at home."

# Chapter 38

As the four of them entered Tess and Eva's apartment, the overhead lights flashed on and a cacophony of familiar voices shouted "Surprise!" Tess took a step backward and bumped right into Luca, who instinctively put his arms around her.

She relaxed into him for the briefest of moments, then moved forward and looked around, holding his hand on one side, and Eva's on the other. She was stunned. Here were the people she cared for most in the world: Kit, beaming beside Marshall; Cecilia, sitting on the sofa with Just Jasper purring on her lap; Glory, holding onto a wiggly Samuel; Max and Mimi Pearl, perched on the loveseat; Carolina, with her flaming red hair and glamorous dress; beloved Eva, Luca and Teo. "What is all this?"

"It's a surprise party for YOU!" Eva let go of Tess's hand and ran across the room to Cecilia and the cat. "Happy birthday!"

Tess held both hands over her heart, her eyes brimming with tears. "I . . . thank you . . . I'm overwhelmed!"

Kit gave her a hug and kissed her on the cheek. "Happy birthday, dear."

She turned to Luca and Teo. "Did you guys know about this?"

"We did," Luca replied, and Teo agreed eagerly. "It was all Eva's idea."

"But . . . back at the theatre, on the patio . . . what if I—"

"We would have come anyway," Luca reassured her. "But I am glad that the 'what if' never happened."

"Me too," she replied and kissed him lightly on the lips, to the scattered applause of the small gathered crowd.

"Mom! Mom!" Eva bounced off the sofa and raced back to her mother's side. "I forgot the most important thing! We're all here except for Micah!"

"Of course, honey. He can't be here because—"

"But he *is* here . . . "She gestured wildly to Cecilia. "Gram, did you—"

"I did," Cecilia said with a grin. She held up her phone, lowered her voice, and made an announcement worthy of rivaling any sports reporter on ESPN. "Our local hero Micah Gilmore is coming to us live via smartphone from Columbia, South Carolina, USA, land of the free and home of the brave."

Tess took the phone from her mother's hands and sank onto the sofa beside her. Just Jasper jumped down and headed for the safety of Eva's bedroom, limping only slightly. The living room was way too crowded for his taste. As soon as Teo noticed Jasper hop off the sofa, he quickly shut the apartment door; Luca gave him a thumbs-up.

"Micah, is that really you?" Tess stared at her son and Nurse Paloma who was bustling around the room, trying to stay out of the camera's view.

Micah was still chuckling, albeit hoarsely, after Gram's introduction. "Mom, I wish I could be there with you, but . . ." He gestured weakly around at his sterile surroundings. "I'm otherwise occupied at the moment, as you can see."

"It means the world to me that you're able to be with us this way instead." Tess's cheeks hurt from smiling. "Eva, come and say hello to your brother."

"Hi!" Eva stuck her face in front of the phone and waved.

"Hey, Evie-Bee." He leaned closer to the camera. "How did your plan go?"

Eva giggled and pointed to Tess. "Ask her yourself."

"Mom?"

Tess smiled some more. Her cheeks really did hurt. "It went great," was all she could say before Cecilia stood up and passed the phone around so the other guests could say hello.

When she finally got the phone back, Micah said that he had arranged a special gift for her, and that Aunt Kit knew where it was. Hearing her name, Kit ducked into the kitchen and came back with an envelope and a small wrapped box. She handed the envelope to Tess and held the small box behind her back.

Tess carefully unsealed the slim white envelope and took out a gift certificate to Chloe's by the Sea. "Thank you, Micah! You didn't have to—"

"Yes, I did," he replied, taking several focused breaths before continuing, his voice still quite hoarse. "I want you and Luca to have a special night out. Can I talk to him again?"

She beckoned Luca closer. "Hey, Micah! Thank you for your service. I hear you are getting better every day."

"That's what they tell me anyway," Micah replied. He gestured for the water cup and Paloma helped him take a sip. "Luca, please take care of my mom and sister for me, okay?"

"You got it, my friend. We will be taking care of each other." Luca put his arm around Tess's waist.

"Before I go, I have a present for Evie too," Micah pushed himself a little higher up in the hospital bed, wincing with each movement.

"Me?" Eva squealed. "You got me a present? How—"

"Aunt Kit to the rescue," Kit said, handing over the small white box with a tiny green bow on top.

Eva lifted the lid and peered inside, her mouth forming a little round O.

"What is it, hon?" Tess looked over Eva's shoulder and saw a delicate sterling silver feather glistening against the white cotton filler. It was about an inch long, on a lacy silver chain.

"I love it!" Eva held the necklace up for all to see, then held still as her mother draped it around her neck and attached the clasp at the back. "Thank you, Micah," Eva said solemnly. "I'll never take it off."

Micah grinned. "You can take it off, Li'l Sis."

"But I want to wear it always, like Teo wears the medal that his mom gave him."

"Okay then," Micah conceded. "Wear it whenever you want. It's for you to remember the time I went away but stayed with you by sending you all those feathers."

Eva fingered the necklace thoughtfully.

Nurse Paloma's face filled the screen; her blonde curls shone like sunshine in the stark hospital light. "Say goodbye now; Micah needs to rest."

Tess handed the phone back to Cecilia. "Thanks, Mom."

Cecilia brushed away a tear. "We couldn't have a surprise party for you and not have Micah here, could we?"

"Of course not!" Carolina was at Tess's side, guiding her to the doorway into the kitchen. "How are you doing, Tess? Do you need a moment to take a breath?"

Tess nodded gratefully. "It's been . . . quite a night!"

"I'll say!" Carolina replied. "And there's more to come."

"More?" Tess looked back at the others in the living room, chatting amicably with one another.

"Yes, more!" Eva appeared and tugged at Tess's hand. "Jasper and Carlos are coming over after the Gala is over and they're going to sing! Glory was supposed to sing with him after intermission but she said she'd rather come here, that's why she's not still at the Gala." She paused to take a breath.

"Okay . . ." Tess said with an amused smile. "I'm looking forward to meeting Carlos."

"Then everyone I love really *will* be here."

"Except for Chiara and Quinn," Eva replied sadly, wringing her hands. "I called them but it was short notice so they couldn't come. They're going to call you later tonight, after everyone leaves. I made them promise."

"Thank you, Eva, I love that you thought of all of this!"

"I didn't think of it all by myself."

"You didn't?"

"Savannah helped me. When she heard I wanted to give you a surprise party, she gave me lots of ideas, but there wasn't enough time to do *everything* she suggested, like fancy decorations and stuff—"

Luca interrupted them, placing his hand gently on Eva's head. "But Savannah did suggest that we provide a special dessert for you, and to find out if you prefer birthday cake or another kind of—"

"Because not everyone actually likes cake on their birthday," added Eva excitedly. "I didn't know that!"

"Well, I like—"

"We asked Aunt Kit," Eva interrupted.

"She told us how the Chloe's Delight special was Blueberry Peach Cobbler when she took you there for dinner in May," Luca continued.

"That's right, I—"

"Mom!" Eva grabbed Tess's hand and pulled her all the way into the kitchen where a sumptuous-looking dessert stood proudly in the center of their small kitchen table. "We got you Chloe's Delight!" She hopped on one foot, then the other, back and forth, impatiently.

Kit came up behind them and placed her hands on Tess's shoulders. "Do you remember our dinner before you officially decided to move here?"

"I do." Tess moved her hands on top of Kit's and held them there as she thought back to that dinner at Chloe's by the Sea, after her interview at Pearly Whites. Was that only two months ago? She looked around at Luca and Teo, Carolina, Glory and Samuel, Cecilia, and the Pearls. Aunt Kit with her new beau Marshall. And Eva, precious Eva. So much had changed since that interview, since that dinner with Kit. She remembered being hesitant about ordering the decadent "Chloe's Delight" dessert then, as hesitant as she'd been about accepting a new job and moving to Seahaven. The word "delight" hadn't been part of her vocabulary for a very long time. And now—

"It wasn't even on the menu today!" Eva exclaimed. "Chloe made it *just* for your birthday party. Aunt Kit asked her and she did it! See the pretty bowl that it's in? It's handmade by an artist right here in Seahaven. It's Aunt Kit's birthday gift to you. There was no way to actually wrap it because it's holding the dessert!" Eva hugged herself happily. "And we put it on our special rainbow birthday plate!"

Tess pulled Kit and Eva in close on either side of her. "Kit, I love the bowl, and I can't wait to try the cobbler again. Thank you both! This is the best birthday I've ever had."

Luca kissed her on the forehead and joined the group hug, pulling Teo in close. "I promise there will be many, many more."

Teo leaned out of his father's grasp to get a closer look at the dessert which smelled sweet and fruity. "How do we cut a cobbler?" he asked as everyone laughed.

Tess grabbed a large metal spoon from a kitchen drawer and scooped a hefty serving into a paper bowl, then handed it to Teo. "Like this!" she said with delight as Luca gave him a spoon.

While Tess scooped up another serving of dessert, Eva tugged on Luca's arm. "When's *your* birthday?" she asked.

"If I tell you, will you give me a surprise party like this one?" He took the dessert bowl from Tess and passed it to Kit.

"Maybe; maybe not," Eva replied playfully.

"My birthday is February eleventh, so you'll have to wait six months."

Eva gasped. "No way. That's *my* birthday!"

Luca handed her a bowl brimming with peaches, blueberries, and a sugary, crumbly topping. "We will have to plan our party together," he replied. "Did Aunt Kit bring the ice cream like we asked?"

"I did!" Kit strode to the freezer and pulled out a gallon container of Simply Sweets Heavenly Vanilla, set it down next to the cobbler, and began scooping. Luca wandered back into the living room with Teo.

"Eva, did I hear Luca say that his birthday is February eleventh?" Kit asked, dropping a big scoop of ice cream into a bowl and handing it to Mimi Pearl.

"Yes!" Eva replied, happily digging into her bowl of Chloe's Delight. "It's another synchronicity!"

"Speaking of synchronicities, here's another one. Carlos's sister is moving to Seahaven from Boston next week. She needs a place to stay, so guess where she's going to live?"

Eva's eyes widened. "Here? In the apartment over Glory's?"

"That's right." Kit said. "Her name is Elena Jeffries; she's the new English teacher at the high school."

"She wouldn't have known about the apartment if Carlos and Jasper didn't meet because of my cat . . ." Eva ran the back of the cold spoon over her lips, forehead wrinkled in thought. "Wow!"

"That's how synchronicity works, and always when you least expect it." She scooped ice cream into her own bowl. "Another example is you and your mom, and this apartment. You needed it and it was here. The same thing happened with Jasper."

"And Glory and her grandkids." Eva savored another spoonful. This one had more blueberries than peaches. She now liked blueberries as much as she liked living in Maine. "But what about you?" Eva asked, setting her almost-empty bowl down on the table and gazing up at Kit.

"What about me?" Satisfied that everyone's bowls were full, Kit placed the cover back on the container and walked to the freezer. Eva followed.

"You and Marshall. Was that synchronicity too?"

Kit put the ice cream container back in the freezer and took Eva's hand as they walked to the living room. "You could say that. I met him when I was twenty-two. He was married then, of course, and I was still so sad about my Ollie." They paused on the threshold and she looked down at Eva for a moment. "It wasn't the right time."

"But now . . ." Eva prompted.

"Yes, now . . ." Kit's gaze roamed the living room until it landed on Marshall who was laughing companionably with Max Pearl by the window. Marshall caught her gaze and gestured for her to join them. She looked down at Eva. "Now seems to be the right time. Keep on seeing the synchronicities in life, Eva. They're all around. You just have to pay attention."

Tess, on one side of the sofa, beckoned to Eva as Kit joined Marshall. "I was watching you now with Aunt Kit."

Eva sat on the arm of the sofa. "We were talking about synchronicity again."

"I see." Tess smiled. "Remember back in New Haven, when I said that you look like Kit did when she was younger?"

"Yes?" Eva looked puzzled.

"Well, you do look like her, and you also have the same qualities of kindness and generosity that she does. You're pretty darned wise, too, just like Aunt Kit."

"I am?" Eva looked into her mother's eyes. "All those things?"

"You definitely are."

Eva twirled a section of her hair. Could she accept the fact that she *wasn't* plain and ordinary? She used to think that she wasn't as special as Micah and Charli, but here in Seahaven, she'd discovered something she was good at. She knew now that she didn't have to be like Micah or Charli in order to be special. She'd figured out that sometimes people who aren't related come together to make a special kind of family. She'd been smart enough to find a way to get to her brother when he needed her most, and she'd figured out how to bring her mother and Luca back together. "Mom?"

"Mmm...hmm?" Tess pulled Eva closer.

"I'm happy that I'm like Aunt Kit, but I'm also a lot like you."

Astonished, Tess opened her mouth to speak, but no words came out.

Eva giggled a little at her mom's silence. She knew what she was thinking. But everything was different now. Everything.

"What do you mean?" Tess finally found her voice.

"I'm hard-working and smart and thoughtful, like you. I'm a good friend like you, too." Eva continued with certainty. "I'm just like you *and* Aunt Kit." She kissed Tess on the cheek, then bounced up. "I'm going to find Teo to see if he knows when Poppy's coming back!"

"All right," Tess replied, stunned by her daughter's revelation about their similarities. She was completely bowled over by the entire evening. To think that she hadn't even wanted to go to the Gala in the first place!

"A penny for your thoughts." Luca's deep voice startled her as he sat down beside her and placed a hand on her knee which was covered by her new periwinkle dress.

As Tess leaned against him, it felt as if her body was humming with happiness. "Eva just told me that she wants to be like me. I never thought she'd feel that way."

"Life is good, eh?" he whispered against her hair.

She nodded, savoring the feel of his neck against her cheek. He smelled salty like the sea, and sweet like the pines that lined their driveway.

"Hey!" Luca gently moved away from her and took a small tissue-wrapped package from his pants pocket. "I almost forgot to give you your birthday present."

She carefully undid the tape, and found a delicate gold bracelet entwined with bits of aqua and bottle-green sea glass. "I love it, Luca! Thank you."

He affixed the clasp, then took her hand in his and put it over his heart. "It is to match the necklace I gave you all those years ago. Tessa, I am so glad we found each other again."

"Hey, love birds!" Theatre Jasper snapped his fingers in front of Tess and Luca who were kissing as the party swirled around them. Smiling giddily, they broke apart as Jasper, Glory, and Carlos began singing a rousing chorus of "For She's a Jolly Good Friend." The others soon joined in, and Tess slowly looked around at the people who had gathered to celebrate her birthday, her heart overflowing with gratitude for each of them.

After much applause, more gifts were given and received. Tess's eyes glistened with tears when she opened two hardbound copies of *A Brief History of Time* from Cecilia. "One is for you and the other is for Luca," she explained. "You read it together all those years ago; maybe it will give you even more to talk about now." Tess exchanged a meaningful look with Luca before embracing her mother warmly.

Carolina presented Tess with a gift certificate for two massages at Coastal Soul, and Tess realized she was no longer averse to the idea. Kit and Marshall gave Tess an open-ended invitation to stay at Marshall's place in New York City with tickets for her and Eva to attend the Broadway show of their choice. "This is perfect. Eva, look!" Eva did a happy dance and turned to Theatre Jasper to ask him what Broadway show might be the best one to see. The Pearls surprised her with a beautiful watercolor painting of an ocean sunrise by their favorite Asian artist. "I know where I'm going to hang this," Tess said, hugging it to her chest as she thanked her bosses.

Next, Tess opened an elaborately wrapped present from Theatre Jasper and Carlos. She gasped in surprise and held it up for Luca to see. "It's a photo of you and me . . . that night at Simply Sweets. I love the frame!" She looked up at Jasper. "But I don't remember you taking this!"

"I didn't take it. Jake did." He cleared his throat and looked at Carlos whose expression showed only encouragement. "Remember? He took your camera right before Teo—"

"Yeah," Teo interrupted. "Sorry about that. I didn't mean to—"

Jasper reached out and tugged Teo's hand. "Hey man, it's all water under the bridge now, right?" Teo nodded slowly. "Anyway, the present isn't just from Carlos and me. It's from Eva and Teo too. Right, guys?"

"Yes!" Eva ran over and sat next to Tess.

"We're glad you like it," added Carlos with a big grin. "The only thing I did was buy the card!"

"Thank you all so much." Tess's heart was full as she stood, surrounded by thoughtful gifts and loved ones. She opened her arms as if to hug everyone at once.

"One more!" Glory hurried over to Tess. "Kalila, Samuel and I picked this out for you last week but we haven't had a spare minute to wrap it. Samuel is finally asleep and Kalila is still at the theatre." She handed Tess a small wooden plaque with several colored feathers dangling from it. Tess turned it over and happily gasped when she saw the words "Home Sweet Home" engraved in the wood.

"It's for your front door," Glory explained.

Eva clapped her hands in delight. "Look at all the feathers!"

"This is perfect!" She hugged her neighbor and let herself be hugged in return.

Home, sweet home, indeed.

# Chapter 39

"**Mom!** I love these new jeans and I don't care that you got them from a thrift shop!" Eva ran into the living room where Tess was working on her laptop as she absent-mindedly stroked Just Jasper who lay belly-up beside to her.

Tess looked up and smiled. "This weekend we'll go to the Maine Mall and get whatever else you need for school."

"Including the cell phone, right?"

"I already ordered you the GABB phone. It should be here any day now."

"Thank you!" Eva plopped down on the sofa next to her mother and lifted Jasper onto her lap.

Tess bumped shoulders with Eva. "I'm sorry I didn't get you one sooner. If you decide to run away again, be sure to take it with you." She winked mischievously but Eva didn't notice.

"Mom! That's not gonna happen, I promise."

"I'm kidding," Tess replied. She quietly closed her laptop and stretched her arms out in front of her. She hadn't had a headache in more than two weeks.

"I can't wait to see Micah again this weekend!" She rested her head on her mother's shoulder and picked up the remote. They were leaving on Friday to spend Labor Day weekend with Micah who was already starting physical therapy at the hospital, and the best thing was—Luca was going with them. Teo would stay at home with Madison.

"I think Micah's going to get along great with Luca, don't you?"

"I hope so." Tess put her arm around Eva.

"They've both watched *Schitt's Creek* like a hundred times," Eva said happily. "I think they'll have a *lot* to talk about."

"I imagine they'll find more than that to talk about, hon."

"Yeah! I guess they'll be talking about you and me!" She giggled as she turned on the television. "Mom, remember how one of my special things is recommending books or shows for people based on how they're feeling and what's going on in their life?"

Tess looked at her curiously. "I do."

She grinned mischievously. "Well, I found a show that I think *you'll* like."

Tess raised a skeptical eyebrow. "Oh?"

Eva clicked a button on the remote as Tess carefully set her laptop on the floor.

The television finally cleared from the many screens that Eva had casually flipped through, giving way to jaunty instrumental music and a wide-angle view of people going about their business on the main street of Stars Hollow. Then the camera began to track Lorelai Gilmore heading toward Luke's Diner.

Tess closed her eyes for a moment. Was it possible? Her daughter was finally offering to watch *Gilmore Girls* with her from the very first episode? She pulled Eva close. "Are you sure?"

Eva nodded, snuggling against Tess with a happy sigh. "It's a mother-daughter thing. Let's watch as many episodes as we can until we fall asleep, then get up tomorrow morning and go to the beach for another *earthmove!*"

Tess smiled happily. "You know me so well." She turned the volume up and breathed a sigh of contented delight.

# Gratitudes

*R*emember how Tess and Eva played the "Gratitude Game" in the hotel room? Here is my own list of thank-fulls on the completion of this book.

**Jeff**- My heart and soul are thank-full for your love and companionship in this our thirty-second year together. I still can't believe I'm lucky enough to be married to you! You make my daily life easier and my whole life's journey complete.

**My Early Readers**- You know who you are, but I'm going to name you here anyway. Your eager responses, suggestions, ideas, and corrections made a world of difference in the polish and shine that blesses this book's pages. I am thank-full for Carolyn Dumaine, Chigoke Adoma, Dee Relyea, Laura Denton, Marti Beddoe, Paloma Sylvan, Pam Papworth, Sharon Seliskar, Susan Coburn, and Taylor Williams.

**"Last Eyes" Readers**- A special thank-full note to Margaret Banks in Australia and Stacy Green in Kentucky, for being my "last eyes" before I sent the manuscript to my book designer.

**Writing Teachers**- I will forever be thank-full for Jennifer Louden whose online class I stumbled into in 2016. Your teachings about small steps, celebration, persistence, and motivation changed my life as a writer. Also, Jessica Brody, whose *Save the Cat Writes a Novel* book and online courses helped to shape *Feathers in the Sand* in a myriad of ways that surprised and delighted me.

**Writing Community**- My thank-full-ness continues for all the direction, support, and kindness I've received from the Women's Fiction Writers Association (WFWA). I have learned so much from all of you and hope to be able to give back as much as I've received.

**The Towns of Wells and Ogunquit, Maine**- Over the last few years, I've secluded myself in various spots in your lovely seaside towns, in order to create this novel. I am grateful to the staff at The Falls in Ogunquit and Garnsey Brothers Realty in Wells for fabulous accommodations, beautiful views, and excellent customer service. You make my writer's heart happy!

# Book Club
## Discussion Questions

1. Which character did you identify with the most? Why?

2. Was there a time in your life when you had to make a decision to start over somewhere new? What prompted you to make that decision? How did it turn out?

3. Have you seen the TV show *Gilmore Girls*? Why did Tess want Eva to watch it with her? Do you think it's realistic to wish for a mother-daughter relationship like the one that Lorelai and Rory have?

4. What was your relationship like with your mother? How did it affect your relationship with your daughter(s) or other young women in your life?

5. Do you have a big brother who was special to you in some way? What made that relationship unique?

6. *Gilmore Girls* and *Schitt's Creek* have a lasting effect on several characters in this story. Is there a special TV show that has made a difference in your life? How did it change you or the way that you think?

7. Have you ever experienced synchronicity in your life? Share an example.

8. Take some time right now to play the Gratitude Game that Tess played with Eva. What are you most grateful for today? How can playing this game (with yourself or someone else) transform your day?

9. When was the last time you experienced a sunrise? What was it like?

10. Aunt Kit tells Eva about carrying forward the light of someone she loved who died a long time ago. Is there someone no longer with us who lit up your life? How do you carry their light forward?

11. The Sun will rise and set regardless. What we choose to do with the light while it's here is up to us. Journey wisely. ~ Alex Elle What does this quote mean to you? What did it mean to each of the characters in this novel?

# Please Stay in Touch!

I hope that *Feathers in the Sand* touched your heart and soul in some way. If you enjoyed it, you can help me share this book with others by leaving a short review wherever you purchased it.

Please sign up for my free monthly author newsletter, Stories That Stir Heart & Soul. You'll be the first to read about my monthly give-aways of heart & soul-stirring paperback novels, contests, recipes from this book, background info about some of the characters, and information about upcoming novels from the wild wanderings of my imagination. AnneMarieBennett.com/newsletter

**I'd love to hear from you about how Tess and Eva's story touched your heart and soul!**
AnneMarieBennett.com
AnneMarie@AnneMarieBennett.com
facebook.com/annemariebennettauthor
instagram.com/annemariebennett520/

## Additional Books
## by Anne Marie Bennett

### Fiction

Come As You Are

My Other Dad

All You Need is Love . . . and Lilacs

Dragonflies at Night: More Than a Love Story

### Nonfiction

Bright Side of the Road: A Spiritual Journey
Through Breast Cancer

Sunflower Spirit Workbook for Women with Cancer

Through the Eyes of SoulCollage®

Into the Heart of SoulCollage®

Walking the Path of SoulCollage®

Magical Inner Journeys: 44 Guided Imagery Scripts

*The Sun will rise and set regardless.*

*What we choose to do with the light while it's here is up to us.*

*Journey wisely.*

*~ Alex Elle*

Made in the USA
Middletown, DE
16 July 2022

69011337R00205